ACCLAIM FOR PEN

MW01039094

The Empty Chair ~ Murder in the Caribbean

"Penny Goetjen uses the idyllic setting and island culture so effectively, the reader is tempted to savor ocean views from The Empty Chair, but don't pause too long—danger is never too far away."
—Kathryn Orzech, Author of *Asylum* and *Premonition of Terror*

Over the Edge ~ Murder Returns to the Caribbean

". . . a well scripted murder mystery with deceptive characters and an unpredictable path."
—*Suzy Approved Book Reviews*

Murder on the Precipice

" . . . completely transportive, plenty of thrills, with a warm cast of characters that adds a lot of heart to this story."
—Megan Collins, Author of *The Winter Sister*, *Behind the Red Door*, and *The Family Plot*

"Penny Goetjen has that rare ability to quickly capture the reader's attention and keep their interest from scene to glorious scene. There is elegance in her writings. She is a gifted storyteller and never disappoints."
—Martin Herman, Author of *The Will James Mysteries*

Murder Beyond the Precipice

"Goetjen is a competent writer who keeps things moving along, throwing in hints of the preternatural that add to the overall ambiance . . . worth a read."
—*Kirkus Reviews*

"Hard to put this book down. The twists and turns and intrigue never stop. . . . A must-read for murder mystery fans."
—*Readers' Favorite*

Murder Returns to the Precipice
"A richly textured mystery that's both charmingly atmospheric and cunningly staged. Be forewarned . . . this story will lull you in with its seeming tranquility only to sweep you away in the undercurrent. Take a deep breath and surrender yourself fully. Penny Goetjen is a mighty force!"
—John Valeri, *Criminal Element*

The
WOMAN
Underwater

Other Titles by
PENNY GOETJEN

Olivia Benning Mystery Series

The Empty Chair ~ Murder in the Caribbean

Over the Edge ~ Murder Returns to the Caribbean

Elizabeth Pennington Mystery Series

Murder on the Precipice

Murder Beyond the Precipice

Murder Returns to the Precipice

THE
WOMAN
UNDERWATER

PENNY GOETJEN

SECRET HARBOR PRESS

For information about this title or to order other books and/or electronic media, contact the publisher:

Secret Harbor Press, LLC
www.SecretHarborPress.com
secretharborpress@gmail.com

Cover and interior design by The Book Cover Whisperer: OpenBookDesign.biz

Publisher's Cataloging-In-Publication Data

(Prepared by The Donohue Group, Inc.)

Names: Goetjen, Penny, author.

Title: The woman underwater / Penny Goetjen.

Description: First edition. | Charleston, South Carolina : Secret Harbor Press, [2022]

Identifiers: ISBN 9781733143943 (paperback) | ISBN 9781733143950 (ebook)

Subjects: LCSH: Missing persons--Connecticut--Fiction. | Teachers--Connecticut--Fiction. | Wives--Connecticut--Fiction. | Boarding schools--Connecticut--Fiction. | Loss (Psychology)--Fiction. | LCGFT: Detective and mystery fiction. | Thrillers (Fiction)

Classification: LCC PS3607.O3356 W66 2022 (print) | LCC PS3607.O3356 (ebook) | DDC 813/.6--dc23

Library of Congress Control Number: 2022902809

Publisher's Cataloging-In-Publication Data
(Prepared by The Donahue Group, Inc.)

978-1-7331439-4-3 Paperback
978-1-7331439-5-0 eBook

Printed in the United States of America

FIRST EDITION

For my mother . . .

PROLOGUE

SEVEN YEARS CAN BE a blur, and it can also be a life sentence. In the time since Victoria's husband disappeared, it's been both.

Grieving in the traditional sense has not been an option. That would mean she acknowledges he's dead. She grieves, instead, for his absence. The empty side of the bed where the sheets are cold. The silence in the kitchen when there should be witty one-liners as he pours his morning coffee and then a second cup for her. She longs for the warmth of his arm slipping around her waist and pulling her closer, his masculine scent lingering in her nose long after he kisses her lips and slips out the front door for work.

There is a rawness to life—life without her first real love and the father of their children. A ragged edge that can't be smoothed. Something sinister simmers along the fringes, threatening to engulf the lives of everyone who knew Robert.

She's been left to pick up the pieces and go on. But she's not sure she knows how to do that—or even if she should.

And yet the day he disappeared started out much like any other day. If only she'd known it would be their last.

But no one disappears without someone seeing something, someone knowing something.

Chapter One

Seven Years Earlier

Their comfortable routine had been thrown off, and the boys could sense something was different about it. Only thirteen and ten, Harrison and Jameson watched their father flitting between the kitchen and his den, fetching papers and securing them into his weathered leather briefcase—the kind with well-worn, soft sides that looked relaxed even though the person packing it was anything but. Muttering to himself as he gathered what he would need for his overnight in the big city, he accepted a half slice of toast from Victoria on the way by.

"You need to eat, Robert," she gently coaxed.

"Is today your trip with the boys, Dad?" Harrison asked as his father re-emerged from the den.

Robert smiled broadly at his sons at the breakfast table, pausing to engage. "Yes, it is." He leaned in and snatched a piece of cantaloupe from his older son's plate.

"Hey!" Harrison protested and grabbed unsuccessfully at the melon chunk.

Jameson chimed in, "Where are you going again?" His voice was younger and more childlike than his older brother's, and Victoria feared the innocence in it would disappear before long.

With the patience of a father who had explained the details many times before but would do it many more, Robert answered, "To New York City."

"But you'll be back tonight?" Jameson screwed up his face as though he already knew the answer.

Delivering a jab to his little brother's upper arm, Harrison said, "No, dummy."

"Ow!" Jameson protested and punched back at his brother but missed when he dodged the shot.

"You know he's staying overnight. He already told us that. About a bajillion times."

"That's enough, boys. Now finish your breakfasts so you don't miss your bus." Victoria stepped in.

"No, James, I need to stay overnight this time. I've got a very full day tomorrow, so I want to be able to start early. I get to go behind the scenes at the Museum of Natural History and see things the public doesn't get to see."

"Why, Daddy?" Jameson's curiosity about his father's work was boundless.

"So I can use what I learn there in my history classes here on campus to teach my students." Both boys were poised with cereal spoons in midair, their interest piqued. "Then when you guys are students here, you'll get to learn about it too."

"Why do we have to wait until then?" Harrison asked. "Can't you tell us when you get home?"

Robert's smile returned. "You bet I can. And I'd love to do that."

"Okay boys, run upstairs and brush your teeth, and I'll walk you out to the bus stop." Victoria grew impatient.

"Mom, you don't have to do that. I'm old enough to watch out for the little squirt," said Harrison, mussing his brother's hair.

Swatting at Harrison's arm, Jameson whined, "I'm not little, and I'm not a squirt."

"You're *both* getting to be such big boys. But I enjoy my morning walk out to the street with you. I'm afraid you'll just have to indulge me this simple pleasure. Now get upstairs, or I'll have to *drive* you to school, and I know how much you love *that*, Harrison."

"Let's go, squirt." Harrison tugged on his brother's collar and darted for the stairs, Jameson at his heels, protesting the derogatory nickname.

Turning to Robert, Victoria asked, "What time are you leaving?"

"We're planning to hit the road right after we grab an early dinner. Ben invited me to dine with him at his home."

"Oooh, fancy. Dinner at the headmaster's house."

"The kitchen staff does a great job catering the gatherings there, don't they?"

"Yes, and I just love that huge fireplace in the dining room. Looks like something dating from Colonial days that was used for cooking. . . . It will be just you and Ben?"

"I think so. Although Ben has been known to invite an associate along out of the blue. He calls it cross-pollination. Connecting people whose paths wouldn't ordinarily cross and watching what transpires."

"I see. And you're going to drive?"

"Yeah."

She let out an exaggerated exhale. "Really?"

"Yes, Victoria." His expression hardened. "I'm driving. I'm a teacher. Ben is the headmaster. It's expected I will drive."

"Doesn't he realize we only have one car, and so I'll be without one for . . . what, thirty-six hours?"

"More like thirty. But I'm sorry, Tori. Sometimes we have to make sacrifices, and this is one of those times." He paused long enough to calm his voice. "What is it that you have going on that you need the car for?"

"Don't worry about it." She dismissed his question with a shake of her head. "It's nothing important." He didn't need to hear that while he was essentially working overtime, she had nothing of any significance on her calendar. How neurotic would that sound that she wanted to have the car available—in case she needed it to get off campus. He would think her pathetic if she fessed up, so she kept it to herself. "Then I probably won't see you before you go."

Looking up from a handful of papers he'd become engrossed in, Robert said, "Uh . . . no, I guess not. I'll be in classes most of the day, and you've got . . ." He gestured with an open palm for her to fill in the blank.

"I'm meeting Aviva for lunch, and then we're going to go for a hike in her neck of the woods." She paused. "Ha! Didn't mean to make a pun. But anyway, then I'll stop in to see my mother before I head back. Don't worry, I'll have the car back in plenty of time for you. I'll leave it in the usual spot."

"Sounds like a fun day." She glanced his way to gauge his expression, but he seemed genuine in his observation.

"Most of it."

The rumble of muffled footsteps on the center hall stairs announced the boys' arrival before they burst into the kitchen and brushed past her in a race to get to the table to see who could tag it first.

Suddenly the tiny kitchen of their faculty housing was filled with a cacophony of the boys arguing as to who was the winner. Victoria could only imagine what it would have been like if Robert had gotten his wish for four children. He kneeled with outstretched arms, a broad grin on his face.

"All right, boys, let me give you hugs."

The boys embraced their father—Jameson held on a tad longer than his brother—and then scampered toward the front door.

"Have a good day at school," he called after them. "Learn lots of new things. Be nice to everyone. Think for yourselves. Have fun at your soccer practices, and I'll see you tomorrow evening."

"Bye, sweetheart." Victoria blew him a kiss as she hurried to catch up with the boys. "Miss you already," she called over her shoulder.

"Miss you too."

CHAPTER TWO

Seven Years Later

A steady but babbling stream pushed its way through twigs and around sticks fashioned into a home by a beaver and spilled into the shallow stream beyond, trickling past exposed rocks along the way. The hypnotic sound nearly drowned out everything else trying to be heard around her. Chirping wrens and a singular crow with its nagging caw might as well have been miles away. As the gentle breeze played with branches overhead, sunlight dappled her face, painting serenity with a wide brush.

Yet there was something in the air. Something that wasn't right. As she turned to survey her surroundings, her head lurched forward, carrying the rest of her body with it, landing face first in the pond. Water filled her mouth and nose and eyes. She couldn't pull her head up. It was too heavy, as if someone was holding her down.

Bolting upright, gasping, Victoria struggled for air.

She felt a hand on her arm. "Tori . . . Tori, it's okay. It's just a dream."

Vince. He'd made it home. She called it that when he was there because he made it feel that way. But their relationship was complicated—they cared dearly for each other, but Victoria was caught between her feelings for him and her desperate desire to find her husband. She didn't dare ask herself the question, *What would she do if Robert suddenly came back to her.* She was grateful Vince hadn't either.

Victoria grabbed for his other hand and it found its way into hers briefly, then traveled to her back, hunched and trembling with each of her ragged breaths.

"Steady breathing. You'll be okay," he assured her. A quick pat on her back and his hand slipped away.

Wiping sweat off her forehead with the back of her hand, she squinted to see his outline in the dark. "I'm sorry to wake you."

"It's okay, babe." He pulled his other hand away, which left a cold spot on her arm. She ached to reach out and pull them both back, wrap them around her, and snuggle in close to his chest, but she could tell it was the middle of the night. It was always the middle of the night when this happened. And he only had so many hours of sleep before he'd be up and out the door without so much as a cup of coffee in a to-go cup.

"The guest room bed is made up if you want to go in there. I'm sorry. You need your sleep."

Throwing back the covers, she slipped out of the damp sheets into her fuzzy slippers and padded to the bathroom. A hot shower would feel good, take the chill off her skin.

Yanking the curtain open on its oval rod encircling the clawfoot tub, she cranked the faucet as high as it would go. As she waited for the water to get hot, she wrapped her arms around herself, trying to shake off a shiver. She knew better than to look into the mirror at that hour but couldn't help herself—like gawking at an accident scene. Once you do, you can't unsee the tragic mess.

A stranger looked back at her. Dark circles under her eyes seemed worse than usual. Puffy and bruise-like, faded red. Fortunately the intimate—what Vince liked to refer to as miniature—bathroom would steam up quickly and obliterate her image, but she'd have to remember to layer on the concealer thicker than usual in the morning.

The recurring dream only went so far. Was there more for her to see? Would it be revealed if she could hang in there and stay with the dream? She always woke up as she plowed headfirst into the water. Did she lose her balance and fall in? Did someone push her?

Then a more terrifying question crossed her mind; if she did stay asleep and see the dream to the end, would she never wake up?

Balancing on the curved porcelain edge, she peeled off her nightgown and eased her legs up over the side and into the tub, the water swirling at her feet. She leaned into the shower, the beads of water stinging her face. Pulling away to snatch a breath, she leaned in again. She imagined she was under a waterfall in a tropical getaway, willing the nightmare away.

But the images pressed to the forefront of her thoughts. Had the seven years of feeling lost without Robert manifested itself in her dreams? Or was it more literal and a harbinger of things to come?

Turning off the shower, she plucked a plush white towel from the hook next to the sink and blotted the quickly cooling water from her skin. By the time she slipped into her bathrobe, she felt a chill up her back again. Drawing the lingering thick steam into her lungs and letting it out slowly, she envisioned the dream swirling down the drain along with the sudsy water. A clear mind. Only positive thoughts. Restful sleep for what was left of the night. She needed to think it into existence.

Hitting the light switch and tossing her towel on the rack, she returned to bed. Vince's side was empty, and she could hear him sleeping soundly across the hall. Running a hand across the sheet where his body had been, it was already cold. Sliding over to his side, she grabbed the larger of his two pillows and pulled it close, taking in his scent. She lay awake for what seemed like hours, listening to his even, heavy breathing while replaying the dream in her head, the details of which were evaporating from her memory the longer her eyes were open.

CHAPTER THREE

The timeworn wooden box could have been any other vessel used for storing valuables, but this one had been her husband's and was filled with precious memories from his days as a student at the academy—Litchfield Academy or LA—what the boys fondly referred to as La-la Land. Boys whose futures were filled with promise and hope, even if they were too naïve to understand some futures came with a dear price.

"Mom, the car's all packed. We're heading out." His voice came from the bottom of the stairs.

Snatching a breath, she scooped up the box and hurried to the railing along the landing overlooking the small foyer. "Jameson, wait. I want you to have this."

"What, Mom?"

She ignored the impatience in his tone. Her feet touching lightly on each tread, she scampered down the stairs, the third to last one creaking as expected.

"This was your father's when he was a student at Litchfield," she said, presenting the box to him like a trophy at an awards ceremony.

"Why do I need that?" He pulled back as if afraid to touch the relic.

"It's filled with all kinds of memorabilia your father saved that meant a lot to him. I'll bet there's something in there you might find useful. I think there's an old Litchfield pennant you can hang on your wall to personalize your space. I'll bet no one *else* will have one of those. See what's inside," she urged, inching it closer to him.

"Memorabilia." He said it like it was something distasteful, yet he leaned in as if he might slide the patinaed metal hook out of the clasp and open the lid. "Why are you giving this to me now? It's my last year." A honk yanked him back to his posture of indifference. "I gotta go."

As he turned toward the door, she tried again. "Well at least take it. Open it when you have a chance."

"All right. Fine." He tucked the box under his arm—his sizable frame making it appear to shrink in size—and gave her a quick peck on her cheek before punching the latch on the screen door. "See you at Presentation later?" he called back to her.

"Yes, of course. I'll be there. See you then." She caught the frame of the screen before it slammed shut. "Oh, Jameson, did you grab your meds?" she yelled.

Jameson stopped short of pulling open the passenger side door, fist on the handle. Turning toward her, he nodded with his lips pressed firmly together as if holding in words that would hurt her and then slipped into the front seat.

"How about the dress shirts I ironed?" she yelled again after lunging onto the front step. "They were hanging on the back—"

"Yeah, got 'em." He poked a thumbs up through the open passenger window.

"And your ties?" Laughter spilled from within the car. She watched as his friend punched Jameson in a playful jab on the shoulder.

"Yup, all set. Thanks." His smile seemed forced. Her insides twisted at the sound of the two of them snickering at her expense. Her baby seemed a different person when his friends were around.

"Okay . . . text me when you get there." She waved to the boys as they backed out of the driveway, tires catching on the pavement, leaving a patch of rubber before they set off down the street.

Wrapping her arms across her chest, Victoria's eye caught the glint of sunlight reflecting on a puddle on a worn slate stepping stone as she let herself get lost in the ache from the vacuum of her son's absence. She stepped back inside, letting the screen door slam into place. Even though she'd expected the sound, it made her body stiffen.

The air in the house suddenly grew cold, and the stillness had a ringing in it that filled her head. Her younger son didn't need her to help him move in for his senior year. After being a part of the process for the past three Septembers, she hadn't imagined him not needing her there. Or was it not wanting her there? That would feel even worse, if that were the case.

And instead of having one last evening to spend with him, Jameson had invited his buddy Lance Martin—the headmaster's son—for a sleepover of sorts and one last hurrah, saying it was the least he should do after Lance offered to pick him up with all of his stuff and help him move in—the school being an hour's drive away.

It was Jameson exerting his independence, she told herself—after all, he'd be heading off to college in a year—but it didn't make it hurt any less. With a lump in her throat that couldn't be swallowed away, she had to set her sights on, and settle for, heading to campus later that evening.

It was a time-honored tradition at Litchfield Academy. After a day of parents and siblings swarming the campus to help their sons and brothers settle into its quaint English-cottage-style dorms on the two-hundred-year-old campus, they were all treated to a family-style meal, served by the students, at long wooden tables with seating on uncomfortable benches.

Once the parents' meal was cleared, students partook of their own dinner while the parents enjoyed cocktails out in the courtyard strung with festive white lights to commemorate the venerable occasion. The few siblings that had been dragged to the affair were whisked away to be amused by members of the drama club.

Victoria had decided to skip the dinner festivities so she could forgo having to mingle as a single in a room full of couples, struggling to maintain a confident, contented face. When she mentioned it to Jameson, he didn't seem broken up about it. She would only have to worry about getting into and out of the auditorium with minimal interaction.

Following dinner and cocktails, Presentation of the Senior Class was held in the auditorium, which was where she would catch up with Jameson. There, the young men would be treated to a barrage of directives from the headmaster as well as other senior educators who felt compelled to lay out weighty expectations and objectives for the year ahead. Getting through the evening seemed to be a rite of passage to senior year. Skipping it was not an option—certainly not under Headmaster Martin's watch.

With the departure of one son, Victoria yearned to reach out by text to the other, who had already begun his college classes on the West Coast. Texting was the one format the boys seemed to respond to. If she called, they wouldn't always pick up and, only if they remembered, would they text later.

// Hey, Harrison. How are you doing? Jameson left for move-in day at LA. House is kind of empty now. I imagine you're settling into your classes by now? //

She waited and considered texting Jameson, but he'd just walked out the door. Too soon.

To her surprise, she got a reply right back.

// hey mom yup doing gd wlkng to clas now //

// Oh! Good to hear from you, Harrison. Which class are you on your way to? //

// histry of architctre //

// Whaaaat? Why are you taking that? That can't be in your plan of studies for pre-med. //

// lol its not but it fills a gen ed req // // prtty intrsting. //

// That's good. //

// yeah we have a project coming up i tink im going to do it on LA //

// Litchfield Academy? //

// yea //

// Oh! Interesting. I'd love to see it when you're finished. //

// sure // // gotta go. im at my clss //

// Okay, Harrison. Great catching up with you. //

// same and dont worry abt the little squirt. hell be fine //

Victoria grinned. Some nicknames you just didn't outgrow—especially when it's your older brother who has bestowed it upon you.

// I'm sure you're right. All right, have a good class. Love you. //

// thx u 2 //

When her cell vibrated in her hand again, she thought it was another text from Harrison. Instead, the refrain of Simon & Garfunkel's "Bridge Over Troubled Water" spilled from the speaker, the ringtone she'd assigned to her best friend.

"Hey, Veeve. What's going on?" Victoria tried to keep her voice steady but knew her friend wouldn't be fooled. She and Aviva went way back. Back to their flight-attendant days with Southeast Airlines. During training they'd become fast friends and still were close. Maybe too much so.

"Hey, girl. How are *you* doing? Has he left yet?"

"Yeah, just now." Victoria leaned over to take in the infectious perfume of coral-colored roses gracing the demilune table in the foyer. They were dwarfed by the substantial antique mirror hanging above it.

Robert had figured out early on in their marriage how much she liked that particular shade of pink rose and, without fail, had them delivered every year on her birthday. When they continued to arrive after he disappeared, she was stunned. Each time she called the florist—a different one each year and located in a circumference of towns at significant driving distances throughout New England—without fail, the flowers had been purchased with cash, so there was no way to track their origin.

She wanted to think her sons were responsible, but since her birthday fell around Labor Day, when the boys were heading off to school or were already there, her day was often forgotten. If they thought to text her to acknowledge her day, she felt fortunate.

Victoria finally decided the only other person who knew her well enough to know what to send was Aviva. But she denied it—more vehemently each time.

"So, you doing okay?"

Victoria knew her silence spoke volumes, but she couldn't put the words together fast enough. Reality was crashing in on her. She was alone—completely and miserably alone.

No one was in the house that needed her care. Not even a goldfish. No one to bake their favorite lasagna for. No one who needed her to run a forgotten lunch over to school. No scraped knees to nurse.

Admittedly the last two were in the distant past, but she missed being the one to take care of them—terribly.

"You're not, are you?" Aviva tried again. It was more of a statement than a question.

Drawing in a lung-filling breath, Victoria let it go before saying, "No . . . no, I'm not." Her voice wobbled. "I know it's silly. Most women in my shoes would be—"

"But you're *not* most women. These are *your* shoes. You feel how you feel. That's all there is to it."

Her friend's truism made her smile. Aviva always seemed to come up with the right words to say, until she didn't.

"Thanks, Veeve. Appreciate that. I know I'll get over it and move on." She cringed at the way that sounded like they were talking about a death in the family and quickly added, "I still have the Presentation tonight—which I'm looking forward to."

"Good to hear. Are you going alone?"

Victoria couldn't envision how else she would be going. Vince had yet to set foot on campus for Jameson—he hadn't for Harrison, either—always having work as an excuse. She didn't expect him to suddenly show up for this. And Victoria had always let it slide. Litchfield Academy had been their father's domain—as a student and later as a revered and respected educator—one who seemed an obvious choice and on track to be headmaster.

"Yes, I'm going alone." She could hear an edge of annoyance in her words but did not regret them. She needed Aviva to back down on her ongoing contempt of Vince.

"Well, I'm happy to go with you if you'd like company. I don't fly again for a couple days."

"That's very generous of you, but I wouldn't dream of asking you to sit through this snooze fest. It would be one thing if it was a drama performance or even a concert. But this will be an excruciatingly boring ordeal. Thanks, but I'll go it alone."

"All right. If you're sure. But keep me in mind for next time."

Victoria had an inkling her single friend was dying to get onto

campus to meet and perhaps catch the eye of one of the eligible bachelors—divorced and rolling in it. There were a surprisingly large
number of them there. What was it about certain guys who seemed
to age gracefully?

"And I know you'll get over it, like you said. You need a little
time—or a diversion."

"Aviva . . ." Victoria knew her friend would broach the topic again.
She just didn't expect it to be minutes after her house had suddenly
grown eerily quiet.

"This may be too soon, but you should *seriously* think about getting
your wings back. How fun would it be to fly together again?"

It wasn't a new proposal by any means; Aviva had brought it up
on numerous occasions. Victoria had turned in her wings at Vince's
urging not long after they'd started seeing each other, and it was the
right thing to do. Having been involuntarily thrust into single parent-
hood, she couldn't be a proper mother from thirty thousand feet and
hundreds of miles away, although letting that career go made money
inexorably tight.

"Aviva. No. That's not going to happen." Even though it was fun
to imagine, Victoria would *never* be able to compete with the young
single women vying for one of those cute blue-and-red-fitted uniforms
with the heart pin over the left breast. That ship had sailed—or in
aviation-speak, that plane had not only left the gate, it had taken off
and was halfway across the Atlantic.

"Why not?" she protested. "Your house is empty. I know you're a
fixer—a problem solver—but there is no one left to fix things for. At a
minimum, it's time they figured out how to solve their own problems.
They'll never learn if you keep doing it for them."

This, from the woman who'd been married and divorced before
the ink was dry on the marriage license and didn't have children but
was quick to offer "fixing" advice of her own when it came to them.
She didn't seem to understand that fixing was what mothers did. It
was in the job description, not to mention a mother's instincts. But
Victoria wasn't going to throw that in her face. Aviva undoubtedly

would love to have kids, even though she insisted her career was all she'd ever wanted.

"You need to redirect your energy." Aviva wasn't going to let it go.

"Do you think I'm too controlling?" There, she'd said it. Enough of the dancing around what her friend really meant.

Aviva paused before answering, "Yeah, I do. As far as your kids go. I mean, I wouldn't call you a helicopter mom. Maybe you were when they were younger. You're happiest when you're in control . . . but they've outgrown the need for that kind of control."

Relieved Aviva couldn't see the burning she felt creeping onto her cheeks, Victoria wondered if she *had* been too domineering with the boys. Was that why Jameson was so hell-bent on leaving her behind today? Because he finally could? But who could blame her as a single mother? Had she been that way before she'd lost Robert?

"All I'm saying is it's time for you to pull back and be more selfish. Think about yourself for once. It's your time now."

Her time?

"This didn't exactly happen overnight. Your boys have been pretty independent for quite some time now."

Victoria silently pleaded with her to let it go.

"And how about your travel agency? Is that as profitable as you'd hoped? How many hours a day do you spend on that?"

Not enough, Victoria answered to herself. What had seemed like a logical next step—starting an online travel service with her extensive, first-hand knowledge of the industry—fizzled as more and more people booked their own trips on the burgeoning number of DIY websites. It was disheartening to have her business fail before it really got off the ground.

"And your baking business . . . you seem to put an awful lot of time into it. Every time I call, you're either pulling cookies out of the oven or frosting a cake. Is that profitable?"

"Aviva, I'm not going to discuss my finances with you."

"You're right. I'm sorry. I was over the line with that one. I'm just trying to be your friend here. I bet you would make a lot *more* money if you got back into flying. And probably spend less time at it than you do at your two businesses now."

"Perhaps," Victoria was slow to admit.

"And what do you do for fun? Anything? You know, besides when you hang out with me."

"Well, of course. I've got tennis and my book club." Victoria crinkled her nose at how defensive she sounded.

"How the hell can either of those be that much fun? You need some excitement in your life, girl."

Victoria acknowledged to herself her book club had turned into more of a wine club, which had its merits in the form of diversion. But she dragged herself to each gathering, clutching the book she'd devoured from cover to cover, knowing most of the ladies hadn't cracked the spine.

Tennis was the one saving grace, although lately she'd realized she was the oldest member on the team—in some cases by decades—as many of her friends had faded to the sidelines with lingering injuries, reprioritized their leisure time after the arrival of grandbabies, or moved away to a warmer climate. Victoria had taken a break from tennis for the summer; she preferred playing indoors with consistent conditions—no wind, sun, or bugs to worry about. She'd hoped to get back into it come fall but had yet to hear from the team captain about the practice schedule. Had she been left behind on that venture as well?

Maybe Aviva was right—she certainly had a more objective perspective—maybe there was no longer any fun in her life. Even so, she wasn't going to let Aviva tell her what to do. *She* would make that decision. This was under Victoria's control—but there was that word again.

"You don't have to answer that. You already have with your silence. All I'm saying is this is the perfect time to jump back into flying. Get out of small-town Dullsville and see at least a small part of the rest of the world. It would do you good. Your boys are grown. Vince is entombed in his career. Don't lose yourself again."

"Forget it. It's not happening, so get it out of your . . . what do you mean 'again'?"

"Are you worried about what Vince would say?" Aviva ignored her question. "How could he protest this time? Your hatchlings have flown the coop. Hell, you should just *tell* him this is what you're doing. Why should he care? You said yourself, he's never around."

"Aviva." Her voice may have been louder than she'd intended, but Victoria needed to stop her overzealous friend before her rant got out of control, and she said things Victoria would hate her for. "Not now."

"Hell, maybe you'd even meet a guy who'd treat you the way you deserve to be treated."

"Aviva," Victoria snapped.

After a beat, Aviva conceded. "All right . . . fine . . . for now."

"Oh, and Veeve. Thanks for the roses. So nice of you to remember my birthday."

"Girl." The syllable was drawn out more than necessary. "How many times do I have to tell you? It's not me. Remember? I'm the shitty friend who always forgets."

Victoria chose not to believe that. No other explanation made sense.

CHAPTER FOUR

Having made the drive to Litchfield Falls too many times over the years to count, Victoria was grateful for the sparkling autumn late afternoon to get a renewed appreciation for the sights along the way. It was all back roads and took about an hour door-to-door with plenty of time to get lost in one's thoughts and reflections. Halfway there Victoria realized she'd never heard from Jameson. He meant well, but his track record for texting to let her know he'd arrived safely at his destination was only around fifty percent—if that.

If she could have figured out how to work the controls for the sunroof, Victoria would have opened it enough to bring in the cool, crisp air. The Mercedes—whatever model it was—that Vince had insisted she needed to fit in with the other parents at the academy, seemed so over-the-top to her. He'd been more than generous to buy it for her, but she'd been perfectly happy with her seven-year-old Jeep Cherokee, right up until the day she'd had to trade it in to pick up this light blue sporty sedan that he'd hand selected for her.

So happy, she'd shed tears as she caught the Jeep in her rearview mirror on her way out of the lot. Not just a few tears, gut-wrenching sobs. She was relieved Vince wasn't in the car with her to witness the spectacle. It wasn't pretty.

Rounding the last curve before the gates of the academy, the first of the brownstone structures came into sight up on the hill, replete with their slate roofs and humble wooden doors; the art center with its classroom space and gallery where the boys' work was showcased, and at the top of the bluff, the highest point on campus, the revered chapel where the boys endured vespers on Sunday evenings dressed in their navy-blue jackets with the gold insignia on the pocket and gray wool trousers.

Victoria found it amusing that the strict dress code seemed to end at the ankles though. If you were to glance down the dimly lit pews with a flashlight in hand, you'd see all manner of shoe coverings and in all manner of conditions. Clearly the standards were set by the male counterparts of the administration and enforced by the male members of the faculty. Some of what they let pass as appropriate must have kept the few female teachers struggling to retain their composure. The occasional mud-caked work boots or fur lined moccasins brought a smile to Victoria's face, although she would never have permitted her sons to don either, in flagrant disregard of the intent of the rules, as some boys did.

The gates were splayed wide open to welcome students and all who chose to venture onto campus for opening day but would be secured once the festivities had concluded in the evening. A smaller, less grander side entrance a quarter of a mile down the road was used when classes were in session—one with a gate that could be raised and lowered by security that staffed the booth.

Not expecting anyone to be exiting the campus, Victoria jammed on the brakes when a truck pulled through the gates, cutting her off. Throwing her arm across her nonexistent passenger to keep her from going through the windshield did nothing to keep her purse from sailing off the seat and slamming into the glove compartment before dropping to the floor with a dull thud.

"Jesus," she barked. "That was close." And to the offending driver, she said, "Try looking next time." Not that the driver could hear her, but it made her feel better.

As the double "S" on the back of the truck disappeared around the bend in the road, she added, "Stockwell Sanitation, if you were anywhere else, you'd have to get your shit together and watch who you've got driving your trucks. Good thing you have an in with Headmaster Martin."

Once through the grand wrought iron gates, a series of campus security guards in reflective vests guided her like aircraft marshallers past the brimming main parking lot to the field down the hill she recognized as the one used by the thirds soccer team. Those who had gotten there early and partaken in opening day move-in got to enjoy the added perk of parking in the paved lot. Those who had ducked out of it—or were precluded from it—were relegated to the outskirts of campus.

Shoving the shift into park and cutting the engine, she retrieved her phone from the console and texted Jameson to give him a light-hearted poke.

// Hey Jameson. I trust you found your way. I'm here. //

She didn't expect an immediate response, but when her cell buzzed with a call, she didn't hesitate to hit the answer icon.

"Oh shit." It was only then she realized the caller ID read Brookhaven. And there were two missed calls from them as well. How had she not heard it ring? Hopefully she could keep it brief. The Presentation would be starting shortly, and she didn't want to have to walk all the way to the front to find an open seat.

"Hello," she said, and then pleaded with the universe. *Please don't let it be something urgent. Nothing serious. Please let her still be alive.*

"Mrs. Sands?"

"Yes, but please call me Victoria." How many times did she have to ask? Perhaps it was their protocol, but it was annoying to have to correct them every time they spoke.

"Victoria, this is Barbara, the head nurse here at Brookhaven. I'm calling to uh . . . I'm afraid we need to discuss your mother's situation." Her sing-songy intonation sounded forced.

"Is she okay?" What had she done now? Sliced her finger open in arts and crafts class? Left her wet clothes sitting in one of the community washers too long, and they had a major mold problem on their hands?

"Yes, she's fine. I'm sorry to have alarmed—"

"Then what's going on?"

"I'm afraid this facility may not be a good fit for her any longer."

Already? Victoria hadn't seen that coming. Or had she and simply chose to ignore the signs?

"When your mother arrived, her dementia hadn't presented itself in the way it does now. She seems to be transitioning into a phase of her disease that we're not equipped to handle. We don't have a separate Alzheimer's unit."

The "A" word hit her firmly in the gut. The word dementia didn't seem as much of a death sentence as the "A" word, but she knew she was just fooling herself.

"What's going on?" Victoria bit the side of her lip as she braced for the news.

"She's taken to wandering around the halls—which, in and of itself, wouldn't be a problem—but now she's taking it upon herself to enter other residents' rooms. She makes herself at home, so when the other residents return, they get upset and it turns into quite an explosive situation. She doesn't seem to get bothered by all the fuss the other residents make, but you can understand how it would be upsetting to them."

"Does she do anything when she's in their rooms? Take anything?"

"Well, not that we can tell, but that's not the point. It's very upsetting to the other residents, and we can't seem to make her understand that."

Having received too many of these calls, Victoria pushed out an audible exhale. They'd become more frequent lately. Couldn't they find a resolution on their end? How about restricting access to other hallways with a push button code? What did they expect her to do? She hated that they were dumping this in her lap.

"So, what do you want from me?" She felt her shoulders sag as she asked the question she knew the answer to.

"Mrs. Sands, we need to talk about her options. Could we make an appointment to sit down and chat?"

Chat. That was their euphemism for being grilled by the director of nursing, the director of resident services, and the managing director of Brookhaven. Three against one. Not exactly her idea of a good time, and she had no one to drag along to join the fun.

"Of course. I'd be happy to stop in." Why can't adults say what they really mean? Like: *No. I don't want to make an appointment so you can confront me—gang up on me—only so we can dance around the issue until I offer to pull my renegade mother out of your uncompassionate facility. You* can't *find a solution for this? Or you have no intention of finding one?*

"That would be wonderful. Could you stop in early next week, say Monday morning at 9:00?"

"Monday morning? No, actually. I can't." She had nothing going on, but she wasn't about to let them push her around.

"Okay, no problem. What works for you?" The lilt in her voice had all but disappeared.

"Uh, let me take a look." She paused long enough to feign checking her busy schedule. "Well, I could probably swing by later that afternoon. Say three o'clock?" There. It was her calling the shots. Let's see what they do with that.

"That sounds fine."

That was too easy. *Damn it.*

"Okay."

"Great. We'll see you then, Mrs. Sands." Click.

"Victoria," she shrieked at the silence on the other end. "Damn it." She slammed her phone into the back of the passenger seat. "Damn it," she sputtered, smacking the steering wheel, which elicited an unintended toot. Not venturing a glance around her to see if she'd aroused anyone's attention, she fetched her abused cell and checked to see if Jamison had responded. He hadn't.

Why did caring for your aging parent have to be so complicated? Why couldn't the facility you entrusted with your family member's wellbeing figure it out? Was she being insensitive about this? Maybe a better question was, considering she had a brother, why was looking out for her mother left entirely up to her?

Those were questions for another day—next week, to be more accurate. For now, Victoria was going to focus on the evening ahead and catching up with her son. She could use a Jameson hug right now.

CHAPTER FIVE

Cursing her choice of shoes, Victoria tiptoed to keep her heels from sinking into the muddy field the academy was using to accommodate the overflow vehicles. If it wasn't still light out, she would have considered dispensing with the pumps all together and running barefoot. Maybe on the way back.

In spite of her best efforts, her calves grew tired and her heels dropped lower with each step, poking a series of holes in the soft dirt in a random, zig-zag pattern.

"I'll bet you weren't expecting to hike across campus tonight." His deliciously British accent sounded familiar, and when Victoria turned toward the voice, she saw the father of one of Jameson's friends—one of the recently divorced, well off, available ones. Not to mention, extremely good looking. Maybe too much so. Was that possible? Thank goodness she'd told Aviva she'd come alone. No telling where things would have led if she hadn't.

Victoria couldn't recall if they'd formally met, but with both sons in their senior year, they'd crossed paths many times, her noticing him but not the other way around. In the past, his then wife—perfectly vivacious in her size two Dolce & Gabbana pantsuit or dress—was wrapped around his arm as if she was afraid someone might steal him if she let go. Looked like he'd successfully broken loose.

"Not at all. Could you tell from my shoe selection?" They both laughed and paused where their paths converged.

"I'd offer to lay down my jacket for you, but I'm afraid that wouldn't get you very far." He chuckled at the suggestion. "And it would take forever to get there if I had to keep picking it up and moving it closer." She felt a flutter in her gut at his doting and sense of humor. *Was this the kind of treatment Aviva was referring to?*

"Generous thought though, thank you. But I've already made a mess of them." She lifted one foot and took a swipe at the mud on the heel. "No sense taking out your jacket too."

"Fair enough." He extended his hand. "Emerson Kittridge."

"Victoria Sands," she countered.

"Ah, yes, Victoria Sands." He was the touchy-feely type who grasped firmly with both hands. She may have held on a little longer than necessary. His touch was tender. A crisp white cuff peeked out from his tweed jacket. Her eyes landed on a square gold cuff link with some sort of insignia or initials on it. "You're Jameson's mom." Behind him and across the field a helicopter sat on the pad with its rotors still rotating, but slowing.

"That's right. And you're—"

"Asher's father." He'd filled in a blank she hadn't created. Annoyance flared up inside, but she reigned it in.

"Right." Even in the waning daylight, his chiseled cheekbones and perfectly coifed light brown, wavy hair with just a touch of gray along the edges of his face gave him the look of someone well-educated and well-traveled with just the right family tree. Or maybe it was the silk scarf draped effortlessly around his neck, one end tucked inside his jacket. But it was certainly the sleek, tan Italian loafers that allowed him to pull off the dark denim jeans. She was intrigued by his sun-kissed ankles peeking out between the two. Where had they been soaking up the sun recently?

"Going my way?" He nodded toward the auditorium, light spilling from the open doors along the front.

"Let's." She half expected him to offer an elbow, what with the chivalrous talk about sacrificing his jacket, but she was relieved he hadn't. Her soiled shoes were enough of a spectacle. And the unexpected tingle in her abdomen was . . . well, enough too. She couldn't remember the last time a man's attention had made her feel that way.

"I see you missed the dinner too," Victoria said.

"Yes . . . ran into a bit of traffic getting out of the city."

She caught his wink and they shared a laugh.

As they approached the steps to the bustling auditorium, a familiar grin shifted into view. Jameson's. And to his side was his friend Asher. No one could tell Victoria the Fates were not a thing.

"Hey, Mom." He slipped his arms around her and hugged her tight—a welcome change in temperament from earlier in the day. Had it only been a few hours? Hopefully the embrace wasn't something the students were instructed to do. It was warm and lasted just long enough, either way.

"Mr. Kittridge." Jameson extended his hand to his friend's father. Emerson's handshake looked firm, but he didn't use the two-handed technique he'd used on her. Asher followed with a handshake of his own for his father. Victoria found this rather common behavior between fathers and sons on campus a bit too formal. Distant even. She wondered if Robert were still around if Jameson would have hugged him in this situation or followed suit and kept it by-the-book for appearances.

"Victoria . . . Emerson." The approaching voice bordered on booming, drawing out their names like he was announcing them in a raffle, as though the increased volume would make up for his modest stature. Jameson took a step back to allow room for Headmaster Martin to join their circle. "Good to see you both." One of his hands ended up on Victoria's middle back, the other on Jameson's shoulder in what had a remarkable resemblance to a raptor's grip with Martin's hand higher than his own shoulder. Jameson appeared to be doing his utmost to stifle a flinch.

Martin's eyes traveled from Victoria to Emerson and back again, no doubt having seen them approach the gathering together. He removed the hand from her back and extended it to Emerson, and they shook.

"Boys, you'll want to run along and take your places on stage," Martin said, dismissing them and leaving no room for discussion. They knew not to run counter to the headmaster and scampered through the doors like two bunnies frightened by a fox in the woods.

"Fine young men, both of them," he offered, wringing hands that were so dry you could hear the friction he was generating. "This is going to be a banner year. So much ahead of them. They will no doubt both be up for the Headmaster's Scholarship. Tough competition for that, for sure, but they'll be in it."

The Headmaster's Scholarship was the largest and most prestigious of all the awards presented to the boys toward the end of their senior year—so sizable, the names of the committee members charged with selecting the recipient were not revealed until after the award was announced. Deliberations were held behind closed doors, and the word on campus was that security was tight.

"It will be exciting to see whose name joins the company of a long line of academy elite up on the plaque outside my office."

It went without saying his son Lance—an overachiever like his father—would be the frontrunner. Victoria was fairly confident Jameson would be in the running, but the headmaster was being generous by adding Asher's name to the mix, no doubt to stroke Emerson's ego.

"And I hope that the Parents Committee can count on you two this year. Your experience and knowledge as parents of seniors is . . . well, they could use your input. And fundraising efforts this year could use a boost. How can a freshman parent refuse a call from either of you? When you tell them how Asher and Jameson grew from mere boys coming here out of junior high, into young men with their picks of impressive colleges to attend—all because of their years here at Litchfield, they'll be lunging for their checkbooks to support the fine institution that made it all possible . . . and will make it possible for their sons." His incessant nodding reminded Victoria of the bobblehead bulldog on the dashboard of her father's old Chevy Skylark. As a young girl she would mimic it from the backseat and giggle.

Emerson took the lead and answered, "I'd be happy to help."

With a side glance to the dapper man in the tweed jacket, Victoria felt she had no other option than to agree. "Sure thing."

"Great to hear. Thank you both for your undying support. Missi is the chair this year. I'll be sure to have her get in touch with you."

Victoria struggled to wriggle her grimace into what she hoped looked like a grin. Parents weren't supposed to go against the headmaster's wishes either. Few tried it. Better to say yes now and dodge the Parent Committee chair later. The only problem with that strategy this year was that Missi was his wife. His second, much younger, wife who seemed to be out to prove herself as a legitimate member of the administration to the tuition-paying parents.

"Well, I must be off as well and get things started. Good to see you two," he repeated. "See you in there." He patted them both on their upper arms in unison.

"Always a pleasure," Emerson called after him. Turning to Victoria, he gestured toward the entrance, "Shall we?"

"Can't think of anything I'd rather do," she said, feeling her shoulders tense as they approached.

Accepting a program from a bright-eyed young man at the door, whose right-off-the-ironing-board blazer and trousers screamed freshman, Victoria entered the hall with Emerson right behind her, which begged the question: Were they going to sit together? And more importantly, if so, how would that be perceived by others? A recently divorced man and a woman whose husband—she wasn't sure how to describe him. Missing, but might still be alive? Some probably assumed she was divorced too. The rest, who knew her situation, assumed Robert was dead. Victoria refused to utter the word—certainly not in the same breath with his name.

Suddenly it seemed as though every head had pivoted, and all eyes in the brightly lit auditorium had turned to watch their next move.

Her concerns were soon doused like a bucket of water on a match when she heard Emerson answer someone who'd called his name and then felt a tug on her sleeve. "I'll catch up with you later—" He nodded toward a guy with a bad case of receding hairline waving him over. "—to help you find your car in the dark, if you'd like."

Victoria had to admit there was something stirring within her from the attention he'd showered on her. Okay, maybe not showered. Perhaps a healthy sprinkle. She hadn't realized she'd been so thirsty.

Victoria allowed herself a laugh—as much for him as others within earshot—and then focused on finding a place of her own to sit. Thankfully she only had to go about a third of the way down before finding one, and just in time. After shuffling past a couple engrossed in their conversation with another couple in the row behind them, she plunked her backside into the next available stadium-style seat as the lights went down.

CHAPTER SIX

By the time the lights came back up, Victoria had started to nod off. Allowing herself to get swept up in the enthusiasm of the rest of the parents, she rose to her feet and clapped along with them. In veritable facial calisthenics, she began raising her eyebrows and letting them drop repeatedly, hoping to get rid of any signs of sleepiness. She longed to be the young girl two rows in front of her who was snoozing contentedly—her head nuzzled into her coat bunched up on the arm of her chair—in spite of the exuberant parents towering all around her.

Making her way down the aisle toward the stage, Victoria wove through a maze of vaguely familiar faces. Only a handful of people spoke—mostly men. It was remarkable she'd had two sons go through Litchfield, and yet had no real friends there—just a few acquaintances. How had she become so disconnected? Would it have been different if Robert were still alive? Of course it would have. He had a gentle way with people, including the students. Everyone loved him. He would have been the headmaster by now. And Victoria would have been at his side, supporting him, doing whatever he needed her to do—even heading up the Parents Committee. They'd always been a team that way. And Victoria didn't mind being in the background, if that was what he needed. Without him by her side, she felt adrift at times.

"Mom!" Jameson's eager voice was a treat to her ears, a lifeline she could latch onto to escape the sea of strangers. She felt a tug on her elbow, and she turned toward his voice.

"Jameson, there you are."

Distracted by a fist plowed into his upper arm, he playfully swatted a passing shoulder. "Hey, Payton, what's up?" Jameson tossed his head back in acknowledgment as the young man responded in kind.

"What an inspirational program. Did you enjoy it?" she teased.

"Yeah, sure. Mr. Martin has a way with words sometimes." It was a half-hearted effort to come up with something positive, but she'd take it. "Listen, Mom, I gotta go. But thanks for coming."

"I wouldn't have missed it." Disappointed at his abruptness, she hoped her words sounded more upbeat than she felt.

"Oh and . . ." He leaned in. "You and Asher's dad . . . You're not thinking about . . ." He scrunched up his face like a small child refusing to eat spinach.

"What? Of course not." *Who was she kidding? She would kill to be "with" a guy like Emerson—unabashed good looks that many a younger man must covet, suaveness that would make his British ancestors proud, and an accent that made her name, when it sashayed off his tongue, sound like it belonged to an angel. Utterly irresistible, not to mention filthy rich. What warm-blooded female wouldn't want to get swept up into his jet-setting lifestyle? But she was just having fun fantasizing about it. He seemed the type who would greet every unescorted woman as he had her. He had a way of making you feel like you were the reason he was there.*

"Okay, sorry. I had to ask. 'Cause, you know, that would be weird and all."

"That would bother you?"

"For my mother to date one of my friend's fathers? Yeah." He dragged out the last word. "Just a little. More than a little."

"Well, I don't think that's going to happen, so don't give it another thought." *You either, Victoria.*

"Okay, great. All right, well, drive carefully home." *Did he have to make it so obvious he was verbally shoving her toward the door?* "Tell Grams hello for me next time you see her." She wasn't going to divulge she'd be seeing her next week, and his grandmother's circumstances would be changing dramatically—and not for the good. "Love you, Mom." He reached out and wrapped his long arms around her.

"Love you too, sweetheart." Her words were nearly lost as she buried her face into his shoulder where it always ended up due to his height.

His hug had always been a particularly tight one, even when he was a little guy and first understood what it meant to hug. They got to calling his embraces Jameson Hugs, that only he could dole out. In fact they used the term when he was little as their secret code should they get separated and someone claimed to be able to take him to her. Thankfully they'd never had to use it. Now that he had grown into a six-foot, well-built young athlete, she felt secure inside his hug, even though, as his mother, she was the one who was supposed to make him feel safe and secure.

Words were spilling from her lips before she'd pulled away from his chest. "Now you buckle down and stay on top of your studies. I know how easy it is to get behind because you think you have the whole year ahead of you. But it goes fast. And you're going to have more distractions this year, being a senior and your college applications and all. So, keep your wits about you."

"Yeah, Mom. Don't worry. I got this."

"I know you do. You're a smart young man. You take after your father. You have a strong sense of responsibility." The last part she added as much to underscore the importance of having one as to speak it into existence. "I'm so proud of you. Your father would be too."

His face tinged with a seldom seen darkness. She hadn't meant to drop a weight on his shoulders, but she had.

Someone called his name from the boisterous crowd of young men milling about with their parents. As he looked in the direction of the shout, she was relieved to see his brief somberness had disappeared. "I'll be right there," he called.

"Okay, one more hug, and I'll be off." She grabbed him around the ribcage and hung on until she didn't dare to any longer. Backing off a bit, she let her hand slip down to his and held on for a moment. "Keep in touch," she added, although she knew she was treading precariously close to nagging. A swallow caught in her throat. The thought of letting go was paralyzing. He took the lead and pulled away first.

"See you at Thanksgiving." With that, he turned and slipped through the crowd, disappearing into a sea of navy-blue jackets.

Getting jostled from all sides, it was difficult to keep her feet planted on the floor. Multiple conversations around her competed for airspace.

In spite of being in a grand auditorium, an overwhelming feeling of claustrophobia swept over her. Eyeing the side exit near the stage that had been propped open to let in fresh air, she pushed through the crowd. A rather rotund man she recognized as the chair of the math department belted out a guffaw on her way by. A few steps later, an errant elbow caught her in the side and nearly knocked the breath out of her. There may have been an apology thrown her way, but it got lost in the din of the crowd.

Victoria was nearly there and could feel the cool air on her face. A few more strides, after side-stepping to keep from ramming into the backside of a woman who had suddenly bent over to pick up the phone she'd dropped, and she crossed the threshold. She pulled in the cool air. Her ears were ringing like they had so many times after rock concerts when she was younger.

This time she slipped off her heels and walked back to her car alone. No one else seemed to be leaving as early, so there was no one to offer his coat or an arm to escort her. She picked up her pace as raindrops started to fall. It was a cold rain. And it did nothing to pull her out of the melancholy state leaving her son behind had brought on.

CHAPTER SEVEN

Since it was a light rain, she cracked the windows to let in fresh air and sucked it in. Leaving behind the campus where she felt more like a visitor than a seasoned upperclassman parent—for the second time, Victoria was grateful Jameson was at home there with dear friends—some of which would end up being life-long friends or so the marketing brochure touted.

Making her way along the winding road that meandered through the dark woods, she found it to be a different experience at night. And not a pleasant one. Victoria's eyes darted from one side of the road to the other, expecting a deer or some other wildlife to dash out in front of her. Screeching brakes, skidding tires, and a well-timed scream made for a heart-pumping scene in a horror movie—not a smooth ride home. She felt her chest tighten at the thought. A call to Vince would provide her with the distraction she needed until she could put some distance between herself and campus. Tapping the screen on her dash a few times, she listened for the ringing and wondered if he would answer.

He picked up on the second ring. "Hey, Tori. How's it going? You doing okay?"

"Hey, Vince. Yeah, I'm fine." It seemed he *had* remembered Jameson was leaving for school after all. "Just leaving campus now." Was she going to let on that she hadn't been there all day, helping him move in and joining in on the festivities? No. She would keep that to herself.

"Did Jameson get settled in okay?"

"Yeah, no problem at all. You know, he's a senior now. Has done it a few times already. I almost didn't need to be there," she fibbed.

"True . . . so, you've had a long day."

Yes, but not for the reason he thought. "The Presentation Ceremony just ended, so I'm heading home."

"Oh, that's right." He hadn't remembered that part. But could she blame him? Jameson wasn't his flesh and blood. And he only had so much time he could devote to his personal life. The fewer people that required his attention, the better. She was grateful when it was her who was the recipient.

"How's your evening going? Will you be heading my way soon?" Victoria refrained from referring to her place as their home—at least not to him—even though he'd logged some quality hours there since Jameson had left for his freshman year at Litchfield. But it didn't feel right. Not yet.

She wasn't expecting an answer in the affirmative, but in her infinite optimism, she figured it didn't hurt to ask. He might surprise her. But when he and his team were working on a criminal case, he rarely came up for air. Which was why he didn't make the forty-five-minute drive from Hartford each night. Instead he kept extra clothes in his office, had scheduled dry cleaner deliveries there, and regularly took a room in the Marriott across the street from his building. She didn't know what he expected from his staff or if he made any accommodations for them. She didn't ask.

"No, I'm afraid not. It's crunch time with two cases. A third just got added—"

"A third? Sounds like a lot." Probably couldn't say no to another client. Cha-ching. Cha-ching. "Couldn't you refer them to another attorney?"

"No, this one I needed to take on myself. And we're making some good progress on all three. So, I want to crank out a couple more hours while we're still going strong." He was never one to bring his work home with him. And she'd never felt comfortable pressing the issue.

"Okay. Well, I hope it goes well for you."

"Thanks, babe. Hey, did you get a call from Brookhaven tonight?"

Victoria eased her foot off the gas. Apparently they'd thought it was such an urgent matter they'd called him—bothered him—when she didn't answer? He was supposed to be a contact for emergency purposes only. "They called you too?" *Damn it*, he didn't need that kind of interruption—or involvement. She could handle her mother's situation.

"Yeah, but Delores didn't put the call through."

"Okay, good."

"So, what's up? Everything okay with your mother? Did you talk to them?"

"They want me to go meet with them. They think her Alzheimer's is getting worse, and she doesn't belong there anymore."

"What kind of nonsensical crap is that? Why doesn't she belong there? Isn't a nursing home the safest place for her? Why did they accept her if they knew her condition would worsen?"

Victoria cringed at his use of the term "nursing home." Technically it wasn't. It was more along the lines of assisted living. But she wasn't going to correct him.

"All excellent questions, my dear. Apparently she's wandering around and walking into other residents' rooms and making herself at home."

"That's it? That's what's concerning them? Sounds like she's just being her friendly self, and it's the other residents that have a problem."

"Could be." Victoria loved how he could take a conflict with potentially stressful ramifications and twist the perspective enough to find an angle that no one else had thought of. "It's just that they don't have a separate memory care unit and don't know how to handle her."

"You know what I think?" he continued without waiting for her to answer. "I think they're right. She doesn't belong there."

Her heart sank. She thought he was on her side. "What do you mean?" Victoria was startled to hear a wobble in her voice.

"I don't think her Alzheimer's has progressed *far* enough where she needs to be in a facility like that. I think it was too soon to put her in there. She's probably bored."

"Too soon?" It had been an agonizing decision—one that was made over many tearful weeks. It was not made without consulting his opinion as well. And now he thought it was the wrong one? Had he thought she'd made the wrong decision all along?

"You've said, yourself, that you have normal conversations with her when you visit."

"Yeah, a lot of the time, we do," Victoria admitted.

"Then pull her out. Bring her home. She's probably dying for some intelligent company."

Sure, he could throw out a flippant solution. He wouldn't have to deal with her. Instead she'd be stuck at home taking care of an eccentric elderly woman twenty-four/seven. Victoria's life as she knew it would be over.

Guilt tugged at her gut with her reaction.

"It might do her good to be in familiar surroundings," he added. The house that Victoria and the boys called home *had* been her mother's home too, for many years. After landing a job as a flight attendant, Victoria began flying out of Bradley International in Windsor Locks but grew tired of the hour-long commute to the airport from their apartment in Bridgeport.

Leaving the Park City and her incarcerated brother behind, she'd purchased a modest dwelling she called her cottage in sleepy Talcott-ville, just west of Hartford, and moved in with her mother, reducing her drive to fifteen minutes. It was on one of her flights to Charleston that she'd met Robert.

After they married, Robert moved in with them, and it was a relatively smooth transition. He and her mother got along famously. They shared a love of cigars and bourbon. The two would steal away after a big dinner and light up in a corner of the brick patio, each with an old fashioned in hand, the sound of their laughter wafting inside. Victoria pretended not to notice—often had to stifle a giggle at the two of them—but it was hard not to when they'd slip back inside, reeking of tobacco and Wild Turkey.

As Robert's career flourished at Litchfield, he felt the need to move to campus so he could take on more responsibility, and Victoria moved with him into faculty housing. They continued to pay the mortgage so her mother could live in the cottage.

Victoria pushed back in her seat, away from Vince's voice projecting from the dash. If it hadn't been pitch-black and in the middle of the woods, she would have pulled over to focus on the call.

Had she put her mother into Brookhaven too soon? She had seemed fine with the idea. Had Victoria talked her into it without giving her a choice in the matter? Perhaps she had.

"Let's see what they say next week," Victoria said.

"You know what they're going to say. And they'll try to move her to another facility they own."

"Well, I don't know. Maybe—"

"For Christ's sake, Tori, bringing her home makes the most sense. At least until you can figure out a better place to put her. She can't be happy there if people are getting pissed at her for stopping by to visit."

Unable to process his suggestion, there was only silence on her end. Everything—no matter what they were discussing—was so black and white for him. Not so for her. Not even close. And the gray areas often threatened to consume her. This gray area brought with it emotional strings.

Although the onset of her mother's disease could test Victoria's patience at times, the two had always been close, particularly after her father's unexpected death. He was a house painter, and Victoria loved to watch him work. He would take her along if he worked on the weekends, and she'd sit quietly, pouring water when needed and, at midday, unpacking the lunch her mother had prepared for the two of them. But when Victoria was in eighth grade, he fell off a ladder in front of her and died from his injuries shortly thereafter. Besides the obvious psychological damage, it changed her family's modest life as they knew it.

Having lost her sister the year before her father's death, the last three remaining members of her family—Victoria, her brother, and mother—moved from their humble cape with a mortgage in a blue-collar neighborhood in Bridgeport and downsized to a two-bedroom apartment not far enough from the projects. It was all they could afford on Millie's paltry wages and tips at a local diner. Victoria took on babysitting jobs in the building to help support their family. She couldn't understand why her brother, older by six years, couldn't find a way to help. She learned later on that he *was* gainfully engaged in making money, in a matter of speaking—robbing local convenience stores to support his habit—none of which found its way into the family coffer, as it were. Through it all, Millie was a loving mother who supported her children the best way she knew how. She tried not to show how heartbroken she was each time her son was caught and thrown back into jail for various infractions. Victoria hated him for it.

It had just about killed Victoria to put Millie in Brookhaven. She kept telling herself it was the best place for her, but she'd never really wrapped her head around it. That nagging feeling in her gut wouldn't go away no matter how many times she rationalized the decision and no matter how many people assured her it was the right thing to do for her mother. It never felt right. Even her mother had tried to convince her. Was she doing what she thought was easiest for Victoria? Millie had been doing that as long as Victoria could remember. Selfless when it came to her children. She also had a way of saying one thing and then waiting to see if Victoria would think for herself and do what was right, even if that meant going against everyone else who had weighed in on the matter. Millie's mind game.

"All right, well, you'll figure it out. You always do," Vince assured her. "I have to go. I'll probably stay downtown tonight. It won't be worth driving out by the time we wrap up." In other words, it's not worth the effort to come to her place, sleep in the same bed, and perhaps share a cup of coffee in the morning.

"Okay, I'll see you tomorrow." Probably not, but Victoria was hopeful nonetheless.

❦

BRINGING HER MOTHER HOME to stay with her . . . well, that would change things. Was it Karma for mourning the loss of someone to care for? It was her sons she'd been thinking of, not an elderly woman with mental health issues. Now she'd end up being a full-time caregiver for a different kind of senior—not what she'd pictured with an empty nest. Vince's impulse to bring Millie home made Victoria realize she'd been seriously considering Aviva's proposal. Trying it on for size, at least. It was sounding more tempting than ever now with the prospect of turning her house into a nursing home with her as the head nurse, recreation director, and safety officer.

CHAPTER EIGHT

Victoria left her car in the driveway, forgoing the temperamental garage door that was becoming harder for her to lift, and took in the stone façade of their humble home on her way up the walk, her heels click-clicking on the slate.

The morning dew still clung to the lower branches of the bushes where the sun hadn't reached yet. She loved her old English-style cottage with its ivy-covered chimney, light blue shutters with a cutout heart near the top of each one, a matching light blue front door with its curved top, and extensive gardens surrounding it. She didn't have the same green thumb her mother had—it was closer to brown—but she gave it her best shot.

Vince had tried to talk her into leaving the cottage behind and moving in with him into a much grander house—a build-to-suit Mc-Mansion of sorts on the outskirts of town—with an in-law suite for her mother. She imagined it was as much to have a place to call their own as his desire to flaunt his success as a criminal defense attorney. But she was happy in her little abode, and so she stayed. She'd insisted on it, knowing she couldn't leave the connection she felt to Robert there. And what if he came back, and she wasn't there anymore?

Understandably disappointed, Vince settled for the next best thing: the largest house in her neighborhood, a couple of streets over. He drove past her cottage as a matter of habit, even though the quickest way in and out would have taken him a different route. Victoria wrote it off as a sweet gesture, him looking out for her.

Setting down her shopping bags to unlock the door, she caught a whiff of the fresh mulch Jameson had helped her spread under the bushes—a task they'd worked on right up until the day before he left for school. The scent reminded her of her father. He'd always been careful moving his ladder around his customer's meticulous landscaping, often stirring up the mulch with the feet of the ladder.

Her uncontrollable thoughts quickly shifted, as they often did, to the image indelibly etched in her mind of his lifeless body at the foot of that ladder. It took stabbing pain for her to realize she was squeezing her keys in a fist, jagged indentations forming in her palm. She would need to consider an alternative to mulch for her gardens in the future. Pine needles? Cocoa shells? River rocks?

Before the screen door could swing back and latch with a bang behind her, she spied the teacup on the coffee table, a small folded napkin under a silver spoon next to it. The porcelain cup with hand-painted, pink roses and matching saucer had been a favorite of her mother's. So was the magenta lip color on the rim.

"Will I be staying with you now?" Millie asked in a tenuous voice, appearing in the doorway into the kitchen.

Victoria began to put the pieces together. Her call with Vince the night before. His insistence her mother should be pulled out of Brookhaven. His natural voracity to move ahead with what he thought was best. And his modus operandum: Ask for forgiveness, not permission.

"For the time being . . . we can talk about what to do next. Let's not worry about that right now."

But how had he pulled it off? Most likely sent a car to pick her mother up and had his assistant let him know when his call went through to Brookhaven. He knew exactly how it would play out, undoubtedly cutting the director's well-rehearsed monologue short, announcing he'd be moving Millie Hernandez out of Brookhaven—that day. After all, they were ill-equipped to care for her, and they were not going to allow her mother to stay in a facility that was sub-par.

After delivering the news to the director, his task complete, he would have returned to his workload without having burned through much unbillable time.

Probably expected a call from her, thanking him profusely. It wasn't going to happen. Victoria hated that he'd made the arrangements. Not only could she have handled it, she *would* have. And it might not have had the same result. In fact, probably not. Now it was in her lap to sort things out and figure out what was best for her mother.

"Join me for a cup of tea?" Millie flicked at her empty cup with a pale, drooping hand, a gesture that looked more like she was brushing flour from her apron. "The kettle is still hot. Won't take long to get it back to boiling."

"Sure. That would be lovely." Victoria paused to embrace the normalcy of the moment. "There are some homemade oatmeal raisin cookies we can have with it," Victoria said. She'd made them for Jameson to take with him, but he didn't seem as interested as he usually was. Weren't they his favorite? Or was that Harrison? Did Jameson prefer chocolate chips to raisins? Lance had offered to take a few. Victoria figured he was just being polite.

Millie's eyes traveled the room, taking it in like it was a grand palace. She looked more hunched than Victoria recalled, her stomach concave. She'd lost weight. Why hadn't she noticed during one of her visits? She pictured her mother lost in the back of one of the stretch sedans Vince often hired, her seatbelt tight across her lap but hanging loose from her shoulder.

But more than her weight had changed. An air of submissiveness hung on her like a heavy cloak. Had age extinguished her mother's fiery spirit? Or had her relatively short time at Brookhaven done that?

"Your home is lovely—just as I remember it."

Strangely Victoria couldn't read her mother. It could have been humility and gratefulness, but something was off about her.

"Thanks, but—" Victoria stopped short of saying it was her home, always had been. Apparently Millie didn't remember it that way. And whether she stayed there would be determined in time. There was much to consider, particularly with her mother's funds getting low. And Vince to consult.

Victoria made short work of putting away the groceries and settled in at the coffee table with a strong cup of Earl Grey. At first their conversation danced around safe topics as if they were getting acquainted for the first time. Victoria was not going to ask about her extraction from Brookhaven, figuring it would come out slowly over time. Perhaps she didn't want to know the specifics.

Nibbling on her second cookie, with crumbs along the edges of her lips, Millie reached over and placed her hand on Victoria's arm—reconnecting—as if she was thanking her and forgave her.

"I'll send for your things. We'll put them in storage until we can figure out—"

"I'm sure you'll do what's best," her mother said, patting her arm before pulling her frail hand back onto her lap. Victoria's eyes locked on her mother's bent frame. Why hadn't she noticed before when she'd visited? Why hadn't someone on the staff noticed? They'd been paying Brookhaven to take care of her mother, yet they'd failed miserably in so many ways. In a softer voice, staring straight ahead, she said, "I'm glad you took me out of there." Victoria waited to see if there was more. Finally her mother added, "Sometimes they weren't nice to me."

That did it. Victoria wasn't sending her back to Brookhaven or anywhere else. She'd find a way to make it work for her to live with her. She'd hire a visiting nurse, if necessary. But that would take money—money she didn't have—unless she changed her employment situation.

Victoria hated that she had no significant income of her own. The second mortgage she'd taken out to cover expenses would come due soon. She hoped to refinance that and pull out more equity.

It had been that way ever since Vince had insisted she stop flying—what she absolutely loved to do. Besides the money, there was something else that drew her to it. There was nothing like the rush of barreling down a runway and hurtling into the air, leaving behind family conflicts, financial worries, and marital stress. Up in the stratosphere her focus had to be one hundred percent on the passengers. She came back refreshed as if she'd been baptized in holy water. And the job was much more than serving soft drinks, handing out pretzels, and calming a fussy baby for a harried young mother. Victoria and her fellow crew were entrusted with the safety of up to one hundred and seventy-five souls—a sobering responsibility they took to heart—even though sometimes it was a matter of saving themselves from their own stupidity.

Like the time on one of her longer flights they had to take the hinges off a lavatory door when an elderly lady inadvertently locked herself inside. Turned out she wasn't stuck—just trying to sneak a cigarette. Had even brought along a shower cap to put over the smoke detector. She was aghast to be greeted by security upon deplaning at their destination.

Or the businessman who'd had a few too many gin and tonics before the ones he drank on the flight and tried to take his leave through the emergency exit. Fortunately he was too drunk to figure out how to open it, and his seatmate alerted Victoria. She and a male flight attendant were able to subdue him, then convince him to switch to a seat at the back of the plane where they could keep an eye on him. It didn't end well for him either.

Victoria was in her element in the cabin of a Boeing 737. Caring for others. Mothering them in a way. Now it looked as though she'd be mothering her mother again. Things had come full circle. She needed to be careful what she wished for.

CHAPTER NINE

Millie became so well re-accustomed to her familiar surroundings in her first few days back home, she seemed to flourish; her robust personality returned. With her puttering around the kitchen, preparing small meals for the two of them, it began to feel as though they had switched things around, taking on roles from many years earlier. Millie, the mom. Victoria, the daughter. It was familiar. It was comfortable. And Victoria was pleased to see her mother functioning independently. She seemed happy. But how long would it last? Was this simply a temporary reprieve from her disease? A remission of sorts? Whatever it was, Victoria was going to enjoy it while it lasted.

Then there were the occasional days where she didn't seem as lucid.

"Will Robert be home for dinner tonight?"

"Robert? Mom, you know he's not . . . here anymore."

A puzzled look crossed her mother's face right before her eyes glazed over.

"Where did he go? I always liked him."

"He's missing, Mom. He's been gone a long time."

"Well, why aren't you looking for him? Maybe he's working late."

"No, he's not working late. We did look for him. For a *very* long time. You helped too. The police looked. . . . No one could find him. Something happened to him." Her words tugged at her insides. So many questions left unanswered and a gaping hole in her and their sons' lives. "It's Vince that's working late."

"Vince?"

"Yes, Mom. Vince."

"Oh, that's right. The guy you met in court."

"Well, not actually *in* court. But in the hall at the courthouse. He's who I'm seeing now." She wasn't about to get into how they'd actually met on one of her flights years earlier; their meeting in the courthouse a reunion of sorts. But her mother didn't need to be privy to the sordid details.

"Why did you have to go to court?" Did her mother not hear her last statement? Or was she simply ignoring it?

Pressing her eyes shut, Victoria gathered what patience she could muster to answer her mother's questions—the same ones she'd answered many times before.

"Mom, Robert had been missing for . . . years. Our attorney advised me to go to court to have him declared dead." Uttering the words felt so callous. She never wanted to admit he wasn't coming back—that he wasn't alive. It pained her to do it—particularly to have to explain to her sons what she was doing. No mother should have to do that.

"Declare him *dead.*" Millie spat out the last word. "Why would you *ever* want to do that?"

"I never *wanted* to do it. But it was something that had to be done. I needed the insurance money." She hated that she had to explain herself. She hated that she was struggling to support herself and her sons. But with Robert's disappearance, he was no longer actively on the staff at the academy. The headmaster had been more than generous offering to let her and the boys stay in faculty housing as long as they needed, but she couldn't bear the thought of staying and enduring the pitying glances from everyone on campus.

Instead, she'd made the move back into the cottage with her mother until she could get on her feet financially. Getting stable emotionally would prove to be a tougher obstacle to overcome.

"Connecticut law says a person can't be declared legally dead—" There was that word again. Why did she have to use it to describe her husband, the father of her children? "—before seven years, unless you go to court and present your case. So that's what we had to do. That's what we *tried* to do. We didn't have any concrete evidence he was actually . . . dead. So, they denied our case. That's why I had to go back to work. And you watched the boys for me after school."

This was her precarious situation: still married to a man who'd vanished without a trace, who everyone around her had decided was dead, and she should move on—for her sake and the boys, as well. Seven long years that left her and Vince in relationship limbo for the past five.

Her attorney suggested an option would be to divorce him, but she couldn't bring herself to do it. She never would have divorced him if he were still alive—how would she explain that to her sons—and she certainly wasn't going to do it just because it was the general consensus Robert had suffered some sort of fatal incident and wasn't coming back.

Vince didn't pressure her to go through with the divorce after the first time he brought it up. But without it, they couldn't marry, if that was where their complicated relationship was heading. In her mind, as long as no one produced conclusive evidence Robert had passed, he could be out there somewhere, trying to find his way back.

"But you're still looking for him, aren't you?" At times, her mother posed questions a young child would ask, but Victoria wrote it off as her disease playing tricks on her mind.

"Absolutely. We'll never stop looking until we find him," she assured her. And there was more than a shred of truth to it.

CHAPTER TEN

Grandparents Day was always the third Wednesday in September, and until Millie had been rescued from Brookhaven, it didn't look like Jameson would have a visitor that day. Victoria was pleased he sounded upbeat about the change in plans and his grandmother's upcoming visit. The day before the big event, Victoria texted him to confirm he remembered he'd be hosting her. He got right back to her that he had and was looking forward to it. Then he added,

// mom could u find my phone chrgr and brng it tomrrw? s/b plgged in nxt to my bed //

And then, as if he could anticipate her next question, he texted,

// been borrwng ashers gettng 2 b a real pain thx //

Grinning, Victoria was pleased there was something he needed her help with.

From the passenger seat her mother snored softly, the side of her head pressed against the window for much of the first half of the ride to the academy. Victoria wondered if the day would be too much for her.

Along a stretch in the woods of majestic pines, the rising sun peeked through the trees, creating a pulsing light on Millie's weathered face as they drove through. She opened her eyes and squinted through the side window, wrinkling her nose.

"Welcome back, Mom. You were so sound asleep I was beginning to wonder if this was a good idea for you to go to this event."

"Oh heavens," she gushed. "I was resting up so I can keep up with all those handsome young men." Her chuckle erupted from the depths of her gut, and she smacked the dashboard. "Can't wait to see my grandson and allow him to escort me around campus. He's such a big man now."

"That, he is." Victoria was glad to hear the childlike delight in her tone. It reminded her of when her mother was younger, and her voice was always a notch louder than it needed to be. She could picture Millie strutting alongside her grandson on campus, one arm laced through his, head held high.

"Besides, he would be so disappointed if I didn't come. And I would never want that."

"No, we wouldn't." Victoria shook her head with a grin.

"Hey, have you seen your friend Aviva lately?"

Victoria glanced across the front seat. "That was random. Why do you ask?"

"Oh, I happened to think of her. Have you two stayed connected?"

"Yeah, we talk frequently."

"How's she doing?" Her mother pulled on her cardigan so it overlapped her torso.

"You know Veeve; she's always doing great. The party starts when she arrives." They shared a brief laugh.

"You always enjoyed flying with her, didn't you?"

"Absolutely. Good times. Great memories."

"Victoria, why don't you go back to being a stewardess."

"Flight attendant, Mom."

"Whatever." She swatted at the air in front of her. "You know what I mean. So why don't you? Your nest is empty—actually has been for a couple years—so it would be the perfect time to go back. Put some fun back into your life."

Victoria wasn't expecting to have to fend off the wild notion from her close friend *and* her mother. She stopped short of reminding her she already had a full-time job: caring for an elderly lady.

A jingling spilled from the dash and the readout announced the caller.

"Oh, look at that. There she is now." Millie sounded as though it was a long-lost friend of hers. Victoria knew it wasn't a coincidence Aviva popped up after Millie mentioned her. It was what her mother did—as if she could conjure up what she spoke about, spoke it into existence.

"I can call her back later."

"Go ahead and answer it. I don't mind."

"No, that's okay. I can—"

Before Victoria saw her mother move, she'd swiped the screen and answered the call.

Serving up an icy glare to the other side of the front seat, Victoria answered, "Hey, Veeve. How's it going?" She hoped her friend couldn't hear her clenched teeth.

"Hey, girl. You know I'm fabulous. Any day I wake up without a chalk outline around me is a good one."

Victoria could sense from her peripheral vision her mother had flinched at the reference.

"Of course, you are. Hey, Veeve, I've got my mother with me and—"

"Hey, Mama Hernandez, how are you?"

"Oh, Aviva, I'm doing really well. Thank you. You're so sweet to ask."

"I hear you got sprung from Brookhaven."

Millie chuckled. "Well, yes, I did. I'm a free woman again."

"Yes!" Aviva dragged out the "s" sound. "Good for you." Victoria could picture her friend with her hand curled into a fist raised high in solidarity. Had everyone been against her decision to move her mother to an assisted care facility? It certainly seemed so.

"You guys should get together to celebrate sometime." Victoria let her cynicism slip.

"Oh, that would be fun," her mother chimed in.

"We could go out for happy hour, Mrs. H."

"That would be fun," her mother repeated, the childlike glee returning.

"I hear Coco Vive has some great apps. And they've got a new signature drink that—"

"Okay, we'll have to make some plans," Victoria chimed in.

"Oh, did you want to go too?" Aviva poked.

"Someone has to chaperone you two."

"Yeah, we could probably use a chauffeur." Her friend's laugh crackled through the car's speaker. Millie joined in.

"All right, you guys. Veeve, I gotta call you back. My turn is coming up."

"Okay. Call me."

Approaching the grand wrought-iron gates as she had done the evening of move-in day, Victoria checked for renegade garbage trucks before pulling through.

"They're having a reception in the lobby of the auditorium—" Victoria started.

"Sounds wonderful, dear. Thank you." Her eyes glistened, and her cheeks took on a peachy-pink glow Victoria hadn't seen in a while. Maybe this was a good idea after all.

"You'll meet up with Jameson there, but I'll walk you in to make sure you guys connect."

"What? Are you afraid I'll get lost on my first day of school?" Millie chortled her signature laugh that Victoria could never distinguish between a nervous reaction or downright callousness for others' feelings.

"Of course not. You can handle yourself. I just thought it would be nice to have someone to walk in with." It crossed Victoria's mind that perhaps it was *her* that felt more comfortable—needed—an escort more than her mother did.

Pulling up to the curb, carefully slipping her Mercedes between a sleek black Porsche and a boxy white Range Rover, Victoria left the flashers going while she rounded the back and opened the passenger side door. The din of grandsons greeting their elders made her pause to survey the sidewalk and steps, her hand on the door handle.

"Victoria!" The voice from the crowd had an overly jovial twang to it. It clearly belonged to someone she'd met before, but she couldn't place it. Having made a few appearances at Parents Committee meetings, Victoria's first instinct was to run in the opposite direction. But her options for evasive tactics were limited, and that wasn't one of them. She decided to keep moving with her task at hand and pulled open the door for her mother, who sprang out onto the sidewalk like there was a tag sale she was late for.

"I thought that was you. So good to see you." The voice was on top of Victoria.

Feeling the imprint of a palm on her back as she shut the car door, it dawned on her who it was. The woman's husband had the same annoying, intrusive habit. Parting her lips to speak but still assembling cordial words in her head, Victoria realized Missi was speaking before she could make a sound.

"Did you bring the cupcakes?"

"Yes, of course. They're in the back." Victoria gestured.

"Awesome! If you pop the trunk, I can have some of the boys carry them to the kitchen for you."

"That's okay, Missi. I can take them down myself. I just need to get my mother checked in first. In fact I'd rather—"

"Don't be silly. That's why I have help all lined up." Swiveling toward the doors to the auditorium, she called out, "Where are my volunteers?"

Victoria followed her around to the back and pressed a button on her key fob, cringing at the thought of someone other than herself delivering her works of art to their final destination and realizing she'd abandoned her mother at the side of the car. Clearly Missi had no idea how much of her heart and soul went into the process of creating the delectable little masterpieces.

What if the boys fooled around like adolescents often do and a box or two were bobbled, ultimately ending upside down on the floor? She blinked and pushed the painful image from her mind.

As if on cue, three young men in navy-blue blazers skipped down the steps in sync toward the car.

"Here, boys, I need you to take these—"

"Please be careful," Victoria jumped in.

"Oh, yes, be ever so careful. This is a special delivery, and we wouldn't want anything bad to happen to them." Missi had a way of making everything sound like she was speaking to a toddler.

As Missi reached in, Victoria tried, "I can do that." But Missi was already fishing out the boxes and handing two or three to each boy.

"Don't be silly. We've got this," she said to Victoria. "Here you go," she said to the boys.

Peering into the windows in the top of the boxes, the students offered up varying versions of, "Mmmm. I want one of these."

"Thanks so much for making them for us, Victoria. And on such last-minute notice. I couldn't believe it when our chef called in a panic after the bakery we usually get desserts from let him know they'd lost power and didn't know when they'd be getting it back. It was so late in the day; I knew I couldn't put in an order for so many cupcakes with anyone I didn't have an *in* with."

"Glad I was able to fit them in."

"How *is* your cupcake business going?" Victoria heard "Micky Mouse" in place of "cupcake."

"Uh . . . good. Thanks. Keeps me very busy."

"These must have taken a lot of time." She motioned toward the boys scampering up the steps with the pink boxes. Victoria didn't dare look to see if any were teetering.

"Well . . . yes, they did."

"Then how could you have fit in making them if you're so busy with regular clients?"

Taking a moment to read her, Victoria couldn't tell if she was genuinely impressed that she'd gotten it all done, or she was questioning if Victoria was really that busy (read successful) with her business. Victoria chose to assume Missi was on the side of civility.

"It's amazing what you can do when you eliminate sleep," Victoria answered with a flip of her hand. She got the intended reaction, which was a brief laugh from Missi.

Appearing from around the side of the car, her mother piped up, "Good morning, I'm Jameson Sands' grandmother—Millie. And you are?" The tone of her mother's question could only be interpreted as coming from a sweet old lady who was sincerely interested in knowing who she was. After all, if this woman was on campus, she was part of her grandson's life—a grandson who meant the world to her.

"Oh, nice to meet you. I'm Missi Stockwell. The headmistress, you could say." She let slip a giggle like a freshman cheerleader after messing up on a routine.

Victoria scrunched her forehead, making no effort to conceal her reaction. She held no such title. Missi's eyes caught Victoria's expression and returned her attention back to Millie. "Well, you see, my husband is the headmaster," Missi offered as a clarification.

"I thought the headmaster's name was Martin." Millie was keeping up. Victoria loved it.

"Uh, yes. Yes, it is."

"But didn't you say your name was Stockwell?" Millie asked.

Victoria moved in closer to her mother, with the side of her mouth turning up. Not many could make Missi Stockwell have to explain herself, but Millie was doing just that.

"Yes, I did. I didn't take my husband's last name when we married."

There was a pause while Millie considered the idea. "Why not? Isn't that what women do?"

Missi chuckled, practically cutting off Millie's words, and it was clearly not the nervous kind of laugh. Missi wasn't capable of that, but she appeared to be losing interest in this particular grandmother. Leaning in, her highlighted bob brushing her cheek, she spoke like she was correcting a child. "Not always. I had made a name for myself in my family's business before I met Ben, so I felt strongly about not losing that connection to my name."

"I see." Millie nodded her head slightly, in a way Victoria had seen many times before, which meant she'd heard you but couldn't possibly understand why you would do such a thing. Victoria made a mental note to fill her mother in on the family business Missi didn't want to lose her connection to—garbage collection. There would be more head nodding in Millie's near future.

Turning to Victoria, Missi said, "So Vicky, thanks again for the cupcakes."

Victoria bristled at the sound of the nickname, her least favorite. If she hadn't already been engaged in conversation with her, she would have come down with a severe case of selective hearing.

"You're welcome." Victoria pushed past her to slam the trunk lid shut. Missi stepped back, but continued.

"On another note—another way of contributing to the Litchfield Academy community—Ben mentioned he'd spoken with you at Presentation and that you are wanting to be on the Parents Committee this year." Victoria half expected Missi to pull out a couple of pom poms and shake them over her head. "That's great news. We can always use new blood to inspire the group—especially a seasoned senior parent, like yourself."

Seasoned? As in *old?* Victoria shook off the implication. Perhaps the thirty-something hadn't meant it the way she was taking it, but at nearly twenty years her junior, Missi would have had to have children at age fifteen in order to have a son at Litchfield. Lance was Missi's stepson.

Victoria knew better than to commit to any Parents Committee responsibilities, and yet she had done so by not bowing out when Headmaster Martin had corralled her the last time she was on campus. If only they lived farther away. An hour wasn't quite far enough to beg off the inconvenience. She often envied parents who lived on the West Coast, or the ones who sent their sons there from Europe—although she couldn't imagine doing that to a child. Those parents weren't expected to show up for meetings or help out by setting up a refreshment table at events or making phone calls to beg for money. They just sent the money. Although with Victoria's anemic checking account, she'd have to continue to suffer through helping in person from time to time. Thankfully it was Jameson's last year.

"Well, he mentioned it. Uh . . . I'll see what I can do to help," Victoria said, hoping that was adequately non-committal. Without taking her eyes from Missi, she looped an arm through her mother's. "Why don't we go find Jameson, Mom. I'm sure he's anxious to see you."

Clasping her hands together like a young girl about to blow out her birthday candles, Millie replied, "Yes, let's."

Victoria put an end to their chat as she moved her mother forward. "We'll catch up with you later, Missi." She hoped not, but it was inevitable on such a small campus.

"Okay. Sounds good, Vicky. I'll put you down for the Fundraising Committee. Nice to meet you Mrs. Sands. Hope you enjoy Grandparents Day," Missi called to them as they got swallowed by the crowd.

Millie whipped her head to look at Victoria. "Did she just call me Mrs. Sands?"

"Yes, she did."

"Presumptuous," Millie spat out, the emphasis on the second syllable.

"That's one word for it."

"And I thought you didn't like to be called Vicky."

"I hate it," Victoria hissed.

"Why didn't you correct her?"

Good question, Victoria thought. All she could come up with was "That's the headmaster's wife."

"So?" Victoria knew she was right, but she had never corrected Missi when they'd first met. It was a little too late now.

Once inside, they made their way over to check-in. The welcome aroma of brewed coffee permeated the crowded space. Two vaguely familiar faces sat at the table with an array of name tags and corsages of some sort of yellow flower splayed in front of them.

As they waited in line behind a handful of gray-haired couples who didn't seem to be in-tow, Millie wriggled out of her overcoat—one that would have been more appropriate for much colder temperatures—like a kindergartener coming inside from recess. She threw the bulging mound over one arm and then unwrapped her scratchy wool scarf from around her neck, tucking that inside her coat. Then she plucked her floppy, red hat from her head and tucked it in with her scarf. As if she could sense her wispy white hair was sticking up at odd angles, she patted it down with thin fingers.

After moving a few steps closer to the table, she wedged her coat and its contents between her legs and used both hands to wrestle with her cardigan, stopping to adjust her coat to keep it from slipping until she'd pulled her sweater free and added it to her other accessories inside her coat. Her eyes grew wide as she patted herself down. A smile sprang onto her face as she saw others were watching her antics, and she couldn't help herself from explaining, "Wanted to make sure I didn't take off too much. My daughter hates when I embarrass her in public. Ha!"

Victoria thought she was long past being bothered by her mother's carryings-on but could feel her cheeks starting to burn. She told herself it was the overheated lobby and the throngs of people in it. Giving her mother a quick once-over, she hoped there were other grandmothers dressed in black leggings, a cheetah print tunic, and black ankle boots. Victoria would have gently suggested something else before they left for the day, but she didn't think her mother owned anything more appropriate. There were no designer labels hanging in Millie's closet or tucked neatly into a fine antique armoire drawer. At least she'd thought to put on her pearls and her favorite magenta lip color.

"Mom! Grandma!" Jameson's voice burst through the crowd of overdressed, out-to-impress, nouveau riche, and blue bloods. He hugged them both—first Millie and then his mom—with his trademark firm embrace. Victoria tried not to hold on too long, but it always felt so good to be in his arms. "Good to see you." He took a step back and threw open his palms. "Wow, nice outfit, Gram." Before she could respond, he said, "Looks cool."

Watching her mother beam at her grandson's approval, Victoria silently urged, *Please don't encourage her, Jameson,* but kept her expression even.

"Glad you could come, Gram."

"I wouldn't miss it, sweetheart," Millie cooed, her weary eyes locked on her grandson's face, then lurched toward him and gave him a peck on the cheek.

"Aw, c'mon, Gram." He brushed at the bright pink smudge and turned to his mother. "Is it gone?"

"Here." Victoria fished a tissue out of her purse and handed it to him. He rubbed until his cheek was red. Victoria figured it matched both of hers. "You've got it now. You're good." He handed the crumpled tissue back to her and turned his attention back to his guest.

"Here, let me take that for you." As he scooped the bundle of clothing she was clutching, making it look much less cumbersome against his thick torso, Millie grabbed onto Jameson's jacket sleeve with one hand as if she didn't want to lose him in the crowd.

"Thank you for dropping me off, Victoria. I'm sure Jameson can take it from here."

"Okay . . ." Victoria started to pull away, feeling the sting of her mother's curt dismissal. "I'm sure he can. You as well." Anxious to take her leave before any other volunteer recruiters in the crowd noticed her, Victoria grabbed one more quick hug from Jameson as he placed a gentle kiss on her cheek. She wondered if his lips could feel the heat from it.

Shoving both fists in her coat pockets, Victoria felt a bulge in one. "Jameson, I almost forgot." She pulled out his phone cord and handed it to him.

Watching Millie slip her arm through Jameson's as it was their turn to check in, Victoria couldn't remember the last time she looked so happy. She beamed as he placed her name tag onto her shirt.

CHAPTER ELEVEN

Back in the safety of her car, Victoria let out a breath she hadn't realized she'd been holding while blazing a trail back through the clamorous crowd and dashing down the auditorium steps. Pulling away from the curb, she caught sight of another familiar face up ahead. The headmaster.

"How about that? First the headmistress, then the headmaster," Victoria said aloud, smirking at Missi's use of the title. She returned his wave but it looked as though he was waving her over as she got close. Rolling down the passenger side window, she greeted him with as much of a lilt in her voice as she could manage.

"Hello, Ben. How are you this morning?"

"Good morning, Victoria. What a glorious day it is. Did you drop off your mother?"

"Yes, just did." She refrained from mentioning the cupcakes. There was no need for any unnecessary back-patting. *Was there ever a need?* She decided, yes. But not this time. She'd save it.

"Wonderful. So glad she can join in the festivities. Jameson must be thrilled."

"He is. Yes. Thank you."

Leaning in, he rested an arm on the window well. "Listen, Victoria, you have a few minutes?"

"Sure thing. What's up?"

"I'd like to have a chat, if we could."

"A chat?" *More volunteering opportunities?* There weren't enough hours in the day.

"Yes, there should be an empty classroom on the first floor of the Rentschler building we can grab. I'm going to head over there now."

Why they wouldn't meet in his office, she didn't understand.

"Okay." She'd never seen the inside of it. Perhaps he reserved that for meetings with men, his good old boys' network.

"You can leave your car out front on the road."

"Okay. Will do."

Even though the science building was completed after Robert's last footfall on campus, both boys had had classes there, and she'd visited on past Parents Weekends, so she found it easily. Ben was waiting out front. He showed her to a lab down the hall on the left and to a two-person workstation, one of only eight in the room. Litchfield prided itself on its small classes and low teacher-to-student ratios.

Plunking her shoulder bag onto the counter, she climbed awkwardly in an ankle-length skirt onto a stool, hooking the heel of her boot on the rung near the floor to keep from toppling off, and looked to the headmaster to take the lead. He didn't waste any time getting started after settling onto his stool.

"Victoria," he said, reaching over and patting her closest forearm. "I wanted to see how you were doing."

"How I'm doing?" she asked, pulling away, looking to him to elaborate.

"You know . . . it's been almost seven years." He didn't have to elaborate any more than that. She knew what he was referring to. It was a painful badge she carried with her. A scar of sorts that made her stand out from all other parents at the private boarding school. "I wanted to see where you stood with moving on."

Moving on? He made it sound more like a junior high school breakup than what it really was; a gut-wrenching loss that had no end.

"Moving on. Is that what you think I should be doing, now that seven years have passed?"

"Well . . . yeah. I do. I think it's time for you to face reality. He's gone. He's not coming back. I hate to be so candid, Victoria, but I hate to see you hanging onto hope that just isn't . . . justified."

Blinking away stinging tears welling in her eyes, threatening to spill over, and run down her cheeks, she swallowed hard and allowed her gaze to rest on his clear plastic seltzer bottle. Tiny bubbles danced their way to the top inside in a random, hypnotizing choreography.

Suddenly she realized he was speaking again. ". . . wouldn't you agree, Victoria? It doesn't make sense to keep holding on."

"How can you say that? You were his friend."

"I still am his friend, yours as well. I've known you both for years. And as a friend, I need to be honest with you. I hate to see you doing this to yourself."

"A friend doesn't give up hope when another friend is missing." She hated that her voice quivered as she spoke. "What makes you so sure he's not coming back?"

"It's just been too long. It isn't feasible."

Then it hit her how he could be so confident.

"What do you know, Ben?"

He pulled away from her slightly. "Nothing, Victoria," he assured her. "Nothing. I think so much time has passed that it's time to be realistic."

She pressed again. "What aren't you telling me? What do you know that no one else does? What happened in New York? You were there. What happened?" A couple of students paused in the hall, near the door and peeked in. She waited for them to move on and then lowered her voice. "To be that certain he's not coming back, you must know something. Tell me."

"Victoria, I don't know anything more. There's nothing to tell. I just want you to be able to move on. Live your life."

"How can I when my husband has disappeared without a trace, and everyone has given up on finding him—except for me?"

"Look within yourself. Really examine your thoughts and your gut feeling. I bet you'll find that you know—deep down—he's gone."

"But where could he be? Why hasn't anyone been able to find him?"

"Victoria, half the cops in New York City were looking for him and came up with nothing. Who knows what happened?"

"Someone has to know."

"We may *never* know." His gaze landed at her feet as his head wagged back and forth.

"How dare you, Ben." Scooping up her purse, she slid off the stool and landed with both feet squarely planted on the cement floor.

"Where are you going? Wait. You need to think about your boys too, Victoria. Stringing them along with false hope isn't good for them. Living in limbo is not good for any of you."

Easing the strap of her bag onto her shoulder, she stared into the headmaster's blank eyes. "It's easy for you to say when you don't live with the loss every day of your life. Shame on you, Ben, for thinking I should forget about him like you have."

Turning to take her leave, she banged her shin on the stool, sending it toppling with a clamorous clanking, and bit her lip to keep from yelling out in pain. She left the stool where it lay, rolling in a semi-circle on the floor, and the headmaster behind her, sputtering something about him not forgetting and her being realistic.

Inside her, hatred churned for the weak man who claimed to be their friend. Not looking back, Victoria slammed the classroom door behind her and made her way back to the car.

⚜

As she pulled back out through the grand gates, her dashboard lit up with an incoming call.

"Aviva!" Victoria's overexuberant voice rattled around inside the confines of the car. She was more relieved to be leaving campus than she'd realized.

"Hey, girl. Whatcha up to? Got time for lunch?"

"Hey . . . uh, sure. I'm actually leaving the academy—"

"What for? Did Jameson forget something he couldn't live without until his next soccer game?" Aviva laughed to herself, undoubtedly thinking there was her proof Victoria micro-managed her boys. She decided to keep the phone charger to herself. Victoria was tickled to be able to come to his rescue—albeit a minor one. She'd take it. It had felt satisfying.

"No, it's Grandparents Day and—"

"Grandparents Day? Never heard of such a thing."

No surprise there. Victoria hadn't either—having gone through the Bridgeport public school system—until she'd been indoctrinated into the world of private schools. And not because she and Robert could afford one for their boys, but because Robert had become a teacher at one—a damn good teacher. She'd felt comfortable—accepted—in the role of the supportive wife of a Litchfield Academy faculty member. She'd thrived in it. But years later, the transition to Litchfield parent, without Robert at her side as a safety net, had been awkward. She would never be able to afford it on her own. But the school—Headmaster Martin—had made a promise to her after Robert's disappearance that the academy would honor their long-standing tradition of waiving the tuition, room, and board for the children of faculty members.

When her older son Harrison had enrolled, she found herself with a foot dangling in two very separate worlds, suddenly thrust into rubbing elbows with some of the most well-educated, extensively-traveled, upper crust whose days were filled with country clubs, nannies, sports cars, and yachts. She'd never really clicked with any of the other mothers. Hard to carry on a conversation with someone whose most difficult decision that day was which color to choose at the nail salon for her mani/pedi.

Victoria kept telling herself the education the boys got there was like no public school could offer and would open doors most young men their age could only dream of. Vince reminded her of this—having come from a modest background as well—when she faltered. She needed to suck it up and ride it out to the end, which was in sight.

"Well, its quite sweet, really. The school enables the boys to honor some of the special people in their lives. They get to show them around campus, take them to their classes . . . even strut their stuff for them in their soccer or football games."

"Sweet." Aviva dropped the word with the thud of a discarded pizza box.

"Okay, well, it is what it is." Victoria was through discussing it. Aviva would never understand. *She* didn't always understand what went on behind the stone walls of the academy. She did her best to go along with it for the sake of her boys.

"So . . . lunch." Aviva tried again.

"Okay, sure." Victoria had time to kill before she had to return to campus to retrieve her mother, but she hadn't been planning to drive all the way back to Talcottville.

"Great! Can you do noon? At Serenson's? We could even eat outside. It's such a beautiful day. We need to enjoy this New England fall weather while it lasts."

"Sure. That sounds fine. See you then."

CHAPTER TWELVE

Known for locally sourcing its ingredients, particularly seafood, even though it was a solid hours' drive from the shoreline, Serenson's was a family-owned café tucked in among an eclectic assortment of boutiques that gave Talcottville's Main Street its charm. It had survived the ravages of a pandemic, when it was forced to temporarily transform its business to take-out only, and a move from a prime corner storefront to a less prominent spot in the middle of the block when rents skyrocketed.

As Victoria approached the hostess stand inside the wrought iron fence corralling the seating out front, Aviva's hand shot up from the far corner. A thick sugar maple hung over that end of the patio, curving not far over her head, with smaller branches drooping down, neatly framing her face. That and her straighter than straight posture gave Aviva the air of royalty holding court from her throne. Victoria made her way over, zigzagging through bistro tables crowded together to get as much seating outside as possible during the pitifully short summer months in Connecticut.

"Hey, girl. You made it." Her friend relinquished her phone, dropping it face down next to her silverware as if signaling lunch had started and she was committing her attention to it.

"Hey—sure I did." Aviva always made it sound like she wasn't sure you were going to show up. Or was that just the way Victoria interpreted it?

On the table were two glasses in addition to the water goblets. A white wine for Victoria and a martini with oversized olives on a skewer for her friend. Aviva's was already half gone.

"I took the liberty. Figured you could use one. Long drive with your mother and all."

Although Victoria doubted she would have ordered wine if she'd been left to her own devices, she wasn't angry with her friend. Tossing her phone on the table in like-fashion as Aviva, Victoria scooted onto the wobbly metal chair and took a sip, ignoring the slim one-page menu card next to her folded napkin. She held the buttery goodness in her mouth before swallowing, reminding herself she had to make the drive back to Litchfield Falls and home again. She'd need to keep it to one glass and nurse it.

A perky redhead with a neatly twisted braid on the side of her head appeared with pad and pen at the ready, and they quickly put in their orders; their usuals. After scooping up their ignored menus, the girl turned to the table next to them to check on their meals.

"So how are you doing?" Aviva took the lead.

"I'm okay," Victoria lied.

"No, you're not. Not even close."

"What?" The word was a whisper floating through Victoria's barely parted lips.

"I'm sorry, Tori. But I'm your friend, and I'm going to play it straight with you. . . . Honestly you look like you're in mourning." Aviva ran her gaze down Victoria's front side. "I mean, just look at you, girl. You've got dark circles under your eyes that you don't seem to be able to cover with makeup. Or maybe you have, and they look much worse than what I can see. And look at those nails. We're not back in seventh grade, you know. When was the last time you had them done?"

Reflexively Victoria curled her fingers under and allowed her eyes to wander over to the tiny, perfectly formed circles of condensation on her water goblet.

"It's been, what, three weeks since Harrison left—?"

"Jameson," Victoria hissed, shifting her gaze to catch her friend's startled expression.

"Right, Jameson, sorry. So, three weeks since Jameson left, and you look like . . ." She let her words trail off.

Victoria leaned back in her chair. "So then let me mourn."

"What's there to mourn? He's an hour away. You haven't lost him.

He's living his life as an eighteen-year-old. He's off at school. Happy. Doing what's normal. What you're doing . . . this isn't normal."

How quickly her friend had transitioned from a halfhearted sympathetic listener the day Jameson left. "How would you know?"

"Okay, so maybe I'm not in your shoes—*specifically*. But it doesn't feel right."

Blinking away the sting in her eyes, Victoria said, "The summer went by too fast. It seemed like he'd just come home when it was time for him to go back. Harrison never came back this summer. He stayed to work with a professor—"

"Harrison's in California, right?"

"Yeah, UCLA." Victoria hated when Aviva cut her off mid-sentence.

"Got it."

"Now Jameson's gone. Why can't you just let me be sad about it and miss him."

"I'd rather see you let it go—"

"And get over it?" Victoria finished for her. Her friend couldn't possibly know what she was feeling—know the loss of having a child at a distance and not needing her anymore. Maybe it was the latter that hurt worse. And she was committed to embracing her mourning period as long as it lasted. This was on top of having her heart torn open with what felt like a jagged shard after losing Robert, which had never fully healed. Scar tissue had started to form, but Jameson's departure reopened the wound.

Aviva shrugged. "If you want to put it that way." She took a sip of her vodka-laden cocktail, the olive stirrer sliding along the rim. "Look, you've done an amazing job bringing them up. And I know it hasn't been easy after Robert . . ."

It stung that her friend struggled to utter the words. She grabbed her wine and filled her mouth with the dry, white elixir and held it there, waiting for Aviva to continue.

". . . uh . . . went missing. But you did your best, and they've turned out to be amazing young men. You should be so proud of them."

Swallowing, Victoria said, "I am. Of course, I am."

"They could *easily* have gotten majorly screwed up with what happened to their father."

Victoria's thoughts went to all the doctors' visits she'd dragged Jameson to, to try to quell his anxiety. At its height, he was nearly paralyzed, unable to drive a car, sleep through the night, or sit still for an entire class. She hated to see him on meds, but he seemed to be doing much better with them.

"All I'm saying is you've brought them up right, now it's time to set them free."

"Like the proverbial butterfly?"

"*Yes.* Tori, you've done the motherly thing. Now you need to trust that they can handle it from here."

That was the part Victoria was having trouble with. Everyone in her life seemed to leave her before she was ready for them to leave. *Are you ever ready?* She prayed the boys would come back.

"Now it's time for you—on more than one level."

"Oh yeah?"

"Career wise and lover wise."

Victoria allowed herself to snicker.

"I'm serious. You're laughing at the latter, aren't you?"

Victoria grinned and nodded, grabbing her glass again, her eyes following the movement of her wine as she swirled it.

"You need to let someone special into your life."

"I've got Vince."

"Really? You think so? Girl, you've been leading him on—"

"I have not."

"What would you call it? You say he's a great guy. How long has he stuck around? Five years."

Victoria lifted an indifferent shoulder. "Give or take."

"Well, I think he's been doing all the giving, and you've been doing all the—"

"Veeve, that's not fair."

"*Exactly.* That's *not* fair." Aviva's eyes connected with Victoria's.

"I thought you didn't like him."

"Tori, I don't even know him. I've only been around him a few times over those five years. I get the feeling you don't see him that often either. Even though he lives down the street from you—which I think is a bit stalker-ish—you still don't seem to get together much."

"He's so busy with work." Victoria ignored her stalker comment.

"Or . . . you're not letting him into your life."

Pushing away from the cramped table, Victoria exhaled. "How can I let him in if I'm still married and have no idea what happened to my husband?"

"Do you think you'll ever find out what happened to Robert?"

There it was. The question everyone wanted the answer to—including Victoria. She let the dust settle from Aviva smacking the question onto the middle of the table. Snatching up her wine glass, she held it in two hands, poised to take a sip but not bringing it to her lips.

"I honestly don't know how to answer that question anymore. People have been asking me that for almost seven years. At first, my answer was a resounding yes. Then it became more of a hedge, like 'I know they're doing their best to find him.' Now I don't know. Part of me doesn't ever want to stop looking for him. I love him. I want him back. I want our life back. But that may not happen. So, then I have to think about the boys—who also want their father back. And then I think about me. Even though it sounds selfish, at this point I start to wonder if I'm being foolish to think we'll ever find him or find out what happened to him. But I'm only human, and I'd like male company."

"Oh, I think you know. You know he's gone."

Setting her jaw, Victoria said, "No, I don't. I have no evidence of that."

"Some things you don't need concrete evidence to know. Listen to your instincts."

Her friend was sounding too much like her old friend on campus earlier.

"Geeze, Veeve. I already got an earful when I got pulled aside by the headmaster this morning—"

"The headmaster? But you and Robert were pretty friendly with him, weren't you?"

"Yeah."

"What did he have to say?"

"He was saying the same thing you are; it's time to move on." She dropped her voice to imitate Ben. *"It's what's best for you and the boys."*

"See? It's not just me, Tori."

"No, it's not just you, and I'm getting tired of it."

"Well maybe you should listen. . . . I mean, get a *grip* already."

"Well that was blunt. Thanks."

Her friend continued. "You stopped trekking to the city to look for him a long time ago. You've tossed in the towel. You've given up looking because you know he's not out there to find."

"I have not."

Aviva allowed a couple of ticks for the heated exchange to cool, fishing the olive spear from her glass and sucking the one on the end into her mouth.

Feeling pressure to fill in the awkward pause and come to her own defense, Victoria asked, "Veeve, can I tell you something?"

Her friend relinquished the empty olive spear onto the table and sat back, arms folded across her torso, chewing.

"I've been having these dreams. . . . They started up not long after Robert disappeared." Victoria imagined her friend replaced the word "disappeared" with "left" or "died." But she continued. "It's always about water. Lately they've been getting more vivid."

"Really?"

"I feel like—and I know this is going to sound crazy—but I feel like he's trying to tell me what happened to him."

"Robert is. . . . Do you really believe that kind of crap?"

It was awkward to answer in the affirmative after her friend had put it so eloquently, but she said, "Yes."

Aviva seemed to be considering the possibility. "So, if you think he's trying to tell you something through your dreams, then you're acknowledging he's no longer alive."

"*No.* No, that's not what I'm saying."

Her friend wrinkled her nose and picked up the spear again, rolling it between her thumb and fingers. "I don't know how you can have it both ways, Tori. If he's alive, he'd be contacting you in person. But, as I suspect, and I think you do too, he's not. So, he has to reach you via other methods—like in dreams or through a medium."

Victoria hated when her totally irrational, illogical friend used logic against her.

"Look, all I'm saying is, you could be right about him coming to you in a dream, but then again, I remember when it first happened, and you talked about how it *felt* like you were underwater. It was so surreal to you. It seemed like a dream. Maybe those feelings and thoughts have manifested themselves *into* dreams, and they're from your imagination."

It was all coming back to Victoria—when she'd first heard the news Robert had gone missing. She'd felt submerged and unable to find the surface, making it hard to breathe. Even conversations seemed like they were spoken underwater. Words were muffled and sounded funny to her. At times she'd imagined air bubbles floating out of the other person's mouth. Held in a veritable state of flux—a sort of purgatory—arms flailing as she reached out to grasp a piece of heaven while the forces of evil had its arms wrapped around her legs.

"Besides, I thought he went missing in New York City. Where could he drown there?"

Victoria considered the idea of him drowning. An accident. Not at the hands of another person—was that preferable? Same result.

"Oh, I guess there's the Hudson River . . . and the East River." Aviva was still following her train of thought.

Victoria added, "Even the lake in Central Park. That's a good size."

"You should call the NYPD." Aviva's attention was pulled away by a police car roaring by with its siren undulating. Then she refocused on Victoria. "Let them know about your dreams. The detective you've kept in touch with."

Their gazes met.

"You already did that."

Victoria nodded. "And he was very gracious, listening to me ramble on about my theory. Said he would look into it. Got back to me and confirmed there were no unidentified bodies found in any body of water around Manhattan—even checked the other boroughs."

"Well, you tried." Aviva's curt dismissal signaled she was finished discussing the matter.

Victoria was okay with that. She was more interested in addressing what she believed was the real reason Aviva invited her to lunch. "So, are you and my mother in cahoots?"

"What are you talking about?" Aviva pursed her lips and turned the corners down, playing with the straw in her water glass.

Victoria filled her in on the timing of her call in the car right after Millie had pressed her to consider flying again. She could have written it off as her mother's uncanny ability to sense something had happened—or in this case something about to happen—or simply a coincidence that two people who loved her were both thinking of the same way to help her be happy. Either was possible, but Victoria suspected there was a bit of collusion involved.

"She's right, you know," Aviva sassed once Victoria had finished, and then let it simmer in Victoria's head, not admitting to any collusion. When Aviva couldn't stand the silence any longer, she added, "God, it would be so much fun, you know. Holding the fussy babies for the stressed-out new moms. Tag-teaming the belligerent passengers."

"You make it sound so tempting."

"Well, you know . . . there's always flirting with the occasional rookie pilot."

"It hasn't really been *fun* since 9/11. Everything changed after that."

"Not everything. You still get that rush every time you take off. And the relief when the wheels touch down safely on landings. Realizing how far up in the air you are when you're walking down the aisle, and you hit a patch of turbulence. None of that has changed."

Victoria remained quiet, unsure how she felt about her friend's proposal. Was she seriously allowing herself to consider it?

"What's your hesitation? Vince?"

"Well . . . that's part of it. I don't think he'd be pleased."

"What's his beef with it?" When Victoria didn't answer, she tried again. "Is he one of those guys that doesn't want his woman to work in a job where she's on display for other guys to see?"

There was so much more to it than that. Victoria had first met Vince on one of her flights, one of the few without Aviva in the same cabin. Also one of the few she'd been scheduled to lay over overnight. Victoria let him talk her into getting a drink after they landed. The drink turned into dinner and then a nightcap in his room. Racked with guilt for succumbing to her need for a man's tender touch, Victoria halted their encounter before it went too far. She never told anyone about it, not even Aviva. But she imagined Vince would think twice about condoning her flying again, whether it was guys like him he didn't trust or her. *Did she trust herself?*

"I think he might see it as a slap in the face."

Aviva puffed out her lips. "Well maybe he should put a ring on your finger."

"You know he can't do that. Not yet, anyway."

"What's the deal with him? You guys serious?" Her friend was back to probing about Vince. Victoria willed their food to arrive, hoping to run interference with the rapid-fire questioning.

Aviva had made it clear early on she didn't click with Vince, and it didn't seem as though she was willing to try, which hurt Victoria. Friends were supposed to have your back—weren't they?

"It's complicated. We couldn't be serious if we wanted to. Legally or morally. I know people look at us and judge us. Judge me, really. I'm the one still married. Everyone thinks they know what I should do, even though they're not in my shoes."

"So, you *are* serious." Aviva tried again.

"Vince and I enjoy being together very much. And I don't want to lose that. So, if getting my job back as a flight attendant will piss him off, I'm not willing to risk that."

"Have you even asked him? Honestly he wouldn't even have to

know," Aviva whispered and then scooped up her martini, clinking Victoria's glass sitting on the table before throwing her head back to drain the last drop.

"What? Oh, I couldn't do that."

"You said yourself he's not around much." Aviva set down her inverted cone on a stem and signaled for the waitress. "You could get your old routes back—out in the morning to somewhere along the East Coast and then back again on the return trip. It might as well be an office job. . . . But you and I both know we wouldn't be caught dead stuck in a cubicle. We fly the friendly skies."

"Well, I think I would need to tell him—ask him." Victoria's eyes went to her water glass as she dragged a finger through the condensation on the bulbous shape.

"*Ask* him?" Aviva grabbed the edge of the table and lunged halfway across. When Victoria didn't react to her outburst, she settled back into her seat. "Tori, that doesn't seem right. He doesn't own you. But I'm not going to pretend to understand your relationship. Whatever you need to do." She raised her palms as if surrendering. "But I don't know how he could say 'no.'"

The waitress stopped by to let them know their meals would be right out. Aviva ordered another vodka martini—*extra* dirty this time with blue-cheese-stuffed olives.

"It *would* be nice to have a more sizeable paycheck. . . ." Victoria found the corner of her napkin and began to curl it toward the center of her lap.

"There you go. That's my girl." Aviva came to life again, poking a finger across the table at her. "You know it would. I say you just do it, and see if he even notices. You know how I operate: ask for forgiveness, not permission."

Vince's mantra too. It was unsettling to hear it spill out of her friend's mouth. She and Vince were a lot alike—maybe that was why Aviva didn't click with him. *Plow ahead and do what you think is best and deal with the collateral damage later, if there is any*—like the way he'd pulled her mother out of Brookhaven.

Victoria allowed her gaze to meander along the branch hanging above them, from the chunky part near the trunk to the end where it was narrowest. A sparrow perched at the very tip, on a twig that didn't seem sturdy enough to support her, nestled in three-lobed leaves of bright gold with tips of orange.

"What's the other part of it?"

"What?" she asked, refocusing on their conversation.

"You said Vince was part of it. What's the other part?"

"Oh, I don't know—"

"Yes, you do. What is it?" Aviva's deep chestnut, doe-like eyes beneath aggressively tweezed brows grew larger, coaxing her to spill.

Victoria tilted her head, twisting a lock of hair a few times through two fingers before flipping it over her shoulder.

Suddenly Aviva's face lit up. "You don't think you're too old, do you?" By her uttering the words, it gave life to the apprehension Victoria had yet to give a voice to.

Damn it. They'd been friends too long for her to be able to keep any secrets. Aviva always figured out what was on Victoria's mind. She could only glare across the table at her. And there she sat with her spunky ebony bob, looking much younger, although there was only a couple of years' difference between them.

"You've got to be kidding. You may be a little older than me, but you've still got it girl—and in all the right places too."

"Veeve, really." She glanced over to the next table to confirm they were consumed in their own conversation.

"You do. Are you kidding me? Are you worried they wouldn't take you back because of your age? They would, in a heartbeat. You're a seasoned professional. They should beg you to come back . . . teach the fresh-faced newbies a thing or two."

"I don't know about that."

"I'm serious."

"Me too."

The waitress arrived with two chopped salads; Victoria's with grilled chicken, Aviva's with roasted oysters. Once they'd assured her they were all set for the time being, she left them to their food and chatter. The young girl had only made it a few steps away when Aviva called her back and asked about her martini. Although she tried to talk Victoria into a second, Victoria declined but asked for more water. Water would have to do. She'd use her imagination.

Aviva picked up where she'd left off, not one to let a good discussion topic go before exhausting all possibilities. "Are you worried about your mother?"

"I can't very well go off and leave her for the day on a regular basis."

"I thought you said she was doing great—seems like her old self—like you're wondering if you should have put her in that nursing home in the first place."

"It's not a nursing home," Victoria corrected, perhaps a tad too loudly. Lowering her voice, she said, "It's assisted living."

"Whatever you call it—" Aviva waved away the discrepancy like she was shooing a New England no-see-um. "—she wasn't happy there." Sucking in a quick breath, she added, "Do you think she deliberately misbehaved so you'd have to pull her out?"

The intimation hit Victoria in the gut like a well-placed elbow. Would her mother pull a stunt like that? She couldn't help but laugh.

"Maybe she did. . . . Oh my God. Millie, the con artist." Victoria wanted to believe it was that simple, but she'd had the cognitive testing done for Alzheimer's. It sounded conclusive. *Could* it have been flawed? It had taken less than an hour. Was that enough time? Should they have taken her to more than one doctor? Or was her diagnosis accurate and her symptoms were delayed and would show up later with a vengeance?

"Well, there you have it," Aviva said with a mouthful of greens. After she swallowed, she added, "Sounds like we've covered it all."

Victoria was still lost in her thoughts about her mother when the waitress arrived with another martini, filled to the brim and precariously close to sloshing over the top.

"If it seems like I've taken away all your excuses, you're right. That's why you don't have a comeback."

In between bites of salad and sips of her second martini, Aviva laid out how her return would work; the abbreviated training, which Aviva thought Victoria could even teach, the new uniforms with extra pockets, and Millie holding down the household, feeling useful like old times, covering for her if Vince got suspicious.

"I can't ask her to do that."

"Are you kidding? Tori, you know that's in her wheelhouse."

"That may be, but I can't ask, and I can't go off and leave her."

"Yes, you can. She'd love to be your partner in crime."

"Maybe. But I don't feel comfortable with it. I can't be sure what her frame of mind will be. She might seem perfectly coherent today, but who knows what tomorrow will bring. The disease is so unpredictable."

"For the time being, she's doing well. So, run with it until her situation dictates otherwise."

"I'll think about it." Victoria poked at a piece of cucumber, trying to think of a new topic to get her off this one.

"You don't have to. I've already talked to your mom, and she's on board."

"*What?*" Victoria slammed down her fork, rattling the rest of the silverware on the table, nearly toppling her water glass. "What did you do that for?"

"Because I knew you would drag your feet." Aviva pushed her bowl away and latched onto the stem of her glass with both hands. "And as I expected, you were going to."

Victoria shouldn't have been surprised by her friend's forwardness—Aviva went after what she wanted with little regard for those posing resistance—but she was irked nonetheless. Then she had another thought. "What else did you do?"

Aviva's twitching brow and clenched jaw told her there was more.

"Well? What other arrangements did you take care of? Who else did you talk to?"

Silence hung between them like fog over snow on a warm spring morning. Victoria could almost hear the seconds ticking away.

"Aviva?" She prodded.

"Okay," she said, finally. "I might have mentioned to Sawyer you were thinking of coming back."

"Oh, Veeve, you didn't." Sawyer was their regional supervisor. He scheduled the flight attendants, and getting on his good side went a long way when it came to putting in for time off, schedule changes, or route requests. Victoria didn't have to work too hard at endearing Sawyer. He'd taken to her right away and seemed to take it as a personal affront when she gave her notice after Robert went missing. Nothing had transpired between them other than what seemed to be an occasional innocent brush against each other. It had felt innocent to her. She had to trust it was for him too.

Pressing her lips nearly out of sight, Aviva nodded. "And he was thrilled." She swatted at the back of Victoria's closest hand splayed on the table next to her salad. "So there. How 'bout that? He would welcome you with open arms."

"Veeve, I know you have my best interests at heart—"

"You know I do."

"And I appreciate that. Really, I do. But I *don't* appreciate you going behind my back and talking to people about something so personal—life changing."

"*Life changing.* Now that's a little dramatic, don't you think?"

"No, I don't. This would change my life as it is right now—"

"Which *sucks.*" Aviva jumped in, blasting the last word.

"Veeve, cut it out," whispered Victoria, her eyes darting to the nearest table. Two women, slightly younger, were finishing their meal. The one facing them paused with a coffee mug at her lips as she held her gaze on Aviva.

"Well, it does. You know it."

Victoria drew in as much air as she could to fill her lungs and released it, dragging it out to give her time to water down her reaction to Aviva's dig.

"Just because my life is different from yours doesn't mean—" A vibration from her phone cut her off. Snatching it up, she was pleased to see it was a text from Jameson. She read:

// hey mom i need my permissn slip signed for the field trip nxt wk //

Victoria felt a breath catch in her throat. The senior class history field trip. She knew it was out there on the horizon and had been reminding herself since his freshman year it was coming. She thought she'd be prepared for it, but the mere mention of it knocked her off the rails.

"What's up?" Aviva rarely attempted to contain her curiosity.

Looking up, Victoria did her best to make the text sound as ordinary and non-urgent as it was on the surface—like so many others. "Jameson . . . has a quick question." Her cell vibrated again.

// srry I frgot to ask whn u droppd grandma off //

As Victoria read, she could feel Aviva's eyes on her.

// mr. jennings is on my case so i dont want to forgt can u remnd me? //

Damn it. The last thing Jameson needed with his anxiety was one of his teachers harassing him for a silly permission slip.

"Tori, go ahead and answer him."

"No, that's okay. I'll get back to him after lunch. It's not urgent." She needed Aviva to keep her nose out of it.

"Seriously, how long can it take?"

"It's okay. Really." The sound of the Doobie Brothers' "Black Water" spilled from the phone she thought would go silent for a while.

"Oh, sorry," Victoria said. "Now he's calling." She glanced around to gauge the annoyance level of those around her, but it seemed minimal.

"Then answer it. Must be more urgent than you realize."

Reluctantly she answered in hushed tones, her hand cupped around the bottom of her phone. "Hey, Jameson."

"Hey, Mom. Just wanted to make sure you got my text."

"Yes, I did. I'm actually at lunch now. But I'll take care of it when I get there later."

"Okay, great. Thanks. Jennings is turning into a real ass about it."

"Jameson, watch yourself."

"Sorry, but he is. So, I need your help to get him off my back."

"Sure thing. Don't you worry. We'll get it straightened out. I'll see you later."

She did her best to tuck the subject matter aside, so she could get back to their lunch, but Aviva couldn't let it go.

"Interesting ringtone."

"Really? You don't like the Doobies?"

"Sure, but 'Black Water'?"

"Yeah . . . I like it," Victoria said, and then added, "Harrison's ringtone is 'Smoke on the Water.'"

"Deep Purple."

"Yeah."

"What's mine?"

Victoria allowed the corner of her mouth to turn up before she said, "'Bridge Over Troubled Water' . . . Simon & Garfunkel."

The two friends guffawed at the implication, which eased the tension that had been ratcheting up between them. Still, Aviva was stuck on Victoria's call with Jameson.

"So, what's going on? Is he okay?" She leaned across the table toward Victoria, the smell of vodka-laced olives on her breath.

"Nothing's wrong." Victoria sent a *back off* vibe across the table.

"Bullshit." Aviva smacked the edge of the table with her palm.

"Veeve, come on." Again she glanced to the next table with apologetic eyes. Both women looked over this time. Aviva ignored them and Victoria's angst.

"I can read you like a book. Tell me. What's going on?" She raised her brows as she cocked her head.

"No. Really. He forgot to have me sign his permission slip for a field trip. It was my fault because I missed an email, but I can take care of it when I go back and pick up my mother. Not a big deal."

Sitting back, Aviva sized her up with a long, icy stare, her arms wrapping across her torso again. Finally she spoke.

"Oh, no. . . . that's *the* field trip, isn't it?"

On the surface it would seem to anyone else—including the ladies at the next table—a simple question. But to Victoria, it was like Aviva had thrust her hand through her ribcage and, with her painted red nails, yanked open her beating heart. The dull pain in her chest hit before she realized her eyes were brimming, and soon her cheeks were wet. With a wobbly finger she brushed away the tears.

Through ragged sobs she struggled to contain, Victoria rasped, "I *can't* let him go, Veeve. I just can't." She could feel poring eyes on her but ignored them, willing the rest of the crowd to refocus on their lunches.

Her friend sat motionless—the space between them felt like a chasm—not uttering a word of encouragement or even needling. At that juncture, she would have welcomed either. So instead Victoria filled the void.

"I can't let him go," she repeated, a little louder.

Scooting to the edge of her seat, Aviva finally spoke, shaking her head ever so slightly. "Tori, what do you think is going to happen? Do you think he'll disappear too?"

Victoria pulled in a quick breath and held it to try to stop herself from crying in front of what seemed like the entire town but knew it would only work as long as she didn't release it.

Aviva had done it again. Pulled out her inner thought—her most painful fear—and announced it to everyone within earshot. She might as well have grabbed a paint brush—the size meant for painting houses—and a bucket of red paint and spelled it out with larger-than-life letters on the front of the building for everyone who drove by to see. Letting out the air she'd trapped in her lungs, Victoria wept quietly and didn't bother to wipe away the tears.

I won't be able to protect him, she was bursting to shout. *I should have protected my sister, but I didn't. I failed miserably. Now I'm not going to be able to protect Jameson if I let him go.*

Aviva fished around in her purse and handed Victoria a tissue as if it could plug the leak.

"Really?" her friend asked. She didn't get it.

"Yes. But you can't possibly understand."

"Because I haven't gone through the same type of tragedy, or because I'm not a mother?"

Victoria considered the question before answering, "Both."

"Okay, maybe you're right. So, tell me about it, so I can try to understand."

Scanning the tables around them, Victoria was relieved to see it was clearing out. Thankfully they'd soon have the place to themselves. The lone, red-headed waitress was clearing tables into a gray plastic tub, clanking them with such deliberate movement, she seemed angry at the crockery. Victoria was grateful for the noise.

"Every year the seniors who are taking AP classes or are on honor roll—which is the vast majority of the kids—have the opportunity to go on a handful of field trips. The one in the fall is to the New York Historical Society—the city's oldest museum. They grab a couple of meals and take in a Broadway show. This year they're also visiting the 9/11 Memorial."

"Didn't Harrison go on this trip?"

"No. We dodged a bullet with him. He ended up with Mono a week before the trip and couldn't go."

"But now Jameson wants to go . . . and he doesn't have so much as a sniffle."

"Right. But I'm terrified to let him."

"Because this is the trip Robert disappeared from, and you think Jameson will too," Aviva restated the obvious.

"I know it sounds totally irrational, but I can't help myself."

"Maybe . . . so, remind me what happened. How long ago was it now?"

"Seven years. Wait . . . remind you?" How could her best friend who was with her when the call came need a reminder about Robert's disappearance?

"Yeah, I need a reminder. Look, I know you relive the horror every day of your life. I hate to tell you, but the rest of the world has moved on. Even your boys, I bet."

"No, they haven't. They still hold out hope he'll be found."

"*Alive?*" They'd officially circled back to Robert's status. Aviva was a pit bull on a bully stick. She didn't let go of a topic until *she* was finished with it.

Victoria realized she'd never answered that question before—out loud, anyway—and had never really allowed herself to ask it. "I don't know. I hope so."

"So where do you think he's been? Wandering around with amnesia?"

"I suppose it's possible."

"Or maybe he started over with a new life in another country and has another wife and kids."

"Aviva, how *dare* you," Victoria snapped. "You know Robert. Do you really think he'd do something like that?"

"Tori, how well do we really know anyone?" Aviva leaned in. "How often do you watch the news, and a guy has done something terrible, and all his friends and neighbors say they never thought he was capable of such an atrocity, yet he did it?"

Victoria let her question go unanswered.

"All right. Enough 'what-ifs.' Remind me what happened that day."

"Robert was looking forward to taking his students to the city. It was a big group. They had to use two coach buses."

"He rode with the kids on the buses?" Aviva recoiled at the distasteful idea.

"Well, no, actually he didn't on this trip. He and Ben drove down together. In Robert's car. Ben likes to drive separately so if there's an issue with one of the boys he has flexibility and isn't stuck on a bus. But on this trip, they left the evening before. They both had appointments early the next day—Robert at the Museum of Natural History and Ben at the Museum of Modern Art—so the plan was to catch up with the boys at the play in the afternoon for the—"

"Oh my God, look at that one."

"What one?" Victoria glanced in the direction Aviva's attention had been diverted. A twenty-something approached the hostess stand—dark features and tanned skin with biceps pushing the limits of the seams on his button-down Oxford.

"He's a hottie, don't you think?"

Victoria turned back to Aviva to confirm who she was looking at. "What? What are you—"

"I've got to get with him." Her eyes darted around the outdoor dining area. "Wonder where our server is. Maybe she could give him my number."

"Aviva, are you serious? He's got to be half your age."

"What's that got to do with anything?"

"And there's the fact that he brought a pretty young thing with him."

"It doesn't mean they're *together*."

Victoria let it go. She'd suddenly soured on being with her friend any longer.

"Okay, sorry. Where were we?"

"Don't worry about it. It's not worth—"

"Of course it is. I know where we left off. At what point did they know Robert was missing?"

Pausing to grab another sip, Victoria could feel the back of her neck tighten with Aviva's interruption. *Why couldn't she just let her tell the story?*

Tracing the base of her water glass in nearly a complete circle and then back again, over and over while she talked, Victoria began. "It wasn't until the end of the day when it was time to head back. Robert ended up never catching up with the boys. He was meeting with someone at the museum to learn how to improve the curriculum at Litchfield and apparently got caught up in it and ended up spending the whole day there. That's so like him, you know?"

Victoria slid her hand from the table and dropped it onto her lap, glancing at Aviva to appraise her interest level. She seemed adequately rapt, so Victoria continued.

"Those boys meant the world to him. He was always looking for ways to enrich his teaching—to enrich their learning experience. He was so happy teaching. He put every bit of himself into it. It was easy as his wife to support that kind of dedication. I'm so proud of him. His students loved him, and the other faculty did as well."

"That doesn't surprise me at all," Aviva said, which pleased Victoria.

"When it got toward the end of the day and Robert hadn't shown up, Ben called his cell but couldn't reach him, so he called the museum but it was after hours at that point. He went back to the hotel and found that Robert had checked out of the room but had left his overnight bag with the bellman. That's when Ben called the police." She looked up with her eyes filling again. "But you know how that works. They don't take it seriously until the person has been gone forty-eight hours. His briefcase was never found."

"Jesus."

"Ben ended up staying in the city to look for him. Understandably he was distraught. He finally convinced the police Robert was missing, but I wonder what they missed during the time they lost. The Connecticut State Police got involved, but no one could find him. . . . And no one found any evidence to point them in a direction."

"No one *found* anything? No one *knew* anything?"

"No."

"No leads at all."

"No."

"How is that possible?"

"I don't know."

Their somberness hung over the table like the stench surrounding a paper mill on a windless day.

"I mean, how do you explain to a thirteen-year-old and a ten-year-old that their father is missing and may not be coming home?" Her glance landing on the spot where the sparrow had been sitting, Victoria shook her head. "We held out hope for the longest time. I called the New York City police detective every day for two years. I even took my mother and spent a few days in Manhattan, retracing his steps."

"You took your mother?"

Victoria nodded, returning her gaze to the table. "That was before her dementia diagnosis. You know . . . she has this ability to sense things that others can't."

Aviva remained quiet, her jaw set.

"I've told you the stories, haven't I?"

"Yeah, and I've seen in her action. She's almost creepy at times. Was she able to sense anything?"

"No. It was so disappointing," Victoria said, twisting a corner of her mouth. "And she felt bad that she couldn't be of any help. I was sorry to have put her through that."

"You had to try. You would have felt worse if you hadn't. So would your mother."

"True." Victoria appreciated when Aviva bolstered her, but those times didn't come close to offsetting the times Aviva spoke candidly, even if Victoria didn't want her to, pleaded with her not to.

"Look, Tori, I need to be brutally honest with you. Can I?"

"Sure, I guess so." She was surprised Aviva had even asked. Usually she plowed ahead with or without permission.

"As you said, it's been seven years—"

"Almost."

"Almost." Aviva nodded her head once and then grew quiet. Finally she spoke. "Tori, honey, he's not coming back. I think you know that. Deep down you do, if you let yourself listen to your gut. Something's happened to him. Something terrible. And I'm sorry that it happened, but, as they say, sometimes terrible things happen to good people. That's just the way it is. You can hold out hope forever, but it's not going to change what's happened. You need to accept that. Stop pining. Get on with your life. Do it for you. Do it for your boys."

Her friend sounded eerily like Ben Martin, as if they were both referring to the same page of a dramatic script.

"Veeve, how can you say all that?" It took everything she had not to ask what kind of a friend said those things. "They never found a body. They didn't even find his car. How am I supposed to give up on him? He's out there somewhere. It's a matter of time."

Her friend's shoulders drooped, and she let her head snap back against an imaginary headrest. "It's been *seven* years. He may *never* be found. Do you actually think he's still alive—after all this time and nothing has popped up?"

Leaning against the back of the chair, Victoria said, "What do you think I should do? Divorce Robert?"

"Soon you won't have to. They'll declare him dead, and you can move on. And you should. You're relatively young, attractive, you have two amazing sons, live in an adorable cottage in a highly sought-after town in upper-class suburbia . . . who wouldn't want your life?"

Victoria wondered if that meant her friend wanted her life. There were times Victoria wasn't sure *she* wanted to be in it—the times it felt like someone else's heavy, soiled overcoat had been draped over her shoulders, wafting of greasy diner food she'd never let pass through her lips.

"And you said yourself there are quite a few good-looking, successful, single guys whose sons go to Litchfield."

"I know I mentioned it, but it didn't mean I was on the prowl."

"Maybe not, but maybe you should be. You're certainly keeping an eye out. Or are you keeping them all for yourself? You're certainly not sharing them with me."

"Aviva, you know I've got Vince in my life, and I'm happy about that."

"But what kind of a relationship could you possibly have? You still feel married to Robert—not just married, tied to him. His memory. You can't let it go. I don't think he'd want that."

"Maybe not, but I also think he wouldn't want me to give up looking for him until we had answers."

Victoria's phone vibrated on the table again, so she grabbed it, expecting it to be Jameson. Instead it was an unfamiliar number with a 212-area code.

"Popular lady today."

"Well, no. And I don't have to—"

"Go ahead. Take it. Maybe it's someone who will lift your spirits more than I've been able to."

Victoria tried to read her face.

"Seriously, go ahead."

"I don't need to—"

"Answer it," Aviva shoved through clenched teeth.

"Fine." And with a click of an icon, she was connected with a familiar male voice.

"Hey, Victoria. Emerson here. How are you, love?" Never tiring of his British accent, she tried to suppress the elation erupting within her from materializing on her face. But soon her cheeks warmed.

"Oh, Emerson. Good to hear from you. I'm fine." She turned to Aviva with wide eyes. "What's going on?"

"You didn't let me walk you to your car after Presentation the other night." He allowed his declaration to dangle, a sort of lifeline for her to grab onto. She opened her mouth to answer but closed it again when nothing came to mind—witty or otherwise. *Why did he make her feel so giddy that her brain ceased to function?* "I mean, it stings a man's heart to have a stunning woman like yourself jilt him."

"Jilt you? Emerson—"

"There! I got you talking." Even his chuckle was entirely lyrical. She yearned to reach through the phone and pull him close. *What did he smell like? Was his cologne designer? Where did he buy it? Was it on a weekend excursion to Europe?*

"Listen, I know it's not the most exciting thing to be ringing someone about, but I'm following up with our rather loose, yet no less binding, agreement to help with the Parents Committee this year."

Rolling her eyes, she did her best to contain a groan. *That was the real reason for his call? Please, Lord, please help me find a way to get out of this. I need an excuse—any excuse.* She knew her silence could be misconstrued, but she struggled to find the words.

"I know, I know. It doesn't sound like much fun, but I think we can find a way to make it a bit more palatable," he said.

"Oh, really? How's that?" A flutter in her gut at the prospect of spending time with none other than Emerson Kittridge made her grin. Catching Aviva's expectant look, Victoria winked before she realized she'd done it and then shifted her gaze to watch an aqua Chevy Skylark pass by. If she'd had a better working knowledge of old cars, she would have been able to come up with the year of the vehicle, but couldn't. Her father would have been able to.

"Well, why don't you and I get together. I think between the two of us we can come up with something. Let's have lunch."

"Lunch?" She stole a glance back over to Aviva whose eyebrows were nearly touching her bangs. "Okay, where did you have in mind?"

"Brooklyn. I know a smashing place there, and the chef is a good friend of mine."

"Brooklyn. Okay, that's a little bit of a drive from here, but okay. I can meet you there."

"You don't have to drive. I'll pick you up."

"Pick me up?" She scrunched her forehead. *Why would he want to pick her up?*

"Where can I put down a whirlybird in Talcottville—or the surrounding area?"

"A whirlybird?"

"You know. A helicopter. A chopper."

"A chopper." Victoria looked to Aviva for an answer, even though she was only hearing one side of the conversation. "Hold on." With her phone pressed against her side, she whispered, "Where can you land a helicopter around here?"

Aviva, not taking Victoria's lead with a hushed voiced, answered, "A helicopter? Jesus. Uh, there's the helipad on top of Talcott Mountain, but I think that's for LIFE STAR emergencies. I can't think of anywhere else. . . . How about someone's backyard? Oh, maybe that would be illegal. . . . Oh, the airport. I've seen one land there."

"Bradley?"

"No, the one here in town. It only handles small planes, but a helicopter could land there."

"That could work. Thanks."

Returning the phone to her ear, she said, "There's a small airport on the north side of town that would work. Talcottville Municipal."

"Okay. I'll make the arrangements."

Smiling, she knew he wouldn't be "making the arrangements." Undoubtedly someone who worked for him would be.

"Talcottville Municipal Airport it is. Next Friday, okay?"

"Friday?" Victoria looked to her friend who seemed to have lost interest in the conversation. Or was it envy?

"I'll pick you up at 11:30. Okay?"

"Uh, 11:30. Sure. That works."

"Brilliant. I'll get reservations at Treviannos."

"Treviannos. That sounds wonderful. See you then."

"Oh, and don't forget your notepad."

"My notepad?"

"I'm sure we'll come up with a lot of fabulous ideas and will want to write them all down."

"Okay, will do. See you then."

With a click, Victoria was left to consider what she'd just agreed to.

"Are you kidding me?" The upper half of Aviva's body lurched toward Victoria again. "Are you seriously getting picked up in a helicopter and whisked off to New York for lunch at Treviannos?" Aviva's brows narrowed and nearly touched as she spoke. "God, why can't I meet someone like that on a flight," she said to herself.

"New York? No, he said Brooklyn."

"Did you think he meant Brooklyn, Connecticut?"

"I did. . . . Are you serious? Treviannos is in Brooklyn, *New York*?"

"Geez, Tori. Wake up. Who's taking you there?"

"Oh, please don't get jealous. This is to talk about the Parents Committee at Litchfield. Completely boring stuff."

"Me?" Aviva scoffed. "I'm not getting jealous. Come on. Get real already. So, who's doing the escorting?" Although she insisted there was no jealousy, her persistent curiosity said otherwise.

"Just a guy." She wasn't about to reveal he was recently divorced, more attractive than a guy his age should be, and entirely breathtaking as soon as he opened his mouth to speak, every luscious word dripping with his British accent. "He's the father of one of Jameson's friends."

"Uh, huh."

"Oh, Aviva. Give it a rest. I made the mistake of getting myself committed to helping with fundraising, and he's just following through on it. I was hoping he'd forget, or I'd fall through the cracks, but clearly that didn't happen."

"Clearly." Aviva regarded her friend from across the table. "You know, Tori, you can't hog all the well-heeled, eligible bachelors. . . . And I would say two is hogging."

CHAPTER THIRTEEN

"Mom, where are you taking me?" The last thing they needed was to get lost in the woods. Neither one of them had a stellar sense of direction. Like mother, like daughter, Victoria guessed. It brought back an uncomfortable memory of getting lost with Robert.

Once, when they were dating, the two set off on a mid-winter hike at her urging in the nature preserve on the fringes of Westport, neither giving a thought to the late hour and the timing of winter sunsets. Victoria assured him she knew the trails like the back of her hand. However, focusing more on their conversation than their surroundings, she became confused when they lost the daylight to guide them. Scant moonlight wasn't much help to discern their way back to the parking lot.

At some point they got turned around and headed in the wrong direction. After what seemed like hours trudging through the dark woods with the sounds of the wild around them and the temperature plummeting with each footfall, they came out onto a narrow, paved road with no buildings in sight. With nothing familiar to help her get her bearings, it became obvious they were nowhere near their car. Flipping a virtual coin, with neither direction a sure thing, they chose one and kept walking.

After a while they came upon a modest dwelling—it was more like a shack—with light emanating from within. They ventured to the front door and knocked. Straining to hear sounds of life on the other side, they knocked again. This time a man answered, pulling the door open far enough to peer out but keeping most of his torso tucked safely behind it. He listened patiently as they asked for directions back to the nature preserve. Shaking his head, he declared they were so far from their destination he should drive them.

Thanking the man for his kindness, they slid onto the backseat of his beat up, old station wagon, pushing aside what felt like damp blankets. The man's Doberman mix took what was clearly his place on the front passenger seat but kept his head cocked toward the intruders in the rear. It was a humbling and quiet ride, except for the grumbling muffler that was long overdue to be replaced, that took more than a few minutes through thick woods.

In the dark, it was difficult to see what her feet were brushing up against on the floor, but the smell that had crawled into her nasal passages was a combination of wet dog, stale cigarettes, and pepperoni pizza. Victoria prayed they hadn't accepted a ride from a serial killer, but they didn't seem to have any other choice.

When they finally pulled into the lot, she'd never been so happy to reach some semblance of civilization, although it was limited to the small building that housed the nature preserve office. She opened her door before the man had come to a complete stop, practically jettisoning onto the packed dirt lot, hoping Robert was right behind her. It was deserted except for a single light on a telephone pole shining down on her car. Clearly no one at the preserve had been concerned to see the solitary car with no one around after hours.

"Keep up. I'll show you." Her mother moved more nimbly than most seventy-eight-year-olds. Victoria kept her eyes on her feet so as not to catch a toe on a root or slip on a particularly wet patch.

"We don't want to miss Jameson's soccer game," Victoria tried, hoping to entice her mother back to campus.

"Oh, we've got plenty of time." She swatted at Victoria's words as if batting them away.

Before long, they'd reached a small waterfall—one Victoria had only heard of and seen in recent yearbook photos. The waterfall spilled into a large pond with a beaver dam on the far side.

"See?" Millie was beaming like she'd surprised herself she'd found it. "Ha!"

Victoria took in the bucolic setting that was right out of a Monet painting. Floating on the still water were flat green lily leaves with dirty white wilted blossoms. The only thing missing was the curved white wooden bridge traversing it.

"Absolutely beautiful. But how did you know this was here? And how did you know how to find it? There weren't exactly signs pointing the way. Not even a marked trail." Thankfully Millie was having one of her lucid days. They still had to retrace their steps, so hopefully it would last.

"Harrison brought me here during one of his Grandparents Days. He'd had enough of the throngs of people on campus, and so he and I went for a walk after lunch. This is where he brought me."

"It's beautiful," Victoria repeated. "I can see why you wanted to come back."

"But here's the thing; I was drawn here. Then with Harrison and now."

"Really?"

"Yeah, I'm sensing something here. I think it reminds me of your sister."

"Jessica? Why?"

"I don't know. . . . Maybe it's because of the woods. And the pond. She always liked to venture into the woods. Go hiking." The brightness of her mother's face dimmed. "And that's where they found her."

Can a mother develop a heightened sense of what has happened to a child? To her husband? And later her son-in-law? Should a mother ever have to endure so many tragedies?

Millie may have been able to "sense things," but in this pond, where the boys came to blow off steam, she could be sensing energy from a variety of benign events. Victoria prayed her mother wasn't sensing a not-so-benign event that had yet to happen. She wished Jameson would steer clear of there. Bad things could happen when adolescent boys started fooling around. What starts out as innocent fun, could turn very quickly into a mishap.

Victoria felt a sharp twinge in her gut as her mother's eyes bored into hers. Her mother was still reflecting on the distant past. It all came cascading back.

Her sister Jessica had been the middle child between Victoria and their older brother, Sean. She never seemed to fit into the family—perhaps she'd never tried. It was like she went out of her way to do things differently and was eager to try things her siblings had not. Jessica and their mother rarely argued, but when they were embroiled in a heated discussion, Victoria did her best to stay out of the way. It was torture to hear their raised voices because she loved them both dearly. It was usually over before long, and Victoria remembered longing to hug them both simultaneously to reconnect their hearts.

One day, after school, Jessica told Victoria to go on ahead home, and she would meet her there. It shook Victoria because they had always walked home together. The high school was located in the same complex with the school Victoria attended that housed kindergarten through junior high. But her big sister was insistent, assuring her it would be all right and to tell their mother she was staying after school for extra help studying for an algebra test.

Victoria was terrified walking home alone. She was only eleven and had always had the comfort of her big sister, a high school sophomore, at her side. That day, it was the longest walk she'd ever taken. And she knew her sister wasn't telling her the truth, which pained her. How would she be able to lie to her mother on her sister's behalf? Victoria hated that she'd put her in that situation and wondered what Jessica was up to that made her willing to lie.

Jessica never came home that afternoon. And by dinnertime, it was clear something was wrong. Her parents called every friend they could think of, but no one had seen her. By Victoria's usual bedtime, two policemen arrived at the front door. Her mother abruptly announced to them Jessica wouldn't be coming home and burst into gut-wrenching sobs. While the police assured her they would do everything they could to find her daughter and her husband tried to console her, Millie wailed and insisted it was too late. She was already gone.

The next morning, when the police returned, Victoria peeked out from behind her father's threadbare, green plaid La-Z-Boy and noticed how drawn their faces were. The men recoiled when her mother confronted them at the door and refused to let them in. The rest of the details were fuzzy in Victoria's memory, but as the events were relayed later, Millie told the officers she knew they had found her daughter's body in the woods behind her school. Because the details she spewed were so accurate, including the pond that few knew was there, Millie initially became a suspect but was later cleared.

Despite several persons of interest in the case, no one was ever charged or prosecuted for the murder of Jessica Hernandez. Her brother blamed Victoria for not making Jessica come home after school like she was supposed to—as if an eleven-year-old could sway a strong-willed fifteen-year-old.

It was the following summer that her father passed—again with Victoria the last to see him alive—and as Victoria recalled, her mother showed up on the job site just as the ambulance was arriving before anyone had called her.

Their father's death, so soon after Jessica's, turned out to be more than her brother could stand. After that, he pulled away from Victoria and her mother, the last two surviving members of his family, living nearby but rarely making contact. She imagined it was guilt that kept him away. Not survivor's guilt. More like guilt for not figuring out how to move on so he could be the brother and son they so desperately needed him to be.

The pounding in Victoria's head—the kind she usually endured after spending more than a short time with her mother—had started up again. All she wanted was to be back at the car with the seat warmers on and her mother dozing in the passenger seat as they made their way back home. Instead, they were in the middle of the woods, and Victoria had to figure out a way to convince her mother to head back to campus. There was a soccer game they needed to make an appearance at. And a permission slip that needed to be signed.

CHAPTER FOURTEEN

"Mrs. Sands. . . uh, this is Erin Myers Hutchinson. I don't think we've formally met, but I'm a history teacher here at Litchfield Academy."

Victoria's first thought was that Jameson was having an issue in her class, which she found perplexing. He didn't seem to have problems with *any* subject, and he loved history. Maybe that came from his father. But he had a genuine interest at an early age.

Trips to Sturbridge Village in Massachusetts were a highlight for him, whether on an elementary school field trip or family outing. Jameson had also asked to make a stop to see Plymouth Rock on a summer vacation to the Cape. In junior high, it was the trip to Gettysburg that got him talking about being a history major in college. Of course Robert was thrilled at the prospect that his son might follow in his footsteps, and Victoria kept her concerns about getting a job with such an impractical major to herself.

Or perhaps Jameson was struggling with his anxiety again. Her first thought was to drive to school and offer to bring him home for a break from the pressures of private boarding school. But if it was that, why wouldn't it be someone in the nurse's office or his advisor who was calling?

"Hello, Erin. Nice to hear from you." But was it, really? "What's going on? Is something up with Jameson?"

"Jameson? No, actually he's not one of my students."

"He's not?" Victoria grew puzzled.

"No."

Victoria waited to hear the reason Erin Hutchinson was on the other end of the line.

"I'm calling to see if we could meet sometime. Maybe have coffee. Somewhere off campus."

Intrigued, Victoria said, "Sure, I'd be happy to. Can you tell me—"

"There's a cute shop not far from the academy called The Daily Grind. I realize it's kind of a drive for you, and I apologize for that, but I can't be off campus for long. Could you meet there day after tomorrow at 2:00?"

"Uh, sure. That would work, but can you just tell me—"

"Please, let me fill you in on Wednesday. Okay, Mrs. Sands?"

"Okay, but you can call me Victoria. It's all right with me."

"Thank you, Victoria. I appreciate your time and look forward to meeting you."

"Wait. How will I know how to find—"

"Oh, don't worry. I'll be able to spot you. See you Wednesday."

Victoria sat motionless with a dull silence droning in her ear. How would she be able to recognize this history teacher from Litchfield Academy? To take a small measure of preparation, Victoria searched for her online and was surprised at how quickly something popped up. She examined her photos, which had been taken over time—none of which made her look older than twenty. The most recent photos showed her with chestnut hair with blonde highlights that fell just past her shoulders. Crystal blue eyes peered out from unblemished, cherub-like skin. Her smile creased her face in all the right places and exuded warmth. Victoria thought of the testosterone-laden boys and how they must clamor to get into her classes and instantly regretted the thought. Her son was one of those boys.

Next, she Googled Erin Hutchinson along with the name of the academy. A short bio indicated she had started as a history teacher at Litchfield Academy seven years earlier—the same fall Robert disappeared.

CHAPTER FIFTEEN

The Daily Grind was a quaint yet bustling shop, set in a strip mall on a busy state road that passed through Litchfield Falls, about a mile or so from the academy. In the same town, but worlds away. It appeared that most patrons were grabbing their afternoon caffeine fix and heading back out the door for destinations unknown. The enticing aroma that grabbed you as you stepped through the front door and clung to your clothes could make a tea-drinker convert on the spot. The bell on the door to alert staff to customers made a pleasant ding-ding sound.

Arriving a few minutes before their appointed time to meet, Victoria ordered a coffee in a to-go cup and eyed the display case while she waited. She imagined what the nearly empty shelves of pastries and cookies would have looked like when the café first opened in the morning. If it wasn't such a long drive, she might have inquired about becoming one of their suppliers.

After surveying her seating options, Victoria grabbed a small u-shaped, dark-velvet-upholstered booth with more toss pillows than Home Goods—farthest from the door, yet with a panoramic view of the whole place. Sitting with her back to the wall, she kept the entrance in her peripheral vision while allowing her eyes to peruse the shelves lining two walls with coffee-themed knickknacks; an old wooden coffee bean grinder with a dark, patinaed handle on top that cranked horizontally and a drawer at the bottom to catch the fresh grinds, a stack of coffee-colored mugs with the café's logo on the sides, and small stretched canvases with cute sayings like "But first, coffee," "IT'S COFFEE O'CLOCK," "Coffee: Happiness in a mug," "Coffee: *Because adulting is hard*," "Great ideas start with coffee," "Never trust anyone who doesn't drink coffee," "A day without coffee is like . . .

sorry, I have no idea," and one that may have been borrowed from a major coffee outlet and paraphrased, "Humanity Runs on Coffee." Worn paperbacks filled in the rest of the space on the shelves.

Before long, a young woman who was the spitting image of her recent online photos slipped inside. There seemed to be an electric connection when they made eye contact—or was it only on Victoria's end? Erin gave a quick wave on her way to the counter. Her long, swishy navy-blue and burgundy print skirt and loose wrap gave her the appearance of an art student from Southern California more than a teacher at a preppy private school on the opposite coast.

After what seemed like an exorbitant amount of time to get a coffee, Erin appeared at the table with an oversized white ceramic mug, the steam from its frothy contents wafting above it and disappearing. She brought a whiff of inexpensive cologne with her as she tossed her floppy canvas tote onto the bench.

"Mrs. Sands." Plunking down the mug, she held out a diminutive pale hand that clearly had spent more time grading papers than basking on the beach.

"Victoria, please."

"Of course." Erin nodded, and they shook. "I'm Erin Hutchinson, although the boys sometimes still call me Ms. Myers. I just got married last spring." Scooting into the booth, she rearranged the pillows to make room. "Thanks so much for meeting me."

Erin fell silent, mesmerized by her steaming mug, and Victoria sized up her young, innocent exterior. Victoria wondered what attracted her to a private school in a remote town like Litchfield Falls filled with young boys, rife with hormones and cocky attitudes, even if their bodies couldn't quite back them up yet.

"No problem. . . . So, you're a newlywed."

Erin grinned and nodded again.

"Where was the wedding?"

"Charleston, South Carolina."

"Sounds lovely. Why there?"

"My parents retired there, and I've absolutely fallen in love with it.

The wedding was right on the Ashley River. A fabulous outdoor venue with amazing Grand Oaks with Spanish moss. All the southern charm you could ask for. And the weather cooperated pretty much. After a brief downpour half an hour before the ceremony, it cleared up and the rest of the day was perfect."

"Sounds magical," Victoria offered.

"It was. Thanks."

"So, what's up?" If their time was limited, Victoria wanted to waste none of it with any further pleasantries.

"Well, uh, as I mentioned on the phone, I teach history at Litchfield." She slipped off her weak-tea-colored wrap that appeared itchy to the touch and tossed it next to her. Victoria watched as a pillow on the middle of the bench seat got bumped and rolled off onto the floor.

"How long have you been there? I don't think you've had either of my sons in your classes."

"That's true. They must have had Ted Jennings instead. I've been there seven years—"

"Seven."

"Yes."

"So, did you know my husband, Robert?"

Erin's gaze dropped to the table. Suddenly interested in her coffee, she wrapped both hands around her mug. After a quick sip, she said, "I met him" and returned her attention to Victoria. "I started a few weeks before he disappeared."

For Victoria, the words still stung when someone else spoke them.

"I see."

"He was so sweet to me. Very welcoming. Made me feel right at home."

"But if you teach history, wouldn't he have hired you? He was the department head."

"I was hired as an art history teacher for the art department."

Victoria was nodding before she realized it, acknowledging the explanation for Erin's outfit.

"I have a minor in European history so when there was a sudden opening in the history department a couple months into the school year, I was a logical choice to fill the spot. I must have done okay because they let me keep teaching history. I've actually enjoyed it very much."

An opening. Caused by her husband's sudden disappearance. How fortuitous for her. How far would someone—jockeying for a position in a prestigious private school—go to create an opening? Victoria hated herself for thinking it as soon as it crossed her mind.

"Will you be going on the senior field trip to the city next week?"

"Yes, and I'm really looking forward to it. It's not always so easy chaperoning two buses full of teenage boys, but somehow—they've assured me—it all works out."

"Did you go on the trip when you first started at Litchfield—the one Robert disappeared on?"

"No." A wisp of Erin's blonder hair slid back and forth across her forehead as she shook her head. "I was brand new, and I think all the plans were set before I started. The teachers who do get to go enjoy the time away from campus, so no one is going to willingly give up their spot."

"So why are we here, Erin?" If she wasn't so likable, Victoria's tone would have been more astringent.

"I didn't get an office right away. Well, what they assigned to me was more like a broom closet, and I didn't want to complain too loudly before I'd had a chance to prove myself. But after seven years, I thought it was time to ask for a proper workspace and a place to have office hours, so this summer I asked. And Robert's was the only one available."

"It's been empty all this time?" Victoria thought it odd.

"Yeah, I'm not sure why. But I'll admit, it felt a bit strange moving in there, knowing the circumstances."

Finding it hard to empathize, Victoria said nothing.

"I've always loved that end of the hall where his office is because of the circular back stairs leading up to it. You know, they're narrow and the stones they're made from make it feel as though it's something out of a medieval castle. I love how the stones are cool and smooth to the touch. The boys seem to like to use the stairwell as well."

Not seeing where this litany was heading, Victoria maintained her patience, trusting the reason for their encounter would be revealed soon enough.

"He—Robert—had this neat old desk, and I've been exploring it lately. I found something." She reached for her wrap and fumbled until she found the right pocket, pulling out a skeleton key and offering it to Victoria in her palm.

Victoria accepted it and examined its intricate antiqued filigree, rolling the thin metal shaft back and forth between her fingertips.

"I can't find anything in the office that it opens," Erin continued. "Not any of the desk drawers. No cupboards or closets. So, I thought maybe it might fit something at your home."

Squeezing the key into her fist, Victoria thanked her but was at a loss as to what it would open.

"But that's not all." Erin had her attention. Snatching a handle on her tote, she pulled out a small manila envelope four-by-six photos would fit into and dropped it on the table between them. "I found these wedged in the back of a bottom drawer in the desk. As if they weren't supposed to be found."

Snatching it up, Victoria pinched together the ends of the metal clasp that secured the flap and slid it open but froze when Erin held up her hand.

"I wouldn't open that here."

Victoria glanced around the empty café. "There's no one here." She let the envelope drop to the table.

"I know . . . I just . . . you never know who might walk in."

As if on cue, bells jingled when the front door to the café popped open and in strode Ben Martin with, surprisingly, no one at his heels.

"Shit," Erin said, only loud enough for the two of them to hear.

A couple of strides and he was halfway to the counter when he noticed the only customers in the place and pivoted on his heels.

Victoria pasted a smile on her face and imagined Erin mentally scrambling for an excuse for the two of them to be having coffee. Victoria lived too far away for it to be a chance meeting. And it wouldn't take much effort for the headmaster to access Erin's class lists to determine she didn't have Jameson in any of her classes. So, what was their excuse going to be?

"Hello, ladies." He didn't seem to have a volume setting other than booming. And in the small space, it was particularly grating. "What brings you to Litchfield Falls, Victoria? . . . And together?" His eyes shifted between them. It was one of the few times she didn't have to bend at the knees to avoid looking down on the headmaster.

Before she could help herself, Victoria began to fill in the answers to his questions. A nervous, knee-jerk reaction. He had a way of doing that to people. "Oh, you know. Parents Committee business is never done." What had she said? Did that make sense? The headmaster nodded but looked for more of an explanation. Erin, however, didn't engage. "Just brainstorming ideas for a fundraiser."

"Impressive. Glad to see you're on top of this, Victoria. What have you come up with so far?"

Really? You couldn't accept that answer and move on? Go get your cup of coffee, damn it. "Oh, we just sat down, so we haven't come up with anything concrete yet."

"But we'll keep you posted," Erin added, finally engaging in the ruse.

Ben seemed to be considering their hastily concocted story, his glance traveling between the two of them again. Victoria shoved her clammy hands beneath her thighs, waiting for him to say something. It felt like he was about to call their bluff. He was too cunning to fall for the thinly veiled pretense they'd thrown out.

"Well, I hate to break up your brainstorming session." He put the last two words in air quotes. "But I need my teachers to be on campus with the boys. Ms. Myers, don't you have office hours now—in your new office?" Apparently the headmaster hadn't caught up with her name change yet. "Perhaps the two of you can get together when you don't have urgent responsibilities."

"Urgent? I left a note on my office door to let my students know—"

"Well, now, that isn't really meeting your responsibilities to the boys, is it?"

"No, sir. I'll get right back."

No sooner had Erin scooted out of the booth than the headmaster took her by the elbow and escorted her to the door in a strangely parental move. Glancing back, he said, "Nice to see you, Victoria. Enjoy your coffee." And he left without his. The ding, ding of the bell on the door as it shut wasn't so pleasant this time.

Erin's frothy mug no longer had steam rising from it. Neither did Victoria's. And the envelope was no longer on the table.

Chapter Sixteen

Turning onto their street, Victoria tapped the brakes and swerved to avoid hitting someone riding a bike in the middle of the road. A woman. She sat erect on the seat, her red wavy hair poking out from under a straw hat bouncing in the breeze. If she'd been pedaling any slower, she would have run the risk of toppling over. The bike looked as though it had been assembled from several discarded parts. Victoria caught a glimpse of lime green, bright coral, and robin's-egg blue. It looked like the back fender had flowers painted on it that nearly matched the ones on her leggings. "Interesting," she said to no one.

Her thoughts drifted to her brief meeting with Erin the day before. What was it she had wanted to show her in that small envelope? Clearly it had something to do with Robert. His disappearance? And why was Ben so eager to end their time together? Victoria would need to reconnect with Erin.

After a couple curves to the section of road where houses were spaced far enough apart to allow for a healthy dose of landscaping in between, Victoria pulled into their driveway, leaving the car in front of the garage. Gathering the empty cupcake boxes she hoped to reuse from the backseat, she headed in, pleased the setup for the baby shower had gone off without a hiccup. One more successful baking job completed. Check.

Once inside the front door, she let the screen shut behind her. "Mom?" She listened but got no response. "Mom?" she said, a little louder, dropping her keys on the table under the mirror and the boxes on the chair. Nothing. Her glance bounced from her mother's favorite chair to the rest of the furniture in the living room. No Millie. "Mom?" Then to herself, she said, "Oh, don't tell me you've wandered off." A charge of panic shot through her to the tips of her fingers. She tried to rub the tingling away.

Climbing the stairs two at a time, Victoria told herself her mother was napping. She poked her head in all three tiny bedrooms, but no Millie curled up under a throw. Just a neatly made bed in each one. Returning to the narrow hallway, she tried again. "Mom?" No answer. The bathrooms. Even though the light was out in the one shared by the guest bedrooms, she leaned in and flipped the switch. It was tighter than the master bath. Stepping across the threshold, she yanked the shower curtain to reveal an empty tub. It was an old porcelain one that was original to the house but didn't have the character of her claw-foot tub. Maybe her mother preferred that one. She dashed back down the hall to her room. Rounding the bed, she could see the light was off but kept going. Flicking the switch with a finger on her way to the tub, she shoved the curtain back and stared at emptiness. *Where could she be?* Retracing her steps to the top of the stairs, Victoria stood and listened to the buzz of the quiet. With her mother around, it shouldn't be.

Then came an unfamiliar rumbling. "What the—" Startled by the sound of the garage door, she bolted back down the stairs and through the front door. Partway down the walkway, she froze.

"Mom! What are you—" Her mother had the garage door handle in her hand and had it raised halfway up. "That door. It's hard to—" Her mother looked at her and yanked it to her shoulder height, then pushed it up the rest of the way, like a weightlifter demonstrating a clean and jerk. Victoria closed the distance between them, not taking her eyes off the bike. "Where did you get that?" she asked, then caught sight of her hair. "Oh my gosh. What did you do?" She realized her hand had found its way to a lock of her own hair, and she let it fall to her side.

"Ha!" Millie threw her head back and giggled like a young girl, clearly pleased she had thrown her daughter off. "Well, what shall I start with first? My hair?" Removing her hat, she pumped an upward palm toward an ear. "Don't you love it? I was getting tired of white. It made me look so much older than I felt. So, I took care of that."

"Yourself?" Victoria couldn't picture it. And like a scene at a horrific car crash, she couldn't pull her eyes from the bright red mop, now in full view. It wasn't a subtle shade of auburn or even a stunning copper, this was right out of a first grader's crayon box.

"Ha! Sure I did. No one was around to help—" Victoria felt the jab in her gut. "—but I didn't really need it. I've done it before."

"I see."

"Don't worry, I didn't make a mess." Her words took Victoria back to when the boys were young, and they'd surprise her by making something in the kitchen. They also would profess they hadn't made a mess, but their definition of clean and hers were on opposite ends of the spectrum. Her mother, however, shared her affinity for a neat space. In their days of borderline poverty, she always said they should take care of what they had. If they didn't, they'd be no better than white trash. Besides, Victoria had just checked the bathrooms, so she knew they were clean.

"I'm sure you didn't."

"So, what do you think?" Millie's cupped hand was back up to her ear, propping up a low hanging curl.

Victoria grinned. "You look fabulous. Twenty years younger," she assured her.

"Ha!"

It would take a while to get used to the vibrant red color, but her mother's glowing face said she loved it. So, Victoria would learn to love it too.

"And where did the bike come from? We had nothing like that in the garage."

"One of your neighbors had it out by the curb. You know, that's what people do when they want to get rid of things. Ha! How about that. I walked past it a bunch of times, and it was lying there, getting rained on, grass growing through it. So finally on one of my walks I decided no one else wanted it, so I wheeled it back here." Victoria noticed she hadn't used the word home. "It looked workable. A little rusty. Tires needed pumping. A little oil."

Victoria stepped closer to get a better look. "Where did you get the paint?" Her eyes landed on the back fender and the intricate daisies painstakingly painted on the length of it.

"Victoria, why do you have to interrogate me so? You're acting like you don't trust me. Do you think I stole it?" She swatted the side of the seat.

"Mom, relax. I'm—"

"Don't tell me to relax. You're the one that doesn't trust me all of a sudden."

"I'm just curious. Clearly you've been very resourceful, which I admire. You always have been. If you don't want to tell me . . . fine."

Their eyes locked and neither flinched. Finally Millie spoke, not breaking eye contact.

"I found the paint in the garage—your garage. There were several cans, not all usable, but I was able to find enough to give this baby new life." She gave the seat a pat—this time more affectionately.

It dawned on Victoria her mother seemed to be going through a rebirth—having been given a new lease on life being sprung from Elderly Alcatraz—and she'd shared that rebirth with the bike.

"I didn't know there was any paint *in* there." When they first moved in, she'd had the best of intentions to clean out the garage, but there always seemed to be something with a more pressing priority. Most of the paint cans had to have been there from the previous owners.

"Well, there was a lot of crap to weed through. But spray paint lasts longer than canned. You just have to clean out the nozzles. I tossed the ones that were all dried up into the garbage can. Hope that's okay."

"Absolutely. Thanks for doing that. Saved me the trouble."

Her mother grinned. Leaning across the bike, she grabbed Victoria by the shoulder. "That's what I'm here for sweetheart. Happy to help."

Given all of her mother's accomplishments, Victoria let herself believe it was going to work out nicely having her stay at the cottage.

"All right. Let's get this pretty bike inside where it will be safe. It's time for some tea."

"Any more of those oatmeal cookies left?"

"I'm sure there are. Let's go take a look . . . and figure out dinner. I think Vince might be coming tonight."

"Well, won't that be fun."

Victoria glanced over to her mother to catch any hint of sarcasm on her face and didn't notice any. She allowed herself a crooked grin in anticipation.

CHAPTER SEVENTEEN

Poking her head into the oven to assess the cupcakes, the whiff of chocolate in her face made her mouth water. Almost done. She wished she had made a few extra. As she ran through the list of ingredients for the coconut frosting, the doorbell interrupted her thoughts. Glancing at the timer, she made a mental note to check back in a few minutes. The doorbell sounded again.

"Coming," she called.

When she pulled open the door, a woman stood on the front step with folded arms and a glare that would scare away the fiercest of foes. A young girl, who couldn't have been more than seven, stood next to her, not looking so fierce, but clearly trying to.

"Are you Mrs. Sands?" the woman asked.

"Yes, I am. Nancy Farnsworth, isn't—?"

"Your mother stole my daughter's bike." The woman put a hand on the girl's shoulder.

"She what?" *Please, Lord, say it isn't so.*

"She stole my daughter's bike," the woman repeated, even though Victoria had heard her the first time.

"There must be some sort of misunderstanding." Where *had* she gotten the bike she was riding earlier? *Oh, Mom, what have you done now?* "What makes you think so?"

"Because our daughter's bike went missing and a few days later we see your mother cavorting around with a bike we've never seen her on before."

"Well, that doesn't mean it's your daughter's."

"Oh, she can paint it all she wants, but we can tell it's Melissa's."

Victoria was at a loss as to how to handle the confrontation. And the woman stood on the front step, hands now on her hips, glaring at her. Her daughter tried to emulate her mother. Victoria had to look twice at her cherubic face with a stern expression and her petite hands on her hips, which she jutted out at an odd angle.

"I think we need to talk to your mother," the woman said.

"I see, well, she's not home right now," Victoria fibbed.

"All right, then open the garage door so we can take a look at the bike."

"Oh, she has the bike with her," she blurted out, fibbing again. Only this time it felt more like the full-fledged lie that it was.

The woman held her ground, and Victoria prayed her next move was not going to be toward the garage. Before she could finish the thought, the mother and her mini-me were striding down the sidewalk. Victoria stepped out onto the stoop. All she could do was watch. This was one of those times she wished there were a man in the house to take charge. If Robert had been there—or Vince—she doubted if the woman would have been so bold.

She watched as the woman bent down and yanked on the handle. But it didn't budge. She yanked again, so hard Victoria thought she was going to dislocate her shoulder. Still nothing. For once, she was grateful it was a stubborn door.

In a voice meant only for her daughter, the mother mumbled something about it being locked. Victoria grinned. It wasn't, but she was relieved they thought so.

"This isn't over," the woman yelled with a clenched fist and a single finger stabbing the air in Victoria's direction. "We'll be back. . . . And next time, we'll bring the police." She grabbed the girl by her shoulder and spun her around, guiding her down the driveway.

The girl put on the brakes. "But Mommy, my bike!"

"Another time." The woman bent toward the girl's upturned face and brushed away a tear. "We can't get it right now, sweetie. But we will. Don't worry. Now, let's go." She yanked on her skinny arm.

"But Mommy!" She continued the protest as they made their way to the end of the driveway, across to the other side of the street, and around the bend in the road.

Finally the bewailing slipped out of range of Victoria's ears. As she went back inside, she knew she'd only bought herself some time. But it was important to talk with her mother alone and not confront her with a couple of strangers looking on. She could only wonder how this situation could possibly have a happy ending and what else her mother would get into that Victoria would have to bail her out of.

"You didn't have to do that." Her voice was low and came out of the dark. It made Victoria jump.

"Geez. Didn't know you were there, Mom." She pressed a hand to her chest.

"Well, I am." Her voice grew louder.

"You heard the whole conversation?" Victoria eased the screen door into place. She wasn't in the mood for another confrontation—especially with her mother.

"Enough to know what was going on . . . and what you did."

"I was trying to protect you from—"

"Protect me? Ha!"

"What I mean is, I wanted to be able to talk to you first—"

"To get my side of the story?" Her mother jutted out her chin and pressed her fragile palms to her hips.

"Well . . . yes. What's wrong with that?" Victoria found it hard to believe they were arguing about Victoria protecting her. Really?

"Absolutely nothing. In fact, I can't tell you what that means to me. I thought after you decided to put me in that home, you didn't really care about what I thought."

"Mother! How could you. We talked about that together. I thought you were in agreement. We—" Victoria felt herself spiraling and on the verge of lashing out at her mother. She pulled back. "I'm sorry. That's a different topic for a different time. Let's keep on this one, if we could." She paused to clear the air. As she did, the oven timer chimed from the kitchen.

"Victoria, why don't we sit and have a cup of tea. How does that sound? Tea always seems to calm the soul." Millie didn't wait for an answer. "I thought we might need one, so I put the kettle on."

Victoria watched as her mother strode into the kitchen. Why did just about everything come down to tea as the solution? She wondered how many cups her mother drank when she wasn't there. Somewhat reluctantly following along behind, Victoria tended to the cupcakes, setting the two pans on a cooling rack while her mother filled a teapot with teabag strings wrapped around the handle.

After gathering cups and saucers and a plate of Italian anise cookies, they settled into the living room and poured tea. Victoria started with a more benign topic than grand theft so as not to put her mother on the defensive.

"These cookies are left over from that baby shower I just did." Victoria held one up and examined it as though she were judging a bake-off. "I love them, and people don't seem to order them as often as I'd like so I made a few ex—"

"They're lovely, dear, but let's get to the point." Millie brushed crumbs from her chin.

"Okay." Victoria dropped the cookie onto her saucer and crossed her legs, clasping her knee with both hands. "Let's." She paused to let her mother begin, but she only stared back at Victoria with a blank expression. "So, tell me where you found the bike. You know, it was embarrassing to have a neighbor come up to my door and make an accusation like that." Victoria could hear her own belligerent tone and backed down. "I'm sorry. Why don't you start from the beginning, and we'll go from there?"

"It's quite simple, really. I was out on one of my walks, and I came across this bike that had been discarded at the end of a driveway."

"Which driveway?"

"I don't know. A few driveways down on the other side of the street."

Victoria created a mental map of her mother's description. Was that near the Farnsworths?

"How did you know it was discarded? Maybe someone had dropped it there to go off and do something else. You know how kids are." Victoria struggled to remain calm and listen to her answers. The running mental images were of her mother taking a child's bike, and after twisting the idea around in her own head, thinking it was okay.

"No. This was definitely discarded. It wasn't ridable the way it was. I had to put air in the tires. It needed painting."

"Mom, just because the tires needed air or you thought it needed painting—"

Millie's hand flew up as she pulled in a lungful of air in an indignant gasp. "You think I stole someone's bike, don't you? Oh my God. My own daughter. Ha! My own flesh and blood. I suckled you at my breast longer than most mothers did back then. And now you turn on me. . . . Well, I guess I should have expected it after getting dumped at the home."

"Mom! That isn't the way that played out, and I'm not accusing you—"

"Oh, but I think you are." Her finger wagged at Victoria. "Why else would you—"

The doorbell cut into the discussion they'd barely begun. Victoria hesitated, not wanting to be interrupted, but the bell rang a second time. She strode to the door, running scenarios through her head of who it could be; the cute girl with blonde pigtails who lived next door and sold Girl Scout cookies (was it that time of year already?), the pimple-faced boy from down the street who tried to talk her into hiring him to mow her lawn more than once during the summer (would he offer to rake her leaves this time?), or maybe it was a couple of annoying Jehovah's Witnesses. With those possibilities in mind, she opened the door to see a man in a dark blue uniform standing on the top step, a hand on one hip, the other on the railing.

"Mrs. Sands?"

"Yes. Victoria."

"I'm Officer Dill." Instantly recognizing the reason for his appearance, she would rather have opened the door and been greeted by the Jehovah's Witnesses she'd imagined.

"What can I do for you, Officer?" She knew it was probably too much to ask for him to be doing a door-to-door check on the neighborhood, but she chose optimism over reality.

"I'm looking into a missing bike."

So much for her rose-colored glasses. "I see."

"I understand your neighbor, Mrs. Farnsworth, stopped by to see if you had seen it."

Grinning, Victoria said, "That's a nice way of putting it."

"Is that so." He allowed himself a chuckle.

She relayed her version of their conversation, knowing the neighbor would have embellished her version and had to give him another side to consider.

"I didn't steal the kid's bike." Victoria jolted at the sound of her mother's voice in her ear. She stepped back and instantly wished she hadn't made room for her to join the conversation. "I'm Millie, Victoria's mother."

The officer introduced himself.

"And I don't like that people think I did." The officer appeared to be listening with a healthy dose of patience, which pleased Victoria, but she wondered how long it would last. When her mother got going, she could test even Mother Teresa. "It was lying at the curb like they'd tossed it out. . . . There may even have been a sign taped to it that said 'free.'"

"Really, Mom? There was a sign on it?" Victoria's optimism grew again. *Or was her mother making it up?*

"There could have been," Millie said, her tone laced with uncertainty.

"So, you're not one hundred percent sure," Officer Dill said.

"I . . . I don't remember. Sometimes I imagine things, you know?" Millie's eyes grew distant as if trying to recall.

Victoria's optimism fell to an abysmal low. *You're not doing yourself any favors, Mom.*

"Well, ma'am, do you remember where you picked it up? What driveway?"

"Absolutely."

"Okay then, why don't we take a little ride down the street, and you can show me where you got it."

"We get to go for a ride in your cruiser? Ha!" The childlike glee in Millie's tone was unmistakable. She practically skipped along behind the officer.

"And you can sit in the front seat," he called over his shoulder.

She clasped her hands together tightly. Victoria followed along behind with a sinking feeling this wasn't going to end well. Not knowing enough to keep her mouth shut, Millie would implicate herself, even if she'd done nothing wrong.

"Actually." The officer eyed the garage. "Could I take a look at the bike you brought back?"

"Sure!" Millie rerouted her feet and yanked up the door. "You should see it. It was in terrible shape. Kids just don't take care of their things these days. They don't deserve the things they have. They really don't."

"That might be true," the officers said, trailing his last word.

"I mean, if you took them away, they'd either not miss them, or ask their parents for a new one, and they'd give it to them. That's the way these kids are handled. There are no consequences for their actions."

Victoria listened to the words tumbling out of her mother's mouth. Was that what this was about? Was she teaching a child a lesson?

"That's not the way you were brought up, was it, Victoria?" Millie didn't wait for an answer. "No, sir." She emphasized both syllables.

Disappearing into the shadows at the back of the garage, Millie knocked the kickstand up with her foot and pushed her pride and joy toward the officer standing respectfully just outside. She was beaming.

"How about this? Huh? I worked hard on it. I think it came out great, if I do say so myself. Ha!"

"Very nice. So, you painted this yourself?"

"Yes, I did."

"Very nice," he repeated, running his fingers across the fenders and then the handlebars. "You did a great job."

Victoria figured his strategy must have been to get on her

mother's good side so she'd trust him and share everything she knew, and Victoria knew it would work like a charm.

Crouching down, he examined the frame, pressed a thumb into one tire and then the other. Victoria knew he was making note of the brand, possibly the model. All he would need from the Farnsworths was matching info and her mother was screwed. "Okay, very nice. Thank you for showing me."

"Sure thing." Millie rolled the bike back to where she'd retrieved it and headed to the cruiser. Victoria slipped into the backseat, wondering what the penalties were for stealing a bike. Jail time? Would her mother's next ride in a cruiser be where she was sitting? Talk about consequences.

Taking his directions from Millie, the officer eased the car down the street, slowing at each driveway and looking to Millie for a reaction. She looked his way and said, "It was on the other side of the street."

"Okay. I'll go to the cul-de-sac and turn around, so it will be on your side."

On the return trip, he kept his speed to a crawl and checked with her from time to time. "Anything look familiar yet?"

"No . . . I don't think so." Her voice trailed off.

"What about this driveway?" He slowed and gestured to a neatly manicured lawn.

"Nope."

Two mailboxes later and Victoria knew they were at the Farnsworth's house. She willed her mother to keep quiet.

"How about this one?" Was he talking her into it?

"Uh . . . it could be. I'm not sure."

Victoria opened her mouth to offer to write a check for a replacement bike when they rolled to the next driveway with a dumpster off to the side.

"Oh, it might be this one," Millie said.

"You sure?"

"No. Not really. I can't remember if the dumpster was there. I'm sorry. It looks different riding in a car versus walking. I just . . . I can't be sure."

Great, Victoria thought. This ride-along hadn't helped her situation. Hopefully it hadn't hindered it.

"Okay, that's fine. I appreciate you taking the time to try." He pulled back into their driveway but didn't make a move to get out of the car. "I'll be in touch when I know more, but in the meantime, if you think of something, please give me a call." He slipped a card from his chest pocket and handed it to Millie.

They'd gotten a momentary reprieve, but Victoria knew it wouldn't last.

Millie couldn't resist getting in a jab as they strode down the walkway to the front door. "At least he believed me. Ha!"

CHAPTER EIGHTEEN

"What a treat to have you here for dinner." Victoria tried to rein in her exuberance so as not to sound overly desperate for Vince's company. But she did miss him—didn't get to be with him nearly as often as she would have liked—and Victoria wanted him to know.

He'd arrived still dressed for the office, looking sharp in his light gray, tailored suit in a subtle windowpane plaid, his silk tie loosened and the top button undone on his white pinpoint Oxford. Although his clothes had absorbed a certain smell from being in the office all day—an innocuous blend of stale air, coffee, and new carpet—she could smell remnants of his cologne. Victoria fought the urge to run her fingers through his dark, sleek hair, parted precisely down the middle, full and brushed back on both sides.

She often marveled at the contrast between Robert's and Vince's appearances. Robert's warm features lent to his laid back and approachable collegiate style with tweed jackets he wore with khakis and paired with a closet full of plaid cotton shirts and solid-color crocheted ties—the ones that were squared off on the bottom. His light brown wavy hair, with the start of a receding hairline, as well as his eyebrows, got bushy when he got too wrapped up in his teaching and administrative responsibilities to take time for a barber. Victoria would gently remind him.

At first meeting, Vince came across as an intense man with a serious (read expensive) wardrobe and little time to waste, having an agenda and much to accomplish. It was best not to get between him and his goals. He worked hard and was going places.

When Victoria searched for what the two men had in common, she could only come up with their drive and ability to help others;

Robert, his students, Vince, his clients. And the fact they both worked hard translated into long hours.

"It's a treat for me too." He shoved another oversized forkful of lasagna into his mouth. Had it been that long since they'd shared a meal that she'd forgotten how quickly he ate? Or was he in a hurry and wasn't planning to stay long?

"I hope the tulips come up next spring," her mother said.

Victoria and Vince exchanged glances.

"Why wouldn't they?" Victoria asked. "They've been coming up for years."

"What tulips?" Vince looked puzzled. Victoria was surprised he cared.

"Oh, they're yellow tulips that come up in a garden near the woods in the backyard. They were Robert's favorite. Mom planted them after he—"

"Ha! *I* didn't plant them. *You* must have." Any trace of joviality vanished from Millie's weathered face.

"What? No . . . I didn't."

"Well, *I* didn't. You did. Who else would have? Maybe you just don't remember."

"I could say the same thing about you." Victoria felt a sudden urge to shoo her from the table. She was spoiling her evening with Vince. Why couldn't they have gone out?

"Well, I found some fertilizer in the garage so I sprinkled it on them to be sure. It would be a shame to lose them."

"That's great, Mom. Thanks for doing that."

The conversation lagged for a couple of beats, leaving them to silently contemplate the tulips and why they were important enough to Millie to bring up.

"So, how are things going for Jameson so far this semester?" Vince glanced at Victoria for an answer, then over to Millie as if expecting her to chime in. Victoria took the lead.

"Nice of you to ask. He seems to be doing well. Has a lot going on. Full schedule of classes. Varsity soccer. Community service. Senior project. Yearbook Committee. Tutoring—"

"*He's* tutoring other students or he's *getting* tutored?" Vince asked.

"Jameson is doing the tutoring. Mostly freshmen and sopho-mores, I think."

"Well, that makes more sense."

"Actually, his friend Asher is one of his tutees."

"Asher? Isn't he a senior too?"

"Yeah, but he's struggled from day one. I'm not sure Litchfield Academy was the right fit for him. It's not for everyone."

"How did he get in? If he's struggling, he couldn't have had the credentials to get accepted."

"Oh, I think his father bought his way in."

"Victoria," Millie reprimanded, and then scooped another lump of lasagna onto her fork.

"Well, it's true. Rumor has it he also bought his way onto the board. From what I understand, he's a huge contributor to the school."

"It happens. Certainly not isolated to private schools," Vince said. "Nice of Jameson to help him out. I'm sure he's busy with his own schedule."

Victoria continued. "And, there's college applications, writing college essays, and soliciting recommendations."

After an abbreviated chuckle, he said, "Well, that should keep him out of trouble, shouldn't it?"

"I got to meet all of his teachers, and they told me he's such a good student. And a nice young man. A pleasure to have in class," Millie piped in, sitting up higher in her chair.

"Oh, that's right. Mom got to spend Grandparents Day with him the other day."

"Grandparents Day." The disinterest in his tone was disappointing to Victoria. She'd hoped he'd care enough to engage her mother in conversation. He rarely saw her and the time they did spent together was usually fleeting; he could at least put the effort in to seem interested. "What was that like, Millie?" He'd redeemed himself.

Slipping away from the table to let Millie share her story with Vince, Victoria busied herself in the kitchen, cutting brownies into squares, spooning vanilla ice cream, and dividing it all onto three small plates. Laughter from the dining room made her smile. The house sounded alive again. If only she could preserve it—keep both of them close to her—forever.

Bring the boys back into the fold. She prayed they would settle down nearby, although with Harrison attending college on the West Coast, she feared the chances of that were slim, but she would do her best to convince him.

She drizzled chocolate fudge, squirted canned whipped cream, and sprinkled walnuts before scooping the plates onto one arm and hitting the brew button on the coffee machine on the way by. As she reached the threshold to the dining room, she was struck by how quiet it was. Her mother sat alone sipping from her water glass. Delivering a brownie sundae to Millie first, she asked, "Where's Vince?"

"I think he said something about a call. He went out in the hall."

"Oh, okay." Victoria dropped off the remaining two desserts and cleared the three dinner plates. As she returned to the dining room, Vince appeared at the doorway to the foyer.

"Oh, hey," he said.

She couldn't read his expression, so she pressed him. "You had a call?"

"Actually, *you* did."

"Me?"

"I heard your phone ringing out on the table in the foyer, so I went to get it for you. It said 'spam risk' so I answered it." He chuckled. "Those clowns don't know when to quit."

"Keep that up, and I'll have to warn Delores you might be gunning for her job," Victoria teased.

Millie burst into laughter that was entirely too over-the-top for the simple jab, but Victoria was pleased to have given her a reason to be amused.

If Vince's hands hadn't been empty, it would have taken a great deal of restraint not to yank her phone from his grip. *How did he think it was okay to answer her phone when it rang? If it was important, they would have left a message.* She was grateful it had been a telemarketer and not the airline.

"Oh, Victoria, I think Sean's going to be getting out soon," Millie said.

Her brother. Had he spent less time while they were growing up being jealous about what she was accomplishing and worked at making something of himself, perhaps he wouldn't have ended up a drug addict and convicted felon.

"Really, Mom?" Victoria let her shoulders slump. Why did her mother have to pick then to bring it up? "Didn't know you were in touch."

"Ha! I'm not, really. I happened to remember how long the sentence was, and it should be up right around now."

Vince considered Millie's announcement and asked, "Who's Sean?"

"My brother."

"Didn't know you had a brother."

"Yeah, well, there's not a lot of positive to talk about when it comes to him."

"I see."

"Let me put it this way: if you were a criminal defense attorney in the Bridgeport judicial system, there's a good chance you would have bumped into him at one time or another." Victoria hoped her brother wouldn't come looking for her with his hand out. The only time he ever showed his face was when his back was to the wall with no other options.

"Listen, you two. I'm going to take my dessert into the den," Millie announced.

"Oh, you don't have to do that, Mom."

"I know I don't, but it will give you some time to yourselves without me hanging onto your every word. Besides, *Wheel of Fortune* is on," she said with a sly wink. Scooping up her plate and napkin, she slipped from the table.

"The coffee should be ready by now," Victoria offered. "It's decaf."

"Thanks, I'll grab a cup on the way by."

"Hope you solve the puzzles before the contestants do," Vince called to her as she disappeared into the kitchen.

Poking her head back out again, she said with a grin, "Ha! I will. Don't you worry" and disappeared again.

"She will, you know." Victoria turned to Vince, her voice hushed. "I honestly don't know how she does it, but she does it *every* time. I can't watch it with her. She blurts out the answers. Drives me nuts."

Chuckling, Vince said, "That doesn't surprise me. She's a smart lady . . . just like you."

"Thanks. That's very sweet of you." She leaned in and allowed him to pull her into a sideways hug.

They fell silent while Victoria dragged a hearty spoonful of brownie through whipped cream and popped it into her mouth. Vince poked at his.

"Why don't we take our coffees into the living room," he suggested.

Getting up to fetch their coffees from the kitchen, she asked, "Or would you rather have something a little stronger?"

"I wouldn't mind a bourbon."

"Okay, no problem." Grabbing their dessert plates, they headed to the farthest room from the den, well out of range. Pulling a stout glass from the cabinet under the built-in bookshelf, Victoria went back to the kitchen to fill it with ice and grab a cup of coffee for herself. Upon her return, Vince was holding a clear cut-glass bottle with brown liquid in it and proceeded to pour a healthy dose into the glass. Victoria settled into her favorite navy floral wing chair with her legs tucked under her and stabbed her brownie with her fork, leaving her coffee on the side table to cool off a bit.

Vince remained standing, gazing out the front window even though there wasn't much to see in the dark. His dessert sat untouched on the coffee table, melting ice cream perilously close to running over the edge.

After a couple of thoughtful swigs, he spoke. "Tori . . . I need to ask a question. . . . I've been needing to ask the question for quite some time, but we never seem to be alone or if we are, we don't have the time."

Her hand with a forkful in it froze midway to her lips. She rested the plate on her knee. "What is it?"

What question? *The* question? Was he going to ask her to marry him? She felt panic rising up inside. She rested the fork on the plate and let go of it. What should she say? What could she say? It was too soon. Nothing had been finalized legally with Robert's situation. But she didn't know if she *wanted* it finalized by a court. That would mean she was giving up hope. And she hadn't. The thing was, she never would.

"Tori, I love you."

Oh no. It was going to be the *question. What should she say?* The last thing she wanted to do was hurt him. She abandoned her plate on the end table next to her chair.

"And I'd like to make more of a commitment to you than what we've had so far."

No. No. No. Please don't ask the question. I can't say yes, and I can't say no.

He took another swig. "But I need to know where you're coming from. What are you able to commit to me?"

With the debate raging in her head as to the right way to respond, Victoria pulled her legs out from underneath her and scooted to the edge of the seat. Wedging her hands under her legs, she finally found a few words she hoped were adequate and wouldn't sound trite or hollow. "Vince, I love you too." There, she'd said it. In the house she'd shared with Robert, the house the boys were conceived in, and the same house they were brought home from the hospital to. But the words felt like a cheater's cheap words to keep a lover close.

"But?"

"Uh . . . I don't know how to answer you. I feel stuck in the middle."

Vince headed for the matching wing chair next to hers and sat down at the edge, mirroring her and inching closer. "Babe, it's been seven years. No one has found anything. It's like he vanished into thin air. Do you really think he's out there? Still alive? And if he *is* alive, why hasn't he returned to you?"

"I can't give up hope." She started to rock ever so slightly, like a mother trying to soothe a fussy baby. His questions stung. He might as well have been scraping away at a newly formed scab from a flesh wound covering every inch of her body with his fingernails. "What kind of mother would I be to my boys if I gave up on their father coming back to us?"

"You went to court to have him declared dead."

"Only so I could get the insurance money so we could survive." Her voice was louder than she'd intended, so she pulled back a bit. "But that didn't work out . . . and if I hadn't tried, I wouldn't have met up with you again." She allowed herself a quick grin, hoping she'd get one in return, but it didn't happen. "I can't believe I'm getting this from you—of all people."

Rubbing his forehead with outstretched fingers, he let out an extended exhale.

"Vince, I love being with you. You've been so good to me over the last few years. Good to the boys too, when they let you in."

"Five years. It's been five years. I've been devoted to you, but not you to me."

"That's not fair. I can't be."

"Maybe not, but it feels pretty shitty to be on this end."

"I'm sorry. I-I don't know what else to say to you."

"Your heart still belongs to Robert, doesn't it?"

A swallow caught in her throat. It killed her to say it—to hurt him. But it wasn't fair to Vince to leave him hanging. "Yes." The word was barely audible.

"You realize you're not being very realistic."

"I can't help it. And I don't think anyone can understand what I'm going through unless they've been through it. I'm stuck in a terrible situation. And I'm sorry if you think I've been stringing you a—"

"No, I don't think that. It's just hard to be on this end for so long."

"I understand. Really, I do. And I'm sorry."

He got quiet, examining the ice in his glass. She pulled her hands out from beneath her legs—they were bright pink from the pressure of her weight on them—and began to play with her wedding band, turning it round and round on her finger. It had an intricate pattern pressed into it, unlike most wedding bands, so the only indication of its significance was its location on her hand. She'd gone so far as to take off her engagement ring and her anniversary ring. Didn't that count for something?

"Can I get you another bourbon?" Victoria tried, pleading with him in her mind to stay.

He searched her eyes with a twinge of torment in his.

"I'll uh . . . I'll have to take a raincheck on that. For the next time we get together." He spoke deliberately. "And that might be a while."

Victoria heard an odd click in her throat. *No! No! Don't do this.*

"I can't do this anymore. I want to be there for you, Tori, but I also thought we'd have a future together by now. I wanted to spend the rest of our lives together. That's why I work so hard, to build a future for us. This limbo thing—and I know it's worse for you—but I can't do it anymore. Five years is a long time." He plunked his glass on the coffee table and then leaned in to give her a kiss on her forehead. He might as well have been tucking a child into bed. Brushing an errant strand of hair from her face, he added, "I'm sorry. You take care of yourself. Let me know if you need anything. I'll still be there for you."

It took every ounce of self-respect she could muster not to snatch the front of his shirt with her fist and hold him there, begging him to stay. *Please, please, please don't go. Don't leave me all by myself. I'll make it up to you somehow. I promise. . . .* Maybe he had said goodnight to a child after all. Was that what this ordeal had turned her into? An immature, insecure child was what she'd become?

As he strode for the door, Victoria rubbed the tingling sensation of his kiss from her forehead. She sat motionless, taking in his acerbic words until the screen door slammed shut, making her jolt.

Something shifted in her mind, and she heard a voice saying, *How dare you walk out like that. Come back here, you controlling, manipulating, son of a bitch. You can't spring my mother and then dump her in my lap.* You *take her.* It was *your* idea. *Not mine.* She gave a quick shake to her head to dispel the repulsive thoughts, but she knew they would creep back in. Like the volatile contents of a snow globe, they could be scattered momentarily, but they'd soon return and settle into the depths of the vessel.

And then the self-berating began.

For God's sake, Victoria, you let him walk out your front door. Do you see any other good-looking, eligible—not to mention successful—men lined up to fill his shoes? That was your chance. He'd had more patience than anyone could be expected to have with your situation, and you'd strung him along long enough, he'd felt used.

"Yup, you screwed this one up—big time," she said aloud to no one but her rueful conscience.

Scooping up the two barely touched dessert plates, his glass, and her cup and saucer, she headed to the kitchen by way of the foyer, easing the inside door shut with her foot. She listened for the rumble of his car starting, the sound of it backing down the driveway, and then fading away into the distance, taking with it any hope he might return to her doorstep again that evening.

In the kitchen, she dumped the brownie sundaes in the trash, poured out her coffee, and loaded the dishwasher. Grabbing an open bottle from the fridge, she filled a glass with a heavy pour of Sauvignon Blanc. She slipped into the den and joined her mother on the couch who didn't seem to notice, intent on the clues being read for *Jeopardy!*

CHAPTER NINETEEN

Never having been to the small rural airport before, Victoria had to ask where she should stand to wait for an incoming helicopter. A small patio with an overhang provided a safe spot. A cool breeze rustled her light wrap, and she pulled it closer with a tight fist.

As she waited, it occurred to her she should call Vince to let him know about the crazy adventure she was setting out on. Not that she needed his permission, and after his abrupt departure the evening before, perhaps he didn't care. But she thought she'd feel better—less guilty?—if she told him.

Her call went right to voicemail so she hastily pulled together a succinct message that conveyed the info and intent she needed him to hear.

"Hey Vince, it's me. Hope your day is going well. Would love to continue our conversation from last night. Just wanted to let you know what I'm up to today since it's a little out of the ordinary—okay, maybe a lot out of the ordinary—and I thought someone should know."

The whir of the rotors announced the aircraft's arrival long before the copter came into view.

"When I was at the Presentation of Seniors, I kind of got roped into helping out with the Parents Committee . . . fundraising. So, the other parent is Jameson's friend Asher's father. And we made plans to meet today to discuss our ideas. Only he's in New York so he's—and I know this is going to sound a bit over the top—he's sending a helicopter to pick me up, and we're having lunch in Brooklyn." She paused, imagining his reaction to what she'd said so far. "I know, that probably sounds silly. He could write a check for whatever the school needs, but I think the idea is to have everyone contribute whatever way they can timewise too."

Hearing herself rambling and starting to sound like she was guilty of something, she yearned to wrap up the message. "So, it might be kind of out there a bit—getting picked up in a helicopter—but I'm actually psyched about it. Seems kind of fun. Just thought someone should know . . ." *Can't tell my worrier mother and give her more fuel to feed her stress. And I certainly can't tell Jameson. He already questioned if I'm seeing his friend's father, so he'd get the wrong idea.* "I don't know, I guess in case anything happened. Well, that sounds terrible. Okay, I'll let you go. Miss you." The last two words fell out before she could stop them. She *did* miss him, but she didn't want to sound entirely pathetic.

She'd no sooner hung up when her phone vibrated—an incoming call from her mother—and she let it go to voicemail. "Not now, Mom. I'll have to call you later. And I'll have something fun to tell you about," she murmured to herself.

As the helicopter neared, the whir became more of a whoop, whoop, and even more staccato as it alit on the tarmac. Emblazoned on the side was **EK Enterprises.** *He has his own helicopter. What a world he must live in. And she was stepping into it.*

Shoving her cell into her bag, she watched as the rotors began to slow. A door popped open, and Emerson stepped out onto the concrete, ducking his head but looking as though he had plenty of clearance. As he strode toward her with the same confidence he'd had on campus, she could feel a corner of her mouth creeping upward. *Was this really happening? Yes, it was, and she was going to have fun. See how the other half lives—or travels.*

"Good morning, Victoria." He waved as if he were hailing a cab in the city, his lyrical British accent creating a tickle in her abdomen.

"Good morning, Emerson. Thank you for picking me up." The words sounded childish as soon as they passed through her lips.

"How else would you have been able to get there?" he poked.

She decided to leave that one as though it were rhetorical.

"Come on." He reached out his hand and took hers, gently leading her to the waiting chariot. Her fingers tingled with his warm touch. Stealing a glance at their interlocked hands, she noticed the sharp contrast between his sun-bronzed skin and the crisp white cuff-linked cuff of his shirt. *Who wears cuff links anymore?* No one in her circles. Apparently Emerson Kittridge did, and he wore them well. Maybe he would start a trend with the commoners. Then again, probably not. But he wore them well. He wore *everything* well.

"What have you got there?" He gestured to the binder with a legal pad tucked inside her tote.

Had he forgotten his instruction? "A notepad . . . for taking notes." His nod and a quick laugh made her realize his suggestion had been in jest.

"It's a gorgeous helicopter." To her ears she sounded as though she was gushing.

"You like it?"

"What's not to like? Has your name on it and everything—well, your initials."

"If you don't have your name, what do you have?"

Victoria nodded and took his hand as he guided her onto the running board. *So true. That was all Robert had left—his name. And it was all she had to cling to.*

Once inside and she was securely strapped in, Emerson handed her a set of oversized headphones she struggled to put on but was grateful he didn't seem to notice until he reached over and adjusted them for her. Aviva certainly would have been jealous if she could see her. Victoria smiled at the thought. What a rotten friend she was for thinking it, she chided herself. But if they had traded places, Aviva wouldn't have given a thought to her friend.

As the pilot fiddled with gauges on the dashboard, the rotors whirred faster above them. The cramped quarters the three occupied smelled like a mixture of jet fuel and a barbershop with a bit of perspiration thrown in—not a combination she'd taken in before. The interior was not as plush as she'd expected from Emerson, but the pristine white leather seats were a nice touch. In spite of the tight space and the fact that much of the fuselage was clear, it didn't bother her a bit. Her mother, however, would never have stepped onto the running board of the helicopter, even just to peek in. She'd *never* flown. That was one of the many ways the mother/daughter duo differed. Victoria's years of flying had numbed her to most inherent risks. For her, a helicopter was an exciting new adventure.

It was hard to tell from behind, and the pilot was wearing sunglasses that wrapped around his face, but he looked to be on the young side. Hopefully he had logged a sufficient number of hours on the chopper to be able to fly it proficiently—and would know what to do in an emergency. The only flight attendant on board had turned in her wings years earlier.

Emerson's voice through the headphones, a grainy version of his otherwise delicious British accent, pulled her out of her thoughts. "Joe, this is Victoria. Victoria, this is my buddy, Captain Joe. Best helicopter pilot you'll meet. Best *any* pilot." Joe gave her an offhanded military salute, and she nodded with a forced smile in response. "I'd trust this guy with my life," he added, laying a playful swat on Joe's upper arm.

"Well . . . you are," Victoria said with a grin, unable to resist the quip. Her voice, filtered through the headset, sounded funny to her.

With a chuckle, Emerson said, "All right, let's get this thing airborne." He formed a vertical curly-Q with his index finger. "Lunch awaits us."

As the craft lifted off and she felt pressed down into her seat, Victoria snatched a breath and grabbed onto the armrests. Emerson laid a gentle hand on her forearm.

The small airport grew tiny as they lifted up and over the trees and soon was in the distance behind them. Seeking familiar sights below, Victoria stepped into the role of quasi-tour guide.

"Check that out." Slipping her arm out from under his hand, she pointed out his side of the helicopter. "That's Heublein Tower. Kind of cool, isn't it?"

"Oh yeah. What is it? Or *was* it?"

"It was built by Gilbert Heublein for his bride as a summer home. I want to say that was in the early 1900s. It's part of a state park now, and if you climb to the top there's an observation deck, and you can see for miles in all directions. First you have to climb the mountain though. It's good exercise and the view is worth the climb."

"I bet that's a fabulous spot this time of year, once the leaves change," Emerson said.

"That's my favorite time to go. It's spectacular."

"You'll have to take me." She glanced his way to read his face. "I'd love to go," he added, as if to convince her of his sincerity.

After that, they let the conversation lag. Victoria allowed her eyes to follow the shadow of the helicopter as it brushed over the treetops below until it slipped from sight with the increasing cloud cover. Emerson busied himself on his phone, having made the trip once already. Apparently the FAA rules about cell phone use didn't apply to private helicopters—or if they did, he simply flouted them.

Not long after they'd flown over Route 8, Victoria noticed some familiar buildings in a clearing come into view and grinned at the sight, not ever having viewed them from above. It almost felt as though she were spying on the idyllic campus. "Look, there's Litchfield Academy."

Leaning across to her side, close enough for her to get a whiff of his tangy aftershave, Emerson nodded. "So, it is. Hope the boys are doing well."

"I'm sure they are." But was she? There was too much to worry about with Jameson there. He was a grown young man. Strong with a sturdy build. His anxieties seemed to be under control. But things could happen. And did. Her mother had her thinking of the dangers that lurked at the pond. And there was that field trip to worry about.

Dark clouds lay ahead in the direction they were flying. Victoria hoped they weren't a harbinger of bad things to happen—metaphorically or otherwise.

As if he was reading her mind, Emerson said, "They've got their big excursion to the city coming up soon. Is Jameson looking forward to it?"

Doing her best to maintain an even expression, she said, "Absolutely. They've all been looking forward to it for so long." Scrambling to find something to say, more than the obvious, she added, "Each year the upperclassmen come back to campus and regale the rest of the students with their stories—"

"Embellished, no doubt," he said through a sideways grin.

"Yes, I bet a few of them are." She thought of how the boys seemed to arrive on campus for their freshman year, wearing their innocence like a warm cloak they could pull tight around their shoulders—innocence that for most would be peeled away gradually over their four years as they matured into men, but for an unfortunate few, would have it whisked away by an unexpected or tragic event.

Grateful he'd left the conversation at that, she turned back to the window and watched miniaturized versions of vehicles, buildings, and trees slip by beneath them. Her eyes glazed over to the point where she wasn't seeing what she was looking at. She held her out-of-focus gaze until she heard Emerson's voice.

"One for you?" She turned to see him holding two fluted glasses, bubbles floating to the top. The tingling returned to her extremities. *How did he do that to her so easily?*

"How lovely. Thank you." Victoria reached out and took the slender glass from him. They clinked and took a sip. It was dry and slipped down her throat easily. Taking a second sip, she realized she might have been gulping and rested the stem on the armrest.

"Here's to a lovely lunch excursion with a stunning companion. And I should add, intriguing as well."

Stunning? Intriguing? He was getting carried away, and it was only his first glass. Or was it? She hadn't heard the cork pop before he'd filled the glasses. She regarded him from across the tiny aisle, narrowing her brows a bit.

"Oh, you're a modest one, aren't you? Or has it been that long since a man told you that? Because you are, you know—both stunning and intriguing."

Victoria didn't trust herself to respond, so she busied herself with examining her glass, watching a veritable bubble ballet, and taking another, longer sip. He took his cue and refreshed her glass.

"Victoria, love. How long has it been . . . since your husband disappeared?"

She hated that Emerson didn't speak his name, and she nearly spit it into the mouthpiece of the headset. "*Robert* . . . disappeared seven years ago."

"*Seven* . . . that's an incredibly long time. I'm sorry you had to go through that." He said it like it was over and done with. And for most people it was. But for her, it would never be over . . . until there was some sort of closure. And that would mean a body. There was a part of her that wished that would never happen. It would steal her hope—the only thing that kept her connected to Robert and made her feel he was still alive.

"Yes, it is."

"Victoria." He leaned over toward her, his forearms on the edge of his armrest. His glass dangling from a well-manicured hand. "Are you ready to move on?"

"Move on?"

"Start another relationship."

Allowing his face to blur in her vision, she looked past him at a darkening sky.

He continued. "I mean, seven years is a long time. At a minimum, you should have companionship."

"Is that what you're looking for?" She heard a snicker in the headset. "How long has it been for you? Three months?"

With the tip of a finger, Emerson flicked a switch on the console between them and added, "Now it's just us chatting. So, you were saying?"

"Didn't you recently get divorced?"

He paused, then said, "It's been six months." He jutted out his chest like a bluebird in mating season.

"I see. Well, no, I guess I'm not ready to move on."

"Really. How long will it take?"

She wished he would back off. "I don't know." And she tossed back the rest of her champagne. He did the same and refilled their glasses. Turning her back against the windows to create more space between them, she said, "Why are you doing this? Why can't you let it go?" She wanted to tell him it was none of his damn business and to butt out, but she had to spend the next few hours with him and didn't want to fight.

"Victoria, someone has to do it. Clearly no one has. You're still young. Not to mention incredibly attractive. You need to live your life."

Shaking her head, she said, "You wouldn't understand."

"Maybe not. But from the outside, this doesn't seem right." He seemed to be still considering her situation. "You should be loved."

In her head, Victoria added, *and you want to be the one.*

"You're beautiful inside and out."

"You don't know me."

"I can tell." His wink made her shift in her seat. There was a pause, but she knew he'd fill it.

"This won't be over until a body is found, will it?"

There, he'd said it. He'd been bolder than anyone else around her. And he was right. "Yes, I guess that would do it."

Turning back into her seat, she gazed out the window and sipped champagne, enjoying the buzz it was building. After a couple of beats of rotors whirling overhead, it was time to change topics. "So, what's the deal with Ben Martin?"

"Ben? What do you mean?"

"I don't know, he's been pretty intense lately. This whole fundraising thing he's all over. I don't remember him being that way, or maybe I didn't have as much exposure to him before now."

"Intense? I guess he can be. He's under a lot of pressure from the board of directors to keep the academy in the black."

"Really?"

"When he was hired, the financial outlook was pretty dismal. The directors had raised the white flag. He was actually brought in to close down the school."

"Close down the school? I had no idea." The reality of how that would have changed their lives hit Victoria in the gut. Above all, Robert might still have been with them. It also hit her that the board must not have believed Robert could rescue the school if they'd brought in Ben Martin as an outsider. Had they approached Robert and he didn't share that with her?

Emerson continued. "I don't think many people knew. That isn't something you want tuition-paying parents to know. They'd be jumping ship and the private schools in the surrounding area would have been salivating to scoop them up."

"You and Ben must be close if you knew about it."

"We go back a ways. He brought me in on occasion . . . asked for my advice."

"So, you gave it to him."

"I did."

"What kind of advice?"

"More along the lines of investments. Together we saved Litchfield."

"How did it go from closing down the school to saving it?"

"He made a deal with the directors. He told them to give him three years to get LA out of the red or else he would pay back every dime they'd paid him to try."

"That was quite a gamble."

Emerson chuckled. "I guess it was. Maybe that's why he and I get along so well. We're willing to take a risk if the payout is right."

"Apparently it worked."

"Indeed." Emerson beamed.

"You like to gamble." It was more of a statement than a question.

"In a manner of speaking. Yes. If the risk/payout makes sense."

"What was the other side of the deal?" He didn't answer, so she tried again. "What did Ben get in return for succeeding?"

Running a finger along the rim of his glass, Emerson appeared to be gauging how much he would reveal. Grinning, he said, "He got to keep his job."

"There had to have been more to it than that. As you said, the payout had to be right to take the risk." Pleased she had caught him in his own explanation, she maintained a straight face and waited for an answer.

Nodding, his somber expression brightened. "You're absolutely right. And I'm sure there was some sort of bonus involved since he not only plucked the institution out of the red but planted it firmly in the black."

She let it go. He wasn't going to reveal any more than he already had.

On the horizon the Hudson River came into view. As it grew larger, Victoria's palms left a wet imprint on the armrest where she was grasping it.

"He's not going to . . . we don't have to . . ." Her heart rate quickened, and she shook her head back and forth in rapid fire succession but barely moving in either direction. Her knees began to ache from pressing her feet into the floorboard.

She felt Emerson's hand on her forearm again. "What's the matter, Victoria? Are you okay?"

"We can't go over the water. He's not going to fly over the water, is he?"

"He likes to follow the river down to Manhattan. Less congestion that way."

"No!" The word blasted through the headset. "Tell him no. We can't go over the water."

Without another word, Emerson flipped the switch on the console, which must have changed it to a two-way conversation with the pilot. She could see his lips moving but didn't hear them talking. Another flip of the switch and he was back.

"There. All set. Joe said he'd fly along the shoreline but not over the water—as best he can."

"Thank you. I appreciate that." But she had a feeling they'd eventually run out of dry land. She counted on the champagne to get her through the rest of it. Hopefully Emerson wouldn't think her silly. It was hard to explain her fear of water. She imagined that was true of most fears.

As they reached the Hudson River, the pilot banked left, keeping the chopper well inside the shoreline. Victoria tried to picture where they'd be going.

"So where does one land a helicopter in New York City?"

"Huh?" She'd pulled him away from something on his cell that had him rapt. "Oh, uh, there are a few options. But we'll be setting down on Pier 6."

"Pier 6?" *They were landing on something out over the water?*

"It's the Downtown Manhattan Heliport."

"Manhattan? I thought we were going to Brooklyn."

"We are. The heliport is right on the East River, across from Brooklyn. A short car ride away from the restaurant."

She knew what the answer would be, but she needed to hear him say it. "So, there will be a car waiting for us?"

"That's the plan."

"You have quite the life, Emerson."

"Do I?" His grin gave away his feeble attempt at humility.

"If you don't mind my asking, what do you do?"

With a sly smirk, he said, "You could say I look for my opportunities where they present themselves. You know, that whole risk/reward concept."

Out of the corner of her eye, she caught a flash of light off to the west. Fixing her gaze on the general area it came from, Victoria's body stiffened when a jagged flash of yellow burst from the clouds and stabbed at the ground.

"Oh!" she grabbed the armrests again. Lightning had always unnerved her during her flying days. Although aircraft were built to sustain a direct hit, an electrically charged bolt could emerge from a benign looking cloud without warning, and she never wanted to test the conductivity design of the craft she was in.

"We're okay," Emerson assured her. "We're at a safe distance." She felt a warm hand on her arm.

"How much longer before we land?" Ten minutes ago wouldn't have been soon enough.

Emerson flipped the switch on the console between them and relayed Victoria's question, looking to Joe to answer who turned back to address them. She wished he would have kept his eyes forward. He didn't have a co-pilot to keep his or her eyes on the dashboard or in the air around them while he conversed with his passengers. "About ten minutes or so. The flight path is to follow the Hudson down and then around the tip of Manhattan. You should be able to see Ellis Island and the Statue of Liberty off to your right as we come around and pick up the East River. We're coming up on the Tappan Zee Bridge now."

From one river to another. *Doesn't water conduct electricity better than most anything else?*

Another flash of lightning. This one seemed much closer. Raindrops began to pelt the windshield and form horizontal streaks on the sides of the craft. Daylight had been vanquished, and a grayness enveloped them that made it feel as though night was approaching. The pilot peeled off his dark glasses, revealing laugh lines on the edge of the eye, which comforted her. He now looked to be close to their ages.

Emerson pulled his hand away and began typing with both thumbs on his cell. After he paused, he looked over to her and said, "Just confirmed the car is there waiting for us. So, you won't get too wet dashing through the raindrops."

She grinned at his thoughtfulness. It felt good.

Situated on the right side of the passenger compartment, Victoria was able to observe the pilot holding onto what she guessed was the yoke or the joystick—whatever it was called—with clenched hands as wind buffeted the craft. They were getting pushed around unlike anything she'd experienced in a 737.

"Here, take this." She handed Emerson her glass and gripped the armrests. *Lord, please get us down safely. I'll take a train back. I promise.*

By the time they'd reached the tip of Manhattan, the rain was coming down so hard Lady Liberty was all but obscured. She glanced through the opposite window, searching for the World Trade Center, but couldn't make out anything that resembled the tallest building in the United States.

The pilot had brought the craft down close to the water, appearing to skim the surface. "We're coming up on the pier," he announced. "Make sure your seatbelts are securely fastened. This wind could make it a rough landing."

Emerson gave his shoulder strap a tug and then reached over to do the same to hers. As the pilot was conversing with the heliport, Victoria glanced around to get her bearings but couldn't see much through the rain-soaked windows.

The splash of red blinking lights up ahead shone through the windshield, which she guessed was their target, and did nothing to put her at ease. The red color seemed to be a sign of danger. STOP. NO ADMITTANCE. TURN BACK. NO TRESPASSING.

As they neared the pier with the pilot wrestling with the wind, Victoria struggled to keep her legs from shaking. *Please, just land already.*

"Almost down. It's going to be all right." Emerson grabbed ahold of her nearest hand, the fingers of which were curled around the end of the armrest, white and matching the other hand. There was no hiding how terrified she'd grown in a short time.

She watched as the pilot wrestled with the joystick. "Damn crosswinds."

In the next moment, that could only be described as a flash, she felt the chopper rise up in a swoosh. She was pinned to her seat. Then the craft hurtled to the ground, like a rollercoaster ride, turning her stomach.

"Downdraft!" the pilot shouted. "We're going down. Hang on."

They landed with such force, her spine slammed into her seat, her head snapping back against the headrest. It sounded like everything around her was breaking into pieces. Scraping and crunching of metal. The rotors still whirled above their heads. Then the craft flipped onto its side. Victoria felt her body being thrown toward Emerson's seat but the restraints held her in. Her head whipped to the side, arms and legs flailing. With a cracking sound, suddenly she was toppling in that direction, only to hit up against something impenetrable. *Had the seat broken loose?* More scraping of metal. *The rotors?* She had a passing thought about how close they were to the water before everything went black.

CHAPTER TWENTY

Victoria woke to the dark and an eerie silence, except for raindrops splattering on the side of the helicopter—what was left of it. She couldn't move much. Her legs seemed wedged between something. They hurt, which she took as a good sign, and was grateful she had feeling in them. Her left arm was stuck too. With her right, she groped around her but didn't connect with anything familiar.

Sirens at a distance grew louder. Then there were voices that seemed like they were inside her head. At first she couldn't discern what they were saying. She tried to listen harder.

"Ma'am, we're here to help." A man's voice. "How many passengers were in the helicopter with you? Can you tell us?" Victoria couldn't put the words together. After a pause he sounded as though he'd turned away and was speaking to a colleague. "This looks like a two-passenger model. So, there may be someone under her. You've got eyes on the pilot?" There were some indiscernible words, but she heard something about being in bad shape. His voice got louder again. "Ma'am, we need to move you out of here. But first we need to get some things out of the way. We'll go as quickly as we safely can."

Again the first responder turned away to give more directions. "Mack, keep an eye on the engine and fuel tank. There shouldn't be much fuel but empty an extinguisher on them to be sure."

What sounded like a chain saw started up and before it started in cutting, someone took her loose hand and held on tightly. It was hard to tell what they were doing or where inside the fuselage they were working. The sound seemed to be coming from behind her. As the tight confines of the broken fuselage closed in around her, a voice gently assured her it would be okay.

It had to be. She couldn't leave her boys behind. And she couldn't leave before her mother did. It wasn't supposed to work that way. And yet, her mother had already lost one daughter.

The saw stopped and started up a few more times and soon she could feel movement around her legs. The sound filled up the small space inside the helicopter and rattled around in her head. She wished she could cover her ears.

The hand holding hers squeezed tighter. "You're doing great. We're almost there. Hang in there." This time, a woman's voice. Victoria took comfort in hearing it. In a strange way, it reminded her of her mother's. "What's your name?"

"Victoria," she managed. "Victoria Sands."

In her peripheral vision was the shadow of a large piece of something being pulled out of the cabin—or had they peeled off a section of the fuselage—which made the inside seem a bit brighter. Then her legs began to throb. She let out a groan.

"It's okay, Victoria. We're almost there. Hang in there. You're doing great."

A male voice behind her comforter said, "We need the seatbelt cutter. Who's got it?"

Soon she could feel the straps on her chest getting pulled away and moving in a brisk back and forth rhythm. With a snap, she'd been freed from her seat, but strong hands grabbed her to keep her from falling.

"All right, let's get her out."

"Wait, my arm. My left arm's stuck." Victoria prayed they wouldn't have to saw again. Her ears were still buzzing from the noise.

Someone crawled into the small space, leaning over her. She could make out the EMS emblem on a shoulder. Another crunching sound as he wrenched a piece of something away from her left arm and it was free. She pulled it toward her and tucked it against her chest. It throbbed.

"Okay, we've got her now. Ready to lift," the same man called. She could sense another face in the opening.

"Okay, if you can, take a big breath on three and then we'll lift. Okay, ready? One . . . two . . . three. Breathe in."

Victoria pulled in as much jet-fuel-laced air as she could and held it while hands pulled her out of the wreckage and onto a stretcher. As her back made contact with the gurney, her body exploded in ragged pain, and she let out another groan. They wrapped her in a warm blanket that felt good on her skin. Only on her face did she feel the rain splattering, which she didn't mind. It camouflaged her tears.

ON THE WAY TO THE hospital, the EMT who rode in the back hovering over Victoria asked questions about where she hurt, poked her toes and heels, flashed a light in each eye, secured a band around her upper arm with Velcro, pumping air in it until it hurt, and pressed a wad of gauze against what he said was a cut over her eye. There was a strong antiseptic smell in the space—another tight space.

She was lucid enough to wonder about Emerson's fate. "Do you know what happened to the other passenger and the pilot? Are they okay?"

"I don't actually know, ma'am. You were the first we could extricate and our focus was you. I do know there were other ambulances on the way."

"Do you know what hospital they would take them to? Is it the same one where we're going?"

"Again, I honestly don't know. But once you get to the hospital, someone should be able to get that info for you."

Victoria hoped he wasn't following some sort of EMT protocol of not breaking bad news to a patient. A sick feeling crept into her stomach. What if Emerson didn't make it? What if neither he nor his friend, the pilot, did?

Before long, the ambulance slowed and the siren cut off. Victoria could feel it making a turn. Slowing to a stop, it began to back up with a muffled beeping all around them. The back doors popped open, and they were greeted by two guys in blue scrubs who didn't look old enough to be out of high school with stethoscopes wrapped around their necks like serpents. They went right to work, asking questions while helping to pull the stretcher from the back of the ambulance.

"What have we got?"

"Helicopter crash victim, white female, forties, possible left arm fracture."

"Vitals?"

"Vitals are steady. BP: 160 over 110. Pulse: 120. Respiration: 30. Pupils are equal, round, and reactive to light bilaterally."

"Do we have a name?" The voice was alongside her now.

"Victoria . . . Victoria Sands," someone said.

Victoria watched the lights overhead whiz by as they wheeled her in. Soon they made her dizzy, so she closed her eyes and listened.

"Okay, right in here."

The stretcher came to a stop, and a male voice appeared overhead. "All right, Victoria, I'm Doctor Glynn. We're going to take good care of you." Turning away, he said to a team who had appeared behind him, "Ready? On three. One . . . two . . . three."

In a woosh, they scooped her up and swung her over to the empty bed and laid her down gently. Victoria let out a whimpering groan at the jarring. She did a quick mental assessment of where the pain had originated from. Her entire body ached, but she was grateful to be alive.

The team checked her out and decided she had fared well for what she'd been through but ordered x-rays for her arm. While waiting for an orderly to take her to radiology, Victoria's eye caught a breaking news report about the crash on a television hanging from the ceiling near her bed. The sound was up enough for her to hear. The graphic photos made it all seem surreal—as if it had happened to someone else. All that was left of the helicopter was a pile of bent metal—compacted to the point it didn't look like anyone would have gotten out alive. How had she?

She listened for word on the fate of the passengers until finally the reporter at the scene filled in the blanks: One dead, two hospitalized with injuries. Speculation from the anchors back at the station questioned whether the pilot should have been flying in the inclement weather and if he'd had sufficient training and experience prior to the flight. Victoria could feel lucidity rushing back into her head.

Emerson's words echoed through her thoughts as she tried to put the pieces together of what happened. *Best helicopter pilot you'll meet. Best any pilot. I'd trust this guy with my life.*

Had he trusted him and lost the gamble? Clearly she nearly had.

CHAPTER TWENTY-ONE

"Victoria?" Dr. Glynn slid open the glass door and popped his head into the small sterile space, hands shoved in the pockets of his crisp white lab coat. Was that a defensive move because he had bad news to deliver? She was sorry she'd lost the fogginess they'd wheeled her in with.

"Yes."

He edged in farther, sliding the door back in place. "I wanted to let you know what we found out." He let a beat or two pass.

Victoria didn't appreciate his dramatic effect. Hopefully he hadn't missed his calling as an actor. *I'm not really a doctor. I play one on TV.* If her entire body didn't ache, she would have gotten off the bed and smacked him. *Tell me already.*

"You've got a clean break on your left wrist that we'll need to put into a cast. From what I understand there are some new neon colors that you might be interested in." His tone got strangely whimsical.

"I see." She supposed it could have been worse.

"Other than that, besides all your cuts, contusions, and abrasions, which will heal before long, I suspect you have a mild case of whiplash, perhaps a mild concussion, but I would have to say you were definitely the lucky one in this mishap."

She wasn't feeling particularly lucky, but assuming the odds of surviving a helicopter crash were terrifyingly low, she'd take it.

"Okay, so how soon can I get this thing encased in some neon?" Playing along, she lifted her arm and the doctor chuckled.

"I'll send in an aide to bring you up to orthopedics, and then hopefully we can get you into a room and let you get some well-need-ed rest. I know the gals are working on that. We've been a little tight with lodging lately, but we'll come up with something. I won't have you hanging out at the end of a hallway."

"Oh, no. I can't stay. I've got my elderly mother at home who depends on me to take care of her, and she has no idea what has happened."

"There must be someone who can look in on her. I'd really like you to stay, at least for the night so we can keep an eye on you. You've been through quite an ordeal."

"I really don't. I'm all she has."

"And the NTSB will want to chat with you—once they're finished at the scene. I'm sure they don't want you going anywhere either. You're a witness—one that's still alive."

Victoria felt a pinch in her chest. She might have been the only one to make it. But why her?

"Well, you can give them my number. I'm not spending the night here. I need to get home."

"Do you have someone to pick you up?"

"Yes, I'm all set," she lied. "Really. Let's get a cast for this thing in the next half an hour, or I'll check myself out without it and find my own orthopedist."

"Victoria, I must protest. It's against my recommendations."

"I've considered your recommendations—and I appreciate everything that everyone has done for me—but I'm going to be leaving within the hour." She had no idea what the train schedule was, but she'd figure it out. There were enough trains running between Manhattan and Connecticut that she should have no problem getting one back. But she needed to give him and his staff more of a sense of urgency so she could get out of there. Soon.

The doctor leaned his back against the glass door and rubbed a temple with the tips of two surprisingly elongated fingers. With an audible exhale, he said, "You're putting me in a rather awkward—"

"No, I'm not. You and I both know a patient can check herself out, and that's what I'm planning to do." Victoria grinned. "I mean, you said, yourself, you have a bed shortage. If I take off, that will free up a bed for someone who needs it more than I."

The doctor's face seemed to brighten. "I certainly can't disagree with that logic. All right, Victoria, I'll have the nurse bring the paperwork to you." He slid the door open and paused. "But take care of yourself. It may not have hit you yet what you've been through. Please call me if you have any questions or if you develop any new or strange symptoms. Can you promise me you'll do that?"

"Yes, Doctor." She nodded.

"All right. Good to have met you. Glad you're going to be okay. Take care of yourself."

"I will. Thanks." Before he could slip out, she caught him. "Oh, and Doctor."

"Yes."

"What . . ." Did she want to know the truth yet? She knew she had to ask. "What happened to the pilot and the other passenger?"

Her stomach clenched as she watched his gaze drop to the floor. Again, with the theatrics?

"From what I understand, the pilot didn't make it . . . and I don't know about the other passenger. He wasn't my patient."

"Is he in this hospital?"

"That, I don't know either. I'm sorry." Without so much as an offer to inquire around, he slipped out, sliding the door behind him.

Victoria did her best to believe Emerson was going to be okay. No matter where he was. She'd have to listen to the news like everyone else, like a bystander.

Before long, a smiley, acne-studded face appeared in her doorway with a wheelchair. A young, twenty-something with spiked turquoise hair and a nose stud. "Mrs. Sands, I understand you have a date with orthopedics."

Missus. After all this time, it sounded odd. But she still checked off the married box when she filled out forms and would continue to do so until anything else could be proven.

"Yes, I guess I do."

After ascertaining which arm was injured, the aide helped her into the chair. Victoria failing miserably at stifling her groans. Every turn in the corridor, bump in the floor, and slowing-to-a-stop jarred her body, stoking pain she'd never endured before. By the time the wheels on the chair crossed the threshold into the cast room, Victoria no longer tried to contain her outward expressions of agony.

Grateful she could stay in the chair, Victoria grew mesmerized as the technician first wrapped her arm and hand with a light gauze, wincing when he got near her wrist. The young man seemed disappointed when Victoria chose a generic white for the color of the fiberglass, which he applied over the gauze in no time. Clearly he'd done it before.

Back in her ER room, she sat on the edge of the bed dressed in her street clothes, trying to convey to the staff she was ready to go, and waited for the necessary paperwork to sign. Relieved to have lived through a horrific helicopter crash with a broken wrist being the worst of it, Victoria set her sights on heading home. If she could get there before the evening news, with any luck she would have a chance to tell her mother what happened before she saw it splattered across the TV screen. Thankfully it was a developing story, so it was doubtful they would mention the names of passengers or the pilot. Fingers crossed.

Taking inventory of her scratched-up and soiled tote the EMTs had salvaged from the wreckage, everything seemed to be intact, including the ever-important notepad Victoria wondered if she would have used if they'd made it to lunch. A voice from behind startled her.

"There she is. Madame Explorer, back from her escapades over the East River."

"Vince. What . . .? What are you doing here?"

"I came to rescue you from the mouth of the angry monster known as New York City that rarely gives up its prey." He stepped inside the door. "Yet in this case, the beast's heart may have softened for such a sweet lady."

"What the hell?" She hadn't missed the irony that she'd nearly lost her life in the same city her husband had gone missing, but Vince's perspective on it bordered on peculiar. "I've never heard you talk like that before."

"Well, you've never been this close to death, at least since I met you." He edged closer, scrutinizing her face—no doubt taking note of her facial bruising and the bandage on her forehead. His gaze dropping to her casted arm, cradled in her other hand, his voice softened. "How are you? I didn't expect to see you up and about. How bad is it?" He gestured between the two areas of her body that had visible injuries.

"I was pretty lucky, considering how it could have turned out . . . considering how it may have turned out for the others."

He appeared interested in only her situation.

"So . . . you have a broken arm?" Vince reached out but didn't make contact with her, as if afraid to cause her pain.

"Broken wrist. Could have been much worse. I—"

"And your head. You had stitches?"

Victoria reached up and touched the edge of the bandage. "It'll be okay. Really."

"I'm so glad to see you . . . and that you're going to be okay. I want to hug you, but I'm afraid I'll hurt you."

She nodded. "That may have to wait. I'm pretty sore, all over."

"Victoria, I thought the worst. I mean, how could I not? I tried your phone over and over. No answer. A helicopter crash, for God's sake. Who walks away from one of those?"

Silence filled the antiseptic-smelling space as they reflected. Finally Victoria found her voice.

"Wow. It's a shock to see you. How did you know to—"

"Are you kidding? The crash has been breaking news on every station."

"Oh, of course it is."

"Besides, how were you going to get home? Train?"

"Actually, yes. It got a little rough up there, and I made a little deal with God that if he got us down safely, I'd take the train home."

Vince grew quiet, any hint of his initial frivolity slipping from his face. "Clearly He didn't hold up his end of the bargain, so I'll escort you home. Get you there safely." He gave her another once over. "Let's get out of here. You ready to leave now?"

"As soon as they bring the paperwork for me to sign, I'm gone."

"Great. I've got a car waiting."

"Thank God. You're awesome, Vince." There was no need to ask how he did it. Vince had a way of being on top of what was going on and knowing how to get the information he needed; who the victims were, and what hospital they'd been taken to.

At that moment, the aide with the whimsical hair burst through the door with another wheelchair, this one not looking very inviting, not that the first one was a cushy ride.

"Mrs. Sands? Ready to get out of this crazy place?" She eyed Vince from his well-coifed dark hair and manicured fingers to his tailored suit and polished wingtips with a nod of approval. "Looks like you've got someone to pick you up after all. Nice."

"Is the—" Victoria gestured to the sorry-looking chair with a sagging vinyl seat and discolored backrest. "Is that really necessary? I can walk. Really."

"I'll bet you can. Probably run, if it meant you'd get out of here faster. But it's hospital policy. And if I let you leave without a free ride to the front door, it would be my job on the line. And I can't afford to lose the pay. . . . Oh, wait. I'm a volunteer." She guffawed like an old man who'd just won checkers against his grandson. "Ah, just kidding. But seriously, though, it's hospital policy. Legal ramifications and all, I guess." She patted the seat and waited expectantly for Victoria to hop in.

A nurse in blue scrubs appeared behind the aide with a fistful of papers in hand. "Need you to sign in a couple of places, Victoria, and then you can be off." As Victoria put her loopy signature in the appropriate blanks, the nurse asked the aide, "She's not giving you a hard time about riding in that thing, is she?"

"Nah, 'course not," the aide assured her. "We already took a ride together to orthopedics. We're tight. She's fine with it."

Hunched over the paperwork, Victoria grinned to herself. If only they knew the devious thoughts that had crossed her mind about dodging not only the wheelchair but the entire hospital.

Vince's cell went off, and he snatched it from his pants pocket. The diamonds in his chunky, gold pinky ring sparkled in the fluorescent lights overhead as he held the phone to his ear. "Yeah . . . are you serious? Okay, I'll be right down. Don't move the car. We're walking out right now. Don't move it, you hear?" He looked to Victoria. "Security is giving my driver a hard time about parking out front. I'll run ahead and get the situation under control."

After he darted from the room, Victoria reluctantly lowered herself into the wheelchair. The aide grabbed her tote, examining it as she placed it on Victoria's lap. "Guess that had a rough ride."

"We both did," Victoria said.

"Bye, Victoria. Take care of yourself," the nurse said from behind.

Victoria gave a half-salute without looking back.

On the way to the elevator, staff they passed wished her well, and she thanked each one.

When the doors opened, Victoria was startled to see Emerson in a wheelchair being wheeled off toward her. His face lit up.

"Victoria, you're okay. So good to see you."

"Emerson . . . how are you doing?" She was surprised at how relieved she was to see him.

The doors started to move and Victoria's aide jammed a hand between them to keep them open.

"I've been better. But considering what could have happened, I feel pretty lucky. I've got a bit of a concussion and a broken leg." He tapped his cast, fully extended and propped up by an extension on the chair. His was a tasteful gray. *Why hadn't she thought of that color?* "Just came from having this lovely accessory put on. I see you have one as well." He gestured with an open palm toward her.

"Yeah. Thank God it wasn't worse. . . . I heard Joe didn't make it."

"He really didn't have a chance, poor guy. When the damn thing flipped, the cockpit rammed into a cement piling."

"So sorry to hear. I know you guys were tight. Sorry for your loss."

"Thanks, that's a tough one."

"Good to see you're going to be okay," Victoria offered.

"Same. Hey, I'm sorry it all worked out the way it did. It was a freak thing, but it shouldn't have happened."

"A simple get-together shouldn't be this hard to accomplish, Emerson."

"You're right. It shouldn't. So, I still owe you a lunch. I need to make this up to you."

Victoria frowned. "I don't think that's possible. Or necessary."

"Maybe you're right. How about just lunch then. I'll come to you this time."

Victoria didn't have it in her. She pressed her lips together and shook her head ever so slightly. "No. I don't think so."

His face fell as if he'd never heard the words before.

Signaling to her aide she was ready to go, Victoria called back to Emerson as they entered the elevator, "You take care of yourself." The doors shut behind them, and they descended to the lobby. There was something about Emerson that worried her. She had the sinking feeling she should put some precautionary distance between the two of them. If not, this tragic event could be a precursor of things to come.

Yet there was something so intriguing about him, she didn't want to deny how she felt when she was with him.

CHAPTER TWENTY-TWO

On the road back to Connecticut, the waning light quickly turned to darkness. Victoria settled into one corner of the backseat of the town car while Vince busied himself with work on his computer in the other. A dark, fuzzy blanket sat between them on the seat, folded neatly and making her realize she'd caught a chill. Perhaps it was her body's reaction to her injuries. Vince must have seen her eyeing it.

"I brought that for you. Would you like it?" He scooped it up and offered it to her like one of the magi in the manger.

"You're so sweet. Thank you." Anxious to get underneath it and wrap her body in a layer of warmth, she wasted no time unfolding it. As she did, something fell into her lap. "What's this?" It was a small, flat, square box wrapped in pink floral paper and a matching pink ribbon tied neatly into a floppy bow.

"Oh, that's for you too."

"For me? What do you mean?" After all, they had, for all intents and purposes, broken up. He'd made that clear when he walked out her front door after letting her know, in no uncertain terms, that he couldn't take any more of being in limbo. Neither could she, but walking out was not an option for her. Had he rethought his position? Was this an apology gift?

"I thought you could use a little cheering up after what you've been through."

He'd taken the time to get her a gift before he'd raced to the hospital? More likely he'd had it on hand before their breakup. He was a very generous man. Just look at the car in her driveway—actually at the Talcottville Municipal Airport. She made a mental note she'd need to retrieve it.

"That's very sweet of you, Vince."

"Well, open it."

Balancing the box against her cast, she eased the ribbon off. With a slip of a finger under a piece of tape, she undid the wrapping. Lifting the lid, she let a soft gasp slip out. "Oh, it's beautiful. Thank you."

"You like it?"

"Are you kidding? It's stunning." Victoria lifted the tennis bracelet and held it up. The passing highway lights caught the diamonds and made them sparkle, on . . . off . . . on . . . off.

"Here, let me help you put it on." Taking hold of her right hand, he slipped it gently onto her wrist. "There, that looks beautiful on you. You wear it well."

"Thank you, Vince. That was so sweet of you. You really didn't have to—"

He held up a hand. "Gifts are never a requirement. They should come from the heart. When it feels right, you do it."

It was hard to argue with that sentiment, but this gift only made her wonder if their relationship had changed again. *Is that what happens when you're faced with a near death experience? Those around you change how they feel about you?*

She sat up straight. "I never called my mother back."

"Did she know what you were doing today?"

"No. I kept it simple. Told her I'd be busy for the afternoon with volunteer work for the academy." Victoria regretted not being completely forthcoming with her mother, but she had thought it best. She still did.

"So give her a call. . . . Things ran over. . . . You decided to grab dinner." He flicked his wrist with each detail of his suggested explanation. "She should go ahead and eat without you, if she hasn't already."

Amused by his suggestions, which he dictated like an old-fashioned telegraph message, she said, "Great idea. Will do."

Yanking her tote from the floor, she held it open with her injured arm and rummaged through it with the other. Her hand finally hit something hard that was the right size, and she pulled it out. The screen was blank, so she pressed the power button. Nothing.

"Damn it."

Leaning in to see, Vince said, "That doesn't look promising. Here, you can use mine." He pulled his out from inside his jacket and handed it out to her, but then pulled it back. "On second thought, I'll call her."

Victoria searched his eyes for a pretense.

"I know you. And I know your mother. She'll ask the right question and the whole thing will come spilling out. Am I right?"

She nodded with a half-grin.

"And I know you'd rather tell her what happened in person, so I'll handle it."

Before she could object, he'd pressed a few buttons and had the cell to his ear.

"Good evening, Millie. It's Vince. How are you?" His tone bordered on condescending. Perhaps that wasn't intentional, but she imagined he would talk to a child in much the same way.

Victoria could hear her mother squeal at Vince's greeting. She'd always liked him.

"Listen, I wanted to let you know that Victoria will be coming home a little later than expected tonight. Her meeting this afternoon ran late, and then I surprised her with an invite out to dinner." He paused to listen, then said, "She asked me to call you because her phone is about to die. I'm in my car going to pick her up now." He winked at Victoria. "Okay, I'll tell her. You have a good evening. Hope to see you soon, Millie."

"That was quick. You certainly know how to get to the point, don't you?" She laughed at her rhetorical question.

"When I have to, yes. Okay, so that's settled. Now try to get some rest. Here." He opened a console in front of them, pulled out two small pillows, and handed them to her. "This might help."

"You've thought of everything, Vince."

"Hope so." He patted her leg, and she did her utmost not to flinch at the ache he'd awakened. "Now rest. I've got to get back to work."

She knew it wasn't a command, and he wasn't irritable, although it might sound that way to someone who didn't know him. He was merely stating a fact. She could tell he was pleased with himself for rescuing her and whisking her back to Connecticut. So much of her life was out of his control. But at the moment, she was under his thumb again. And she was okay with it. Victoria felt safe there.

Drifting in and out of sleep, she listened to the reassuring calmness of his voice on the phone and the clatter of the keys on his computer. The sounds blended into her dreams, which were disjointed. She would stir and wake herself up, but then couldn't remember what each dream was about but figured they were inspired by the crash. Vince didn't seem to notice her fitful sleep.

In a heavy fog, Victoria heard Vince's phone ring. He answered right away, and she listened to his side of the conversation.

"Yeah, Vince Terentini . . . Oh, hey, Dan. What's up? . . . No, I don't think that's the case. . . . No, I don't think so. . . . Hey, look. You know what, I really can't go into it right now. I'll have to call you back another time. . . . Yeah, uh, in the morning. . . . All right, I'll talk to you then. Thanks, Detective."

Victoria startled from her fog with his last word. "Detective?"

"Huh?" Vince asked. "Oh, hey sleepyhead. Did you get a little rest?"

Ignoring his question, she asked, "What detective? Someone who wants to talk to me?"

"No, uh, that was for one of my cases."

"And you couldn't talk in front of me?"

"No. Not at all." He tilted his head toward the driver. "I didn't have my notes from the case in front of me."

"Oh, okay. Sorry. I'll let you get back to work."

He reached over and tugged on an edge of the blanket, so it covered her legs and bare feet she'd pulled up onto the seat. For the rest of the ride, Victoria kept her eyes closed, feigning sleep. But there were no more phone calls to monitor.

CHAPTER TWENTY-THREE

Bagels from the local bakery were a special treat on Sunday mornings. The pungent aroma of her mother's onion bagel and her everything bagel filled Victoria's car on the ride home. Tossing her keys on the table inside the door, she called up to her mother, "I'm back. Rise and shine, sleepyhead."

Millie appeared on the landing; her eyes set on the small white bag in Victoria's hand. She had yet to notice the cast, but Victoria had searched out a sweater that was stretchy enough to fit over it. Her plan was to fill her in—for the most part, leaving out details that would unnecessarily excite her—over a leisurely breakfast. She'd been able to keep it from her for a couple of days so far—with the right clothing, extra concealer under her eyes to mask the bruising, and meticulously styled hair that draped across the bandaged cut on her forehead—but she knew it was a matter of time before her mother noticed or Victoria slipped.

"Oooh, yummy. I love those bagels. Did you get regular cream cheese? You didn't get that tasteless lo-fat, lo-cal stuff, did you?"

"No, Mom. I didn't. I got the kind with *all* the fat in it." She did her best not to reveal even a tinge of annoyance. "In fact, I asked for extra fat," she added, chuckling. As she crossed the threshold into the kitchen to start the coffee, the doorbell rang. She froze. *On a Sunday morning?* She really wanted to pretend they weren't home, but the person had probably watched her pull into the driveway.

"I'll get it," her mother called, clip-clopping down the stairs. She didn't usually wear clogs with her bathrobe.

Listening from the kitchen, Victoria heard, "Good morning, Millie."

"Officer Dill, good to see you. Why don't you come in? Would you like some coffee?"

Victoria peered around the corner to see the officer step into the foyer, his uniform looking freshly pressed. Did she want to know what he had to say? Not really. Especially not on an empty stomach. Reluctantly she stepped into view. "Good morning, Officer." She struggled to sound upbeat. After all, he was there with news of what she'd known all along—what she'd been dreading.

"Good morning. Sorry to bother you on a Sunday morning, but I wanted you to know I've wrapped up the investigation."

Both women fell silent, waiting for his conclusion, one more optimistic than the other.

"Turns out there was a mix-up of bikes."

"A what?" Victoria wasn't sure she'd heard correctly. "A mix-up?"

"It took some prodding, but I got Mr. Farnsworth to fess up. He came home one night last week—might have stopped off on his way for a beer or two with the guys—and he ran over his daughter's bike. She'd left it at the end of the driveway, and he claimed he didn't see it in the dark until it was too late. He was so angry, he said he wanted to teach her a lesson. The next-door neighbors—the Thompsons—had just had a dumpster delivered for some renovations they've got going on, so he carried the crumpled bike over and tossed it in. He wanted his daughter to think it had been stolen. Apparently previous threats to take the bike away if she didn't take care of it had fallen on deaf ears."

"Ha! Good for him. Nice to hear of a parent teaching their child a lesson." The story struck a chord with Millie, but she was missing the point about the father being intoxicated and driving. Victoria shuddered to think it could have been someone's dog or a child he hadn't seen.

"So, you're off the hook, Mom." At least until the next angry neighbor shows up on their front doorstep, looking for something they were missing.

"I think that neighbor of ours owes us an apology."

"Don't think you'll get one," Victoria said.

The officer wasn't finished. "Oh, and I think I figured out where you *did* get the bike from."

Victoria braced for impact. Millie looked to him to continue, beaming.

"Right next door to the Farnsworths. The Thompsons had put a
bike out at the curb. And it did have a 'free' sign on it."

Victoria exhaled. Redemption. She hated herself for doubting her
own mother.

"They'd been cleaning out the garage to make space to store the
contents of their kitchen while it was being renovated and got rid of
a lot of old stuff. Their kids are all grown, and they thought someone
might come along who needed the bike more than they did."

Millie grinned. "Ha!"

"And apparently someone did." Officer Dill grinned back. "You
didn't remember the dumpster being there when we took a ride in my
cruiser because it wasn't. They were pretty sure it arrived the day after
the bike disappeared. So, mystery solved."

Victoria imagined he didn't get a lot of mysteries to solve, not in a
sleepy town like Talcottville. He seemed overly pleased with himself
for handling this one. But she had to admit, she had the urge to hug
him for delivering the good news and redeeming her mother.

"Good day, ladies."

Victoria left Millie to linger in the doorway, watching him go, and
set off to toast the bagels.

"Do you know anyone who drives a gray car?" she called from
the foyer.

"What? A gray car? That doesn't tell me much." Victoria pulled
small plates from the cupboard and mugs for their coffee.

"Well, maybe it's a Taurus."

"A gray Taurus?"

"Or it could have been a Maserati."

"A Maserati." She laughed. "Mom, those are two very different-look-
ing cars. Which was it?"

"I don't know, but it slowed down as it drove by the house. The
driver seemed to be gawking." Millie was still carrying on their conversation from the foyer.

"Well, we did have a police cruiser in the driveway. People always gawk at that. People are nosy."

"Yeah, you're right." Millie appeared in the doorway to the kitchen. "Coffee smells good." There was a smidgen of surprise in her voice, one that seemed to be there more often than not lately, as if everything was new to her.

"Should be ready." Victoria delivered the warm bagels to the table as Millie poured two steaming cups.

Biting into one half of her own crunchy deli delight that could have come from the upper east side, Victoria watched as cream cheese oozed out of her mother's full bagel and plopped to the table as she chomped down, completely missing the plate. She decided she'd deal with her mother's cream cheese mustache once she'd finished eating.

"What'd you do to your arm?" her mother asked with a mouthful.

"What?" Had she heard correctly?

"Your arm. Unless I'm seeing things, it looks like you've got a cast on it. What happened?"

The ruse was over.

Millie laughed. "Ha! You didn't think you were hiding it from me, did you?" Victoria opened her mouth to answer, but Millie continued. "I'm your mother. It's going to take a lot to keep something from me."

"I wasn't trying to keep anything from you. I was waiting for the right time to tell you."

"Which was going to be . . . when?"

"Now."

"Okay, I'm all ears. Go for it." Millie reached for the cream cheese spreader, scooped up a glob, and added it to her bagel.

"All right. Here goes. I've got to say it's a bit out of the ordinary—it might even sound farfetched—but it did happen. Do you remember the other day when I said I would be in a planning meeting for the Parents Committee?"

"I think so."

"Later in the day Vince called to tell you my meeting had run late, and he was taking me to dinner?"

"That was the day we had that awful thunderstorm, wasn't it?"

"Yes, exactly."

"I called you that morning and left a message. There was some bad weather out to the west that looked like it was going to be nasty. I had a bad feeling about it. Wanted to give you a heads up if you weren't aware."

Her mother. Always a worrier. This time it was justified.

"Well, uh . . . the person I was meeting lives in the city. He's got money to burn, so he sent a helicopter to pick me up to have lunch in Brooklyn." *Did she have to admit Emerson was in the helicopter?*

Taking a bite of bagel, Millie listened with surprisingly little expression on her face.

"I thought it was over the top, but he talked me into it."

"Why not? That sounds like fun—for you.. What was it like?"

"At first, a bit claustrophobic, but once we got moving it wasn't too bad."

Her mother's face lit up. "Ha! You're braver than me. So, what was lunch like?"

"We never made it to lunch."

"You didn't?"

"No. We almost didn't make it back alive."

Her mother stopped mid-chew, and her eyes grew wide. "What happened?"

"The weather got bad—rainy, really windy—and when we went to land, there was an updraft or a downdraft—whatever it was—and we crash landed."

"Oh my God, Victoria." Millie reached out and grabbed onto her uninjured arm as a chunk of bagel fell out of her mouth. She began to cough so she pulled her hand back to cover her mouth.

"Mom, you okay?"

Her mother nodded as she coughed a few more times, then took a sip of coffee. "Victoria, how scary. That's how you broke your arm? And got that gash on your forehead?"

"Yeah, it's actually my wrist." Her mother reached over and tugged on Victoria's sleeve to reveal more of the white fiberglass. "That and a few stitches, but I was the lucky one."

Millie pressed her lips into a pout but remained silent.

"The guy I was meeting ended up with a broken leg and the pilot didn't make it."

"Oh, dear."

"It was scary."

"All that for lunch. Geez."

The doorbell startled them, and they exchanged quizzical looks. Victoria prayed it wasn't the officer again. "Here," she said as she rose, handing a napkin to her mother. "You've got a little something." She traced a couple of circles around her own lips with a finger.

This time it was another familiar face at the door but not one she'd been expecting.

"Hello, Victoria. I'm sorry to bother you on a Sunday morning."

"Erin . . . good to see you."

Or was she? It had slipped out before she'd had a chance to think about her greeting. They'd never had a chance to get down to business at the coffee shop. Victoria had no idea why she was so eager to meet with her. Should she be wishing for a Jehovah's Witness again?

"Why don't you come in." Pushing out the screen door to welcome her in, Victoria got a glimpse of her car; a gray Mini Cooper. *Yeah, that could be mistaken for a Maserati.*

Erin's gaze landed on Victoria's arm. "What happened?" She gestured to her cast.

"Oh, got a little clumsy. It's just a broken wrist." Victoria cringed at how easily the little lie slipped out.

"Hope it heals quickly for you."

"Thanks. Come on in. My mother and I were enjoying some coffee and bagels from a great bakery in town. We'd love for you to join us."

"Oh, I don't mean to interrupt you. I should have called. But I saw my out this morning to get off campus, and I took it."

Victoria thought it sounded more like a prison for the teachers than a private school. Or was it for this teacher in particular? "Not a problem. Please join us," she tried again.

"Maybe I should come back another time. I really would like to speak with you in private."

"Well, that's silly. You've come all this way. We can take our coffee out on the patio. My mother will understand." But would she? She was so unpredictable. It could go either way and sometimes to an extreme.

"If you're sure . . . I'd really appreciate that."

"Sure thing. Come on in." Victoria motioned for Erin, who was clutching the same tote she'd brought to the coffee shop, to follow her into the kitchen. "Mom, this is Erin Hutchinson. She's a teacher at Litchfield."

Millie looked up, chewing with a full mouth. She took a moment, which Victoria was grateful for, and wiped her mouth, which she was equally grateful for. "Nice to meet you, Erin. Is everything okay with Jameson? Didn't know teachers made house calls. Ha!" Her outburst made Erin pull away with a jerk, but she recovered nicely.

Victoria stepped in to answer. "Yes, yes. Everything is fine. Erin is here . . . to talk about a Parents Committee project." There, she was using that lie again. How often would that be necessary? "I forgot we had talked about getting together this morning." Yet another lie. Turning to Erin, she said, "Let's take our coffee out in the garden."

"I don't need coffee. We can try to make this quick so you can get back to what you were doing." Quick and painless? Or just quick?

"Okay. No problem." Leaving her coffee on the table, Victoria showed the way to the French doors that led out to the patio, and they settled into the chairs with the metal filigree design on their backs across from each other at the bistro table.

Erin plunked the tote on her lap.

"Have you brought the envelope again?"

"Yes, I have." Her expression grew serious.

Hating to interrupt, but allowing her curiosity to get the better of her, Victoria asked, "So, what was up with Headmaster Martin the other day? If someone else was watching that unfold, they would have thought it was a father reprimanding his daughter. I mean, it was a little odd, you have to admit."

Erin held up a hand and dropped her gaze. "Believe me, I was mortified by his actions. But as soon as we got to the parking lot, he let go and told me he expected better decision making from me, now that I was a seasoned staff member and then he was off."

"Wow, I—"

"But let's not worry about that now. That's water under the bridge as they say. Let's get to why I'm here."

"Of course."

Slipping a familiar manila envelope from her tote, Erin placed it on the table between them but trapped it under her palm. "As I said before, I found these wedged in the back of a bottom drawer in Robert's—your husband's—desk. I'm afraid this may come as a bit of a shock to you, but I thought you should know.

Erin pushed the envelope closer to Victoria and slid her fingers off. Victoria stared at the nondescript envelope with no markings to speak of, just dog-eared corners she imagined were from traveling in the tote.

Victoria pulled it toward her and flipped it over, pressing the brass-colored tabs together and running a finger under the flap. Sliding out a stack of photos whose edges were curled, she examined the top one closely. It was a woman, also a brunette like herself, but younger. She didn't look familiar.

Relegating her photo to the bottom of the stack, Victoria studied the next one; four children sitting on a couch, possibly all boys, but it was hard to tell by how they were dressed. The third was the woman posing with the boys. Going through the pile, Victoria grew more puzzled with each one. There were also candids of the children in various sports; baseball, soccer, and lacrosse.

"Four boys. All into sports," she mumbled. Then to Erin, she asked, "Should I know these people?"

"Maybe. Maybe not. You tell me. Check what's written on the back."

Going through the stack again, this time Victoria turned each one over. On the woman's photo, it read, "Miss you and can't wait for you to come home," in feminine handwriting. On the rest were the boys ages but no dates.

Victoria emptied her lungs through a narrow opening in her lips. "Erin, what am I supposed to make of these?"

She shook her head and set her jaw. "I don't know, but I thought you should have them . . . that you'd know what to do with them."

Dropping the stack on the table and sitting back in the chair, Victoria said, "I don't think these belonged to Robert."

"What do you mean? They were in his desk." Erin scooted forward in her seat. "Wasn't he in that office for his entire tenure at Litchfield?"

"I think so."

"Well, then I think there's a pretty good—more than a pretty good chance—they belonged to him."

Victoria's mind raced. Who were the people in the photos? Why didn't she recognize them? Could Aviva's wild idea of Robert starting a new life somewhere else have a shred of reality to it? Had he already started a new family before he disappeared, but it got to be too much to juggle both? Had the other woman forced him to make a choice? The boys in the photos were younger. Did he choose them because of it? Her racing thoughts snagged on the knowledge Robert had ached for four children, and Victoria had only given him two.

When the boys were very young, they discussed having more children. Although Robert had wanted to have a couple more, Victoria did not, but went along with it to the point of her first miscarriage. Then she pushed back and refused to try again. She couldn't bear the thought of being responsible for another death.

Had Robert found someone who was willing to give him the number of children he desired? Would her Robert do such a thing? She couldn't conceive of it, but as Aviva had pointed out: *How well do we really know someone?* She thought of the coral birthday roses that came from different florists. Was Robert moving around to avoid detection?

Suddenly Victoria realized Erin was speaking.

"I'm sorry to drop this in your lap like this. I'm afraid I've opened up a mare's nest, but I didn't feel right hanging onto them, once I'd found them. I thought you should have them."

"Thank you for going to all the trouble to get them to me." Victoria perked up to deliver her next lie. "You know, now that I've had a chance to think about it, I remember him talking about his brother's family and their four kids. I've never met them, but that must be who they are." In her mind, the lie kept growing and strange words continued to fall from her lips. "He was stationed abroad—Japan, I believe—so I never met them," she repeated.

"That's a relief to hear," Erin said, but her tone didn't back up the words. She didn't believe it anymore than Victoria did. "All right, then. I'll let you get back to your coffee. Thanks for your time." She grabbed the edge of the table with two hands as if she were going to push off and stand up, but froze, her eyes fixed on a spot over Victoria's shoulder.

The voice behind Victoria startled her. "Ha! Hogwash."

Victoria spun around in her seat to face her mother with a glare to silence her. It didn't work.

"Are you kidding me? That's a bunch of hooey." She stepped onto the brick patio with her faded pink bathrobe and matching fuzzy slippers that were showing their age, looking soiled and needing a good scrubbing. At some point, she had switched out her clogs.

"Mom, please."

"Oh, don't 'Mom' me. What have I taught you? You don't lie like that." She'd reached the table and rested a frail hand on the back of Victoria's chair, bearing down on her with an "I'm so disappointed in you" expression only a mother could deliver, which tore at Victoria's heart. Turning to their guest, she added, "I'm so sorry. My daughter's head is all screwed up, and she doesn't know what she's saying—has been ever since Robert left."

"Mom, he didn't leave. He disappeared."

"So, you say. But we don't know that, do we? Maybe you know more than you're telling."

"Mom, enough. You don't know what *you're* saying."

Silence hung between the three women as Millie pulled away from her daughter to glance at Erin, and then her eyes went to the table between them and the photos that had become scattered across it. She scooped up a few and pulled them close to her face.

"Well butter my bottom and call me a biscuit. These boys look familiar—like they could be Harrison and Jameson's brothers." With that, she dropped them back onto the table and shuffled off, back into the house.

"I'm sorry," was all Victoria could think of.

Erin searched Victoria's face, and then opened her mouth, but nothing came out.

"She's . . . not all there." Victoria tapped the side of her own head with a fingertip. "And she says things that are so unexpected. I honestly don't know where all that came from. Please excuse her."

"Don't give it another thought."

"Thanks for understanding." Victoria scooped up the photos and shoved them back where they'd come from, securing the clasp—as if her doing so would make them go away.

"Well, as I said, I should let you get back to your coffee. I've taken up enough of your Sunday morning."

As Victoria showed her out, she clutched the envelope close to her side. Holding the screen door for Erin to exit through, Victoria had a thought. "Oh, hey, could you do me a favor?"

"Sure."

"This might sound silly, but could you send me the itinerary for the senior trip?"

Erin looked to Victoria for an explanation. After all, it wasn't as though she had to know when to pick up her son when they arrived back on campus. He was a boarder, not a day student.

"I'd just like to know where they are and what fun things they're getting to do. Then during the day, I can imagine them in the different places."

"I see." Erin considered her request, and then added, "I know there are limited spots, but I could see if they need any more chaperones if you'd like."

"Oh, heavens, no. Jameson would be so embarrassed if I tagged along."

Chuckling, Erin said, "I'm sure you're right. Wouldn't want that." Heading down the sidewalk she called back, "Guess you'll have to stick with living vicariously through an email."

With a wave, Victoria shut the door behind the history teacher. As she turned back, she caught a glimpse of her mother on the threshold to the kitchen, one hand on a hip, the other on the door frame.

"I didn't know Robert had a brother. Ha! And with four kids."

"No, Robert did not have a brother with four kids. And I'd appreciate it if you wouldn't eavesdrop."

"But then why did you say that to that nice girl?"

"*Mom* . . . let it go."

Chapter Twenty-Four

The enticing aroma of chocolate hit Victoria in the face when she opened the oven to check on the cupcakes. Pressing her eyes closed, she inhaled the decadence only chocolate could provide.

"Who are those for?" Millie appeared in the kitchen doorway. Victoria did a doubletake to be sure she saw what her mother was wearing. Orange sweatpants with a purple Clemson pawprint logo down one leg and a gray hooded sweatshirt with a UConn Huskies logo across her chest. Clearly she'd been shopping in Harrison's bureau. They were souvenirs from his college tour loop. He'd turned his nose up at both. California was more his style.

Sliding the trays out of the oven with mitted hands, Victoria placed them gently onto the stove. It took everything she had not to snatch one up, peel off the liner, and take a bite. She figured her reaction was a good sign. No one else would be interested in her cupcakes if she wasn't.

"Oh, hey, Mom. These are actually for a bake sale. A mother who didn't have time to bake—or just didn't want to—called me, and I said I could do it."

"You're getting paid for it, right?"

"Oh, yes. Yes, I am." Thinking back to her days of baking for the boys' fundraisers, she said, "It's been a long time since I got my apron dirty for a school bake sale."

"It's all about convenience these days, isn't it? Ha!" Millie pursed her lips and shook her head with her stamp of disapproval.

"People are busy, and they don't have the time that you and I had when our kids were little. I'm grateful to get the calls, Mom." She pulled out each cupcake and lined them up uniformly on the cooling rack.

"I get it. It's so different now."

"It is." Victoria pulled out a large bowl and began to gather the ingredients to make frosting; confectioners' sugar from the cupboard and milk from the fridge.

Millie squealed. "Ooooh, I love frosting. That's my favorite part. What flavor are you going to make?"

"My client told me to use my imagination. She wanted chocolate cake, but the rest was up to me. I think I'm going to do a variety of vanilla buttercream, chocolate, and mocha."

"Ha! That sounds delicious. I'll have one of each." Millie guffawed, and Victoria wondered if she was serious.

"Mom, I'm sorry. I don't have any extras."

"You don't? What happens if you drop one—you have to start over again?"

"Well, no. I've allowed for one or two mistakes. It happens."

"Great! I'll take your mistakes."

Victoria laughed to herself. Too bad more of her mistakes couldn't be eliminated by peeling off the wrapper and shoving them into her mouth. Her cell vibrated, so she grabbed it off the counter, excused herself, and headed toward the living room.

"Hello?"

"Hey, Victoria. How are you doing?" She'd gotten as far as the mirror in the foyer when she froze, catching a glimpse of the bruising under her eyes.

"Emerson." Instantly regretting not checking caller ID before answering, she allowed some dead air to hang between them. "How are you? Are you out of the hospital?" She tried not to sound too interested, torn between directives from her head and her heart.

"Of course. That was over a week ago. I'm good as new. Missed seeing you, so I want to take you to dinner."

Not an invitation. More of a declaration.

"Good as new? You've got a broken leg. And a concussion too, wasn't it?" She leaned in to examine the stitches on her forehead. The cut looked redder than she would have expected. Was it swollen?

"I convinced them to put me in a walking cast so I'm good to go. Nothing stopping me now, love."

"That's great news. Good for you." She flopped into the chair under the mirror, one that rarely got used for sitting and usually was full of a couple of days' mail.

"So, tell me where I can treat you to a fabulous dinner in Talcottville. No traveling—for you. We'll keep it simple. And we don't have to talk fundraising, I promise."

"I . . . I don't know. I'm not really up to it."

"Come on, don't say 'no' yet. Hear me out. We'll make it a nice quiet evening. Just the two of us. We can go to your favorite restaurant—wherever you want to go. You name it. We'll take our time. Spread out the courses like they do so well in France. How does that sound?"

"I'm really not up to it," she repeated. "Guess I'm still getting over the crash."

"Aw, you need to get out. Leave it behind. We were lucky. It could have been so much worse."

"Exactly. That's the part that scares me. I relive the last few minutes over and over. I'll never get in a helicopter again." Images of that fateful afternoon flooded her head. The rain beating against the windows. The wind buffeting the craft. The pilot's last words. *Downdraft! We're going down. Hang on.* Then the earsplitting sound of crunching metal. The terrifying feeling of being pinned by the wreckage. "I mean, how would you get here?" She could feel herself softening. *How did he do that to her so easily?*

"I'm in Connecticut all the time on business. That's not a big deal. But you know what? The thing about the crash is, we were supposed to live. We were supposed to move on. You're not having survivor's guilt, are you?"

"I don't know what it is. But it's left me scarred." *As if she needed more scarring. How could he move on so quickly when he'd lost a dear friend?* "I'm going to say 'no' to dinner. Thanks anyway."

"It won't be anything crazy. I won't pick you up in an experimental craft or anything like that. Just a—"

"No."

"You can meet me there, if you want. There's no risk of me providing the transportation this time."

"I said, no. Thanks, anyway. Goodbye." And she hung up.

"You're turning down dinner?" Victoria jumped at the sound of her mother's voice.

"Jesus, you scared me. Please don't eavesdrop like that. I've asked you not to."

"Eavesdrop? Ha! How can I not? I could go anywhere in this house and hear a conversation going on in the foyer."

"Whatever," Victoria mumbled as she brushed past her to get back to the cooling cupcakes.

"Don't 'whatever' me." Millie was at her heels. "You're the one turning down dinner. Maybe he wants to make up with you."

"Sounds like he does, but I'm not ready for it." Victoria pulled out the baker's cocoa from the cupboard and grabbed the stick of butter she'd left to soften on the counter, peeling off the wrapper and dropping it into the bowl.

"At least hear him out."

"Oh, I think I've heard enough." She dumped in the bag of confectioners' sugar.

"Give the guy a chance."

"Why are you pushing me on this?" She grabbed the jug and splashed some milk against the side of the bowl.

"You need a man in your life. Preferably one with money. Ha!" Her mother's tendency to laugh at situations—almost as a punctuation to a sentence—that had no humor in them was an oddity Victoria had never gotten used to. This was one of those times.

"And you think because he's got money, I should chase after him?" Victoria began to stir the ingredients together, white powder bursting out of the top of the bowl like ash from an active volcano.

"Hear him out," she repeated. "It wouldn't be such a bad thing to be with someone with money. Ha!"

"Look, you don't even know him." She stirred faster.

"Victoria, you have to move on."

"That's what he said too. But I'm not ready."

"It's been seven years. Life's too short not to move on."

Millie and Victoria had vastly different ways of dealing with loss—a veritable study in contrasts. Perhaps their age difference at the time of their losses played a role, but Millie had adopted the attitude of living life to the fullest while Victoria developed a fear of losing her remaining family members. Her grasp grew tighter, the farther away they ventured. Millie dealt with her daughter's and, shortly after, her husband's loss as a mature woman. Victoria had to face both tragedies as a relatively young child, which, no doubt, shaped how she dealt with the loss of her husband as an adult. Not knowing if he were ever coming back made the process more complicated.

Victoria looked up from the bowlful of white fluffiness, her hand on the idle spoon handle. "Wait a minute. What are we talking about?"

Millie, whose gaze had been locked on Victoria's hand moving in a circular motion, stuck out her lower lip but kept her sights on the bowl, as if waiting for her to resume. "I think you need to let it go and let another man into your life. Otherwise you'll still be making cupcakes when you're my age. And Vince seems good for you."

"I wasn't talking with Vince."

"You weren't?" Millie broke her trance and looked up.

"No, this was the guy I was in the helicopter with when it crashed."

"And you don't want to see him again because you ended up in an accident together?"

"We weren't on a date."

"But now he's asking you out on one and you don't want to go. What . . . has your mind twisted the event, and you're now blaming him for what happened? Like it was his fault?"

"I . . . I don't know."

"'Cause that would be stupid."

"Mom." Her mother had no filter.

"Well, if he's still interested in taking you out after a near-death experience with you, you might want to consider it." She headed for the door, mumbling, "He's certainly got money to throw around."

Victoria thought to herself, *apparently people as well.*

If she wasn't so annoyed with her mother's meddling, she would have laughed at the sight of her toes sticking out from the bottoms of the orange sweatpants, too long for a four-foot-five frame, as she shuffled across the threshold of the kitchen door.

CHAPTER TWENTY-FIVE

W ater trickled in at first. Tiny drops splashed on her face as it forced its way through the crack in the window. Her toes felt wet in her favorite Sperry's and cold wetness lapped at her ankles. The trickle turned into a whooshing all around her. Panic welled in her chest. She couldn't move. Something held her in place, like a strong hand on her left shoulder. She pushed against an unseen force but could only move a few inches before hitting against something.

As the rising water reached her waist, she shivered but couldn't shake off the chill. The gurgling sound filled her ears as she watched the water swirl around her chest. A strange sense of peace came over her. So, this was the way she would go out. She hadn't pictured her death like this, but then again, who got to choose? She'd thought about not growing old, not watching the boys get married, or even becoming a grandmother. She certainly didn't expect her mother to outlive her. How was that fair?

Victoria didn't want it to be over. Who would cuddle her grand-babies when they were colicky and their parents had reached the end of their ropes? Who would have her sons and their families over for a sit-down dinner on Sunday evenings? Who would keep looking for Robert? No one. Everyone had already given up. He would have to forgive her.

As the water reached her chin, she snapped out of her melancholy fog. Panic returned. Gasping for air, she thrust her head back and could feel the cold water on her neck. She thought she should scream for help—but who was nearby to hear?—only to realize it was too late. Water filled her mouth. She spit it out but more flooded in, reaching the back of her throat. It threatened to go down and choke her. Coughing, she forced her head back farther and focused on breathing through her nose. She didn't want to die. *No! No! Please no!* She gasped for air. *Help!*

She felt pressure on her other shoulder. Someone had a firm grip and was shaking her.

"Victoria . . . Victoria, it's okay."

She opened her eyes to blackness. Blinking to discern her surroundings, it seemed the water was gone. Her feet weren't wet any longer. Neither was the rest of her body. The hair on the back of her head was wet, but with sweat. Moonlight filtering in the front windows created shadows throughout the room and allowed her to start recognizing shapes. She was in her bedroom. Had she left the water running in the tub before falling asleep, and it was overflowing?

Then it hit her whose voice it was. Emerson was next to her. In bed. Her thoughts went to Jameson and what his reaction would be. He spoke again.

"Victoria? You okay?"

She scooted into a sitting position and dropped back against the headboard while the details from the night before, like the water in her dream, swelled up around her, filling every crevice in her head. Emerson mirrored her movement and adjusted the pillows behind her, then reached for the lamp on the bedside table nearest him. She flinched at the blinding light.

"Sounds like you were having quite a dream . . . a nightmare." He rubbed the back of her neck, sending a shiver down her spine. She fought to keep her entire body from twitching but was miserably unsuccessful. Emerson was quickly seeing firsthand the pitiful, psychological mess she was. Victoria could only stare straight ahead, her jaw set. No words came.

"Love, what's the matter?" He wrapped a strong arm around her, pulling her into his bare, rippled torso, her lips landing on a taut nipple. Warm against her cheek, the skin on his chest was covered in just the right amount of bristled tawny hair and smelled of a recent shower—no doubt with a fine bath gel he'd picked up from Harrod's on a recent trip to London. *How did he always smell so good?* He ran warm fingers down her back, causing her to shiver again. It was only then did she realize she was naked.

He'd spent the night. . . . Images of them having sex floated through her mind. *Had they used protection? Could she get pregnant at her age? Thank goodness Jameson wouldn't know.* Her back stiffened when Vince's face, crimped with a hurt expression after discovering the secret lover in her bed, shifted into her thoughts. *He would be devastated to know. But he didn't have to find out. Besides Vince had just dumped her, hadn't he? It was more of an ultimatum. Same thing.*

Emerson had shown up at her front door after she'd declined his offer over the phone to take her to dinner and announced he would wait while she changed. Clearly Emerson didn't have the word "no" in his vocabulary; he didn't use it and didn't hear it when someone else did.

While she freshened up and then ripped her closet apart trying to find something that would work—didn't say too frumpy, too old, or too suggestive—he'd found his way into the kitchen where he joined her mother. Apparently they'd clicked, which was no surprise to Victoria. Her mother liked most men—especially rich men—and those who were doting on her daughter.

Victoria appeared in the doorway to find the two of them elbow deep in flour. They looked up in unison before she had a chance to react to the smears of white powder on their noses and the ill-fitting, orange-and-yellow-flowered apron Emerson was donning—a favorite of Victoria's when she was growing up.

Barely stifling a giggle, she asked, "What are you two up to?"

"Victoria." She loved how his face lit up each time he saw her and her name rolled off his tongue. With his accent, he made it sound melodic. "Don't you look absolutely lovely. Ravishing, I would say." If only Aviva could witness the attention Victoria was getting from this entirely ravishing—to use his word—Brit.

Suddenly with all eyes—in particular, his—on her, the solid Robin's-egg-blue cashmere pullover and stretch black jeans felt woefully inadequate, even though she'd accessorized with gold bangles, gold hoops, and dressy black ankle boots. She felt her cheeks burning and could barely utter a thank you.

"All set?" He untied the apron strings behind him, pulled it over his head, tossed it onto the counter in one swift movement, and stepped back with palms up as if he'd just roped a calf.

"Wait. What were you guys doing?" Victoria looked from Emerson to her mother. Surely *she* would level with her.

"Oh, your mum was so gracious to let me barge in to throw some flour about the kitchen." He chuckled. "Great fun, you know?"

Victoria returned her gaze to her mother, who was uncharacteristically silent. Millie shrugged and plastered a grin that said, *I like this one. Hang onto him.*

Millie shooed them off to the car waiting out front, and they headed out to one of Victoria's favorite restaurants in town—Abigail's, where the food was always good, the service attentive but not smothering, and the atmosphere bordering on festive.

It was a popular gathering place—and had been for over two centuries after a tavern was built on top of the foundation for a former stagecoach stop—situated at busy crossroads that dated back to colonial days. It was common to run into one or two acquaintances there and several familiar faces you couldn't place. Victoria had purposely paraded him through the upstairs bar before finding a corner at the far end to hang out in with a drink until their table was ready downstairs.

Two drinks in, the waitress retrieved them and the rest of the evening blurred into snippets of conversation, restaurant noise, and the tables on either side of them emptying and filling up again. She must have offered to do coffee and dessert back at the house. Then it came to her. Cream puffs.

When Emerson joined her mother in the kitchen, she had been making cream puffs—even though her mother didn't have a drop of French blood in her. Millie hadn't been up when they returned, but they helped themselves to the plate of French delights she'd left for them in the fridge.

"I'm okay." She pulled out of his grasp, grabbing a handful of the covers up to her chest. Her head rocked in the wake of all the wine the night before. Then her gut woke up, rolling with more than its usual morning stomach acid. She pressed her lips together, willing the contents to stay put. "It happens."

"These nightmares? They happen a lot?"

Not wanting to appear as screwed up as she felt—and certainly not looking for pity—she said, "Sometimes . . . I mean, they happen from time to time. Not often."

Liar!

"How absolutely dreadful. I'm so sorry. Is it the same dream? Or a different version of it each time?"

She wished he would stop prying. It was probably genuine concern for her, but Victoria didn't want to get into it with him. She felt painfully vulnerable.

"If you don't mind, I don't really want to talk about it."

He seemed to let it go, and she was grateful. Her thoughts returned to the prior evening, trying to piece it together from the grainy images drifting through her throbbing head.

Victoria remembered hearing her phone vibrate in her purse, after another round of drinks had arrived, and she'd pulled it out enough to see who it was. "Oh, look at that. It's Harrison. He never calls me."

"Go ahead and answer it, love," Emerson encouraged.

"That's okay. I can call him back later."

"No, really. It might be something important."

"You're right. But I never answer my cell when I'm with someone else—I don't want to be rude."

"Go ahead." His luscious wavy mop flopped as he nodded his approval.

Tickled to be getting to talk to her son, she answered, "Harrison, so good to hear from you. Is everything all right out there in sunny California?" She restrained herself from saying how long it had been since he'd last called. She needed to sound happy when he did call—not clingy and lonely.

"Yeah, Mom. I'm okay. I need to . . . uh . . . tell you about that project I'm working on for my architecture class."

"Your architecture class?" She looked to Emerson for a dismissive reaction but didn't get one. "Oh, well, dear, I'm actually with some- one right now." *With someone she wanted to get back with.* "Can I call you later?"

"Um . . . this is pretty important, Mom. I don't think you'll want to wait."

"Harrison, you know how proud of you I am, and how much I love to hear all about your classes, but I need to call you back in a little bit. Actually, tomorrow morning."

Emerson looked like a baseball umpire, calling the runner safe at home, crisscrossing arms back and forth over his appetizer plate, signaling to her it was okay.

"Mom, listen. I think I may have found out what happened to Dad. Well . . . I may have found his car."

Victoria allowed his words to sink in. How could he possibly have connected to what happened to his father? Harrison was all the way over on the other coast. It didn't make sense.

She couldn't think of the right words to respond, distracted by Emerson looking expectantly across from her, listening to her side of the call. She was torn between wanting to hear Harrison out and not keeping Emerson waiting. *Please don't let her blow this . . . whatever this was with him. She'd already lost Vince, and this guy was . . . well, he was a hot commodity. So hot, she wondered how he could possibly be there with her.*

"Mom? Are you there?"

"Uh, yes. I'm here. Harrison, so what are you thinking? He drove out to California?"

"No, Mom. I found something on Google Earth."

"Google Earth?" He'd been playing around online, and now he thought he'd found his father's car that had been missing for seven years. A white Toyota that was as common as Queen Anne's lace alongside country roads in New England. It couldn't possibly be Robert's car.

It would have been found already if it was findable. And she wasn't about to interrupt her time with Emerson any longer than she already had by entertaining Harrison's wild notions.

"If it's his car, it seems as though he didn't drive to New York like we thought, Mom. You need to take a look at this. I don't think things happened the way Headmaster Martin said they did."

"Okay, well, maybe it's not what *you* think it is. Why don't we talk about it when you get home next week for Thanksgiving?" *Please don't let it be his car. How about a stolen car that someone ditched there? But please not Robert's car.*

"I don't think we should wait that long. We need to tell the police."

"Sweetheart, as far as they're concerned, it's a cold case. They're not going to have any urgency to deal with it."

After a ration of silence on his end, he finally said, "Okay, well maybe I'll come home a few days early."

"That sounds wonderful, dear. See you then. Thanks for calling."

In spite of the terrifying images careening through her mind, Victoria tossed the phone back into her purse and composed herself for Emerson's benefit. She hoped he hadn't heard too much of what Harrison was carrying on about.

"Everything okay?" He leaned closer with a concerned look.

"Oh, yes. He's just excited about a class project he's working on and about coming home for Thanksgiving." She hoped he had accepted that explanation.

Content to have remembered the details of their phone conversation, Victoria tried to think past it but couldn't come up with what she'd had to eat after she'd scoffed down the warm brown bread Abigail's was known for.

Scanning the room for something—anything—to throw on, her eyes landed on her sweater hanging off the arm of her reading chair in the corner. Had she tossed it in a hurry the previous evening? Her pants weren't in sight. She hoped they'd made it into her bedroom and weren't dangling across the banister in the foyer.

Then her gaze landed on a framed photo on the table next to her, taken at the celebratory dinner for Robert's promotion to department head. Cringing, she wanted to knock it flat, but chances were, Emerson had already seen it or any of the many others on display throughout the house. "Sorry, Robert," she said to herself.

"I think this might be yours." She turned to watch Emerson gingerly pulling her bra off the lampshade on his bedside table.

"Oh, God. What have we done. . .?" It was more of a whisper, yet Emerson answered her.

With a crooked grin, he said, "We had fun."

"Emerson, I'm sure we did—I know we did—but I didn't expect the evening to end up here . . . this morning."

She rubbed her temples with outstretched fingers. She didn't want to offend him, but she honestly couldn't remember the night before. She wondered if this was how the women who were slipped the date-rape drug felt the next day. *Damn chardonnay.*

"God, I had way too much wine—it was just wine that we had, wasn't it?" It suddenly occurred to her that with his sky's-the-limit lifestyle, there may have been something else mixed in there.

"What? Do you think I would engage in such other frivolities?" He wasn't denying it, but she wanted to believe he had good intentions.

"I'm just asking. I don't really know you, Emerson." And yet she'd invited him into her bed and let him stay the night. Well, less of an invitation and more like the gate was left open and the owner was in no condition to monitor the property, much less keep anyone out. When one was inebriated, others got to make decisions for you, whether they were in your best interests or not.

"Well, let me assure you. Besides a fabulous time together, all we had was wine last night. No worries, love. The headache you're experiencing is from the chardonnay . . . and you falling in love with me."

She kept herself from making eye contact with him. Uncomfortable with the direction of the conversation, she bit her lip to give her mouth something to do other than reply. *Could this really be happening? And so fast?*

"Okay, I know. I know that was probably going too far, but I guess it's wishful thinking on my part," he continued. "I can't help myself. I adore being with you. You light up my world—okay, maybe that was borderline corny." He propped himself up on one elbow. "If it's too soon for a comment like that, please don't be offended. It's probably a cultural difference. Nothing more."

Cultural difference? Practically proclaiming your love for someone you just had your first date with? (Hopping into bed with, notwithstanding). She thought Brits were more restrained than that. Maybe he had a little Italian in him.

"No? I don't want to take it back because I meant it. Go easy on me, Victoria. My heart is fragile. It's been broken before."

Looking into his crystal blues, the pupils dilated due to the light, she thought, *and mine hasn't?*

He got the message without her uttering a sound. "You're right. It's not all about my heart."

"I didn't say that, Emerson. You just . . . surprised me by getting all gushy on me. I wasn't expecting it."

"No, it's okay. I get it." He pushed an errant strand of hair from her face. "I had a fabulous time with you last night . . . for the most part."

Victoria searched her memory for something she'd said, something she'd done that offended him, or was inappropriate. "For the most part?"

"All except when your ex made his presence known."

"My ex?" She ran through what she could remember of the prior evening but was unable to conjure up even a foggy image of Vince.

"You don't remember that?"

Planting a scowl on her face, she shook her head.

"He was rather passive/aggressive about it. He was camped out at the first-floor bar, apparently with a clear view of our table. Sent over a couple of lava cakes."

"Those were from him?" She didn't recall knowing where they'd come from, just the vague recollection of warm chocolate fudge oozing from the center of the cake as she cut into it with her fork and how it felt on her tongue.

"The waitress said they were from a friend so when you got up to go to the ladies' room, I took a stroll over and had a chat."

"How did you know—"

"Every time I looked in the direction of the bar, he had his eye on us. Kind of creepy, if you ask me." He pushed himself up into a higher position, back against the pillows. "Victoria, I'm concerned this guy might be stalking you."

"Oh, I don't think so. Abigail's is a very popular place in town. Everyone goes there."

"That may be . . . but I don't believe in coincidences. Some guys don't know how to handle breakups. And if they can't have you, they can't stand the thought of anyone else being with you. They're control freaks. Who knows, maybe there's a connection between him and Robert's disappearance."

A breath caught in her throat at the mention of Robert's name.

"I can assure you, that's not what's going on here." She wasn't about to go into how Vince had broken up with her. Not his business. "Please don't give it another thought." She flashed back to when Vince convinced her to stop flying. *Was that his way of exerting control over her?* He'd always been generous with his money, but it left her with a meager income and little say in their finances as a couple. *He'd better not ruin her chances with Emerson.*

"It's probably time for me to head out anyway." He threw off the covers and swung his legs out of the bedding. Clearly he'd had enough of his wits about him the night before to find his boxer briefs and put them on. "Breakfast conversation with your mum might be a bit awkward." He chuckled and glanced at his Rolex. "Let's see if I can sneak out the door to save you from any unnecessary explanations." Slipping on his trousers and pulling on his now-slightly-wrinkled but originally impeccably-pressed pinpoint Oxford, he buttoned his shirt and tucked it in neatly. Her face grew hot when she realized she was watching his hands intently with each foray into his pants. She fought off a smile when she noticed a smudge of flour on his belt.

"Will I see you again?" *Wait, was she falling for him?* Her teeth found her bottom lip again as soon as the desperate words had left her mouth. She couldn't take them back, but he didn't seem put off.

Instead, his face lit up, and he said, "I'd love to. Can't wait."

Relieved he hadn't laughed and made a non-committal comment, she slipped out from the mess of covers the bed had turned into and began dressing; first the bra he'd rescued, then her panties from the floor next to the bed. Instead of putting on the previous evenings' outfit—seriously, what says I slept with my date louder than wearing the same clothes he'd picked you up in?—she grabbed jeans and a sweatshirt from the dresser.

After she straightened up from slipping on her Rothy's, he pulled her into his arms, and they kissed—passionately—one more time. Then she led him down the stairs—him clomping in his walking boot and her wrist cast clicking on the railing—past her mother's closed door to the front door, checking for errant pieces of clothing along the way.

As Victoria grabbed the knob, she felt it turn in her hand and move toward her. In stepped her mother, halting to read the room. Victoria sensed Emerson retreating a step or two behind her.

"Well, good morning," Millie chirped, her sing-song voice rattling inside Victoria's head, strumming the beginnings of a migraine. Her mother gave Emerson a once-over.

"Mom, what—" Victoria wasn't sure what to ask. "Where have you been?"

With an indignant shrug of her shoulders, she said, "I left you a note on the counter. I had a date."

"A date?"

"Ha! Yes, a date. I'm sure that seems out of the realm of possibilities for me, but I did."

"With who?"

"Jacob."

"Jacob who?"

"Oh, I don't know. I can't remember his last name. He's the lovely gentleman who picked me up at Brookhaven."

"I see. So, you guys had a date . . . last night?"

"No, silly. We went out for coffee this morning."

"Oh."

"He knew he'd be coming here to pick up your friend, so he came early, and we went out for a bit."

It made Victoria wonder how far in advance Emerson knew he'd be staying over. And if the driver had been the one who had picked up Millie from Brookhaven, did that mean Vince and Emerson hired cars from the same company or did the driver work for more than one company?

As if anticipating Victoria's next question, Millie added, "Yes, I gave him the phone number here when he brought me home the first time."

Victoria couldn't miss the warm glow on her mother's cheeks, her lips pressed into a crooked grin she seemed to be struggling to keep from turning into a full-fledged toothy smile.

Good for her. If Emerson hadn't been breathing down her neck, Victoria would have dusted off her pompoms to cheer for her.

After an awkward moment of Emerson excusing himself, Millie left them to their goodbyes. He stepped onto the front stoop, taking Victoria's hand in his in a smooth, effortless movement. He turned back and placed another warm kiss on her lips. "I had an amazing time with you last night. Hope we can do it again soon." Then he repeated what he had said in the helicopter. "You should be loved." He gave one last squeeze before sliding his hand away, hanging onto the tips of her fingers, and then letting them go. They grew cold with the absence of his touch.

As he headed toward his hired car, idling smack in the middle of her driveway, she watched him from the doorway, holding the screen open, and wondering when he'd arranged to have his driver stop back to pick him up. Surely he hadn't waited in the driveway all night. No, Emerson wouldn't have expected him to do that. *What would the neighbors have thought?*

With a final wave, Victoria let the screen door swing to, catching the latch before it banged shut. Pulling on the inside door, she paused to peek through the sliver of an opening and watch the rear end of the black Caddy disappear around the bend. She hoped she would see him again. Hopefully he'd had a good time. He said he did, but he could have been putting on a good act. She hoped she hadn't come across as too pathetic.

Stepping back, she did a doubletake when she noticed another car had come up behind Emerson's, following in the same direction. She tried to tell herself it wasn't anyone she knew, but it looked remarkably like Vince's black Mercedes. Or was it dark navy? She couldn't tell one model from another—just the general color—so it could have been anyone driving that car. Anyone who wasn't interested in who Victoria entertained at her home.

"So . . . who was that?"

Victoria jumped at the sound of her mother's voice. She stood with hands on her hips in the doorway to the kitchen, silently demanding an answer.

Stepping out from behind the front door, Victoria pushed it closed and said, "Emerson. Remember, you met him last night in the kitchen? He took me to dinner."

"Oh, I guess it was the mussed bedhead hair that threw me off. Ha! And then you slept together?" Her mother's judgment splattered across the small foyer as she spit out each word.

Pulling in a lungful of air, Victoria paused to let her mother hear the intrusive question that had erupted from her mouth and caromed off the walls.

"I'll take that as a yes."

"It's none of your damn business," Victoria snapped. She resented her mother being there to witness when she had a male visitor and every misstep she took.

"Well, I hate to be so blunt, but it's kind of obvious when you parade through here with your gentlemen friends." Her mother's expression turned puzzled. "What happened to the other guy? What was his name?"

"Vince?"

"Yeah. He seemed like a nice guy. Did you dump him?"

"Oh, come on, Mom. Let it go."

"Let it go? What's that supposed to mean? I see one guy who you seem serious with, and then he disappears. And now this English chap shows up—it's almost like he was waiting for you to break up with Vince."

She'd remembered his name this time. Was she angry that her mother was getting too nosy or that her observations were spot on?

Chapter Twenty-Six

"So . . . how are you doing? Still have bruising under your eyes?"

Leave it to Aviva to hone in on the area Victoria was most sensitive about.

"I'm fine. Healing nicely. Thank God for makeup."

"That's good. How long do you have to have the cast on?"

"It will be several weeks."

"That sucks."

"Yeah."

"So what's up with your new guy? The British chap. What's his name?" Aviva had never been good with names, but Victoria didn't mind filling her in.

"Emerson." Just saying it out loud sent a flutter through her abdomen.

"Oh my God, I can hear you smiling on the other end of the phone. Tell me about him. Clearly he's got you giddy."

"I don't know about giddy, but he's certainly . . ." None of the adjectives that were coming to mind seemed adequate. And a single word wouldn't do.

"What?" Aviva pressed. "Who is he? What's he like?"

"Oh, Aviva, I feel amazing when I'm with him. It's like—even in this ridiculously large, impersonal, very distracted world—I'm his only focus. He is always present when he's with me." And she didn't want to blow it with him like she had with Vince.

"How fabulous is that!"

"He showed up at my door the other day and surprised me with flowers. It was the largest bouquet I'd ever seen. Could barely see around it to see who was holding it. Another day he whisked me off to Mystic in a limo for lunch at my favorite seafood restaurant.

Afterward he chartered a boat for just the two of us, and we sailed along the coastline, admiring the foliage."

"Yeah, I'm sure the two of you were leaf peeping. Nothing like a little afternoon delight. *And on a boat.* Good for you."

"We had another dinner out at this—well, you get the idea. He makes me feel amazing," Victoria repeated, ignoring her friend's teasing.

"That's what a guy should do. The right guy."

The fact that the advice was coming from a divorcee, who was not in a current relationship, amused Victoria.

"I've never experienced that before. It almost seems like . . ."

"What?"

"I don't know."

"Yes, you do. Just say it."

"Like it won't last, or . . ." Victoria fingered a chain around her neck with a diamond pendant. She had discovered it there after their first date, the latter part of which was a blur and ended with the two of them waking up in the same bed the next morning.

"Why wouldn't it last?"

"It just so exciting being with him. I feel incredible. It seems to be mutual. How can we sustain it?"

Aviva snickered. "I wouldn't worry about that now. Enjoy the ride. What if this one's a keeper?"

"I don't know. We'll see."

"The guy is loaded. Gives you gifts. Clearly the sex is good."

Victoria could feel her cheeks warming. "So far. . . . He's traveling now and I can't wait to see him when he gets back."

"What does he do?"

The only thing that surprised Victoria about Aviva asking the question was that she hadn't asked sooner. It made Victoria realize how little she knew about Emerson.

"I . . . I don't know, exactly. Investments or something along those lines."

With little to grab onto there, Aviva jumped to another question she'd been dying to ask.

"Are you feeling guilty about Vince?"

"A little." She acknowledged to herself it was more than a little. And not just about Vince. Her husband was still missing, and yet she couldn't deny she longed for a man's companionship. A man's soft touch. His attention.

"Hey, does that mean Vince is available?"

Leave it to Aviva to go after her ex while his side of the bed was still warm. Then it hit her that she'd allowed Emerson onto that side.

"Really, Aviva?"

"Just thought I'd ask . . . for a friend."

"Sure."

"I mean, Vince is nice too. Also loaded. Brought you gifts."

Victoria could hear herself saying, "Yeah, but he doesn't have time for me. It's as if all the lavish gifts are a deposit, a promise to make good on in the future."

"You've had some interesting guys in your life, Tori. And they all seem so different. Vince, while rough around the edges, especially when he lets his Long Island accent slip, is a real go-getter. And sweet to you. Robert was Mr. Academia with an obvious soft side, successful in his own right. Not very exciting, so busy with everything he had going on, on campus, but everybody loved him."

Victoria hated that her friend spoke of Robert in the past tense.

"But this new guy seems perfect from what I'm hearing. I'd *love* to meet him. Successful, suave, incredibly good looking, well-traveled, treats you like a queen—like you should be treated. I'd hang onto that one, girl. If you're not careful, I might snag him up." She snickered again.

Silence on the other end gave Victoria a moment to consider the irony of it all. She couldn't commit to Vince because Robert could still be out there, so she'd lost him. Emerson showed up and picked up where Vince had left off, showering her with gifts and, more importantly, time together, and she'd let him seduce her. Yet the guilt she was ravaged with for indulging with other men was twisting her insides. What she really wanted was Robert back. She wanted their life back.

And Harrison's call during dinner with Emerson was still on her mind. Although she found it doubtful Harrison had actually found Robert's car by searching satellite images—after all, there had to be an unfathomable number of similar cars, and why wouldn't someone else have noticed it?—still, it knocked her in the gut when she realized what it might mean. A more likely explanation was that Harrison ached to have his father back, and he'd convinced himself he'd found his car. If there was any validity to his discovery, it could indicate foul play. And she wasn't ready to accept that.

CHAPTER TWENTY-SEVEN

Water poured in all around her. At first it was just around her feet. It was cold and rose quickly. She tried to get her head above it but something was holding her back. Panic took over and she flailed with her arms, only to splash water onto her face and into her nose.

Her thrashing became more difficult as her arms grew tired. She woke up tangled in the sheets, trying to throw them off her. The cold sweat was all too familiar. Glancing to the empty side of the bed, part of her was relieved Vince wasn't sleeping there anymore—or that last night was not another date with Emerson.

Unwrapping herself, Victoria pulled her legs out of the wadded up Egyptian cotton, swung them around, and plunked her feet on the bedside rug. Leaving her fuzzy slippers behind, she shuffled to the bath and turned on the shower for another middle of the night cleansing. It would only be a temporary fix, but after her nightmare, there would be no more sleeping until perhaps an afternoon nap on the couch.

THE RINGING ON THE OTHER end of the line buzzed in her ear. Once, twice, three times. Why wasn't she picking up? *Come on Veeve,* Victoria urged. After the fourth ring, there was a click, then some indiscernible rustling.

"Yeah . . ." Aviva's voice was ragged.

"There you are. Oh, Veeve, did I wake you?"

"No, I always sound this crappy when I answer the phone."

"I'm sorry. Did you fly yesterday?"

"Yeah. Got stuck in Toledo because of a massive storm front that hovered. Haven't seen a light show like that in a while." She laughed. "And I spend a lot of time up in the sky where they happen."

"That sucks. Toledo?"

"It wasn't so much *where* we were stranded. It was more a matter of how long. We didn't get clearance until almost midnight and got into Bradley around 1:30 this morning."

"Do you have to fly today?"

"No, thank God."

There was a pause while Victoria considered if she should ask.

"So, what's up? I'm sure you didn't call just to wake me up."

"Aviva, I'm sorry. I didn't mean to—"

"I know you didn't. Tell me what's up, so I can go back to sleep."

Victoria hesitated.

"Tori, what do you need? If you don't tell me I'm going to hang up, so spill."

Victoria said, "Today's the day."

"What? What day?"

"The field trip."

"The field trip? . . . Oh, God. Did they leave yet?"

"No. I don't think so. I think they're supposed to leave around eight."

"What are you going to do? Follow the bus down there and trail his every move?"

"No, I can't do that."

"So, what do you need from me?"

"I thought maybe you might want to . . . go out for breakfast."

"And lunch and dinner?" The roughness had returned to Aviva's voice. Part of Victoria felt badly for waking her up after a late night at work, but the rest of her needed her friend to suck it up and be a friend today.

"I need some company today."

"And a distraction?"

"Yes, that would be helpful."

"You could come over here and watch me sleep."

"Funny. Okay, forget it. Obviously I've caught you at the wrong time. I'll find someone else to be my friend today."

"Oh, Victoria, you're killing me. Of course, I'll hang with you today." She exhaled noisily. Rustling in Victoria's ear suggested Aviva was dragging herself out of bed. "Just give me . . ." Victoria waited for her to continue. "Could we make it lunch? I would love to catch a little more sleep. Maybe you could text Jameson throughout the morning to confirm everything is all right."

"I can't do that either. He'll think I'm hovering."

Silence on the other end told her Aviva agreed.

"Just tell him you're thinking of him, and you hope he has a fun trip—however you would say it in your own words. And you could ask him to text you when they got there."

Victoria shook her head. Jameson was terrible about remembering to text, even when asked.

"Wait a minute. Isn't there something you can activate on your phone to track his? Find a friend or something like that?"

"Well, yes, but the other person has to enable you to do that. Besides, I already tried that—I asked—and he didn't want to have anything to do with it."

"Kids." This from the expert, even though she'd never had any.

"All right, I like your idea of texting him. Hopefully he'll respond. Where would you like to have lunch?"

"How about someplace closer to you?" Aviva offered.

"That's very sweet of you. Serenson's again?"

"Sure."

"Noon?"

"Uh . . . how about 1:00?"

"Okay, see you then. And, Veeve, thanks. I appreciate it."

"I know you do."

VICTORIA AND JAMESON EXCHANGED a couple of texts, but it did little to ease her anxiety about him in the Big City on the same field trip his father—her husband—disappeared from. She found herself pacing from the kitchen to the living room and back again with wild scenarios scrolling through her head. Why had she let him go? She'd had no choice; he probably would have forged her signature if she hadn't signed his permission slip.

Pulling up the email with the field trip itinerary Erin had sent to her, Victoria could see the boys' first stop was at the 9/11 Memorial for a solemn tour through the museum, commemorating the terrorist attacks that occurred before the boys had been born. Afterward, they would scarf down a boxed lunch on the bus on their way to the New York Historical Society. There she imagined them shuffling through the exhibits, jotting down notes, and nodding at appropriate times to convey rapt interest for the tour guide. Grinning, she knew Jameson was genuinely interested in the subject matter, even if some of the others were not.

Late afternoon, dinner would be at Antonio's, a three-generation Italian restaurant at Broadway and West 52nd Street, that could fill up the stomachs of teenage student athletes with pasta and bread without breaking the budget, before getting dropped off at the Richard Rodgers Theatre for the play.

Her phone pinged and Victoria snatched it off the counter. It was Aviva asking if they could push their lunch to two-thirty.

"Damn it, Veeve. I'm starving," she barked at no one. Dropping her cell onto the counter, she yanked open the refrigerator door, gazing inside without actually seeing what she was looking at. Finally leftover pizza in its original box came into view, so she grabbed it. Before the door swung shut, she latched onto the wine bottle on the door and slipped it out. A glance to the wall clock told her it was early afternoon. "As they say, it's five o'clock somewhere."

Silently reprimanding herself as she poured the chardonnay into one of her larger wine glasses, she countered, "Don't get me started. I held out that long. I can't do it any longer. I tried to get a distraction for today, but she didn't show up for me." Closing her eyes, she took a long sip and enjoyed the sensation of the alcohol trickling down her throat. Her fingers were crossed her mother didn't wake from her midday nap earlier than usual.

Day drinking. She promised herself it was just for today. Today was different than any other. After sliding a large slice of pizza into the toaster oven, she returned to her glass while she waited for the bell to signal her lunch was ready.

Her phone buzzed again, and she realized she'd never responded to Aviva's text.

// so is that okay?? //

Victoria answered:

// No I got hungry. I'm eating now. How about an early dinner? //

It took a couple of beats before she responded:

// okay //

A few minutes later, she added:

// ill pick up Serenson's and bring it to your house. //

// Sounds good. //

VICTORIA WOKE UP ON the living room couch to dishes clattering in the kitchen. The dull ache behind her forehead and the pastiness on her tongue reminded her of her beverage choice with lunch. Had she finished the bottle? If so, did she tuck the empty into the bottom of the trash so her mother wouldn't notice?

A quick check of the time told her Jameson and his friends were in the throes of plodding through the New York Historical Society. She imagined their bodies had already burned through their boxed lunches, and they were anxious to go to dinner to hold them over during the play—the Broadway production of Hamilton. It reminded her how much she wanted to see the performance, and she put it back on the top of her mental wish list. Some day. She'd drag a friend and go to the city for the day. Robert would have gone with her without hesitation. Maybe she would ask her mother.

Shuffling into the kitchen, she paused at the island and braced herself with two hands, watching her mother unloading the dishwasher, catching a whiff of apple crisp she'd whipped together earlier to use up the apples occupying the fruit bowl and to pass the time. Clutching a stack of white ceramic plates with both hands, Millie shrieked as she caught sight of Victoria and let them slip from her grasp. They hit the floor with a thunderous crash to which Victoria let out a yelp. Instantly Millie burst into tears.

"Oh, look what I've done. I'm so sorry. I didn't know you were there."

Leaping to her aid, Victoria said, "Mom, I'm sorry. I didn't mean to scare you. Don't worry about it; they're just plates. And they're cheap ones at that."

"I'm sorry," she wailed.

"Mom, it's okay. What's more important is: are you okay? Did you get hurt?"

"Oh, look what I've done. Please don't be mad. I don't want you to kick me out."

"Mom! I would never do that. I'm not mad. It was an accident. You didn't mean to."

"No, I didn't. I'm so sorry."

"It's okay. Really. It was my fault anyway. I startled you. But as long as you're okay, that's all that matters."

Fetching the broom and dustpan from the closet, Victoria swept up the mess and continued to calm her mother. The larger pieces of ceramic clunked when she dropped them into the trashcan from under the sink. Millie stood idly by, wiping her tears and watching Victoria work. When the doorbell rang, they both jumped.

Before they'd had a chance to get out of the kitchen, Aviva appeared in the doorway holding up a brown paper tote emblazoned with a Serenson's logo sticker in each hand. "Hello! Hello! Hello! Dinner has arrived, ladies." As an aside to Victoria she mumbled, "Sorry it took so long to get here. You okay?"

Not wanting to clue in her mother to the anxiety-ridden day she couldn't wait to get past, Victoria brushed off the question. "Just great." She returned the trash can to its spot beneath the sink but left the broom leaning against the island. "Thanks for bringing dinner. Good to see you."

The three settled in at the kitchen table, scooping takeout from cardboard containers, sharing three different entrees and generous sides. Victoria pulled out a bottle of wine from the wine rack and chilled it in the freezer for a few minutes. Impatient to wait until it was adequately cold, Victoria announced she was adding ice to their glasses and waited for a reaction but got none. The palates she was serving to weren't all that sophisticated; no one complained about the temperature or the watered-down wine. They were too busy winding the conversation in and out of safe topics until the room grew quiet.

At one point, Victoria caught her mother's gaze, in it a realization she'd figured out the need to be killing time together. Thankfully she didn't speak about it.

In the time they were at the kitchen table, it had grown dark. Victoria glanced at her watch. Just past eight-thirty. Within the hour, they would be boarding the buses soon to head out of the city and back to campus.

Victoria got up to refill glasses, opening another chardonnay, and returned to her seat, leaving the bottle on the table where it would be convenient to grab.

The conversation sputtered and died at times, but no one seemed to care. They were doing their best to keep it going and fill in the silence between them, but as the evening wore on, there were more gaps than words. The long dinner and unspoken worries had drained the threesome of their usual jocularity.

Victoria fetched plates of apple crisp, warmed adequately in the microwave, and topped with a generous mound of whipped cream sprayed from a can she'd found in the back of the fridge. She crossed her fingers it was still good.

Just before ten o'clock, her phone pinged, causing a collective jolting among the three ladies. "Oh." She surprised herself she'd said it out loud.

"Who is it?" Aviva asked, always delving into other people's business. But in this case, Victoria didn't mind.

"It's Jameson."

"Really," her mother chimed in, inching forward on her chair.

"Yeah, he says they're boarding the buses and will be heading back soon. Wanted me to know so I wouldn't worry."

"There now, see? Everything is fine. Everything worked out," said her friend, the eternal optimist—after the fact.

Victoria could breathe again. The trip she'd been losing sleep over had gone off without a hitch. She'd stressed for nothing; her neurotic worrying nearly paralyzing her.

"Ha! What a good boy to let you know." Millie beamed with pride for her grandson.

Catching her mother's eye, Victoria said, "He sure is . . . *such* a good kid. He knew I would worry." She sent him a quick reply, thanking him for letting her know.

"All right, let's clean up this mess." Aviva stood abruptly, as if she were coming to attention, and clapped her hands together before gathering the empty containers. "I've got to hit the road."

"Oh, you don't have to do that, Veeve. We can get it. You went out of your way to order it and pick it up. And let me get my wallet so I can pay you for—"

"It's my treat. No problem." The three had the table cleared in no time, and Victoria walked her friend to the door.

"Hey, I'm really glad everything worked out today. Sorry if I wasn't much of a friend until late in the day. I was spent after last night." She reached out and hugged Victoria.

"As you said, it all worked out. That's all that matters." Victoria stopped short of lashing out at Aviva. Her friend had done what she could for her with the time and energy she had.

Instead, Victoria blamed herself for her own momentary lapse of judgment that occurred right before she grabbed the chardonnay bottle that afternoon. It wasn't the first time she'd dived head first into a bottle of wine when the heartache grew too much to bear. She couldn't let it become a habit, although she feared it already had. She'd had to fight against it in the past.

Pushing the inside door closed behind her friend, Victoria reflected on how well the day had turned out after all.

Jameson and all of his friends would be exhausted but had had a memorable day. She imagined the bus would be a veritable shouting match as they all shared their reactions to their experiences but would grow quiet once everyone had settled in, probably before they'd reached White Plains. By the time they made it to Litchfield Falls, most of the boys would probably be sound asleep and end up stumbling off the bus to find their dorms. The morning would bring refreshed bodies, but with minds that had been expanded by their excursion into a new world they'd had the privilege of visiting.

IN THE MIDST OF a wine-induced sound sleep, one that Victoria hadn't experienced in a while, her cell chirped to life on the bedside table. It wasn't a familiar number, but it was a Connecticut area code, so she did her best to shake off her slumber and grab it.

"Hello?" It came out uneven—more like a croak than a word—so she put a hand over her cell and cleared her throat.

"Victoria?"

"Yes." She cleared her throat again. "Yes."

"This is Ben Martin." She didn't recognize him at first. It wasn't the robust, in-your-face, booming-like-an-auctioneer voice per usual.

"Hi, Ben. Uh . . . what's going on?"

"I . . . I don't know how else to tell you. . . . Jameson is missing."

CHAPTER TWENTY-EIGHT

"What? How can that be? He texted me . . ." Her heart raced. Her breathing became hard to control. Panic rose in her chest. "What's going on? This can't be. Oh, God. Not again."

"I'm still in the city, talking with the police, trying to figure out what happened."

"What *did* happen? How could you let this happen, Ben?" She could hear herself shrieking. "For God's sake, you're responsible for our children. How could you let him out of your sight?"

"It wasn't that simple."

"I'll tell you what is. You take a group of kids to the city, and you keep an eye on them. Too many bad things can happen there. How could you let this happen?"

"Victoria, I assure you, I was keeping an eye on the boys—Jameson, in particular."

"How could this happen? What did you do?"

"It had to have been during the intermission at the play. He left to go to the restroom and I didn't see him come back. I thought I saw him come back to his seat after the lights went back down, but apparently not. Or if he did, he left before the end of the play."

"You son of a bitch. How could you let this happen?" She sensed someone in her doorway and expected it to be her mother, but no one was there. Millie could sleep through the worst thunderstorm. "Find him, damn it. Find him."

Collapsing onto the bed, she let the phone slip from her hand and buried her face into the pillows, sobbing. *Her son. Now her son was missing. Not again. Not Jameson. Oh, God, please bring him back safely. Please let him be all right. Bring him back to me.*

Gasping for breaths between sobs, Victoria could sense someone talking near her.

Wiping her eyes, she picked up the phone and said, "Hello."

"Oh, there you are. Mrs. Sands, this is Officer Webster."

"Yes."

"Ma'am, we're going to do everything we can to find your son." The words sent a chill through her. They echoed what she was told during the search for Robert. "When was the last time you talked to him?"

"The last time? . . . Uh . . . we text more than talk."

"When was the last time you saw him face-to-face?"

"That would have been at Grandparents Day," she said, more to herself than the officer. "That was a couple weeks ago."

"Can you tell me if you had any contact with him today. I know he's a student at a boarding school, but did you speak to him or have any contact at all?"

"No . . . oh, wait. He, uh . . ." She struggled to push down a sob. "He texted me tonight and said they were boarding the buses and would be leaving the city soon."

"What time was that, ma'am?"

"Oh, God, let me see. . . ." She rubbed her forehead, took a few steps and turned back, retracing them. "Uh, I think it was around ten o'clock. Yeah, I remember looking at the time. And I thought they'd get back to campus around midnight."

"Ten. Okay."

"But, wait. How can that be? Ben Martin said Jameson went missing during the intermission at the play."

"Yes, ma'am. He mentioned that. We're still putting all the pieces together."

"Well, that doesn't make any sense. How could he have gone missing during the play and then text me later to say they were getting on the buses?"

"I don't know, Mrs. Sands. But we're working hard to figure it all out." More of his words spilled from her phone but grew muffled. Her eyesight blurred and the phone slipped from her hand. She felt her knees bending and the floor rushing up toward her.

Chapter Twenty-Nine

As black asterisks popped in and faded out of her sight, she blinked them away and pulled herself up onto her bed. The call with Ben came rushing back to her. Her baby was gone. Just like she said it would happen, but no one would listen. Now they were both gone. Her insides ached. It felt like something dark and virulent was eating away at her, coming after her.

Shuffling to the door, she left her robe draped across the end of the bed and ignored the chill that brushed against her skin. Her thin sleeveless negligee provided little coverage, her bare feet hitting the cold, hardwood floor in the hall.

Her mother's room was dark, the door ajar. Victoria could hear her heavily nasal breathing. It reminded her of a getaway to Cape Cod they'd taken not long after Victoria had started her job as a flight attendant. Not willing to splurge on separate hotel rooms, they slept in side-by-side twin-sized beds—rather, Millie slept. Victoria struggled to catch enough sleep to function. After a couple of days she couldn't stand it any longer. They cut the mini-vacation short by a day.

A rush of frigid air hit her in the face. She made a note to herself the ice cube trays were nearly empty. How had she gotten there? The freezer wasn't where she'd meant to go. She closed the door and opened the refrigerator. On the door was a nearly full magnum of chardonnay. She grabbed it by the neck, unscrewed the top, and put it to her lips. There was no taste, just coldness. She shook off a shiver and headed back to the stairs, the bottle bumping against her leg with every other step. A toe caught on the bottom of her nightgown, and she stumbled, landing sprawled on the steps. Still hanging onto the neck of the bottle, yanking her gown up over her knees, she gathered herself and headed up the stairs.

Stopping at her mother's door, Victoria listened for her beathing, the silence feeling like a smothering hand. Why was there no sound? Then a snort and back to snoring. Relieved, Victoria slipped back into her room, eased the door shut behind her, and headed for the tiny bathroom.

Taking slugs from the bottle, Victoria sat on the edge of the tub and played with the water spilling from the faucet with undulating fingers. The temperature got hotter as she flicked it. *Her precious son was gone.*

Soon the tub was nearly full and Victoria eased her body into it, her nightgown clinging to her legs and torso. The heat took her breath away in a gasp. A quiet voice told her she should get out; it was too hot. But she ignored it and settled into the ceramic enclosure, pulling her legs up so she could rest the bottle on one knee. *Sweet Jameson was gone.*

The water gushing from the faucet held her gaze. The rest of the bathroom in her periphery was a blur. More slugs from the bottle. Was it already past half-empty? She regretted not bringing more than one. She would go get another when this one was gone. A few more slugs. She could see the water level had reached the top edge of the tub. Sliding deeper, her eyes rested just above the water. *Why was he taken from her?*

One more long slug and the bottle was empty. *Damn it!* Hurling it at the back of the door, she slid under the water. The bottle hit with a thud and crashed to the tile floor. The shattering across the tiny bathroom was muffled in her ears.

CHAPTER THIRTY

Waking to dim light, Victoria felt her arms wrapped tightly around her legs, pulled close to her chest. She listened to hushed murmurings nearby and recognized her mother's and Aviva's voices.

Victoria recalled their dinner together at the kitchen table. The text from Jameson. Saying goodbye to Aviva after dinner.

Then the middle-of-the-night call came rushing back to her. Her mother must have summoned her friend to her bedside in her time of need.

"Mom?" She forced the word to come out.

"Oh, she's awake," Millie said softly and approached the bed, taking Victoria's hand. "I'm here."

"What's going on?" Fishing her arms out of the blanket wrapped around her, she glanced down at her nightgown. It stuck to her like the scales on a fish. Her shoulders shook as a chill ripped through her.

"What's going on? I'd like to ask that question too, Victoria. You gave me such a fright. I woke up to a bang and then breaking glass. I thought someone was breaking in."

It was only then that Victoria noticed a policeman standing out in the hall, one hand on the doorframe, leaning in, looking half-interested.

"I called out to you, but you didn't answer, so I called 911. Before this nice gentleman came to my rescue—" She gestured toward the man in blue. "—I found you in the tub." Her eyes grew wide, revisiting the scene permanently etched in her memory. "Victoria, you were underwater. I thought you'd drowned." Her voice faltered, and she swallowed before continuing. "It was all I could do to pull you up to get your face out of the water. There was water and broken glass everywhere. I turned off the faucet and held you until the tub drained enough." She pressed her eyes closed as if fighting off the image of her daughter unconscious and submerged in water. *Would the pain and loss ever end for this family?* "When he came to the door, I screamed, and he broke it down to get in."

Victoria recalled a muffled scream.

"He was able to pull you out and get you to the bed. Miraculously you started to breathe on your own." Millie flopped onto the end of the bed, one hand grasping the footboard as if she'd been drained of every last bit of energy and had nothing left to hold herself up. She fell silent but didn't make eye contact with Victoria, a frail hand motionless in her lap.

The gravity of what she'd put her mother through started to sink in.

"What the hell were you thinking, Victoria? For God's sake, you can't keep drinking like you do. What do you think would have happened if I hadn't been here? . . . I'll tell you what would have happened; you'd be dead right now. If I hadn't walked in when I did, you'd be dead."

"Like Jameson?" The self-induced fog was clearing, and a torrent of pain came crashing over her like white water in a raging river.

"What? Don't say that."

"It's probably true. Tonight I got a call from the headmaster that Jameson had gone missing from the field trip." Victoria could sense another figure in the doorway.

"Oh, dear God. No." Millie covered her mouth with a pale, age-spot-covered hand. Some sort of throaty groan emanated from Aviva nearby.

"Did the New York police call back?" Victoria asked but already knew the answer.

"No, not while I've been in your room," Aviva said.

"Maybe they've found him by now." Victoria was hopeful.

"Tori." It was Vince from the doorway.

She rolled over toward his voice. "Vince. You're here."

He pushed past the cop and perched on the edge of her bed. "Of course, I am. Come here." He scooped her top half off the bed and hugged her. She felt her wet nightgown stuck to her body like a second skin. "It's going to be okay."

Pulling back to look him in the eye, she asked, "How can you possibly say that? You don't know. It didn't turn out okay last time."

"This will be different; you'll see. Different situation."

"How is it different, Vince?" She pulled farther away, out of his arms, and propped herself up on the pillows behind her. "It *is* the same situation. Robert disappeared on this trip to New York seven years ago. And now Jameson has. I *knew* I shouldn't let him go." She gasped between sobs. "I *knew* it."

"I'm sure they're doing everything they can to find him," Vince continued.

"Don't say that. That's what they said last time, and it wasn't true."

He reached out to pull her into another hug, and she scooted across to the other side of the bed out of reach. "Leave me alone." Sliding her feet onto the floor, she got up and pulled jeans from her dresser.

Aviva stepped toward her. "Tori, what are you doing?"

Shoving one leg into the pants, she kept her gaze on her task. "Going to go look for Jameson." Nearly losing her balance as she jammed her other leg in, she caught herself by grabbing onto the dresser.

Everyone started talking at once—all trying to reason with her. *She was being irrational. It was the middle of the night. She couldn't take off for New York City by herself. Where would she look? Let the professionals do their work.*

"And how did that work out last time? I'm going. I can't sit here idly, hoping they'll get lucky and find him."

Turning her back to everyone, she whipped her nightgown over her head, sending a chill through her, and pulled on the first sweater she put her hands on in the middle drawer, a heather teal green cable knit—not her favorite but it would do. And ordinarily it wouldn't have seemed odd to be dressing in front of any one of the individuals in the room—but all three at once? She didn't care. And the cop in the doorway didn't seem to either.

"What if the police need to talk to you?" Her mother attempted a fresh angle.

"I'll have my cell with me."

Millie could only shrug in response.

"I'll go with you then," Vince insisted.

"What are you going to do, drive down to the city?" Millie protested.

"It's not even light yet," Aviva added.

"It will be when I get there," Victoria said.

With a slight shake of his head, Vince mumbled, "I'll call for a car."

Millie followed with, "Aviva and I will stay here in case Jameson comes home."

A muffled chirping came from under the bedcovers. Victoria dove in the direction of the sound before anyone else could move. Frantically burrowing into the sheets, her hand made contact with her cell. Sliding it out, she answered. "Hello?"

"Victoria, Ben here."

"Did you find him?"

"Not yet."

"For God's sake, Ben. Find him. Where could he have gone?"

"Listen, you told the officer Jameson texted you around ten to say we were boarding the buses. Correct?"

"Yeah. Why do you ask?"

"I'm trying to make sense of it. No one saw him after intermission at Rodgers Theatre."

"Who was he hanging out with yesterday?"

"In talking to the boys, several seemed to think he and Asher were sitting together on the bus, at the back of the bus."

"Asher . . ." Emerson's son, Victoria noted. "That would make sense. They're good friends."

"Yeah, but Asher wasn't as definitive about it. Sounded more like they rode down together but then split up once they got to the city."

"So, who else said they'd hung out with him?"

"No one."

"Who did he sit with at the play?"

"We were scattered around the theater, but from what I could tell he sat next to Collin Drysdale, but apparently the kid fell asleep and didn't realize Jameson never came back to his seat. When he woke up, the play was over, and he figured Jameson had headed for the bus without waking him up."

"And you talked to all the boys?"

"I believe so."

"Ask them all again. Someone knows something."

"I can't."

"Why the hell not?"

"The buses headed back to campus."

"What?"

"I stayed behind to be available to the police."

"Oh my God, why did you let them go? Someone must know something."

"Victoria, did you try calling or texting him after you heard from him? Have you tried since I first called?"

"Hold on. Let me try."

Putting the headmaster on hold, Victoria tried Jameson's cell. It rang a few times and went to voicemail. Hanging up, she banged out a text to him:

// Jameson I know its late but plz txt me to let me know your ok when you get this ok? Thx //

She stared at her phone but got no response.

Taking Ben off hold, Victoria said, "He's not answering."

"Okay. Glad you tried."

"Hey, why don't you ask the police to trace his phone or whatever it is they do."

"They already did. They pinged his phone but got nothing. He may have turned it off."

"That doesn't sound right. What teenager do you know of, Ben, that turns off their phone? They're available to each other 24/7."

"Some do when they want to sleep uninterrupted."

"Well, I don't think that's what's going on here."

Victoria thought of two reasons Jameson's phone was off: either he didn't want to be found or something terrible had happened to him, and there was nothing left of him to be found.

CHAPTER THIRTY-ONE

Vince stayed by her side initially, for the first couple of days. Their midnight ride to Manhattan proved to be an exercise in futility—one she surmised Vince knew in advance how it would play out but went through the motions for her anyway. Victoria retraced the events of that night, over and over, trying to discern if they'd missed something.

By the third day, Emerson called to assure her everything would be okay. He regretted not being able to be with her, having run into some sort of a snag on his business trip to Brussels that required him to stay longer.

After that, days blurred into one another. *How long had he been missing?* Victoria texted and left voice messages for Jameson until she could only listen to the compassionless voice informing her his mailbox was full and to try later.

Her nightmare of water pouring in on top of her wouldn't go away. Instead, it got worse. It took longer for her to wake up out of the dream into a cold sweat. And what had been a once-in-a-while occurrence, suddenly became a nightly event. Jameson's disappearance had exacerbated her uncontrollable and deep-seated fears that had set in after Robert had gone missing.

A fog hung in her head, making it difficult to function, like she was slogging through chest-deep water, ankle deep in mud.

Conversations turned into snippets that came to her later, sounding familiar, but she wasn't entirely sure they'd occurred:

Vince: "Have you told Harrison yet?"

Victoria: "Harrison? No . . . no I haven't told him."

Vince: "Don't you think you should?"

Victoria: "No, I don't want to interrupt him. He's so busy with his coursework. There's nothing he can do anyway."

Vince: "That's true, but he really should know."

VICTORIA: "MOM, THERE'S A cupcake missing. I told you I didn't have any extras."

Millie: "What, Tori?"

Victoria: "The cupcakes for the bridal shower. There's one missing. Did you take it?"

Millie: "Ha! I can't believe you're accusing me. You said there wouldn't be any extras. I listened."

"Victoria: "Well, where is it? I'm one short."

Millie: "Why are you even worrying about this? You've got more important things going on."

Victoria: "Mom, I can't just say sorry, I didn't feel like it."

Millie: "I think they'd understand."

Victoria: "Maybe. But that isn't the point. I made a commitment."

CHAPTER THIRTY-TWO

Victoria felt herself falling forward as if someone had pushed her. Who was behind her? It was as though she was moving in slow motion. She could sense someone near her . . . speaking, but couldn't make out the words. They were muffled. She was falling in a space she thought should be familiar to her. What would she land on?

Then the impact. She winced when her head connected with something hard. She didn't have time to wonder what it was before blackness filled in where light had been.

As she lay there, stunned from her fall, her eyes adjusted to the dim light of the room. She was back in the dark-wood-paneled den with the navy and burgundy striped curtains pulled back with coordinating navy cords that had come with the house. Robert had liked them, so she'd left them at the time. She'd been meaning to update the window treatments and paint the room to brighten it up but had never gotten around to doing it.

Another dream that had pulled her out of a sound sleep. But this one was different than the rest. There was no water surrounding her, threatening to fill her lungs and extinguish her last breath. Someone had struck her or caused her to fall and strike her head. She had the sense it was someone she knew and the attack came out of nowhere. Entirely unexpected.

Swinging her legs off the couch, she plopped her feet in the general direction of her flip flops and slid them in, cradling her chin in her upturned palms. Maybe the afternoon naps weren't such a good idea. They seemed to invite more of the nightmares. She couldn't escape them.

CHAPTER THIRTY-THREE

The soft glow from a full moon filtered through the trees and into the kitchen windows that ran along the back of the house, painting it all with dappled light. Victoria didn't bother flipping on the light switch. She could see to grab the handle of the refrigerator and, once the door was open, there was more than enough light to navigate the small space.

"What the—?" The shelf where she'd put the leftover lasagna to thaw—the one she'd frozen from the last night Vince had dinner there—was empty. She hadn't felt like cooking. Her mother must have beaten her to it. A late-night snack? "But the whole thing?" There had to have been three full servings left. Yanking open the dishwasher, Victoria pulled out both drawers but didn't see the decorative plate she'd transferred the leftovers to after dinner, her favorite blue and white toile pattern. "Mom, you know I don't like you eating in bed," she scolded her in absentia and made a mental note to retrieve the plate from her mother's bedside table in the morning.

With no lasagna to satisfy her empty stomach, she grabbed a package of microwave popcorn from the cupboard and tossed it into the countertop oven. As the turntable went round and round, she wandered over to the window and gazed out into the yard awash in speckled moonlight.

As the microwave started to beep, she caught sight of movement in the shed. It looked like a small light bobbing inside. At first she thought it was the light of the moonlight as the tree limbs swayed in the breeze. But she kept an eye on the trees, and when the limbs stopped moving, the light kept bouncing.

"What do you see?" Her mother's voice from the doorway made her jolt.

"Mom!" She grabbed the neck of her nightgown and smacked the edge of the counter with her free hand. "You scared the shit out of me."

"Hey, easy with the language. I didn't bring you up to say things like that."

"All right. All right. But look." She took hold of her mother's arm and pointed to where she'd seen the light bobbing.

"What?"

"Look out in the shed. There's someone there."

Victoria could see her mother's expression change, even in the dim light. "Oh my God, Victoria, call the police. Call the police. If they don't find anything they want there, the house will be next." Anxiety was building with each word.

"Okay, okay. Take it easy. The doors are locked."

As she bolted for the kitchen door, Millie turned back. "Like that will keep them from getting in. Ha! Use your head, girl." Not long after her mother disappeared into the foyer, Victoria heard her footsteps thumping up the stairs in quick fashion, the door to her room slam, and the sound of a piece of furniture sliding across the floor, presumably in front of the door. Millie wasn't taking any chances.

Acknowledging her mother's valid point, Victoria plucked her cell from the pocket of her robe and punched in 9-1-1. The dispatcher asked the nature of her emergency and just the word brought back a deluge of images from years earlier. It took her a moment before Victoria realized the woman was asking if anyone was on the line.

"Oh, yes, I'm sorry. Yes, could you send someone out? This is Victoria Sands. Someone has broken into our shed, and they're still there. I can see a light of some sort inside and it's moving."

"All right, ma'am. And what's your location?"

"My location?" Suddenly she couldn't think straight.

"Yes, ma'am. Your address. You're at home. Correct?"

"Yes." Her eyes were trained on the bobbing light in the shed, but whoever was inside never seemed to get close enough to the window for her to see anything.

"Okay, then. What's your address?"

"Uh . . . it's . . . twenty-two . . . uh . . . Twenty-two Peony Farm Rd."

"Okay, ma'am, I will send an officer right out."

"Thank you. Please hurry. My husband isn't here, so I'm really scared."

"Yes, ma'am. We can stay on the line if you'd like."

"Yes, I'd like that. Thank you."

"Hold on a sec while I dispatch the officer."

In seconds, the friendly voice came back on the line. "So, what are you seeing now. Do you still see a light in your shed?"

"Yes, it's still there." Victoria watched as the light bobbed a few more times and then went out. "Oh!"

"What's going on?"

"The light, it just went out."

"Did you see anyone leaving your shed?"

"Well, hard to tell in the dark, but I don't think so."

"Okay, you stay put."

Victoria had no intention of going anywhere while there was someone lurking in her yard but didn't bother to answer her.

"The officer will be there soon."

Staring into the darkness, she had to blink every so often to bring her eyes back into focus. Victoria listened for her mother upstairs but didn't hear a sound. She pictured her holed up in the closet, the comforter from her bed on top of her, and her eyes glued shut.

Before long, there was movement along the side yard, and Victoria jumped again, only to realize it was the responding officer. She glanced between the shed and the cop creeping toward it until he'd reached the small structure they used to store the lawn mower, an assortment of tools, and gardening odds and ends. Nothing of importance. Certainly nothing worth stealing. She couldn't imagine it would take someone long to figure out there was nothing of interest to them.

The officer yanked the door open and flipped on his flashlight, a powerful stream of light that illuminated the inside of the shed as well as his face. He seemed to be conversing with the intruder. Then he stepped inside.

"Oh, no, don't go in by yourself," Victoria pleaded. There was nothing to watch. No movement. No one close enough to the window for her to see anything.

"What's going on?" The voice behind her gave her a start again.

"Mom, what the hell. Don't walk up behind me like that."

"Hey," she barked. "What did I tell you about that mouth?"

"Okay, okay. Just don't scare me like that."

"What's going on?" Millie pressed.

"The police are here. I can't tell what's going on, but he went into the shed."

"Just one cop?"

"Yeah."

"What? No partner to back him up?"

"No, Mom. I guess this was a low priority tonight. Must be something much more interesting than a shed break-in going on in town." Then Victoria's gaze dropped to what her mother was holding to her side. "Whoa, where did you get that?"

Holding up a small black pistol dangling from her fingertips, Millie answered, "This? This is our backup. Our best buddy, Colt."

Victoria took a step away from it. "But where did you get that? Is it loaded?"

"Of course it's loaded. Ha! Wouldn't be any good to us if it wasn't."

"But where did you get it?"

"It was Robert's. He showed me where he kept it and where the bullets were."

"Robert's! How could that be? He never said anything—"

"He knew you'd act like this."

"My God, I had no idea. But you can't—"

"Look." She motioned toward the window with a floppy hand—her empty hand. "They're coming out."

"Go put that gun away before you get arrested for carrying without a permit."

"I have every right to have this in my home if someone is intruding."

"Get rid of it *now*," Victoria shrieked at her mother.

Victoria watched the officer with his hand on the forearm of a sizeable man, guiding him toward the back of the house. "What's he doing? Why isn't the guy in handcuffs? And why aren't they heading to his squad car?"

A few more steps and Victoria gasped, running to the door that led out to the patio.

"Tori, what are you doing?"

"It's him, Mom. It's him." She burst into tears as she opened the door and held it for the two men. "They found him."

"Ma'am," the officer was the first to speak. "I believe you know this guy?" He released his grip on the perp's arm and handed him what looked like a wallet.

"Yes, I do." Victoria struggled to piece together what was happening. Lunging toward him, she took him by the hand, pulled him close, and hung onto him like she'd never let go. She breathed in the scent of someone who'd been outside for a while. Mustiness, sweat, and green grass were the first aromas she could distinguish.

"I'm so sorry, Mom. I didn't mean to make you worry."

"Should have thought of that part sooner," the cop couldn't resist a poke.

Behind Victoria, her mother said, "Jameson?"

Jameson and his mother pulled apart, just far enough to be able to lock eyes. "What are you doing here? Oh, I'm so happy you're safe. Was that you in the shed?"

He nodded.

"What were you doing in there? I thought the worst. I thought you were gone like your father. Oh, is it really you?" She brushed away raindrops glistening on his cheekbone with the tips of her fingers.

"Did you have fun on your field trip, Jameson?" Millie chimed in. Victoria had all but forgotten her mother was still standing there.

"Mom, not now. Butt out." She pulled away from Jameson, allowing her to take in his full frame. He was back safe and sound, and it didn't matter why he didn't get back on the bus.

"I can ask him a question," Millie said, one hand on a hip.

Returning her focus to Jameson, she asked, "How was the play? Was it everything they say it is? Did you get to see Lin-Manuel Miranda? Oh, he so dreamy. I'd love to—"

"Mom, let it go. We can talk about that another time."

"But I'd like to know." She kept her focus on Jameson. "What my grandson does is of interest to me."

"Mom, cut it out." Victoria resisted the urge to smack her mother to snap her out of her nonsensical babble. "We need to talk with the officer right now."

"He's got a lot of explaining to do," the officer piped in. "He might be looking at some charges too."

"Charges? He was in his own shed. I'm sure there's a logical explanation. Give him a chance."

"Mom, I think we might need an attorney."

"An attorney? What do we need an attorney for? Don't be silly. Tell the officer what happened, and I'm sure everything will get straightened out. Both of you come inside." She motioned for them to follow her into the kitchen.

"Oh, don't you dare, Jameson." Millie pointed a crooked finger toward her grandson. "You keep your mouth shut. I'll call Vince. Don't you say another word, Jameson." Allowing time for her words to sink in, she shifted the aim of her wagging finger toward the officer before letting it drop. "Zip it." She nodded toward Jameson and ran an imaginary zipper across her lips with a thumb and forefinger pressed together.

Slipping the cell from the pocket of Victoria's robe, Millie headed for the dining room, but stopped in the doorway. "Not a word. Got it?"

Jameson nodded.

The kitchen got quiet while they waited for Millie to return. Victoria took hold of Jameson's hand again with the resolve to never let go. Hers grew clammy, but she wouldn't let up. She'd finally gotten him back, and nothing was going to take him from her again.

The officer excused himself and stepped out onto the patio. Victoria had to fight the urge to deadbolt the door behind him as he lit up a cigarette in the glow from the back porch light. Through the window, she watched as he leaned into his shoulder mic. There was some back and forth. After a final drag on his smoke, he flicked the butt into the garden and stepped back inside, announcing he'd be taking Jameson in.

"What? No!" Victoria let go of Jameson's hand long enough to wrap her arms around one of his and pull him closer. If it hadn't been such a sober situation, it would have looked humorous the way his hulking frame took up most of the cramped kitchen with his mother clinging to him like she'd been caught in a raging river and had grabbed onto a sturdy tree trunk, waiting to be rescued.

"I'm sorry, ma'am, but I've got orders."

"I think we can wait until his attorney gets here," she pleaded.

"No, ma'am, we can't. That's not the way it works."

"What do you mean, that's not the—"

"Okay, he's on his way." Millie burst back into the kitchen, snapping the tension for a split second, only to rachet it up again. "He said to stay put. He'll handle it. Ha!"

The officer chuckled. "Well, that's not going to happen." Before he'd finished his sentence, he yanked Jameson's arm out of his mother's grasp and turned him toward the back door.

"No! Please don't take him. She lunged for Jameson, but the officer pulled him just out of reach and through the door. "Let's go."

Victoria followed them to continue her protest, and the officer's free arm shot out toward her. "Ma'am, don't come any closer. Don't make this any worse than it has to be. You're going to get *yourself* into trouble." The two disappeared into the darkness once they'd cleared the limited reach of the sixty-watt bulb outside the kitchen door.

"I just got him back. . . ." Her words drifted off into the darkness.

She let the screen door slam shut.

"Give me that." Victoria snatched her phone from her mother's hand. Glancing to her other hand, Victoria was relieved to see it was empty. "Did you put the gun away?"

"Yes, dear."

"Back where you found it?"

"Not exactly, dear."

Victoria noticed a bulge in the pocket of her robe.

"Mom, not there. Put it back where you found it. I don't want it around."

"Okay, okay. I will. I had to put it somewhere while the cop was here."

Grateful her mother had had enough sense to conceal it, she added, "And leave it there. Don't take it out again."

"Of course, not . . . unless we need it."

"We *won't*. Mom, I don't want that gun around. It could easily be turned on us. I didn't even know Robert kept a gun. Is it registered? Well, even if it was, I imagine the permit would have expired. . . ." She let it drop to refocus on Jameson. "I'd better let Vince know to go straight to the police station."

CHAPTER THIRTY-FOUR

"All right, Jameson, spill," Victoria said, grateful he'd been released into her custody with no formal charges as of yet. She prayed law enforcement would see he'd made a silly mistake. A minor lapse of judgment. No one had gotten hurt.

"It was something that Martin said—"

"Mr. Martin to you."

"Not anymore. Just listen. At our field trip meeting a couple days before the trip, he told us to stick with the group and follow the rules for our off-campus excursion so we wouldn't get separated from the group and be lost forever. I swear he was looking right at me when he said it. That's when I realized that must have been the trip Dad went missing from. And I had this feeling that Mr. Martin had something to do with it. I wanted to pay back that son-of-a-bitch—at least scare the shit out of him."

"Oh, Jameson, he had nothing to do with it. They checked the phone records, and Ben had been in touch with your father a few times during the day, just like he'd said. They checked with the man at the museum he went to see. His story checked out—matched up with what was on your father's phone. He had taken photos throughout his visit. It wasn't until the end of the day when he didn't make it back to the bus that they thought something was wrong. A mugging gone bad. A random violent act. Something like that."

"No, there's got to be more to it. You'll see."

"Jameson . . ."

"And all day in New York, every time I turned around, Martin seemed to be right next to me or had his eyes on me from nearby. It was creepy. I mean, to the point I wondered if he had it in for me. So, I knew I needed to get away from him. During the play, we were spread around the theater. Martin kept turning around to make sure I was there, but I made my move during intermission. I bolted for the men's room and kept on going. I ran to Grand Central—"

"You ran?"

"Adrenalin took me most of the way, but it really wasn't that far. You know me, Mom. I've got soccer legs. You wouldn't let me play football," he poked with a grin, adding a bit of levity Victoria could have done without. "Had enough cash on me to buy a train ticket to Waterbury. From there I grabbed a cab to campus. At that point, I was low on funds, but I had just enough to pay for the cab. I figured if there was no credit card trail of me leaving the city, they wouldn't know where to look."

"They, who?"

"Whoever," Jameson snapped. "The police. Martin."

"Okay. Then what."

"When I got back to campus, I slipped into the dorm. They weren't back yet so it was pretty easy. I grabbed some things from my room, including that wooden box you gave me that was Dad's, and went up to the third floor—the attic—into the room where all the trunks and suitcases are stored during the year. No one ever goes in there, at least not until the end of the year when we have to pack up our rooms and schlep everything back home."

A smile brightened his face. "I just wish I could have seen Martin's expression when he realized I was gone."

"What about your roommate? How could you do that to him?"

"I didn't do anything to Asher. I told him my plan. He was a good bud and helped me out with it. Brought me food. He wasn't going to say anything. He owes me."

"How do you figure that?"

"All the tutoring I've done for him? I singlehandedly kept him in school. . . . Not just *in* in school but with good enough grades to go on the field trip."

Victoria considered the trade-off and which one of them made out better. "When did you get here?"

"After a couple days, I was going stir crazy, and Asher started to freak out about getting caught, so he stopped bringing me food. That's when I headed out during the night. Walked into town and grabbed an Uber."

"So, you camped out in our shed?" Her brain conjured the image of an empty refrigerator shelf where the lasagna had been. "And you snuck in to grab food?"

His face brightened again. "Yeah. You still make the best lasagna, Mom. Although it's not as good cold. But I was starving, so I didn't care."

"But why? Why did you do this? What were you trying to accomplish?"

"I figured if both Dad and I disappeared from the same field trip to New York City, Martin would be the only common denominator, and they would have to reopen the case—"

"It's never been closed."

"Well, you know, take a deeper dive into a cold case. And look closer at him this time. I mean, for Christ's sake, it's been seven years already. Why haven't they arrested anyone yet? I mean, you're ready to give up and move on—"

"I have *not* given up."

"You're going to marry . . . what's his name." He gestured toward her as if eliciting a response. "Vince."

"Jameson, how dare you."

"Well, it's true, isn't it? And you don't even know what happen to Dad. How could you forget—" The last word caught in his throat. She could see him struggling not to lose it in front of her. "He could be out there somewhere."

"Is that what this is about? You don't want me to get married again? Look, I don't even know if that's going to happen." She wasn't going to mention her breakup with Vince or divulge the fact she was infatuated with his roommate's father. "But even if it did, no one is going to replace your father."

"Mom, I don't need the canned speech that future step kids get.

That's a bunch of bullshit anyway, and you know it. But that's not what I'm talking about. Dad went missing, the police couldn't figure out what happened, everyone gave up, and no one is being held accountable."

Weighing her options for how best to rationalize with him, she began, "Do you really think your father is alive after seven years, and no one has come up with any evidence he is?" Victoria shuddered at how much she sounded like everyone around her who tried to convince her to move on.

"There's no evidence he isn't. Maybe he's just afraid to come back. Maybe coming back would put us in danger. If he came back, he'd have to point a finger." Pausing, he seemed to be considering the scenarios he was throwing out. "Hey, maybe he'll come back after I graduate, so he doesn't screw anything up for me by pointing a finger."

It tore at her insides to see her son having to endure the agony of not knowing what happened to his father. It wasn't fair. Childhoods weren't supposed to be about missing persons with no leads. And they certainly weren't supposed to be about suppositions of murder with his father's name as the subject. A mother was supposed to protect her child from all that, and she hadn't been able to.

"If he isn't alive, someone is responsible for what happened to him," Jameson continued. "And that person in Ben Martin."

"But why, Jameson? Why would Ben—who is our friend—why would he have anything to do with it? It defies logic . . . and reason."

"I don't know. I haven't figured it out yet. It's just something I sense."

Victoria eased herself onto one end of the sofa, perched at the edge. "Oh, Jameson, what have you done? You can't accuse the headmaster of being a murderer—or even take off from a field trip like you did—and not expect consequences. You've attacked his reputation. He'll revoke your scholarship. He'll find a way to kick you out of school. Then what?"

"But Mom, I know he had something to do with it."

"You don't know that."

"Yes, I do."

"I'm sure it was an accident." Her voice came from the foyer, and then Millie appeared in the doorway. "But Martin *was* involved."

"Oh, the two of you are nuts. The man is our friend—Robert's and mine—and he's also your headmaster, Jameson, at a prestigious New England boarding school where you are fortunate to be going—if you haven't completely screwed things up."

"Mom, I need to show you something."

"*No, Jameson,*" she shrieked. "Now, enough of this. You had better hope you haven't ruined your entire future—everything your father made possible for you. What do you think he would say to you right now? How disappointed do you think he would be?" Tearing up the stairs, she couldn't get away from the two of them soon enough. She slammed her bedroom door and locked it.

"MOM?" HIS VOICE WAS muffled through the door.

"Yes, Jameson."

"Grandma thought maybe you'd calmed down by now. I really need to talk to you."

Well, if Grandma thought it, it must be true! After all, she's omnipotent, omnipresent, and omni-whatever else there is.

"Mom?"

Please go away, Jameson. You've been so naughty my head feels like it's going to split open, and I need time to think about how I'm going to get you out of trouble.

"Are you okay? Now you're getting me worried. Please say something."

"Yes, Jameson. I'm fine." *Fine as I'm going to be with a son who pulls a stunt like you did.* "Please leave me alone."

"Mom, there's something I need to show you."

"Not now."

"It's important."

"Not *now*, I said. Just go away."

As a dull pain crept up the back of her neck, his footsteps faded away.

CHAPTER THIRTY-FIVE

"Ben, thank you for seeing me." Now that the police had dropped charges against Jameson, Victoria was at the academy to grovel to try to keep him matriculated.

"Certainly, Victoria. Please sit down. He motioned in the general direction of an antique settee upholstered with a burgundy and gold paisley—clearly not the original fabric to the piece—and a wingchair done up in a coordinating solid burgundy corduroy. She was convinced his office had been decorated without the help of his second wife, Missi—and after his divorce from his first. It may have been a retribution of sorts to be able to have his space the way he'd always wanted it, and at the time, there was no one around to give him grief for it. She chose the settee and perched on the edge, her glance catching on a charming snow globe. Inside was a beaver sporting a navy-blue school blazer and holding a hockey stick. Victoria resisted the urge to snatch it up and shake it vigorously to get the fake snow to scatter inside.

As Ben fiddled in a desk drawer for his pipe and snuff, she allowed her gaze to travel along the walls of the room. Her back was to a bank of windows, but the other three were dark-wood paneled, which seemed to absorb the natural light and sucked the life out of anyone who crossed the headmaster's threshold. His massive desk blended right in with the dark and depressing theme he had going on. His desk lamp shed little light beyond the small circle around it. Framed diplomas and certificates plastered nearly every inch of the space behind his desk chair. Imposing bookshelves spanned another wall that appeared to be a collection of every black, brown, or navy covered book he could find. A few framed photos were propped up throughout that she assumed were of family but were too far away to discern. The opposite wall held an assortment of sports banners awarded after championships. She thought it odd they'd been placed in the headmaster's office and not the corridors of the sports complex or somewhere the students could see them and share in the pride derived from the accomplishments.

"We've had quite a run over the years." Ben had noticed where her eyes landed. With his pipe in hand, he made his way around the desk and stood before the wall, shoulders back, beaming.

"For sure."

"So proud of my boys—on and off the sports fields or courts, in and outside of the classrooms." Victoria could hear his next words, *so this is why what your son did was so egregious.* She thought it best to make the first move.

"Ben, I'm just going to get right to it. What Jameson did was wrong. And he knows that now. But at the time, he was working with the knowledge he had. He was—as I have been for the past seven years—desperate to find his father or, at least, what has happened to him." His expression read "I'm listening," so she kept going. "He got it in his head that you were somehow responsible for Robert's disappearance, for lack of anyone else to point a figure at."

With a nod, he settled into the wingback chair and said, "That was what I figured. He loved Robert. We all did. It's been such a painful loss for all of us—obviously more so for you and the boys—but we've all felt the loss deeply. So, I got it that he was lashing out. I'm so thankful he was found alive and unharmed."

"Oh, Ben. Thank you for understanding. I know he put you through a lot that night and the couple days until he showed up."

Raising a palm to her, he said, "This is one of those situations where, thankfully, the ending was what we were all praying for. Yes, he caused a lot of people some stress and heartache—especially you—but in the end, he came out of it alive and well. I couldn't have asked for a better outcome."

"I can't tell you how relieved I am to hear you say that. Thank you for being so understanding. I was afraid you were going to kick him out of Litchfield." Victoria let slip a nervous giggle and instantly regretted it.

He looked up from the pipe he had started to light and regarded her.

There was still one remaining question she knew she had to ask, if only so there would be no misunderstanding. "Ben, I need to know. . . . Is he going to face disciplinary action—or worse—is he going to lose his scholarship?"

Averting his gaze, he pressed his lips together until the color had drained from them.

"That's a different matter altogether. There is a Disciplinary Committee that will review his case. They'll make that determination."

"But why does it have to go to the committee? Can't you make a judgment? I know he has every intention of apologizing to you."

"The fact that I've forgiven him has no bearing on his disciplinary action. Technically he disobeyed school rules. We have very specific rules the boys must follow when we're on field trips that are in place for their safety. And if one person decides he doesn't have to follow them, it puts the whole group at risk. So, we can't take these things lightly. There have to be consequences so that he and all the boys learn from it. And he took the situation way too far."

Victoria grabbed the edge of her seat. She suddenly felt as though she was sliding down a ravine, clawing to get a grip, but unable to grab onto anything. Under her breath, she pleaded, "This can't be happening." For his ears, she said, "Ben, please . . . I need your help with this. He can't lose his scholarship. I can't afford to send him here. You know that—"

"Yes, I know. That's quite clear."

"And if he gets kicked out, he'll never get into a decent college. His whole future depends on you right—"

"Victoria, everything you are saying is true, but you have to stop and think about what he did. *He* certainly didn't before he embarked on that childish stunt." He rose, shoving a hand in his pants pocket, and wound his way out of the seating circle, toward the windows that looked out over the quad. *His* quad. Where *his* boys were no doubt crossing on their way to and from classes. It wasn't until then that Victoria realized how personal everything that happened at the academy was for him. Victoria pivoted on the settee to maintain eye contact, but his were focused on something beyond the windows. She continued.

"Ben, I thought you were our friend, Robert's and mine. I'm begging you to help."

As he turned back to her, removing the pipe from his mouth, she was startled by his odd smirk. "Begging. Well . . . that's certainly not very attractive, Victoria. And it's not going to help much in this situation. I'm afraid my hands are tied."

"You're the headmaster, for God's sake, Ben. You can't just throw him to the wolves. He did it out of love for his father." She was losing any semblance of dignity she had walked in with. *Why was he being so uncooperative?*

"Perhaps . . . but the fact of the matter is he broke some strict rules—rules that, as a functioning community, we can't afford to allow anyone to break. There is a process when that happens, and that's when the Disciplinary Committee takes over."

"You can't tell me you have no influence over them."

He returned his gaze to the quad below. Victoria prayed he was softening. Finally he spoke. "I'll see what I can do, but I'm not making any promises."

"Ben, thank you. Thank you. I appreciate it. Jameson appreciates it. Robert would—"

"I said I can't make any promises. . . . Now, if you'll excuse me, I have another appointment I don't want to keep waiting any longer."

"I understand. Thank you for taking the time." Victoria rose and padded across the rug. Halfway to the door, she pulled up short. "Oh, I forgot. There's something else I needed to ask." She returned to the settee but didn't sit. Pulling an envelope from her purse, she began, "This may not be the appropriate time, but I don't know when it will be."

His brows pinched together at the sight of the envelope in her hands.

"This was in Robert's old desk. Erin Hutchinson passed them along to me, thinking they belonged to him." He reached out and she handed it to him. "They're photos. Mostly kids. I don't recognize them."

Ben raised a brow. "And you think I would?"

"Please. If you could just look at them." *Tell me this is not Robert's other family that you've known about all along and kept his secret.*

He peeked in and fingered the edges of the photos. "I'm sorry. Like I said, I have another appointment. Leave them with Missi on your way out, and I'll take a look at them when I can."

Allowing her shoulders to drop, Victoria knew she'd already asked too much of Ben. Now she may never learn about what Erin found.

As she headed for the door for the second time, an old, framed photo of Beaver Pond hung to one side of the doorjamb as if plucked from her recurring nightmares.

When she looked back, Ben had returned to watching over the activity in his quad, pipe pinched between clenched teeth. Letting herself out, she glanced around the small reception area. Besides the unoccupied assistant's desk, there were two black leather club chairs on either side of a small table. Both were empty. She dropped the envelope on the desk.

CHAPTER THIRTY-SIX

"Mom?" Jameson's voice came from the other side of her locked bedroom door.

She didn't make a sound.

"Mom, I heard you come in."

"Yes, Jameson. I'm here. What do you want?"

"Then can I come in? I really need to talk to you . . . and I'd rather not have to do it through the door.

"Okay, just a minute." She dragged herself off the bed and un-latched the door.

Jameson took in her appearance from her tear-stained cheeks to toes that hadn't seen the inside of a nail salon in months, but she ignored his outward concern and flopped back onto the bed, longing for a glass of wine.

"Mom, please listen."

"Jameson, I'm all ears." She threw an arm up over her head, onto the pillow behind her.

Out of his pants pocket, he pulled a flattened roll of brown paper and sat on the edge of the bed near the footboard. "Mom, do you remember that old wooden box of Dad's that you gave me the day I was leaving to go back to Litchfield?"

"Yeah, did that come out of it?" She nodded toward his hands.

"Yes." He unrolled it. "We've got to see what's on it."

Scooting into more of a sitting position to improve her perspective, she squinted. "It looks blank."

"That's just it. I couldn't figure out why he would put a blank sheet of parchment in there. But I got to thinking about the fact that it might not be an ordinary piece of paper."

Victoria felt her patience waning. He needed to get to the point, and fast.

"Do you remember what movie Harrison and I used to watch with Dad, over and over again when we were growing up?"

"Jameson, I'm in no mood for guessing games. Spill it."

"*National Treasure.* Remember?"

"Yes, I do. What's that got to do with this?"

"Remember after they stole the Declaration of Independence," he continued, "they used lemon juice and heat to reveal a secret message on the back of it?"

"What . . . do you think your father left you a secret message?" She had nearly reached her limit with his nonsense. "I thought your father said the movie wasn't accurate . . . and the lemon juice wouldn't have worked."

"Exactly." He jabbed the air with his index finger, clearly pleased she'd remembered that detail. "That's true. He said the lemon juice would have been used to *write* the secret message in the first place."

"Okay. So, movies don't always get it right."

"And then heat would have been used to bring out the message once it had dried."

"So, what are you saying? You found a secret message on this parchment paper?"

Jameson looked her in the eye and took a beat before saying, "Yes."

Victoria heard a click in her throat. "What did it say, Jameson?"

"Uh . . . I don't know."

"You don't know—"

"I haven't actually tried to reveal the message yet. But I know it's there."

An audible clunk came from within the deepest region of her head. "You mean to tell me you came to the conclusion your headmaster was responsible for your father's disappearance, and you were willing to throw away everything you have at the academy because you found a blank sheet of parchment that you think *might* have some sort of message on it from your father, and you're *guessing* at what that message might be. Did I get that right?" By the time she'd finished, she'd pulled herself to a sitting position, leaning forward, glaring into his eyes.

Scooting back to lean against the footboard, Jameson threw up a hand to put some space between them and said, "Whoa, take it easy. Think about it, Mom. It all makes sense."

Victoria had smacked his upper arm before she realized her hand was moving. "You've *got* to be kidding me." She flopped backward onto the bed, this time face down. She let out a wail into her pillow.

"Mom, look. See the lower corner here?"

When she'd flipped back over, he was holding out the parchment and pointing to a scribble.

As she leaned closer and squinted, she recognized the familiar initials RLS with a circle around it. He'd redeemed himself. That was, until she had another thought.

"Those are definitely his initials, and that's how he signs them." Victoria refused to talk about Robert in the past tense. "But that doesn't mean there's anything else on the paper. Maybe he writes his initials first and then composes the narrative on the paper."

"Nah. I don't buy it. I'll show you." He jumped up and headed for her bathroom, calling back, "Mind if I borrow your hair dryer for a sec?"

She was already on her feet and following him into the small space; the two of them filled it up. Yanking the top drawer in the vanity, she pulled out a small, black personal dryer and plugged it in.

"C'mere," she motioned, and he followed her back out to the bedroom, to the other side of the wall from the sink. "Lay it down here." She pointed with the nozzle of the dryer to the flat surface of a low bureau.

Just as she flipped the switch and the dryer roared to life, he took hold of her arm. "Mom, let me do it, okay?"

Considering his pleading eyes, she switched it off again. Even though it was several years earlier, he and Robert had played around with this sort of encryption. There was no need for her to be experimenting. Though her insides were amped up to see if Robert had left them a message, she acquiesced and handed the dryer to her son. She figured they had one shot at retrieving it.

"Thanks, Mom." He flipped the switch and talked over the noise. "You have to be careful you don't get too close with it." He ran it back and forth across the parchment, about four inches from the surface. "You don't want to get it too hot. Just enough to bring out the letters. I'll do a couple lines at a time."

Victoria grew mesmerized by the movement of the dryer, back and forth, until Jameson spoke.

"It doesn't seem to be working."

"Maybe you need to turn the heat up."

"Good idea." As Jameson flipped the switch, the low hum grew to a high-pitched blare. He resumed his methodical back and forth movement.

Stepping closer, she peered around his side to watch. The seconds ticked away. Nothing seemed to be happening.

"No, it's not working," Victoria said.

Apparently in agreement, he shut off the dryer. "It must not be hot enough." He kept his gaze on the paper as if hoping against hope the words would appear if he wished hard enough.

"Oh, for God's sake, Jameson. There's not a message to find." Running fingers through her hair, she lamented, "What have you done? . . . What have you done?"

"No, Mom. I don't believe that." He laid the dryer on the top of the dresser. His hands found their way to his hips, but he grew silent.

Victoria headed back to flop on her bed, wondering how her son would ever get out of the mess he'd created. Apologizing to the headmaster might not be enough.

"Fire."

"What?" She suddenly realized he had said something.

"Fire. We need a flame. How about a match?"

"Jameson, stop. It's not working. There's no message from your father. And no matter what you do to try to—" He was rummaging in the drawer of her bedside table. "What are you doing in there?" She lunged to pull his arm out—she didn't need him to find her stash of condoms—but he'd already pulled out a lighter and flicked it on and began running it under the parchment. He wasn't listening to her. He'd have to find out for himself, the hard way.

A top corner of the paper caught fire.

"Oh!" They shrieked in unison.

Dropping the lighter, Jameson slammed the paper down onto the comforter, smacking the corner with the palm of his hand. "Damn it!" Once the flame was out, he shook out his hand, the palm a deep red. Ashes were scattered across the bed and stuffing peeked out of a small hole with a black tinged edge from the hydrangea pattern.

"Sorry, Mom."

A strange calm came over her. And a sudden yearning to try one more method. *Was Robert giving her a nod to proceed?* "Look, if you want to use an open flame, try lighting the candle." She gestured toward the jar on the bedside table. "You'll be able to use both hands to hold the parchment and run it across the flame at a steady height."

"Great idea." Jameson snatched up the lighter from where it had landed, partway under the bed, and lit the candle. Holding the parchment along the edges, he began to run it back and forth slowly.

"Careful. Don't let it get too close. You may have only one shot at it."

As Jameson concentrated on his task, Victoria listened to her own breathing, whispering a prayer that something was there, and Jameson would be able to retrieve it.

"See, it's starting to appear."

"Oh my God. Look at that." She watched as brown rudimentary letters formed on the otherwise blank page.

"Hey, grab your phone and take pictures. I don't know how many times this will work."

Sliding her cell from her pocket, Victoria pulled up the camera app. The first two lines were now clear enough to read. She clicked the photo icon twice—a habit of hers in case one was blurry.

I am Robert L· Sands
History Dept Head at LA

"It's him, Jameson. It's your father." In her excitement to see his name, she grabbed Jameson's arm and held on, leaning in to watch him work.

"Pretty incredible, isn't it? All right, I'm going to do the next two lines . . . but I need you to let go of my arm."

"Oh, sorry." Victoria reluctantly pulled her hands off. "But look, the words aren't disappearing."

"Awesome. Okay, looks like they're burning into the parchment."

Slipping her phone back into her pocket, she watched him methodically move the paper back and forth. Mentally urging the letters to appear faster, she couldn't stand how long it was taking. She wanted to force Jameson's hand closer to the candle to speed up the process but feared setting it on fire. She kept her hands off and let Jameson perform the task.

Finally the next two lines began to appear.

I have found a copy of a stmnt
stapled to the back of a handout
I had sent for copying.

The letters weren't the childlike scribblings rendered from a cotton swab that the kids had scrawled as children reenacting the movie scene with their father; Robert had meticulously etched the words with a finer tip like a quill pen, or perhaps a toothpick. Apparently he'd had a lot to say and needed to fit it all in on the page.

"Look at that." Victoria couldn't take her eyes from the letters appearing out of thin air. Jameson kept focused on his task.

Funds trnsfrrd from LA to a
discretionary acct only Ben has
access to. A crippling amt.

"No . . ." Victoria had to read the last phrase a second time.

Jameson continued, scooting the candle closer to the edge of the table, so he could move down the page, and revealed:

I confronted Ben Martin. He said
It was a temporary move.

Then came:

I asked for proof· Was warned to stay
out of it· I suspect gambling debts· (Ben's)

Then the next two lines:

A copy of what I found is in hidden
Comprtmnt in LA box· If I'm right he won't

Then:

let me live long enough to confirm·
Look for me in newly disturbed

Then came the final two lines:

earth· BIL has trucks/backhoes·
Robert L Sands 9/28/15

Victoria swallowed hard. His signature was a looser version of what she remembered him signing. It had to have been the best he could construct with a toothpick and lemon juice.

Jameson blew out the candle. A wisp of smoke rose from the wick and vanished. The gravity of the story it had revealed lingered.

All the fears she'd amassed since Robert went missing, but fought every day to push away, flooded over her. All the images of him lying in places no one had thought to look, put there at the hands of someone who held a wicked secret. Her eyes brimmed with tears, and her son pulled her into his massive arms where she sobbed. Finally she pulled away, wiping her cheeks with the back of her hand.

The fact that their friend may have betrayed Robert hit her in the gut. "How could he do this? He and your father were friends. Friends don't do this."

"Money has a way of coming between people—even friends. Sounds like we're talking about a lot of money. That will wreck any relationship." He sounded wise, well beyond his years.

"And the school . . . what has he done to the school? And why?" Her voice trailed off as she considered the extent of Ben's carnage.

"Secret compartment . . . in the LA box."

"You were smart to grab it before you left campus."

"But I didn't find any hidden compartment. There's a hole on the back that might be a keyhole but—"

Pushing past Jameson, Victoria lunged for the drawer in the bedside table, pulling out the skeleton key Erin had given her in the coffee shop. Holding it up, she said, "Try this."

"Awesome, Mom. Thanks." He pocketed it in his jeans.

Still hanging onto the last line of the message before his father's signature, he said, "What do you think he meant by: 'BIL has trucks and backhoes.'"

"BIL? Brother-in-law. Ben's second wife—Missi Stockwell—her brother has a sanitation business and a construction business. Not long after we moved back here, after your father went missing, Ben offered to have him come and clear a section of the yard, so in the spring, you and your brother could plant a garden. He said it would be good to keep you guys busy."

"I remember that. I don't think we ever did much with it."

"No, I couldn't get you and your brother interested. We planted some tomatoes and string beans the first year, but the squirrels got to the tomatoes and what beans I could salvage after the bugs got to them, you guys didn't want to eat. So, I didn't bother after that. And you two didn't seem to care." She reflected on their failed attempt at horticulture. "The one strange thing about it was the yellow tulips that came up that next spring and every spring after that. We hadn't planted them. I asked Ben about them—if his brother-in-law had planted them for us after preparing the garden—and he assured me the guy wouldn't know one end of a tulip bulb from the other, so it wasn't him. I have yet to figure out who did it. But neighbors were doing all sorts of nice things after your father disappeared. Dropped off food, flowers, offered to babysit you and your brother."

"So did they bring in a truck when they made the garden? I don't really remember."

"You don't remember because they did the work in the evening, after your bedtime. Ben said his brother-in-law was doing him a favor, and it was outside of his regular jobs."

"Working under the cover of darkness." Jameson's words had an accusatory tone; his voice, raspy.

"At the time it didn't occur to me that it might seem like an odd time to rototill; the growing season was over. Now it seems odd. . . . Oh my God. You think he's been there all this time?"

"It certainly makes sense. If Ben needed to keep him quiet and dispose of his body where no one would think to look, why not right in our backyard? And now that I see Dad's prediction, I need to get out there."

Flinging the parchment onto her bed, covering the ashes and scorched hole, Jameson pushed past her and disappeared through her bedroom door. As his feet thudded down the foyer stairs, Victoria pulled jeans and a sweatshirt from her dresser—clothes to get dirty in.

⋘⋙

VICTORIA AND JAMESON DUG for hours. Millie ferried food and drinks to them, standing along the side, watching in silence for a spell with each trip, early on cautioning them about steering clear of where the tulips came up every year along the far edge of the original garden layout, near the woods.

By dark, they'd been able to dig down a foot all the way across the twelve-by-fifteen-foot plot and kept going by the light of the moon and the spotlight over the door of the shed.

"Anything?" Millie had arrived with a warm dinner of pot roast and mashed potatoes, much welcomed nourishment and a justified reason to take a break. Piles of dirt ringed the garden. From where Victoria was standing below the level of the yard, her mother's slippered feet were obscured.

"No, nothing yet, Mom. But we're not finished."

"Hell no," Jameson spurted. "They had heavy machinery and would have gone down much deeper than this—and easily."

"Well, how long are you going to be at this?" Millie asked, but it was less of a question and more sharing her concern for the two of them.

"When we find what we're looking for." Jameson was a pit bull after the vulnerable neck of a ground squirrel, much like his mother. He wasn't about to quit before they'd answered the burning question. Neither was she.

"Mom, don't feel like you have to stay up with us." Victoria wiped beads of sweat from her forehead with the sleeve of her sweatshirt. "Go to bed. It's probably time. Right?"

"Not quite. I'll stay with you as long as I can . . . get you what you need."

"Mom, really. You don't—"

"I'll stay up and help you any way I can," she repeated, her voice booming from somewhere deep within her petite body.

Victoria took a step back. "Okay. That'd be great. Thanks."

The three of them pulled an all-nighter; Victoria and Jameson piling the dirt around the garden higher and higher, Millie delivering water and oatmeal chocolate chip cookies.

By sunrise, Millie had collapsed in one of the bistro chairs on the patio and was snoozing with her top half sprawled across the table, a couple of blankets wrapped around her shoulders. Jameson and Victoria estimated they were four feet down but had found nothing of significance other than enough fieldstones to build a wall from the garden to the back door, pottery shards that might have some historical significance, and enough acorns to keep a family of squirrels fed for an entire Connecticut winter. But no body.

Exhausted, Victoria acknowledged to herself she was relieved. To her it meant Robert could still be out there somewhere and still be alive. Jameson had other thoughts.

"Damn it!" He thrust the point of the shovel into the packed dirt at his feet. "Do you think we need to go deeper?"

"Oh, I don't think so, Jameson. We're pretty far down. I think we would have found something by now."

"Then what the hell did he do with him?"

"Sweetheart, just because we didn't find anything doesn't mean there is anything for us to find."

"Are you kidding? You saw Dad's note."

"It doesn't mean anything happened to him at the hands of Ben Martin."

Jameson let his shoulders drop, then lowered his head, resting his forehead on the handle of the shovel still stuck in the dirt.

To see her son so disheartened tugged at Victoria's heart. "Why don't we go get a little sleep. We'll be better able to think about our next step if we've had some rest. Okay?"

Reluctantly Jameson pulled the shovel out of the ground and climbed out of the pit, turning to offer his mother a hand up.

Just because they'd hit a wall there didn't mean there weren't other places to look.

Chapter Thirty-Seven

Her eyes were barely above the level of the water in the infinity pool. She'd never seen this perspective before. Now she understood the idea behind the name. She'd lost track of time but it must have been a while because her head felt groggy. But the warm water was so soothing she didn't want to get out. She didn't care if she looked like a prune when she did emerge. A few minutes back in the sun, and she'd be back to normal.

Victoria could sense him behind her. She wanted to say Robert's name but couldn't make a sound. She anticipated him wrapping his arms around her from behind. It made her smile. But there was no gentle touch—only his palms firmly on her shoulders. No soft words whispered in her ear. The smile slipped from her face.

She struggled to speak his name again but there was no sound. She yearned to reach out and take his hand, let him lead her out of the pool. He wasn't coming into sight. She'd been sure it was him. Why wasn't he saying anything? Why did he remain behind her?

His firm hands pushed her below the surface of the water. Her nose and mouth filled. She squirmed to get out from under his grip, but he held on tighter.

Her thoughts shifted from memories of a vacation with Robert to more recent events. *Had she been out with Emerson and drank too much? What was he trying to do to her?* Her lungs burning, she had to get air, but he was keeping her down. Victoria wriggled and thrashed under the water. In a flash, the hands pulled off her shoulders, and she surfaced, clinging to the side, coughing and pulling in ragged breaths.

Someone was yelling. Victoria didn't recognize her mother's voice at first. "What are you trying to do, Sean? You're high on drugs, aren't you? Ha! You no-good, useless drug addict."

Victoria looked up in time to see the pale, scrawny shell of her brother take a swing at their elderly mother, the back of his hand making contact with her jaw, sending her stumbling against the open door. Searching the small space to find something to use as a weapon, Victoria snatched up the empty wine bottle next to a clawfoot and banged it against the back of her brother's head. He dropped to the floor in a sickening plop.

Stepping over him, she grabbed her robe from the hook. "Mom, are you okay?" She reached for her arm and helped her to her feet.

"Where's your phone? Call the cops on him. The scumbag."

Victoria dashed for the nightstand where she'd left her cell and dialed 9-1-1.

After the dispatcher assured her an officer would be right there, Victoria grabbed an ice pack from the kitchen and led her mother to her car sitting in the driveway, locking the doors. She figured they were safer there than in the house when her brother regained consciousness.

The police couldn't arrive soon enough, and when they did, they retrieved a belligerent felon from the bathroom, leading him out to their cruiser in cuffs.

Victoria acknowledged she and her mother had come dangerously close to losing their lives at the hands of their flesh and blood on some sort of a drug-fueled trip.

THE INCIDENT WITH HER brother shook them both to the core. Neither had required medical attention, but they slept in the same bed for a few nights after that. Victoria made a mental note to look into getting a burglar alarm for the house. She hoped they never saw her brother again, but that was entirely unrealistic.

Chapter Thirty-Eight

Victoria had pieced it all together. Harrison's call. His Google Earth discovery. The nightmares that haunted her and seemed to be pointing her to a body of water—the pond on the Litchfield Academy campus.

With Jameson reinstated, Victoria had come alone and she thought it best that way. No sense involving Jameson if nothing of value were to come of the day's venture. Besides he couldn't risk asking for time away from classes. He'd missed the previous two weeks while waiting for the Disciplinary Committee to decide his fate, enduring a fortnight of daytime pacing and sleepless nights until ultimately they decided in his favor. Victoria sensed it was a nod to Robert and everything he'd contributed to the school.

Arriving early, she'd left her car in the academy's parking lot meant for visitors and walked down to Beaver Pond, staking out a spot on a hill across the street. Her sneakers, soaked from the morning dew in the long grasses, turned a disappointing grayish white, but she barely noticed. Under the protective, low-hanging boughs of a weeping willow, she watched the local police arrive and set up orange cones down the road to detour traffic away from their work area. First responder vehicles began to arrive and line the sides of the road.

Litchfield Falls police had enlisted the help of the Connecticut Police Dive Team and a local towing company with a state contract and a monster rig to conduct the extraction. First the thick brush and small trees that had filled in the area during the last seven years had to be cut out.

Victoria stayed out of sight, watching the men work. Chain saws buzzed, sometimes in unison, other times answering each other. Men wearing bright yellow hard hats and reflective vests dragged limbs and brush up the bank, where they were fed into a wood chipper that roared with each insertion, returning to the scene to grab more. Up and down the hill, limb after limb. After a couple of hours, the small dump truck the chipper was emptying into was nearly full. Victoria's vantage point was a flat spot high up on her side of the road, but the action down by the pond was still blocked from view, even after so much brush had been removed.

By midmorning she grew weary from sitting still, feeling helpless, bouncing between thoughts of elation at the prospect of them pulling the car out of the water and devastation if they confirmed the body inside was Robert's. If it was him, how did he get there? Distracted driving? *Please, Lord, don't let it be suicide.* If it was him, how did he end up in the pond when he was supposed to be on a field trip to New York City with his students?

She shifted in place, untucking her legs and then tucking them again. Her stomach let her know that skipping breakfast that morning had not been such a good idea. She'd been anxious to get there before the roadblock went up and didn't take the time.

Leaning against the trunk of the tree, Victoria felt drowsiness overtaking her, that was until movement up the road caught her eye; a man walking toward her.

He wasn't wearing the uniform of a first responder, and he was dressed more casually than a detective. A white paper bag—the kind you'd get from a bakery—was grasped tightly in his right hand, swinging in cadence as he walked. In his other, he balanced a tray of to-go cups, the cardboard kind you'd get with take-out. There was something familiar about him. Sitting up straighter, Victoria squinted to see more clearly.

Snatching a quick breath, she realized she was watching Robert walk toward her. Jumping to her feet, she called, "Robert," and waved a hand over her head to draw his attention. *Was it him? Had he found his way back?* Her thoughts returned to the activity in the pond below. "Oh, God, no," she whispered. It was him in spirit. "No, no."

Could others see him? No one else seemed to be looking his way.

Refocusing on the approaching man, she realized the absurdity of where her thoughts had taken her. She called, "Harrison," and waved a hand over her head. His face lit up, and he broke into a jog, balancing the drinks and storming the hill.

Easing the tray of coffees onto the ground, he pulled his mother in and wrapped her with his long, strong arms.

"Oh Harrison, it's so good to see you. Did you just get to Connecticut?"

"Yeah. Took the red-eye."

"I can't get over how much you look like your father now. Such a handsome young man, you are."

"Thanks, Mom. I'll be sure to put that on my resumé."

She ignored his quip. "Thanks for cluing me in. I'm so glad you're here." Warmth spread through her. With the three of them together at the house for Thanksgiving, they would feel like a family again.

"Are you kidding? I wouldn't have missed this." His gaze slipped past her, and his face filled with a grin. "Hey, Squirt."

Pivoting, she watched Jameson trudging up the hill toward them in his blue blazer, khakis, and brown Sperry's. Jameson's expression grew rigid, and he said, "What are you . . . twelve? Enough with the juvenile nicknames."

Harrison reached out to muss Jameson's hair, but he dodged the swipe. Instead Harrison settled for offering his hand and pulled him in for a one-armed hug with the other tucked between them. She loved to watch them greet each other. Her grown sons looked more like wrestling bears when they embraced.

"I see they let you back in school." Harrison tugged on the lapel of his blazer.

"I apologized. . . . and I've got a break in classes."

"Jameson, how did you know to come?"

With his head cocked toward his brother, he said, "Harrison texted me." Then asked, "What's that?" thrusting his chin toward the bag in his brother's hand.

"I stopped by The Daily Grind and picked up some scones."

"Solid." Jameson reached out to grab it.

Extending a splayed palm, Harrison said, "Hold on. I gotta make sure Mom gets her favorite first."

After he'd divvied up the baked treats and drinks—Victoria's, a hot chai tea latte, the boys, iced coffees with caramel swirls—they sat in silence while they nibbled, the boys finishing long before Victoria.

Watching them lick their fingers, she poked, "You guys really should learn how to chew."

They joined in laughter together, but then fell silent, distracted by the buzz of activity below. Unable to gauge the progress, Victoria grew impatient.

After a ping, Harrison said, "Oh my God," his eyes intent on his cell.

"What?" Victoria asked.

"There was a fire in my dorm last night."

"What? A fire?" Jameson leaned in for a closer look at Harrison's phone.

"Did anyone get hurt?" Victoria offered up a prayer of thanks Harrison had come home early.

"I don't know. I just got a text from the guy across the hall." His phone pinged again.

"Oh, no." He looked up and his gaze connected with hers. "My roommate was rushed to the hospital."

"Please let him be okay," she pleaded with the universe.

Jameson's eyes focused on the ground between his feet, the solemnity of the news not lost on him.

"Harrison, that could have been you," she whispered. Images flashed through her mind. *How did it start? Was it an accident? One of the kids cooking in his room even though it was against the rules?* She couldn't bring herself to consider arson as a possibility. *If so, why?*

"I know." His gaze drifted down to where the men were working to fish out the car he'd found. She grabbed him around the shoulders and hung on tight. *She could have lost him too.* "Thank God you came home early."

"Okay, Mom. I know. You can let it go now."

She loosened her grip and pulled away, swiping at a pesky tear that had made it to her jawline and threatened to drip off.

The three remained silent until about midday when a man stepped away from the work area and trudged up the hill toward them. When he got within earshot, he said, "Mrs. Sands?"

Getting to her feet, she brushed loose dirt and small twigs off her backside. "Yes?" Her stomach grew tingly. Could they be ready to pull out the car?

"I thought that might be you." He introduced himself as the detective in charge, Dan Perry. "I'm sorry you're having to go through this. Really, I am. Hopefully we'll be able to get the dive team in there soon to take a look and see if it's feasible to attach a cable—an axle would be ideal."

"So, when will we know if that's possible?"

He watched the men moving about down the hill and said, "Looks like they're bringing in the dive team now."

Both of the boys scrambled to their feet.

"Detective, these are my sons. Harrison and Jameson."

He extended his hand to them both. "Good to meet you. Sorry it's under these circumstances. Harrison, I understand you were the one to locate the car. Well done."

"Thank you, sir. It was actually thanks to a school project."

"Really? How's that?"

"I had this assignment to identify the origins of the architecture of a place in my hometown or someplace that had meaning for me. So, I selected Litchfield Academy. I've always loved the brownstone buildings. Part of the process was to do a search on Google Earth to show the overview of the location we were writing about. And when I did, something odd came up."

"I see. Well, no telling how long this would have gone undetected if you had chosen a different class."

"For sure." As he gave a quick nod, a breeze pushed a healthy clump of his wavy chestnut hair across his forehead and obscured one eye, which he brushed away a couple of times before it stayed.

"I took a look at the satellite images you found and, honestly, I wouldn't have come up with the same conclusion you did. It was just a faded white rectangle, partially obscured by vegetation. Not much to go on. Your instincts were spot on."

Harrison nodded without making eye contact with the detective.

The detective turned back to Victoria. "As you know, I've been working with your attorney—"

"My attorney?"

"Yes, uh, Vince. . . Vince Teren—"

"Terentini. Yes, of course. Vince. Sorry, my mind went blank for a sec there." She wasn't going to let on to the detective or the boys that something might be amiss. But what was Vince up to—masquerading as her attorney?

The conversation quickly shifted to small talk, and they commented on how long it was taking to clear out the brush.

"If it is the car we suspect it to be, all those years of growth alongside the road kept anyone, walking or driving by, from noticing it. Anyone on the trails on the other side of the pond wouldn't be able to see it either. Too far away. It landed in relatively shallow water so it didn't flip. That will make extracting it much easier than if it had."

The wood chipper shut down, sending a hush over the pond. One of the divers emerged from the water, and his chatter with the others drifted up the hill. "All the windows are closed and intact. Front axle is accessible." A guy in a reflective vest whistled, motioning to the tow truck driver. Victoria jumped to her feet.

"Whoa," the detective said, latching a firm grip onto her upper arm. "You need to stay clear still. Let us do our job."

"Detective, I've got to see. I have to know and see it with my own eyes."

"I understand. But ma'am, there is *nothing* you'll want to see. Just let us get it out of there first. I don't want anyone getting hurt during this extraction. Okay?"

"You have to let me see—"

"Look, I'm sorry to be so crass, but after all this time, there's not going to be much left to him."

He loosened his grip, which allowed her to take a step back. "Then how will you be able to identify . . ."

"We'll do our best."

"All right," she conceded but had no intention of sitting on her hands much longer. Seven long years she'd waited for this moment—not this *particular* moment—but a long-awaited answer. She'd hoped it would have a happy ending. But however it was going to end, Victoria was not going to be sitting by the phone, waiting to hear. She was going to be on the front lines, boots on the ground, as they say.

She and the boys watched Detective Perry jog back down the hill to where the tow truck had backed up to the edge of the road. He stepped up onto the running board and leaned in, exchanging a few words. Before long he jumped off and cupped his hands around his mouth and yelled something toward the water. Waiting for a response, he then gave a thumbs-up toward the water, and then climbed back up onto the running board and poked a thumbs up through the window.

Hopping off and putting a few healthy steps between himself and the big rig, he watched with hands shoved in his pockets as the tow truck lurched forward. Yells emanated from below, and Perry signaled for the driver to halt. After an excruciating pause, the detective gave the signal to go again.

The truck moved forward, this time more slowly, and kept moving forward.

"Oh my God, this is it." Dropping her latte at the base of the tree, she tore down the hill toward the tow truck. She could hear the boys' footfalls behind her.

When they'd reached the double yellow line in the center of the road, the front bumper of a white car came into view. She froze. All matter of pond plant life plastered the sides and hood, falling off as it was dragged up the embankment and onto the road.

"It's ours" slipped out with an exhale. Her pulse quickened. The last time she'd seen the car, she'd left it parked in their reserved parking spot near their on-campus house.

Her mother had been right. On their hike through the woods on Grandparents Day, she had brought Victoria to the pond and said something bad had happened there. She could sense it.

One of the boys was speaking. She caught the end of it. ". . . sure it's the one?"

Victoria turned to take in what Harrison was saying. "Well, yes. Your memory of it is probably fuzzy. Of course, it's our car. What else—"

"But there are a lot of white cars out there. Same make and model. I mean, this one's got a bashed in front end."

"It probably got smashed when it entered the water . . ." She couldn't finish her thought. To picture her husband in the driver's seat, behind the wheel, causing his own death was more than she could handle. Was it a case of distracted driving? Had he swerved to miss a deer that had darted out from the edge of the woods? If it was him in the car, why wasn't he in New York with his phone?

"One way to find out. The license plate," Jameson said and then started for the assembly of first responders now crowding around it. Harrison and Victoria fell in behind, forming a "V" like migrating geese.

Jameson pushed between two firefighters to clear an opening. His mother and brother pushed through behind him. The front plate was faded but the numbers and letters were still legible. It confirmed what Victoria had feared.

The windows of the car were opaque with some sort of coating—on the inside? Outside? Victoria took a few steps closer but couldn't see in. She reached out to wipe the passenger side window but her arm met with resistance. A meaty hand had a hold of her forearm.

"Don't touch it," a gruff voice barked.

Shifting her focus away from the fogged-up window, she felt the eyes of every man circling her.

"Victoria, please." It was the detective. "Please let us do our jobs." She felt the bear claw slip off her arm. Perry moved in closer and, with a gentle touch on both arms, spun her away from the car. His next words were meant for her ears only and were barely audible. "Believe me, you don't want to look in the car."

❧

VICTORIA TOOK A FEW strides away from the gruesome scene. The detective was right. She didn't want her last memories of Robert to be the decaying corpse he had become. Perhaps she'd seen enough. It was time to let the professionals do their jobs.

Feeling a warm hand on her back, she turned to look into a familiar face—but not one of her sons.

"Victoria, let's get you away from here. This is not a place for you to be." It was Emerson, his British accent not sounding as chipper as usual. She allowed him to pull her away but only a few yards. Then she remembered her manners and introduced Harrison to Emerson. "He's a . . . a friend of mine." She couldn't bring herself to look at Jameson.

Pleased to watch both sons shake hands with her latest love interest, Victoria wondered if they would let him into their lives, if that was where she and Emerson were heading. She dearly hoped so.

"Excuse me, Mrs. Sands?" It was the detective at her side. "We found this. Would you like to open it?" He handed her what appeared to be a wallet, faded brown and dripping. He pulled off a slender drooping leaf before handing it to her. She didn't recognize it, but so much time underwater could render anything unrecognizable.

"Are you sure you want to do that?" Emerson's concern for her was touching.

"Better me than someone who didn't know him." She nodded toward the men in reflective vests surrounding their family car.

With the boys' gazes intent on her hands, Victoria gently pulled open the wallet. She could feel the detective hovering nearby. The left side contained credit cards, each still neatly stored in its own slot. On the opposite side, the plastic covering the license had turned opaque so she couldn't make out the writing or discern the photo. Pinching the edge, she wriggled it out. It was surprisingly clear. But it wasn't Robert's.

She froze.

"Ma'am?" the detective asked.

Not fully understanding what she was looking at, "It's not him," was all she could manage.

Someone grabbed the license from her. She looked up to see Emerson peering at it. "I *knew* it. That *bastard*."

"What? Who?" Harrison asked.

Emerson touched her arm. "Victoria, love, I'm so sorry. Who could have known?"

The detective snatched the license from Emerson's grasp. "Martin . . . Benjamin Martin."

CHAPTER THIRTY-NINE

Seeing their family car pulled from the pond triggered something inside of her. Something she'd suspected all along but couldn't acknowledge, even when Jameson insisted Ben was somehow responsible. But the wallet clinched it. Had he been in the car with Robert that fateful night? Had he been able to get out but left Robert behind?

Victoria began to run.

"Mom!" She could hear Harrison's voice behind her, but she kept running. There were other voices—someone said to let her be—but she kept going. Her feet hit the pavement, and she followed the road back to campus. It wasn't far. And once she got through the front gates, she cut across the grassy expanse leading up to the front of the building that held the Student Admissions Department, her thighs burning. A siren wailed in the distance.

Her breathing labored, she didn't let up her pace. Heading for the archway that connected Admissions to the Cornwall Dorm, she tore through to the open quad past a group of boys who were milling about, brushing against the closest navy-blue jacket—a startled "Hey!" was thrown her way—and straight for the Administration Building. Yanking the door open, Victoria went for the stone steps that spiraled to the second floor, her feet barely touching each tread.

Missi Stockwell looked up as she rushed toward her desk. "Vicky, what's—"

Not there for a social call, Victoria threw her weight against Ben's door and stumbled into his office.

"Wh—what are you doing?" Missi had caught up to her, but hung back in the doorway. Victoria's focus was on Ben, slouched in his chair behind the expansive desk, appearing as a smaller version of his former self.

"Liar!" Victoria spat at him. Only one of his hands was visible, and it was resting on a revolver on the blotter. "Oh no you don't. Not before you tell me why."

"Ben . . . what's . . . going on?" his young wife sputtered behind Victoria. She'd crept closer.

"Missi, honey, it's okay. Why don't you give us a few minutes?" His tone was eerily calm. Victoria kept her eyes trained on the gun but heard the door click shut. Missi couldn't have noticed what was under her husband's hand.

"Ben, you *son* of a bitch," she started, but then paused, watching his finger twitch. She wanted answers but wouldn't get them if either one of them ended up dead.

"Why don't you sit down." He took his hand off the gun long enough to gesture toward the wingback and settee facing his desk.

Grabbing the back of the nearest chair, she said, "I have no intention of sitting." She had a fleeting thought about how much protection the upholstery would provide from a live bullet. "You tell me what happened."

She watched as his hand slid from the revolver and slipped out of view behind the desk. He pressed his eyes shut and shook his head slowly.

"Tell me, damn it. You owe me that," she said.

"I knew you'd come." He kept his eyes averted from hers. "I knew they were at the site this morning. I knew it was a matter of time before you got here."

"*Tell me,*" she demanded.

"It was all a terrible accident."

"An accident . . . Robert's car ending up in Beaver Pond was an accident? I don't think so."

Ben continued; his words soft and nearly indiscernible. "But you have a right to know. It all happened so quickly. If he had just kept his nose out of it . . . but he kept asking questions." Ben's fingers were back on the gun, tracing the barrel.

She leaned in. "What kind of questions? What did he uncover?"

His Adam's apple undulated as he swallowed hard. "Let's just say there was a misunderstanding."

"A misunderstanding."

As if breaking his trance, he blinked and made eye contact with her for the first time since she'd entered the room.

"He thought he found something . . . a misappropriation of funds. But time will reveal what needs to be known."

His gaze was fixed on the pistol again. Victoria kept watch on his hand.

"Stop being so cryptic. Tell me."

But the headmaster grew silent and let his gaze return to the gun.

He couldn't admit he'd taken Robert's life. At that moment she didn't care if her former friend, soon-to-be former headmaster, put a bullet through his brain. "You pathetic son of a—"

Behind her, the door burst open and the room filled with blue uniforms that swarmed the desk. Victoria felt herself being pulled across the room and through the doorway. "Wait . . . but why, Ben? I need to know."

Ben wasn't finished. "Victoria, I'm sorry," he called. "I won't be able to send roses on your birthday anymore."

She pulled up, the male officer's hand still locked on her arm, to watch the headmaster get swallowed up in blue shirts.

Once in Ben's reception area, a female cop took the handoff and gently led her away. Missi sat behind her desk sobbing, the arrest procedure playing out in the headmaster's office emanating from the intercom. No doubt she'd heard their conversation.

Just as Victoria and the officer made it to the top of the stone stairs, Victoria reached for the railing. A shot rang out. Someone screamed. And Victoria lost her footing.

⚜

"MRS. SANDS, ARE YOU all right?" The officer had caught up to Victoria, clinging to the fire extinguisher she'd managed to grab on her way past, and was pulling on her arm, as if to keep her from rolling the rest of the way down.

"Yes . . . I'll be fine. Let go of me." She yanked back her arm—the one with the cast on it—and tucked it against her side.

"Here."

Victoria let go of the extinguisher and took the officer's hand.

"Up you go."

As they reached the bottom of the stairwell, shuffling on the stone steps echoed from above. Victoria and the officer stepped back as Missi appeared, led by a man in uniform, her head hung low with swollen eyes and a red nose.

Victoria felt she should say something to her, but nothing intelligible came out. Just a guttural animal-like grunt.

Missi stopped with her heels barely balanced on a stone step and lifted her head. Her eyes met Victoria's.

"Vicky, what's going on? I have no idea."

Victoria said nothing, offering only a slight shake of her head.

Watching Missi plod down the last few steps as the mustiness in the stairwell filled Victoria's nose, she wondered, had Ben pulled the trigger? Or did he make a move toward the gun and one of the officer's reacted to his sudden movement. Either way, same satisfying result. But Victoria would never know why her precious Robert had been killed.

CHAPTER FORTY

Having both boys home for Thanksgiving break was a welcome distraction for Victoria, though she struggled to feel any semblance of thankfulness, her heart reeling from the recent discovery of Robert's car. The holiday, which they shared with Vince and her mother, came with a healthy serving of somberness alongside the cranberry sauce and stuffing. When it came time for Harrison and Jameson to head back to school, they seemed reluctant to go. Victoria assured them she would let them know as soon as she'd heard from the medical examiner.

It took some time for the autopsy results, and Victoria wondered how much they'd really been able to determine since Robert's body was submerged for so long. She'd done her best to shore herself up, in preparation for what she might hear. She thought she was ready for anything. But was her imagination capable of thinking of all the grotesque possibilities? She doubted it. This was her beloved Robert they were talking about. And what happened to him on that fateful night would finally be put into words for all to know. It was the closure—not the outcome, but the closure—she'd been yearning for, for seven years.

Vince had offered to be there when she got the official word. She needed his strength and cool head as she listened to what had happened to Robert—if they'd been able to make a determination. He held the certified letter in his hands, still in the envelope. She'd been unable to bring herself to open it. She surmised it held the answer to how Robert died, but she may never know the why.

Squeezing his hand that had found its way over to her thigh, she pressed her eyes shut.

"Okay, are you ready?" he asked.

Just read it already. I want this over with. "Yes."

Victoria watched as he wedged a pudgy finger under the flap, tearing it open. Sliding the letter out, he began to read from the report.

"The autopsy performed on the seventeenth of November by the Connecticut State Medical Examiner's Office in Farmington determined the body found on the fifteenth of November in a 2011 white Toyota Supra that was pulled from Beaver Pond in Litchfield Falls, CT was that of Robert L. Sands. Dental records were used to corroborate the findings from DNA testing of bone samples."

All the air in her lungs emptied, a breath she didn't realize she'd been holding.

"At the time of his death, Sands had been the head of the History Department of Litchfield Academy."

Vince may have been skipping over the technical jargon and perhaps paraphrasing a bit. "The victim suffered from a posterior skull fracture that could not have been caused by the car's impact with the water. Any injuries sustained by the crash would have been located on the anterior of the skull.

"And while the decomposition of the body since it entered the water precludes ascertaining the exact cause of death, it is the opinion of the Medical Examiner that the C.O.D. was blunt force trauma to the head or blunt force trauma that led to drowning. Given the severity of the head injury, even if Mr. Sands were still alive upon entering the water, he would have been incapacitated, preventing him from saving himself, and thus drowning."

Victoria had no more tears to shed. She prayed he hadn't been trapped in the car and drowned. That was hard to wrap her head around. What a horrible way to go. Was that what he'd been trying to show her in her dreams? But how would they ever be able to pin it on anyone? Had the person responsible died in the headmaster's office the day Robert was found?

"In addition to the skull fracture, there were other signs of foul play. Evidence found inside the car indicated the accelerator had been rigged with a five-pound stone to keep it pressed to the floor."

Victoria took in a breath and held it again. *Damn you, Ben.*

"Physical evidence found on the victim's body pointed to an altercation prior to the car entering the water."

Victoria slumped against the back of the chair. Vince squeezed her hand and continued.

"A cuff link was found in Mr. Sands' pants pocket with initials that didn't belong to him. The cuff link was still attached to the lower quarter of the sleeve, including the cuff, that had been ripped from a white pinpoint Oxford shirt. The initials were EK."

"Emerson Kittridge." His name was barely a whisper across her lips. *What was his involvement? What kind of a monster was he under that suave exterior?*

Vince set the papers on the coffee table, having delivered the final report.

Victoria took a moment to take in the ME's findings, and then asked, "So how did you get wrapped up in all of this? I understand you were in touch with the police."

"As fate would have it, I happened to be at your house—the last night you had me over for dinner—when the state police detective called. I answered your phone. You weren't in the room, and I heard it ringing in the foyer."

Victoria remembered the evening. It hadn't ended well. Vince had come for lasagna with her and her mother, but it ended with him essentially dumping her and riding off into the night.

"The detective was actually calling to remind you the seven-year anniversary of Robert's disappearance was coming up and to offer to go with you to court."

"He was?" Seven years, the magical number that—in the state of Connecticut—would have allowed her to have Robert legally declared dead. She didn't need anyone to remind her of the anniversary.

"I let him believe I was your attorney so, from that point on, I had an in. Thought it might be useful. Later, he called to let me know about the car they'd discovered in the pond."

"That *Harrison* discovered in the pond," Victoria corrected.

"Yeah . . . apparently his professor contacted the state police about it . . . but I told the detective to hold off on mentioning it to you. No sense upsetting you before they knew definitively whose car it was. And I offered my assistance if they needed any."

"You didn't think I'd hear about it from Harrison?"

With a resigning tilt of his head, he said, "Thought it would buy some time."

"Guess not."

Pressing his lips together, he nodded. "Plus, I didn't have a good feeling about him."

"Him, who?"

"Kittridge."

The image of a car, similar to Vince's, tailing Emerson the morning after he'd spent the night popped up from her memories. "Did you follow him?"

"Not intentionally. At least, not at first. One morning on my way to work I came up behind a car pulling out of your driveway. I'll admit I was being protective of you—and curious—so I followed him to the airport and watched him get into a helicopter waiting on the tarmac. It had EK Enterprises on the side. It was easy enough to look up who he was.

"Once I knew you two were involved, I started digging—in places law enforcement hadn't looked before. So, I was able to clue them in on what looked like questionable financial dealings, figuring there was a connection somewhere with the academy after I found photos his son had posted on Facebook that made it obvious he was a student there. That's Jameson's friend, Asher. Isn't it?"

"Yeah."

"And then the night Jameson went missing, I noticed a cuff link—kind of a flashy gold one—on the floor next to my side of the bed."

Victoria liked the sound of him claiming his territory. From the day their paths crossed and they reconnected outside of the courtroom, she had kept him at arm's length, not letting him get too close, like he so desperately wanted to be. Yet he'd been her rock throughout her lowest of lows. With his patience tested for years, he'd only thrown in the towel once, and it was only half-hearted. There just hadn't been enough room in her heart to let him in. Perhaps now there would be.

"I knew it wasn't mine, 'cause I don't wear them, but when I picked it up I noticed it had an **EK** on it. It confirmed it was him you were seeing."

Victoria braced for an I-told-you-so, but none came. Vince wasn't the type, which Victoria admired about him.

"What's that?" Vince nodded toward an envelope in a clear plastic bag wedged partway under her thigh.

"I don't know exactly. I haven't read it yet. It's from Ben Martin."

"Ben?"

"Yeah. It's postmarked the day he died. As soon as I received it, I turned it over to the police. Just got it back." She slipped it out and studied the front of the envelope, *Office of the Headmaster, Litchfield Academy* emblazoned on the top left corner. Victoria's name and address were handwritten in the addressee section.

"Are you going to see what he had to say?" Vince looked poised to take the handoff and perform the same service of reading it to her that he'd done with the autopsy report.

"I guess I should. I don't know that I want to." Vince offered an upturned palm, but she ignored it, turning the envelope over and flipping up the flap. She imagined it had been steamed open in order to extract DNA from where Ben would have licked it.

Vince pulled his hand back and hooked the thumb through a belt loop.

The letter was also handwritten, no doubt unseen by anyone else's eyes before he mailed it. She began to read aloud.

Dearest Victoria

You and Robert have been such precious friends over the years and it rips at my heart to write this to you. I never wanted things to turn out the way they did. Although I may not get a chance to explain in person, you need to know exactly what happened to Robert.

She felt a breath catch in her throat. Would he provide the answer to why from beyond the grave? Would he finally tell her the truth?

This is an accurate account of the events leading up to Robert's death and the day that followed. This is For Your Eyes Only.

Too late for that now, Ben. The moment she'd pulled the envelope from the mailbox, her instincts had been to hand it over to the police, and she didn't regret that decision.

Ten years ago, I was brought in to shut down the school. The board of directors thought the financial situation seemed too dire to recover from.

Yet I was confident I could turn things around and I did.

I also saw it as an opportunity to be a hero in my sons' eyes by rescuing the very school they'd lived down the street from their whole lives and wanted desperately to attend. After divorcing their mother, they were very angry with me so I saw this as my chance to redeem myself.

I reached out to alumni and drummed up their support—even I had underestimated how generous they would be—and within three years the school was not only out of the red but sitting firmly in the black.

But at that point I had gotten myself so deep in debt. I was desperate.

Victoria looked to Vince. "How is that possible? He was the headmaster at a prestigious private school." She didn't want to think about how much he earned in that position. "On top of his salary, his housing was paid for. So were his meals. His first child doesn't start college until next fall, and I would imagine he'll have a free ride, coming out of Litchfield with his academic record. What the hell could cause him to get into debt?" Was it gambling as Robert had suspected? She continued to read.

My gambling did me in. (That's why my first wife left.) I got too deep into debt to recover on my own. My ass was in a vice grip. My creditors threatened to take legal action and garnish my wages. I couldn't have anyone on campus privy to all that, certainly not my family, my sons.

"Geez," Victoria said. "Missi had no idea what she was getting herself into when she married him. Poor thing."

The excess funds the alumni donated to the school became too tempting to pass up. So I helped myself to get the creditors off my back, but I had every intention of paying it back. I just didn't know how.

When it became obvious I couldn't repay the money to the school, I enlisted the help of Emerson Kittridge, one of the more successful alumni. I wasn't exactly sure how Emerson made his money, but he exuded wealth and assured me he could guide me with investments and turn my situation around. I was so impressed with my short-term results, I convinced the board to invest a chunk of the academy's funds with his investment company. Perhaps deep down I thought if I could recoup the amount I had taken, I wouldn't have to pay it back.

She flipped the page over.

Well, we thought he had an investment company separate from EK Enterprises, but he doesn't. He seduced us and plowed our money into risky ventures—certainly nothing the board would have approved of. But all the quarterly statements we received looked very professional and made it look like our investments were paying off handsomely and consistently, so we invested more. And for a while things were going well until the investments went south. I'm not sure exactly when. He's been covering up the losses with phony statements and telling me the investments would come around, that the board didn't need to know. It would all work out. I believed him. I needed to believe him.

So I ended up putting the academy back into a dire financial situation because of these risky investments. And it all started with my initial scoop from the till that I couldn't keep my hands out of.

By sheer bad luck, Robert ended up with a statement left by mistake in the copy machine showing the large transfer to the headmaster's discretionary account, and he confronted me. I told him it wasn't what it looked like, and it would resolve itself in time. But I could tell he wasn't going to let it go.

I was desperate to save the academy (again), and I really thought Emerson could help. I know he seems to be such a risk-taker, but that's what a professional gambler does. And he's very good at it. Just look at his lifestyle.

Victoria paused to take in the revelation. "A professional gambler."

Also Emerson and his organization donate more money to the academy than the top ten percent of contributors combined.

Then at the dinner in my home, the night before our trip to NYC with the boys, I had invited Emerson to join us. His powers of persuasion work on just about everyone, and I needed his help to convince Robert of the merits of our venture.

Victoria did her best to keep her expression even, having been under Emerson's seductive powers.

Emerson and I tried to reason with Robert, make him understand that we had a plan and his investment guidance would solve the situation, that it wouldn't matter if I couldn't pay back what I had taken. But he wouldn't listen.

Robert threatened to go to the board about the inappropriate transfer and what he inferred were questionable investments. Emerson lunged at him and they got into it. Fists were flying. It was quite a tussle. I don't think Emerson had ever had anyone question his ability to make money. And I think even after all these years, Emerson is still sore that Robert beat him out for the Headmaster's Award when they were seniors.

I pulled them apart and I thought it was over. I didn't realize Emerson had grabbed an anvil from the fireplace. He hit Robert on the back of the head. He went down and just lay there. He wasn't moving. Emerson started talking about how we would dispose of his body. All I could do was stand there. My friend was dead. At the hands of Litchfield's largest alumni donor. And I let it happen. In my home.

Victoria let the page fall onto her lap, shifted in her seat, and continued with the second page.

We waited until after dark. Took your car over to the curve on the hill by the pond, got him into the driver's seat and rigged it with a stone so the gas pedal would stay down and pulled the emergency brake. When the car hit the water, Emerson said, "Just as I'd pictured it."

No doubt they found my wallet in the car. I discovered later it was missing and surmised Emerson tossed it in.

We drove down to the city that night. Checked into the hotel as planned. We brought his briefcase and overnight bag with us. You're probably wondering how all those pictures from the museum got on his phone. That was Emerson. He was on the board at the museum, and he stepped in and took the place of the Director of Acquisitions who was supposed to be the one to show Robert around, behind the scenes, so he went through the motions as if Robert was actually there. I called his phone a couple times during the day and Emerson answered. We were establishing a timeline for the police.

It was awful, Victoria, and I'm so sorry it happened. I can't *ask for forgiveness, but I do ask for the sake of the boys who have traversed the sacred grounds of Litchfield Academy—and who, I pray, will do so in the years to come—please keep Emerson's involvement in Robert's death our secret. I know that's a tremendous burden to place on you—and unfair as well—but if the funds that he and his organization so generously pledge dry up, the academy will no longer be the institution we all love and cherish. I trust he will continue to donate. He's one of our alumni who has made it big and knows he is indebted to Litchfield Academy. Plus I got the board to agree to name the next new building on campus after him.*

Victoria pulled her eyes from the note and found Vince's gaze. "Ben didn't know about the cuff link in Robert's pocket."

Vince shook his head but remained silent.

"And he was willing to protect Emerson right up to the end to save the school." She continued to read.

If only I'd listened to Robert when he first came to me and I had fessed up. Emerson wouldn't have needed to know who had discovered my indiscretion. Robert would still be alive, and we could have been digging the academy out of its financial hole sooner.

I'll take the fall for the sake of our beloved Litchfield Academy.

Yours in eternity,

Ben

P.S. The photos from Robert's desk that you were asking about were of my kids and my first wife. I used the desk before Robert did until I moved into the headmaster's office.

They sat in the stillness of the room, the gory details of Robert's demise having been filled in with intricacies only a fine paintbrush could render.

But why would Emerson—a ruthless killer who took Robert from her—have wanted to get into a relationship with her? What kind of twisted mind would have manufactured his affections? Was it one more way to hurt Robert? He had seemed so genuine. She felt dirty. Used. Yet Emerson could thank her for his current lodging accommodations at the New Milford Prison, stuck there while he awaited his trial.

Victoria shrugged off the chilling thoughts and found her voice. "What will happen to the academy? What if they've run it into the ground?"

"I doubt that's the case. It doesn't sound like the financial situation is anything like when Ben was brought in to shut down the school. It's teetering between red and black ink. And from what I understand, the alumni at Litchfield are now quite active and generous in their support, thanks to Ben Martin. They would never let the doors close."

"That's good," she said but wondered if it would be enough.

"And . . . I think I could make a generous donation as well—in Robert's name—to make sure the institution stays in the black."

Victoria sprang to her feet. "You would do that, Vince?"

"Of course." He barely got the words out before she dove at his chest, wrapped her arms around, and squeezed.

"Thank you. I don't know how I'm so blessed to have you in my life—and how you put up with me." He'd been by her side, seeing her through some of the worst times of her life. In exchange, she'd allowed him to take over some of the control—probably more so than she should have. If they were going to move forward together, though, they would have to make some adjustments in that area.

Chuckling, he said, "Hopefully we're through traversing the raging rapids, and the waters will be calmer going forward."

"Hope so."

"And with your permission, I'd like to bring a wrongful death suit against Kittridge. He's got deep enough pockets to handle that, which will put you and your family back on solid financial footing. He owes you that."

Thundering footsteps brought Victoria back to the days when the boys only knew one speed when they traversed the foyer stairs in the compact cottage. She pulled out of Vince's embrace.

"Victoria, where are you?" Her mother darted into the living room, her hair in a wild mess.

"Mom, we're right here. What's the matter?"

"Victoria, the water . . . it's coming." As she stepped farther into the room, her faded pink robe, which had been loosely secured, fell open with the ends of the tie dropping to her sides and dragging on the floor, revealing a light blue, calico print flannel night gown. Victoria grew concerned her mother would trip on the errant tie closure.

"What water? What are you talking about?" Her mother had to be disoriented from waking up.

"The water is going to cover the town. Everyone is going to drown."

Victoria's body bristled at the sound of the word *drown* again.

"What? Millie you can't be serious." Vince wasn't having any of her mother's nonsense. "You've been reading too much about climate change."

"No!" Her mother's eyes grew more piercing, dark with intent. "No, that's not it at all. *Listen.* I just saw it in a dream."

"Mom, calm down. It's going to be okay." A quick mental scan of Talcottville and the surrounding area assured her there were no large bodies of water nearby that could threaten to take out the town. This time her mother's dream was simply a dream—not a premonition—and dreams couldn't always be explained.

"No, it's *not.*" Millie latched onto Victoria's forearm like a raptor snatching its prey. "We need to warn them," she said, forcing the words through clenched teeth. "I saw it. I don't know how much time we have."

"Why don't we make a pot of tea and sit for a bit," Victoria suggested.

"This isn't going to be solved with a cup of tea. Ha!" She loosened her grip on her daughter's arm. "For God's sake, Victoria, we're losing time standing around talking like this."

Vince spoke up. "Millie, there is no large body of water anywhere around us that—"

"I'm not talking about us." She shifted her wild eyes to Vince.

Then Victoria's thoughts switched to Jameson and the boys at Litchfield Academy.

The reservoir. Picturesque Beaver Pond was a small outlet of a much larger system. Bantam Reservoir was part of that system and had been formed many years ago by damming up the river that led to it. There had been talk of replacing the earthen dam with a concrete fixture, but the funds never seemed to get appropriated, despite concerns over the stability of a dam put in place so many years earlier. The most popular objection to the project was the loss of access to the reservoir during the dam's construction. Residents of the surrounding towns enjoyed the manmade beaches and a plethora of watersports on it. Litchfield Academy's own crew team practiced on the reservoir. Could the dam be on the verge of breaching?

"God, no. Not the boys." Victoria formed the words but barely heard them.

"*Yes*, we need to warn them."

Vince took a step back. "What? You two can't be serious. . . . You're going to warn them about what? That a dam that has been around for decades—perhaps close to two hundred years—suddenly might spring a leak? All because of a dream?"

"This is no leak, young man. And clearly you don't know me well enough to know my dreams are more than my imagination having fun while I sleep. Ha!" Turning to Victoria, she asked, "Where's your phone?"

Victoria slid her cell from her pocket and stared at it. Was she getting sucked into one of her mother's outlandish notions? Would Jameson even listen if she did warn him? What if he did and then nothing happened? He'd never forgive her for making a fool out of him in front of his peers.

It took her a moment to realize her mother had snatched it from her hand.

"I'll call. He'll answer because it's coming from your phone, but he'll listen to the message because it's coming from me." Millie tapped the face of the phone a few times, then put it up to her ear.

Vince busied himself at the liquor cabinet, filling a stout glass halfway with a brown liquid. Taking his first sip, he regarded Millie in the doorway, phone to her ear.

"He's not answering," she reported.

Victoria figured he saw who was calling and let it go to voicemail.

"Jameson . . . Jameson I hope you listen to this soon. This is Grandma."

She went on at length telling him about her dream and how he and all the students and faculty were in danger, and they needed to run for their lives. Get to higher ground. The highest possible. The length of her message no doubt ran past the time limit on the phone, but Jameson would get the idea.

The highest ground possible. . . *the chapel.* It was built on the highest point on campus and looked out over the reservoir.

"Call him back, and tell him to get to the chapel if he can," Victoria instructed.

Millie obliged and left a second message.

Vince, who'd been observing the action from the fringes, said, "Are you guys finished? Anything else we need to do to get the word out?"

Victoria couldn't tell if he was poking fun or if there was a shred of sincerity in his questions. Millie was in the latter camp.

"Oh, heavens, *no.* We're not finished. I'll throw on some clothes, and let's get out there. People in Litchfield Falls need to be warned too." She disappeared around the edge of the doorway in a pale pink flash. "I'll keep trying to reach him in the car on the way," she called on her way up the stairs.

"Tori, how far are you going to let this go?" Vince had returned to her side, his glass nearly empty. She could smell bourbon on his breath.

Examining his face, she said, "As far as my mother says we need to. She's rarely wrong about her premonitions. This one seems pretty vivid."

"Okay, I'll jump on, for the sake of discussion. But what if she's having a premonition of something that's going to happen down the road . . . even years from now?"

Victoria allowed his question to dissipate into silence, and then answered, "It doesn't usually work that way. Usually it happens right before the event . . . or as it's happening."

"Well, what if this time is different?"

She considered his words, then said, "I'm not willing to take that chance."

THE PAIR HAD ONLY made it to the Talcottville town line before Victoria began to question their methods. There were faster ways to communicate her mother's concerns. Had Victoria not bought into the premonition?

Keeping their mission contained to spreading the word to Jameson alone minimized the fallout when—if—her mother was mistaken. But what if she was spot on? Like she had been so many times before . . . and hundreds of souls were in danger of perishing.

Victoria's cell, secure in Millie's clutches, began to play The Doobie Brother's "Black Water." Victoria's eyes traveled to the dashboard, expecting the call to appear there, but it didn't seem to be synced with her phone anymore. "Odd . . ." Had her mother been playing with her phone and inadvertently changed a setting?

"Oh, it's Jameson. Ha!" Millie announced.

"Put it on speaker."

"I don't know how to do that."

Victoria tore her eyes from the road long enough to tap the screen a couple of times to make it happen.

"*Jameson*," they shrieked in unison.

"Mom . . . Grandma." He sounded winded.

"Are you all right?" Victoria asked.

"Of course, I am. What the hell do you think is going on?"

"*Jameson*," the two ladies reproved in unison.

"Look, all I'm saying is everything is fine here. I don't know what you saw in your dreams, Grandma, but we're good."

Victoria pulled the car to the side of the road and leaned back against the seat. She'd gotten sucked in. This was one of the dreams her mother couldn't discern from a premonition.

"What are you doing?" her mother demanded.

"Mom, this time your dream wasn't a premonition."

"What are you talking about? Of course, it was."

"No, Mom. Sorry to break it to you."

"Victoria, how dare you. You know I have the ability. Why are you questioning it now? Let's go." She lunged the top half of her petite body forward, poised with ten fingers outstretched toward the windshield like a superhero off the comics page. "There are other people to warn—even if Jameson thinks everything is fine there."

"Mom, we warned him. He's been informed. If something starts to happen, he can alert the others. I think that's all we can do right now."

Millie's gaze fell, her hands folded in her lap. Her lips began to move as if she were praying. Victoria couldn't tell if her eyes were shut, but she was clearly enlisting the help of a higher power—as if that would help. Victoria had given up on that a long time ago.

Victoria turned the car around and headed back to Talcottville, torn between being embarrassed to have gone along with her mother's silly notion and regretting having alarmed Jameson. How many times would he tolerate that before completely dismissing her concerns without even listening? She needed to pick her emergencies to report, just as she had learned, as a parent, to pick her battles to fight.

As they pulled into the driveway, Victoria's phone buzzed from her emergency app. Snatching it up, she read multiple messages alerting the public to stay clear of the Litchfield Falls area—in particular, the Bantam Reservoir area.

CHAPTER FORTY-ONE

It took several agonizing hours before cell coverage was restored and Victoria could reach Jameson.

"So, you're all right?"

"Yes, Mom. I'm fine. I think most of us are."

"You were able to warn everyone?"

"No, actually I didn't need to."

"No?"

"As soon as everyone felt the vibration on our feet, we knew what to do. We'd practiced so many times."

"What? . . . What did you practice?"

"Headmaster Martin would run these drills. He did it at different times of the day so we'd be at different spots on campus. But he'd ring the bell in the quad, and we had to drop what we were doing and head straight for the chapel. It was the only safe place if the dam were to give way. The rest of campus is below the level of the dam."

"Drills . . . really? I don't remember hearing about this."

"You wouldn't have. We were supposed to keep it a secret so we wouldn't worry our parents." He chuckled. "I think he was more concerned about parents pulling kids out of LA if they knew the danger."

"Really."

"Yeah, so he told us that if we ever felt a rumbling under our feet to do what we'd practiced over and over."

Victoria acknowledged, in spite of having a hand in the murder of her husband, Ben was responsible for saving the lives of the young souls he'd left behind and had been entrusted to care for.

"But it was crazy though. We were all up at the chapel—we didn't all fit inside—and we had an amazing view of the water blasting its way through the dam."

"Have you heard if there were any casualties in town?"

"No, but they had their own warning system, and it sounds like it was just a few holdouts that stayed behind who are now unaccounted for."

"I see." Victoria allowed herself to feel relieved. It could have been so much worse.

"I'll never forget watching that. It was like something out of the book of Genesis."

"Like God was flooding the campus because of all the horrible things that have taken place there."

"Exactly." Jameson was on the same page.

"That sounds about right." Victoria felt a rush of positive energy from within, as if they'd been through the worst and had come out the other side. Robert could now rest in peace. Those who had taken his life had been exposed and justice would be served—in different ways, but served.

"The campus is trashed so we'll have to finish out the semester online. But I'm okay with that. I'd like to spend some time at home—with you, Mom."

"I'd like that too."

"See you soon. Love you."

"Love you too, Jameson."

As soon as Victoria hung up, she could sense someone behind her.

"I know where the yellow tulips came from." Her mother stood in the doorway, hands jammed into the pockets of her robe, her gaze resting on no particular spot across the room.

"Where, Mom?"

"Robert put them there for us. Well . . . for you, mostly, I would imagine. You knew how much he loved them, and he wanted you to know he'll always be with you."

"I think you're right. And I will enjoy them."

❧

EMERSON HAD BEEN SWIFTLY apprehended after Victoria turned in Ben's letter and later convicted of second-degree murder as well as concealing a human corpse, the impetus for which was confirmed with the document hidden in Robert's wooden box, kept safe by Jameson and procured with the skeleton key Erin Hutchinson had found. Emerson would later be tried and convicted of attempted murder in California for the fire he'd arranged in Harrison's dorm room that severely injured his roommate.

EPILOGUE

They say true love endures all. That it can even survive death. But what happens to that love after death? Does the person who's passed take it with him? How does the surviving heart carry on alone? Is it possible to heal and love again? Fully? And when is it the right time to give your heart to someone else? How much time needs to pass? Will you simply sense when it's right?

But what if the person you love has gone missing, and you don't know what's happened to him? No one does. You don't want to give up hope, but with each passing day, each passing minute, there's nothing new to keep you hoping. Is there a time limit for holding out hope?

As a mother, you look into your son's eyes, full of the expectation—albeit unrealistic—that his father will return. How can you take that hope away from him? You love him with all your heart; you can't. And if you were to move on and give your heart to another man, you would be yanking that hope out from under your son. How can a mother do that?

And as days turn into months, months into years, and there are no more answers than the day he disappeared, you don't love him any less. Instead, your heart has had to make room for an ache that won't go away. An ache you're afraid is going to push out the love you had for him because of the emptiness and uncertainty he's left behind.

Yet the heart doesn't always listen to reason. The heart yearns to love.

NATIONAL AWARD-WINNING AUTHOR PENNY GOETJEN writes murder mystery and suspense novels where the settings play as prominent a role as the engaging characters. A self-proclaimed eccentric known for writing late into the night, transfixed by the allure of flickering candlelight, Ms. Goetjen embraces the writing process, unaware what will confront her at the next turn. She rides the journey with her characters, often as surprised as her readers to see how the story unfolds. Fascinated with the paranormal, she usually weaves a subtle, unexpected twist into her stories. When her husband is asked how he feels about his wife writing murder mysteries, he answers with a wink, "I sleep with one eye open."

Find out more about the author and her books:
www.pennygoetjen.com

Sign up to hear about upcoming releases, events, giveaways, and other news:
www.pennygoetjen.com/contact

Connect on social media:

Book Club Questions for
THE WOMAN UNDERWATER

1. What did you like most about The Woman Underwater?

2. What did you like least about it?

3. Did you read it quickly, or did you tend to savor the story?

4. Were there any sections you went back and reread?

5. Do you have a favorite section you'd like to read out loud to the group?

6. Which character did you relate to the most?

7. If you could talk to one of the characters, which would it be and what would you say?

8. Did any of the characters remind you of someone you know?

9. If you could insert yourself into the story, which character would you like to become—an existing character or a new one of your creation?

10. Victoria describes feeling as though she's underwater after receiving the news of Robert's disappearance. What feelings did the story evoke in you as you read it?

11. If you could read the story from a different character's perspective, who would it be?

12. If you could ask the author a question, what would it be?

13. Would you read another book by this author?

14. What did you think of the cover? Does it fit the story?

Disappear in the Pages of a Mystery on the Coast of Maine

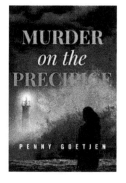

Caught on the rocks in the crosshairs of the storm

After a former all-girls school gets transformed into a cozy inn on the rugged coast of Maine, the unsolved case of a student's disappearance years earlier is all but forgotten—until a young female guest goes missing.

"... *completely transportive, plenty of thrills, with a warm cast of characters that adds a lot of heart to this story.*"
—**Megan Collins, Author of** *The Winter Sister,* *Behind the Red Door,* **and** *The Family Plot*

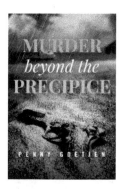

Dearly beloved becomes dearly departed

An historic seaside inn set in a sleepy harbor town may seem like the perfect place to have a summer wedding, until a ruthless killer crashes the party.

"*Goetjen is a competent writer who keep things moving along, throwing in hints of the preternatural that add to the overall ambiance.... worth a read.*"
—*Kirkus Reviews*

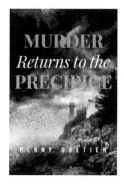

When murder checks in, don't expect mints on your pillow

Returning to her roots on the rocky coast of Maine, Elizabeth endeavors to reopen her family's inn, newly restored to its original New England charm after a powerful hurricane nearly destroyed it. However, unseen forces seem hellbent on derailing her efforts or worse—taking her out of the picture. It becomes clear the inn's dark past has resurfaced.

Disappear in the Pages of a Mystery in the Virgin Islands

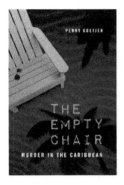

When Paradise Isn't a Sexy Character

Young Olivia travels to St. Thomas to settle affairs after receiving word her mother, a highly-acclaimed photographer, has perished in a boating accident, but island police have no record of her death or even the accident. Could her mother still be alive? Olivia desperately needs the truth, if she has to find it herself. Entangled in the same dark web of crime that may have ensnared her mother, Olivia is low on cash, high on mistrust, yet must rely on the ruggedly handsome stranger who seems to surface when she most needs saving. But is he her rescuer-turned-lover or her deadly foe?

"Penny Goetjen uses the idyllic setting and island culture so effectively, the reader is tempted to savor ocean views from The Empty Chair, *but don't pause too long—danger is never far away."*

—Kathryn Orzech, Author of *Asylum* and *Premonition of Terror*

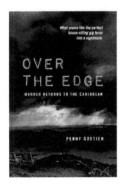

The perfect house-sitting gig turns into a nightmare

Returning to St. Thomas to rebuild her mother's bungalow after it was destroyed by fire, Olivia searches for Colton, her on again/off again love interest from her previous visit, but is left with more questions than answers, his whereabouts unknown. With nowhere to stay, she accepts the offer from an older, wealthy man to house-sit his spacious villa overlooking the Caribbean Sea while he sets off on an extended sailing trip. But what seems like a perfect arrangement turns into a nightmare. Before she can unpack her suitcase in the posh digs, Olivia stumbles upon the man murdered in his own home and becomes the prime suspect.

". . . a well scripted murder mystery with deceptive characters and an unpredictable path."

—*Suzy Approved Book Reviews*

CPSIA information can be obtained
at www.ICGtesting.com
Printed in the USA
LVHW020045160323
741732LV00023B/423

9 781733 143943